BROTHERBAND

www.**brotherband**.co.uk

BROTHERBAND

SLAVES OF SOCORRO

JOHN FLANAGAN

CORGI YEARLING

BROTHERBAND: SLAVES OF SOCORRO
A CORGI YEARLING BOOK 978 0 440 87080 7

Published in Great Britain by Corgi Yearling,
an imprint of Random House Children's Publishers UK
A Random House Group Company
Originally published in Australia by Random House Australia (Pty),

This edition published 2014

1 3 5 7 9 10 8 6 4 2

The Random House Group Limited supports the Forest Stewardship Council®
(FSC®), the leading international forest-certification organisation. Our books
carrying the FSC label are printed on FSC®-certified paper. FSC is the only forest-
certification scheme supported by the leading environmental organisations, including
Greenpeace. Our paper procurement policy can be found at
www.randomhouse.co.uk/environment

Set in 12/15pt Caslon Classico by Midland Typesetters, Australia

Corgi Yearling Books are published by Random House Children's Publishers UK,
61–63 Uxbridge Road, London W5 5SA

www.**randomhousechildrens**.co.uk
www.**randomhouse**.co.uk

Addresses for companies within The Random House Group Limited can be found
at: www.randomhouse.co.uk/offices.htm

THE RANDOM HOUSE GROUP Limited Reg. No. 954009

A CIP catalogue record for this book is available from the British Library.

Printed and bound in Great Britain by CPI Group (UK), Croydon, CR0 4YY

For Leonie, again.

A FEW SAILING TERMS
EXPLAINED

Because this book involves sailing ships, I thought it
might be useful to explain a few of the nautical terms
that are to be found in the story.

Be reassured that I haven't gone overboard (to keep
up the nautical allusion) with technical details in the
book, and even if you're not familiar with sailing, I'm sure
you'll understand what's going on. But a certain amount
of sailing terminology is necessary for the story to feel
realistic.

So, here we go, in no particular order.

Bow: The front of the ship, also called the **prow**.
Stern: The rear of the ship.
Port and starboard: The left and right sides of the ship,
as you're facing the bow. In fact, I'm probably incor-
rect in using the term 'port'. The early term for port
was 'larboard', but I thought we'd all get confused if
I used that.

Starboard was a corruption of 'steering board' (or steering side). The steering oar was always placed on the right-hand side of the ship.

Consequently, when a ship came into port it would moor with the left side against the jetty, to avoid damage to the steering oar. One theory says the word derived from the ship's being in port — left side to the jetty. I suspect, however, that it might have come from the fact that the entry port, by which crew and passengers boarded, was also always on the left side.

How do you remember which side is which? Easy. Port and left both have four letters.

Forward: Towards the bow.

Aft: Towards the stern.

Fore and aft rig: A sail plan where the sail is in line with the hull of the ship.

Hull: The body of the ship.

Keel: The spine of the ship.

Steering oar: The blade used to control the ship's direction, mounted on the starboard side of the ship, at the stern.

Tiller: The handle for the steering oar.

Beam: The side of the ship. If the wind is abeam, it is coming from the side, at a right angle to the ship's keel.

Yardarm or yard: A spar (wooden pole) that is hoisted up the mast, carrying the sail.

Masthead: The top of the mast.

Bulwark: The part of the ship's side above the deck.

Gunwale: The upper part of the ship's rail.

Belaying pins: Wooden pins used to fasten rope.

Oarlock or rowlock: The pegs that hold the oar in place.

Telltale: A pennant that indicates the wind's direction.

Tacking: To tack is to change direction from one side to the other, passing through the eye of the wind.

If the wind is from the north and you want to sail north-east, you would perform one tack so that you were heading north-east, and you could continue to sail on that tack for as long as you needed to.

However, if the wind is from the north and you want to sail due north, you would have to do so in a series of short tacks, going back and forth on a zig-zag course, crossing through the wind each time, and slowly making ground to the north. This is a process known as **beating** into the wind.

Wearing: When a ship tacks, it turns *into* the wind to change direction. When it wears, it turns *away* from the wind, travelling in a much larger arc, with the wind in the sail, driving the ship around throughout the manoeuvre. This was a safer way of changing direction for wolfships.

Reach or reaching: When the wind is from the side of the ship, the ship is sailing on a reach, or reaching.

Running: When the wind is from the stern, the ship is running. So would you if the wind was strong enough.

Reef: To gather in part of the sail and bundle it against the yardarm to reduce the sail area. This is done in high winds to protect the sail and mast.

Trim: To adjust the sail to the most efficient angle.

Halyard: A rope used to haul the yard up the mast (haul-yard, get it?).

Stay: A heavy rope that supports the mast. The **back-stay** and **forestay** are heavy ropes running from the top of the mast to the stern and bow (it's pretty obvious which is which).

Sheets and shrouds: A lot of people think these are sails, which is a logical assumption. But in fact, they're ropes. Shrouds are thick ropes that run from the top of the mast to the side of the ship, supporting the mast. Sheets are the ropes used to control or trim the sail — to haul it in and out according to the wind strength and direction. In an emergency, the order might be given to 'let fly the sheets!'. The sheets would be released, letting the sail loose and bringing the ship to a halt. (If *you* were to let fly the sheets, you'd probably fall out of bed.)

Way: The motion of the ship. If a ship is under way, it is moving. If it is making leeway, the wind is blowing it downwind so it loses ground.

Back water: To row a reverse stroke.

So, now you know all you need to know about sailing terms, welcome aboard the world of *Brotherband*!

John Flanagan

PART ONE

HALLASHOLM

CHAPTER ONE

'I think we should reset the mast about a metre further aft,' Hal said.

He peered down into the stripped-out hull of the wolfship, rubbing his chin. *Wolftail*'s innards were bare to the world. Her oars, mast, yard, sails, shrouds, stays, halyards, rowing benches, floorboards and ballast stones had been removed, leaving just the bare hull. She rested on her keel, high and dry on the grass beside Anders's shipyard, supported by timber props that kept her level.

A plank gantry ran along either side of the denuded hull, at the height of her gunwales. Hal knelt on the starboard side gantry, accompanied by Anders, the shipwright, and Bjarni Bentfinger, *Wolftail*'s skirl and owner. Hal and Anders wore thoughtful, reflective expressions. Bjarni's was more anxious. No ship's captain likes to see the bones of his craft laid bare for the world to view. Bjarni was beginning to wonder whether this had been such a good idea. It wasn't too late, he thought. He could always pay Anders for his work so far and ask him to return *Wolftail* to her former state.

Then he thought of the extra speed and manoeuvrability the new sail plan would give his ship. He shrugged and looked anxiously at Hal. The young skirl was so . . . young, he thought. And here Bjarni was, entrusting his precious *Wolftail* to Hal's hands for a major refit. Of course, Anders was a highly experienced shipbuilder. He ought to know what he was doing. And Bjarni had seen proof of the effectiveness of the fore and aft sail plan that Hal had designed for his own ship, the *Heron*.

Bjarni took a deep breath, closed his eyes and bit back the request that was trembling on his lips. Between them, these two knew what was best, he thought.

'The mast goes where the mast support is,' Anders said doubtfully. 'How do you plan to move that?'

The mast support was a squared piece of timber, a metre long, that stood vertically at right angles to the keel. It was used to hold the mast firmly in place, and was an integral, immovable part of the keel itself. When the original shipbuilders had shaped a tree to form the keel for *Wolftail*, they had trimmed off all the projecting branches, save one. They left that one in place, shortening it and trimming it so that it formed a square section that projected up at right angles to support the mast. Its innate strength came from the fact that it hadn't been fastened in place. It had *grown* there.

Hal shrugged. 'It's not a problem.' He climbed down into the hull and knelt beside the keel, indicating the existing support. 'We leave this in place, so that the strength is retained, and we shape a metre-long piece to match it, and attach it behind the existing support.'

Anders chewed his lip. 'Yes. I suppose that'd work.'

'But why set the mast further astern?' Bjarni asked.

'The new fore and aft yards will reach right to the bow,' Hal explained, 'and that will put more downward pressure on the bow when you're under sail. This way, we'll compensate for that pressure.' He indicated with his hand, describing an angle behind the mast support. 'We could even slope the edge of the new piece back a little towards the stern. That'd let us rake the mast back and give us even better purchase.'

'Hmmm,' said Anders.

The worried look was back on Bjarni's face. He hadn't understood the technical details Hal had spouted so confidently. But he understood 'hmmm'. 'Hmmm' meant Anders wasn't convinced.

'Never mind raking it back,' Bjarni said quickly. 'I want my mast to stand square. Masts are supposed to stand square. That's what masts do. They stand . . . square. Always have.'

After all, he thought, a raked mast would be a little too exotic.

Hal grinned at him. He'd overseen the conversion of four square-rigged wolfships to the *Heron* sail plan in the past months. He was used to the older skirls' conservative views.

'Whatever you say,' he replied agreeably. He stood and clambered up the sloping inside of the hull towards the gantry. Anders reached down a hand to help him.

'Now, have you made up your mind about the fin keel?' Hal asked. He knew what the answer was going to be, even before Bjarni's head began to shake from side to side.

'I don't want you cutting any holes in the bottom of my ship,' he said. 'She might sink.'

Hal smiled reassuringly at him. 'I did the same to the *Heron*,' he pointed out. 'And she hasn't sunk so far.'

Bjarni continued his head-shaking. 'That's as may be,' he said. 'But I don't see any good coming from cutting a hole in the bottom of a ship. It goes against nature.' He noticed Hal's tolerant smile and frowned. He didn't enjoy being patronised by a boy, even if he suspected that the boy might be right.

'I don't care that you did it in your ship,' he said. 'It might just be luck that she hasn't sunk . . .' He paused, and added in a meaningful tone, 'So far.'

Hal shrugged. He hadn't expected Bjarni to agree to a fin keel. None of the wolfship skirls had done so thus far.

'Suit yourself,' he said. He turned to Anders. 'So, can you get your men started on an extension for the mast support? I can send you over a design sketch if you'd like.'

Anders nodded slowly. Anders did most things slowly. He was a deliberate man who didn't leap to decisions without pondering them. That was one of the things that made him an excellent shipbuilder.

'No need for a sketch,' he said. 'I can work out how to manage it.'

Hal nodded. Anders was right, of course. The design work involved would be a simple matter for an experienced craftsman. He had really only offered out of politeness.

'Well then . . .' he began. But he was interrupted by a booming voice.

'Hullo the ship!' They all turned to see Erak, the Oberjarl of Skandia, on the path that led from the town. Anders's shipyard was set outside Hallasholm, so the constant noise of hammering and sawing — and the attendant curses as fingers were mashed by incautiously wielded mallets — wouldn't disturb the townfolk.

'What's he doing here?' Bjarni said idly.

Anders sniffed, and wiped his nose with the back of his hand.

'He's on his morning constitutional,' he said. Noticing Bjarni's puzzled glance, he added, 'His walk. He walks along here most days. Says the exercise keeps him slim.' A ghost of a smile touched the corners of his mouth as he said the last few words.

Hal raised an eyebrow. 'How can it keep him something he's never been?'

Erak was an immense bear of a man. 'Slim' was not a word that sprang readily to mind when describing him. The Oberjarl was striding across the grass towards them now, flanked by Svengal, his constant companion and former first mate.

'What's that he's got?' Bjarni asked. Erak was wielding a long, polished wood staff in his right hand, using it to mark his strides. The staff was about a metre and a half tall, shod with a silver ferrule at the bottom and adorned with a small silver knob at the top. At every third or fourth pace, he would twirl it between his powerful fingers, setting the sunlight flashing off the silver fittings.

'It's his new walking staff,' Anders explained. 'There was a delegation in from Gallica two weeks ago and they presented it to him.'

'But what does it do?' Hal asked. In his eyes, everything should have a practical use.

Anders shrugged. 'He says it makes him look sophistic-ated,' he replied.

Hal's eyebrows went up in surprise. Like 'slim', 'sophisticated' was not a word that sprang readily to mind when thinking about the Oberjarl.

Erak and Svengal paused at the foot of the ladder leading to the gantry.

'All right if we come up?' Erak called.

Anders made a welcoming gesture with his right hand. 'Be our guest,' he said.

They felt the timbers of the gantry vibrate gently as the two men climbed to join them. Erak was huge and Svengal was built on the lines of the normal Skandian wolfship crewman — he wasn't as big as Erak, but he was tall and heavy-set.

Perhaps, thought Hal, it had been wise of Erak to ask permission before mounting the ladder.

The two men approached down the gantry, peering with professional interest into the bared hull below them.

'Getting one of Hal's new-fangled sail plans, are you, Bjarni?' Erak boomed. 'Old ways not good enough for you any more?'

'We've done four other ships before this one,' Anders said. 'Been no complaints so far.'

Erak studied the shipwright for a moment, then switched his gaze to the young man beside him. Secretly, he was proud of Hal, proud of his ingenuity and original thinking. On top of that, Hal had shown leadership and determination in pursuing the pirate Zavac halfway across the known world. Erak admired those qualities, although he considered himself to be too set in his own ways to adapt to the sort of change that Hal represented. Deep down, he knew that the sail plan the young man had designed was superior to the old square rig of traditional wolfships. He had seen it demonstrated on more than one occasion. But he loved his *Wolfwind* as she was and he couldn't bring himself to change her.

'Time for a change, chief,' Bjarni said, as if reading that last thought.

Erak thought it was time to change the subject. 'They've really ripped the guts out of her, haven't they?' he commented cheerfully.

Bjarni looked as if he might argue the toss, but then he subsided. In fact, they *had* ripped the guts out of her. It was strange, he thought, how when craftsmen set about making improvements to anything — be it a ship, a house or an ox cart — their first step almost always involved practically destroying it.

Erak paced along the gantry, his walking staff clacking noisily on the timber walkway.

'There's a plank or two could use replacing,' he said, peering keenly to where several of the planks were showing wear between the joins.

'We've noted those,' Anders replied. Still, he was impressed that Erak had spotted the problem from a distance.

Clack, clack, clack, went Erak's staff as he paced further. Hal caught Svengal's eye and winked.

'Decided it's time for a walking cane, have you, Oberjarl?' the young man asked, his face a mask of innocence. Svengal turned away to hide a grin as Erak turned slowly to face Hal.

'It's a staff of office, young man,' he said haughtily. 'They're all the rage in Gallica among the gentry.'

'The gentry, you say?' Hal asked. He knew the Oberjarl had a soft spot for him and he knew how far to push things. Or at least, he considered ruefully, he *thought* he knew. Sometimes he overstepped the mark — and then a hasty retreat was advisable. 'Well, I can see why you'd have one — you being as gentrified as you are.'

Erak twirled the staff, the sunlight catching the silver-work again.

'It makes me look sophisticated,' he said. There was a note of challenge in his voice.

'I've definitely noticed that, chief,' Svengal put in cheerfully. 'I was only telling the lads the other night, "Have you noticed how sophisticated the chief is looking these days?"'

'And what did they say?' Erak asked, with just a hint of suspicion.

'Well, they had to agree, didn't they? All of them. Of course, then they spoiled it by asking what "sophisticated" meant. But they did agree — wholeheartedly.'

Bjarni let out a short bark of laughter, and Anders's shoulders appeared to be shaking. Hal had found something fascinating on the handrail of the gantry and was studying it closely.

Erak snorted. 'People never appreciate sophistication,' he said. He *clack-clacked* his way along the gantry once more towards the ladder, his old friend following a few paces behind. At the head of the ladder, Erak turned back and called to Hal.

'Drop by and see me tomorrow morning, young Hal. Might have a project for you and that band of misfits of yours.'

Hal's interest was aroused. Life had been a little on the slow side lately, with nothing but routine sea patrols to fill in the time.

'What do you have in mind, Oberjarl?' he asked. But Erak only smiled sweetly and tapped the side of his nose.

'I never discuss business in public, Hal,' he said. 'It's so unsophisticated.'

CHAPTER TWO

Lydia was hunting.

She had trekked up into the mountains behind Hallasholm, following the winding game trails, looking for tracks and signs of animals. There had been rumours of a boar active in the area, but so far she had seen nothing to indicate that the rumours were true.

On a previous trip, she had discovered a rough hunter's cabin high in the hills and she set up camp there. The roof was holed in several places and she spent the first afternoon repairing it, and filling chinks in the warped planks of the walls. It was obvious that nobody had been here for some time.

After she set the cabin to rights, she stowed her gear, replaced some of the rotting ropes that formed the net mattress on the bed and set the old battered kettle to boil on the fireplace. The eager flames sent a cheerful, flickering light through the cabin. Even though it was summer, the nights were cold in the mountains and she was grateful for the fire's warmth as the evening wind whistled round the uneven walls.

She noticed that several past residents had carved their names into the timbers of the hut. None of the carvings were fresh, she thought, as she traced them with her fingertip. *Arn. Johann. Detmer.* One name was carved on a wall opposite the others and was obviously not Skandian. Nor was it a male name. She studied it curiously.

'Evanlyn,' she said to herself. She wondered who Evanlyn might have been, and what a woman was doing here in the first place.

'Maybe hunting, like me,' she said. She took her small utility knife out and deftly carved her own name under the other woman's, studying her handiwork with satisfaction. *Evanlyn. Lydia.*

'We girls have got to stick together,' she said.

She ate a quick supper of bacon and boiled potatoes, then turned in for the night.

The following day, early in the morning, she set out a series of snares for small game and birds. Her atlatl was too brutal a weapon for such prey. It would tear them apart, leaving nothing for eating. She saw some deer tracks and followed them. But they were several days old and she caught no other sign of the animal that had made them. That was hunting, she thought. Sometimes, no matter how skilled you were, you came back empty-handed.

Not that she cared too much. The hunting trip was merely a ploy to get her out of Hallasholm for a few days — and away from the attentions of Rollond.

Rollond was a contemporary of Stig and Hal. He had been the leader of the Wolf Brotherband, who had competed with Hal and his Herons two years ago. He was tall and well built, and extremely handsome. She knew from idle conversation that the members of the Heron Brotherband liked him and respected him. She had heard vague stories about how he had helped them during their brotherband training period. In addition, he was popular throughout Hallasholm. His crew had come third in the competition, but that hadn't prevented the Wolves being chosen to join one of the leading wolfship crews in the port — and Rollond had been appointed as second in command.

Trouble was, Rollond had a massive crush on Lydia. She had been pleasant to him at first, because he was a nice person — and an attractive one. But she didn't reciprocate the depth of his feelings for her.

He was constantly asking her out: a picnic, or a fishing expedition, even a hunting trip from time to time. Occasionally she agreed. More often, she cried off. But it was getting harder and harder to find believable excuses, and she certainly didn't want to hurt Rollond's feelings. After all, he *was* a very likeable person.

It was just that she didn't want to like him too much. Casual friends? Fine. Anything more than that, and she felt constricted, confined.

Lydia was a free spirit, and something of a loner. She had spent her early years largely by herself, hunting, tracking and wandering in the dense forest that crowned the cliffs above her hometown. As a relative newcomer to Hallasholm, she resisted the concept of being known as 'Rollond's girlfriend', as she knew she would be. She didn't want to be defined in terms of some other person.

She was still trying to establish her own identity in her new home.

Of course, she was known as a member of the *Heron*'s crew and that had gained her a certain level of respect. She still enjoyed the company and camaraderie of the Heron Brotherband. They made her welcome whenever she joined them — at festivals or feasts or other social occasions. And she knew that to them, at least, she wasn't an outsider, but a tried and proven member of their brotherband. She still wore her knitted watch cap, emblazoned with a white heron symbol, with pride.

But since the *Heron* had returned from her triumphant voyage to Raguza, Lydia had little to do on board. After a long winter lay-up, the crew had been engaged in short cruises in local waters, keeping a protective eye on the Skandian trading fleet. Since Lydia was part of the fighting crew rather than the sailing crew, using her deadly accurate atlatl darts to bring down enemy crewmen, the day-to-day task of escorting the trading fleet left her sitting idle in the stern of the little ship. Stefan and Jesper looked after the raising and lowering of the tapered yards. Ulf and Wulf seemed to have mastered the intricacies of sail trimming, working together, with that instinctive sense of oneness that twins so often share, to produce the most efficient sail shape, wringing every possible knot of speed out of the ship.

She supposed she could learn to steer. But with Hal, Stig, Edvin and even Thorn more than capable of doing that, the *Heron* was well served with helmsmen.

Even big, short-sighted Ingvar had his position on board. His immense strength was put to use helping

Jesper and Stefan. And of course, he was the only one who could cock and load the massive crossbow they called the Mangler.

'I need a long cruise,' she said. If they were sent on another mission, like the hunt for Zavac and his black ship, the *Raven*, she knew she'd find plenty to do. For a start, the mere fact that they would be a long way from Skandian home waters raised the odds of encountering hostile ships. Also, her hunting skills would be put to good effect as she could provide food for the crew. And a long cruise would solve the problem of having to continually avoid Rollond.

For now, she'd have to resort to hunting expeditions like this to keep her distance from him. He'd already inveigled her into agreeing to be his partner at the upcoming haymaking festival. But at least there'd be plenty of other people around — the entire town, as a matter of fact. And Hal, Stig and the other Herons would be on hand as well.

As she turned these thoughts over, a separate part of her mind was taking note of the terrain around her, searching for hoofprints, broken branches on low-lying bushes, scraps of fur caught on thorns, scars in the bark of trees that might indicate a stag had been rubbing his antlers against them to rid them of the irritating 'velvet' that coated the horns, or to mark his territory — searching for anything, in fact, that might indicate the recent passage of a large animal.

She saw none of these things, until she rounded a bend in the narrow game trail, stooping to make her way under a tangle of thorny vines. She straightened and found herself looking at a large tree several metres away, with marks on its trunk that set her senses jangling.

Something had gouged two sets of parallel scars in the thick bark — four in each set. She looked around warily, her left hand automatically dropping to draw one of her darts from the quiver at her belt. Her right hand already had the atlatl ready.

The marks were those made by a bear, tearing its claws through the bark of the tree, to sharpen them or strengthen them, or just out of sheer contrariness. She knew that bears would be abroad at this time of year but this was the first time she had seen evidence of one so close to Hallasholm.

She took a pace or two towards the tree, touching the scars on the trunk. The sap in the torn bark was still tacky, meaning the bear had been here sometime in the past one or two hours. Again, she looked all round her, but there was no sign of a bear anywhere she could see.

'It's the one you don't see that's the problem,' she told herself. It occurred to her that she had been talking to herself a good deal lately. 'That might not be a good thing,' she said, then realised she was doing it again. She frowned and shook herself. She would have to stop this.

The bear was a big one. She had to look up to see where the scars on the tree trunk began, well above her head. From their position, she estimated that the animal would stand half a metre taller than her own height. And it would be correspondingly bulky. She wasn't armed to fight a bear, so she turned and retraced her steps down the game path.

On the way back to the cabin, she detoured to check the snares she had set several hours earlier. She found two plump plovers, a grouse and a rabbit in the snares.

A good haul, she thought. Obviously, nobody had hunted this area for some time. She gathered them into her game bag and made her way to the cabin. Her full attention was turned to the woods around her as she stayed alert for any sign of that bear. She considered what she would do if she saw it. Initially, remain very, very still and hope it would go away. But if it charged her — and if it had cubs it might well do so — her best chance would be to climb a tree. Accordingly, she continually made note of suitable trees within reasonable running distance.

She reached the cabin and breathed a small sigh of relief. Bears were not animals to tangle with. They were unpredictable. And they were big and strong and had claws. That was not a reassuring combination, and the fact that there might be one somewhere in the vicinity had set her nerves on edge.

She shut the door, and smiled as she realised how false was the sense of security it gave her. The wood was old and warped and the leather hinges were dried out and fragile. One good shove from a bear would undoubtedly smash it open, tearing it from its hinges. But, flimsy as it was, it was a psychological barrier and, as far as she knew, bears did not tend to enter buildings — unless they smelled food.

She moved outside again, and away from the cabin. She skinned and dressed the rabbit, and cleaned and plucked the birds she had taken from the snares, throwing the residue into the bushes that fringed the clearing where the cabin was set. She hung the birds from the edge of the verandah and took the rabbit carcass inside.

While there was still light, she made a hurried trip to the stream that ran nearby, cleaning the blood and feathers from her hands, and filling the old water bucket that she had found in the cabin. By the time she returned, the shadows were lengthening. She shut the door again, dropping its locking bar in place, and lit a candle from her pack. She had other items there as well — basic cooking ingredients. She jointed the rabbit, rolled the joints in seasoned flour and stoked up the fire once more. There was a big black iron frying pan hanging behind the fireplace. She set it on a grate over the flames to heat up.

She cut a large pat of butter and dropped it into the pan, tilting the pan from side to side to coat it with the sizzling, spitting butter. Then she quickly placed the joints of rabbit onto the pan, swirling the pan to roll them around in the butter, watching as the joints quickly sealed and browned in the heat. She moved the pan to one side, away from the direct heat of the flames, and set the rabbit pieces to cook through, shaking the pan every so often to move them around. The steady sizzling sound continued and a fragrant smell filled the cabin. When she judged that the rabbit was almost cooked, she took a handful of wild bitter greens that she had picked the day before on the way up the mountain, and tossed them into the pan. She watched as they wilted down to a third of their original bulk, then took the pan off the heat and spooned several joints and the greens onto a platter.

She burned her fingers and her lips as she tried to eat the rabbit. Having learned her lesson, she left it to cool for several minutes, then devoured it hungrily. The meat was tender and full of flavour, and the bitter, astringent taste of the greens cut through the butter taste. She ate quickly. Nothing sharpens an appetite like a day hiking in the fresh, clear air of the mountains. She picked the last strands of meat off the bones and sat back, replete. She put her feet up on the table and let out a most unladylike burp.

'Delicious,' she said to herself, sucking the last of the butter and grease from her fingers. She recalled hearing somewhere that an unrelieved diet of rabbit would not sustain life in the long term. The meat was too lean, and free of fats and oils. She shrugged. Maybe not. But in the short term, it was delicious.

Remembering her earlier thoughts about bears and their reluctance to enter buildings, she tossed the remnants of her meal out into the clearing. Even if there was no bear around, she knew there were plenty of smaller creatures who'd dispose of the scraps before dawn.

A short while later, she prepared for bed. It had been a long day. She snuffed the candle, wrapped herself in her blankets, stretched out on the bed and sighed happily. The glow of flames from the fireplace flickered on the inside of the cabin. It was a comforting sight and before long she was asleep.

The flames had died down to a dull red glow when she suddenly snapped awake. Something was moving on the warped boards of the porch. Something big. It brushed against the wall of the cabin. The wall creaked and the cabin shook. Carefully, she pushed the blankets back and reached for the dirk that hung in its scabbard from the bedhead. There was a small window set in the wall looking onto the porch and she stepped towards it.

And, in the unfamiliar surroundings of the cabin, blundered into a small stool in the middle of the room, sending it clattering over. Instantly, there was a rush of movement from the porch, as a large body moved quickly away. Rubbing her shin, Lydia made her way to the window and peered nervously out.

There had been three birds hanging from the porch when she went to bed. A grouse and two plovers. Now there was only the grouse. The other two had gone. She pursed her lips thoughtfully.

'I think I'll head down in the morning,' she said.

CHAPTER THREE

Hal left Anders to continue working on *Wolftail*. The shipwright, after his initial doubts, had eventually come round to his way of thinking and was considering the best way to fit an extension to the mast support, so that the mast could be stepped further back in the hull.

Bjarni hovered anxiously over Anders's shoulder, watching the craftsman at work and constantly querying what he was doing. Eventually, Anders turned to him, his patience exhausted.

'Bjarni, don't you have anything else to do?'

Bjarni shook his head, a blank expression on his face. 'Not really.'

With great deliberation, Anders persisted. 'What would you normally be doing on a day like this?' he asked.

Bjarni gestured towards the stripped hull below them. 'Normally, I'd be at sea, on board my ship. But that's not really an option now that you've torn it to pieces.'

Anders thought about that for a second or two. There was really no argument with Bjarni's logic.

'Why don't you go fishing?' he suggested, adding quickly, 'Off the harbour wall. You don't need a ship for that.'

Bjarni looked blankly at him. 'I don't like fish,' he said. 'My mam made me eat it all the time when I was a boy and I just don't like it now.'

'Well, there's no need to eat them,' Anders told him. 'You could just catch them and throw them back.'

'What's the point of that?' Bjarni said. 'Why throw them back if I catch them?'

'Because,' Anders said, with grim determination in his voice, 'you don't like eating them.'

'Then there hardly seems any reason to catch them in the first place,' Bjarni said, somewhat puzzled. He was beginning to wonder whether Anders was the right person to entrust his beloved *Wolftail* to. There seemed to be a definite lack of logic in the shipwright's thinking, and Bjarni assumed that a person who worked with tools and wood and precise measurements might need to be logical.

'There is a very good reason,' Anders told him, stepping closer so that they were chest to chest. Unconsciously, Bjarni gave way, but Anders followed him, maintaining his invasive position. 'If you stay here and keep driving me crazy by asking "What are you doing now?" and "Why are you doing it that way?" and "What's that for?", there is an excellent chance that I will brain you with a mallet.'

He gestured with a heavy wooden mallet that he used to drive his chisel. Bjarni regarded the mallet, and the shipwright's well-muscled right arm.

'Well, you only had to say,' he said in a slightly aggrieved tone. He backed away, casting one last look at his beloved wolfship. 'Be careful with her, won't you?'

Normally, Anders would be incensed at the suggestion that he wouldn't take care of any ship left in his hands. He was a meticulous craftsman. But the tactless question seemed a small price to pay for getting rid of Bjarni's hovering presence.

'I will treat her as if she were my own,' he said, with a smile that tried to be reassuring — and failed miserably.

Bjarni noted the strained expression and wondered whether Anders might be suffering from indigestion. But wisely, he elected not to comment.

'All right then,' he said. 'I'll be on my way.'

Hal's home, and the restaurant run by his mother, lay on the far side of Hallasholm. Rather than take the long, looping path home from the shipyard through the town, he chose a short cut that went up into the hills, cutting across a ridge, through the woodland above the town itself. It was peaceful and quiet in the woods and he enjoyed the patterns of light and shade thrown by the trees. This close to the coast, there was a mixture of growth, although pine trees predominated. As a result, there was a pleasant smell of pine needles in the air. He wondered what Erak wanted to see him about. He hoped there was some sort of mission in the offing. He and his crew were becoming stale and bored with short patrols.

Maybe we should go back to raiding, he thought, although he wasn't serious.

For years, the Skandians had raided coastal settlements along the Stormwhite Sea and down into the Narrow and Constant Seas. Hal's own mother had been captured in such a raid, in Araluen.

But the treaty Erak had struck some years back with King Duncan of Araluen had included a proviso that the Skandians should desist from that particular pastime, diverting as they might have found it. With their primary activity curtailed, Erak had searched for something else to occupy his restless men. It soon became evident that neighbouring countries would pay, and pay well, for ships and men who might protect their own trading and fishing fleets from predators. As a result, the Skandians had become a de facto naval police force, hiring out their ships to other countries to protect them from raiders and pirates from Sonderland and Magyara, among other less amenable countries. It had proven to be a good decision, with the revenue they received far exceeding the amount that they had made from raiding.

Of course, that had all happened when Hal was a mere child. But there were many older Skandians who remembered those old raiding days — some with a certain amount of nostalgia, it had to be admitted.

He spotted a bunch of yellow wildflowers growing beside the track and he paused, stooping to pick them for his mother. Karina loved having flowers in the house. As he stopped, he heard a rustling noise in the bushes behind him. He paused, his hand on the stems of the flowers.

'Who's there?' he called. The thought occurred that it might be Stig or one of the other crew members, playing a joke on him. It was the sort of thing Jesper would do.

The former thief loved to practise his old craft, sneaking around without being seen or heard.

Hal straightened up, half turning to look at the thick bushes where the sound had originated.

'I can hear you, Jesper,' he called, a trace of irritation in his voice.

The only answer was a rumbling growl from the shadows beneath the trees. The hairs on the back of Hal's head stood on end. That definitely wasn't Jesper, he thought. His hand dropped to the hilt of his saxe knife. As it did, he realised how insignificant that weapon would be if the sound was what he thought it was.

Namely, a bear's snarl.

He had never heard a bear. But he assumed that a bear's growl would be pretty much what he had just heard — deep, resonant and threatening. He began to back away along the path, stumbling on a protruding tree root and hastily regaining his balance, his heart in his mouth. Instinct told him that it would be best to move slowly. Yet every nerve in his body was screaming for him to run.

The bushes moved, as whatever was in there kept pace with him. Or was that why they moved, he wondered. It could be he was imagining things and it was simply the wind moving the branches.

Except there was no wind.

Kloof!

The sound was short, abrupt and threatening. He stopped, peering into the shadowy spaces between the thick bushes, trying to get some sight of what was following him. Nothing moved. He took another step backwards. Then another. Now fear was winning over instinct and he began to move faster, putting as much distance as possible between him and this growling, *kloofing* bear.

Kloof!

There it was again. Peremptory. Commanding. The bear obviously didn't want him to get away. He stopped, and now he could see the bushes moving again. He could hear the passage of a heavy body shoving the undergrowth aside. It seemed to be moving at about waist height, and he estimated that a bear moving on all fours would be about that high.

He saw eyes glowing in the shadows beneath the bushes, then a face pushed through into the open.

Not a bear, he sighed with relief. A dog. But a dog bigger than any he had ever seen. So big, in fact, that it might well have been a small bear.

It was black, with a white muzzle and a white blaze that ran up between its eyes, so that it looked as if it were wearing a black mask. The body was black, with a white chest and a white underbody. The legs were black to about halfway down their length, where the black fur gave way to tan socks and white feet. There were tan markings on its jowls as well, and a tan spot above each eye. With its eyes evenly bisected by that white strip, and the two identical markings above them, there was a pleasing symmetry to the dog's looks. Everything seemed to be just right, correctly in place. Its ears were floppy and black, again with tan highlights at the tips.

Kloof!

The dog spoke again and Hal sensed that it was hesitating about coming any closer. He dropped to one knee and held out his right hand, palm down and fingers loosely curled, towards the animal.

'Kloof yourself,' he said in a gentle, welcoming tone. 'Come and say hello.'

The dog edged out from the bushes, then retreated half a pace, eyes fixed on Hal. He remained unmoving, still with his hand outstretched. The dog took another pace and emerged fully from the bushes. The big, heavy tail wagged tentatively. No, it didn't wag, Hal corrected himself. It waved. Back and forth, back and forth, gaining conviction as it did so.

'Don't be frightened,' he said, thinking how ironic that was. When he'd thought it was a bear, the dog had nearly caused him to lose control of his basic functions.

The dog shook its head. *Kloof!* it said again.

Hal nodded approvingly. 'That's quite a bark you have there,' he told it. He wriggled his fingers and the dog moved a pace closer. Then two more.

It stopped just out of reach of his outstretched hand.

'Don't know what you're scared of,' he told it, speaking in a low voice. 'You could bite my arm off at the elbow if you had a mind to.'

The dog moved closer still. He could feel its warm breath huffing onto his knuckles. Then the tongue came out and licked his fingers. The tail wagged more convincingly as the dog decided it couldn't taste any threat on his hands.

'You know,' he said quietly, 'my knees are killing me. I might have to stand up.'

He opened his fingers, touching the dog lightly under its chin, rubbing the soft hair there. Its eyes half closed and he reached further, to fondle it under the neck. The dog tilted its head to enjoy the touch.

'All right,' he said, 'I'm going to stand up now.'

Slowly, he rose from his crouching position. As he began to move, the dog's eyes snapped open and its ears pricked up in alarm as it reared back half a pace, both its forepaws coming off the ground as it did so. He kept his hand extended, and continued speaking softly to the dog as he stood.

'Nothing to worry about. Nothing to be afraid of. It's still just me.'

The dog eyed him warily, then its ears went down and it sidled forward again to be patted. It let out a low-pitched gurgle of pleasure as Hal fondled its ears, then turned and rammed its heavy body against his lower legs, nearly throwing him to the ground. It sat on Hal's foot, trapping him, and held its chin up for more fondling. He obliged.

'You're a big one, aren't you?' he told it. 'What's your name?' He put a little playful urgency in his tone as he repeated the question, ruffling the fur on its head and ears. 'What's your name, eh? What's your name?'

The dog stood abruptly, tail lashing back and forth.

Kloof! it said. He considered the sound.

'Well, I suppose that's as good a name as any,' he told it.

CHAPTER FOUR

On closer inspection, Hal determined that Kloof, as he now called the dog, was a female. She led the way back to his house, or rather, she pranced ahead of him, turning back from time to time to make sure she was heading in the same direction he was, wagging her tail to encourage him to keep up.

They approached the side door to the restaurant kitchen, where Hal would normally expect to find his mother, preparing for the evening's trade. He gestured to Kloof to sit and, somewhat to his surprise, she did.

'Wait here,' he told her. She thumped her tail once on the ground. Some instinct told him that it might be unwise to let such a large animal come into the restaurant — particularly the part where his mother did the cooking. He mounted the steps to the side door and pushed it open, peering inside.

'Mam?' he called tentatively, rehearsing his next words. He wasn't sure whether to start with 'Look what

I found' or 'Can I keep it?'. Either choice was a risk. 'Look what I found' left itself open to a reply along the lines of, 'Fascinating. Now go and lose it,' while 'Can I keep it?' invited the terse rejoinder, 'No.'

There was no answer, and he edged inside the kitchen, turning back to make sure that Kloof hadn't come any further. She sat watching him. Her tail thumped once or twice on the ground.

'Good girl,' he said softly. 'Stay.'

He held up a hand to reinforce the command, then moved through the kitchen to where he could peer into the restaurant itself.

'Mam?' he called softly.

There was no reply. He tried again, a little louder this time.

'Mam? Are you there?'

'She's gone to the market.'

The voice was right behind him and he leapt in shock, spinning round to see Thorn standing only a metre away.

'Orlog's breath, Thorn! Don't sneak up on me like that!' he said, his voice rising to an undignified high register.

Thorn shrugged. 'I didn't sneak up. I just walked in here, while you were bellowing for Karina.'

'Well, you might have let me know you were there!' Hal said, regaining his composure and trying to cover his embarrassment with righteous indignation.

Again, the old warrior shrugged. 'I did. I said, "She's gone to the market." You seem a little jumpy today,' he added, eyeing the younger man curiously.

'Jumpy? Not at all,' Hal replied. He looked around the kitchen, moving to the bin where Karina threw meat offcuts. It was nearly full and he took a large handful of beef scraps out.

Thorn raised an eyebrow. 'Your jumpiness wouldn't have anything to do with that whacking great black and white horse you've got parked outside, would it? By the way,' he added, gesturing to the meat in Hal's hands, 'last I heard, horses don't eat beef. They eat grass and oats.'

'It's not a horse. It's a dog,' Hal told him.

'Could have fooled me,' Thorn replied. 'Although the floppy ears have a doggy side to them.'

It occurred to Hal that Thorn must have come past the dog to enter the kitchen. 'How come she didn't bark when you came in?' he asked.

'Horses don't bark. And besides, they like me. I have a way with horses.'

'Is that right?' Hal said. He stepped past Thorn to the door and elbowed it open. Kloof was still sitting where he had left her, eyeing the door and thumping the ground with her tail. 'And I keep telling you, she's not a horse.'

He descended the stairs, and held out the meat to Kloof. Her ears came up and she reared back off her forepaws with excitement, bringing them thudding back to the ground together.

'Horses do that,' Thorn observed.

Hal tossed the meat onto the grass in front of Kloof. She trembled expectantly, eyes riveted on him, until he gestured to the meat.

'Go ahead,' he said, and she immediately dropped her head, snuffling and whuffling as she gulped up the meat in great mouthfuls. He looked sidelong at Thorn. 'Horses don't do that,' he pointed out.

Thorn tilted his head to one side in mock surprise. 'Well, what do you know? Maybe it is a dog after all. Where did you find it?'

'She found me, up on the mountain track. Came out of the bushes and frightened three years' growth out of me. I thought she was a bear.'

'Bears don't grow that big,' Thorn said. 'Any idea who might own her?'

Hal shook his head. 'Haven't seen her around the town,' he said. 'And she'd be a bit hard to miss. My guess is she got lost in the mountains and wandered over the ridge.'

'She's pretty scruffy,' Thorn said and Hal nodded.

'Needs a brushing. I'll get onto that.'

Kloof had finished the meat and was sniffing around experimentally, hoping that another piece might have materialised out of thin air. Hal clicked his fingers and she looked up instantly.

'Come on, Kloof,' he said and started to walk towards the back of the building, where he and Karina had their living quarters. Thorn, of course, still lived in his small lean-to against the side of the building.

'What did you call her?' Thorn asked, tagging along with Hal and the dog.

'Kloof,' Hal said.

Thorn frowned. 'Kloof?'

The dog reared her forepaws off the ground again. *Kloof!* she barked.

Thorn made a moue with his mouth. 'Forget I asked. Well, I've got work to do. I was varnishing some benches when you came in and started bellowing for your mam.

Better get back to it. Oh, and good luck with Karina,' he added, as he turned away.

'Why would I need good luck?' Hal asked. He had a vague feeling that pretending not to know what Thorn was alluding to would make it less likely to happen.

'You'll need it when you ask her if you can keep Choof there,' Thorn said.

Kloof! said the dog.

Thorn bowed in her direction. 'I stand corrected.'

'I don't need to ask my mam if I can keep her. I don't need anyone's permission. I'm a skirl. I have my own ship and my own crew. I don't ask permission. I give it. And I hereby give it to myself. I may keep the dog.'

Thorn grinned. 'Let me run a few possible reactions past you,' he said. He thought for a few seconds, then quoted, in a reasonably accurate imitation of Karina's voice:

'I won't have it here. It'll get hair all over the place. And it'll smell. And it's too big. It'll eat us out of house and home. Take it back where you found it.' He paused. 'How's that for starters?'

'She'll be a great watchdog,' Hal said in reply. 'She'll keep thieves away from the house and the restaurant. And she'll keep pests away too.'

'All excellent arguments,' Thorn said, turning to go.

Hal caught his sleeve, betraying his underlying anxiety about Karina's reaction to the dog. 'Do you think they'll convince her?'

'Not for a second.'

Hal pursed his lips as his friend strolled back to the front of the building, where he had been working. He looked critically at Kloof.

'Maybe I should tidy you up. If you're brushed and shining, she'll see what a good dog you are.'

He went into their living quarters, looking for something to brush the dog with. Needless to say, he found nothing in his own room, but in Karina's dressing room he came upon an old hairbrush and a carved wooden comb. He nodded to himself.

'She's had these for ages,' he said. 'She won't mind my borrowing them.'

He went back outside and set to work on Kloof's coat, dragging the comb and brush through her matted fur, gradually clearing the tangles and brambles that she had collected, and stripping out the old, dead hair. She grunted with pleasure at the touch of the brush, only complaining when he attacked the thick tangles around her ears, pulling her head sideways as he did. Being an alpine dog, she had a double coat, and there was twice as much work to do. But after a good hour of brushing and combing, when his arms were aching from the effort, her black coat was shining and lustrous. He looked at the pile of loose hair growing around her, marvelling at the sheer volume.

'I've nearly got enough for another dog here,' he muttered.

Kloof grunted at him.

'Where in the name of Boh-Raka did you find that? And what is it?'

Karina's voice cracked like a whip. Hal turned nervously and rose from the low stool where he had been sitting. His mother was a diminutive woman by Skandian standards, and she was still beautiful by any standards. She could also be extremely intimidating when she chose to be.

She was choosing to be now.

'It's a dog,' he said, trying for an ingratiating smile. He gestured with the hairbrush. 'Look how shiny her coat is.'

Karina's eyes widened with rage as she saw the brush in his hand. 'What have you got there? Have you been brushing that . . . cow . . . with my hairbrush?'

He looked at the brush as if noticing it for the first time. 'It's an old one,' he said. 'You've had it for years. I knew you wouldn't mind.'

'Does it occur to you that I've had it for years because it is my favourite hairbrush?' she said icily.

Hal actually backed away. Kloof looked worried.

'Your favourite?' he said, desperately tugging at the thick wads of dog hair caught in its bristles. 'I'm sure it's all right.'

'It's ruined.'

'No, no,' he said, discarding huge handfuls of dog hair, tossing them behind him as if that would prevent her seeing them. 'It'll be good as new, I promise. I'll clean it up in a jiffy. See?' He held it out to her, realised that it was still heavily laden with dog hair, and snatched it back again, tugging more tufts of black and white fur out of it.

'What makes you think I'd want to put it anywhere near my hair now?' she asked. 'I'm surprised you didn't take my good sprucewood comb as well,' she added bitterly. He glanced down at the comb, lying on the ground beside the stool. Hastily, he covered it with his foot.

'Well, I have to admit, I did look for it. But I couldn't find it anywhere. I think it might be lost.' And if it's not, he thought, it will be the minute you give me a chance to lose it.

'That's beside the point,' Karina said, realising she'd been sidetracked from the main subject. 'Where did you find that . . . monster?'

'She followed me home,' he said.

She snorted derisively. 'Well, I hope you didn't feed her,' she said. 'If you fed her, we'll never get rid of her. You *didn't* feed her, did you?'

Hal found it very difficult to meet her penetrating gaze. He looked up at the sky.

'A bit,' he said finally. Then, desperate to change the subject, he asked, 'Mam, who is Boh-Raka?'

Karina's eyes narrowed.

'She's a Temujai demon who delights in beating stupid sons with a hickory branch,' she said. 'Hopefully, you may meet her soon.' Then she gestured at Kloof. 'Anyway, I'm not having that brute here. It'll get hair all over the place.'

'No!' Hal protested. 'She doesn't shed a lot.'

Karina gestured at the yard. 'Hal, look around, we're knee deep in dog hair right now. You've brushed enough out of her for two more dogs!'

'We-ell . . . one, perhaps. A small one. Two is a bit steep.'

'And who's going to clean up after it?' she demanded.

He pointed at his own chest with the hairbrush, hastily tossing it aside as he realised he was only drawing attention to it again. 'I will!' he exclaimed. 'I promise!'

'Hah!' Karina's voice soared into an upper register of disbelief. 'For the first week or two, I'm sure. Then it'll be me doing all the work. Well, I'm not having it here. Besides, it'll eat us out of house and home. And it'll smell.'

From the other side of the house, they heard an explosive snort of laughter.

'Shut up, Thorn!' Hal shouted, but the laughter only redoubled. Then he pleaded with his mother. 'Please, Mam. She'll be a great watchdog. She'll keep pests away.'

'We've got Thorn for that,' Karina said. The laughter from the other side of the house cut off abruptly.

'Mam, please. She was lost on the mountain, she has nowhere to go. She was so lonely and miserable. Look at that face.'

Karina looked. Unfortunately, Kloof chose not to look lonely and miserable. She grinned and lolled her tongue at Karina. She shuffled forward a few paces, stretching her neck out to be patted. In spite of herself, Karina reached out and ruffled the fur under Kloof's chin. She was a remarkably handsome dog, Karina thought.

'Please, Mam? She'll come on the ship with me. She'll be a real sea dog. And we could use a watchdog on board.'

There was a certain amount of sense in that, Karina thought. A lot of the wolfships had dogs on board. And a brute this size would keep sneak thieves away when the *Heron* was in a foreign port.

'Well, maybe . . .' she said, relenting. Then she realised she was giving in too easily, and felt a need to reclaim the high ground. 'But the first time she bites a customer, she's gone.'

'The first time she bites a customer, the customer will be gone — in one gulp!' Thorn called from the far side of the house. Hal and Karina exchanged a glance.

'Shut up, Thorn,' they chorused.

CHAPTER FIVE

The following morning, Hal walked briskly down to the harbour, with Kloof lolloping along ahead of him. From time to time the big dog would galumph back to look up at him, as if making sure that they were heading in the right direction. Then she would galumph off, staying five to ten metres ahead of him, stopping occasionally to sniff at something fascinating and smelly — like a dead gull or a mummified field mouse.

Hal thought it was best to take her with him. He'd noticed that Kloof had a tendency to chew things — he'd already lost one shoe as a result — and he thought it might be wise to keep her away from his mother as much as possible. Karina had consented to letting Kloof stay, but her attitude was a long way short of enthusiastic. One disaster round the house or restaurant and he knew that Karina's permission would be instantly cancelled.

Heron was pulled up above the high water mark on the beach inside the harbour. She was chocked either side to keep her decks level and, as he approached, Hal could see that the crew were already swarming over her, although he wondered if 'swarming' was the appropriate word for seven people.

On their last trip to sea, he had noticed that some of the rigging was fraying and in need of repair or replacement. As a result, Jesper, Stefan and the twins were re-rigging the ship with new stays and halyards throughout, smearing thick tar on the new rope to preserve and protect it.

'Why don't we just replace the bits that are frayed?' Jesper asked as Hal approached. 'Why replace everything?'

Of course, it would be Jesper who asked that, Hal thought.

'Because if some of it is already frayed and weakening, it won't be long before the rest begins to go the same way. It was set up at the same time, after all,' Hal explained. 'This way, we get it all done at once, instead of in dribs and drabs — and we don't risk having something give way at an embarrassing moment.'

'What's a drib?' Ulf (or perhaps it was Wulf) asked. It seemed he understood what a drab might be, but the term 'drib' puzzled him. His twin gave him a long-suffering look — the sort of look you'd give a little child.

'It's the same as a drab, only the other way around,' Wulf said.

Ulf considered that answer for a few seconds. 'Wouldn't that be a bard?'

Now it was Wulf's turn (or perhaps Ulf's) to look puzzled. 'Wouldn't what be a bard? A bard is a poet.'

Ulf shook his head, clinging stubbornly to his point.

'You said a drib was a drab, only the other way around. A drab the other way around is a bard.'

Stig and Hal exchanged looks. 'Do you ever understand anything those two talk about?' Hal asked his second in command. 'Or is it just me?'

Stig shook his head. 'It's them. They do it on purpose to confuse people — and to annoy me.'

Hal turned to study the twins, where they were kneeling amidships, greasing one of the blocks that the halyards passed through. They did seem to be a little smug, he thought. Stig was probably right.

'Ingvar!' he called. The giant crewman was in the bow. He had dismounted the Mangler and was greasing the thick axle and circular rail that the giant crossbow turned upon.

'Yes, Hal?' Ingvar replied, looking up and peering myopically at the figure on the beach. It might be blurred, but the blur was a familiar one and he recognised his skirl.

'If anyone mentions a drib or a drab . . . or a bard,' Hal added for good measure, 'I want you to throw him overboard.' It was the standard punishment he asked Ingvar to carry out.

'We're ashore, Hal,' Ingvar pointed out.

Hal nodded, conceding the point. The ship was some five metres from the water. 'In that case, drag him down to the water and throw him in from there.'

Ingvar touched one finger to his forehead in assent. 'Anything you say.'

Satisfied that he'd shut down the argument, Hal turned back to Stig to tell him about Erak's summons.

'I only wanted to know what a drib was,' he heard one of the twins say, in an aggrieved tone.

Hal cast his eyes to the heavens. 'Right!' he said. 'Ingvar?'

'On my way, Hal.' Ingvar moved down the deck with deceptive speed. He might be bulky and short-sighted, but the confines of *Heron*'s deck were familiar ground to him. Before the twins could escape, he had grabbed them by the scruff of their necks. They wriggled and squawked, trying to escape. But his grip was like iron.

'It wasn't me!' they both protested.

Ingvar held them up, close to his face, peering at them, looking for some sign that one of them was lying. The twins continued to protest their innocence.

'Throw them both in,' Stig suggested.

Ingvar looked to Hal for confirmation. 'Hal?'

Hal was beginning to smell a rat. He looked suspiciously at the other crew members. Jesper was watching the tableau with interest. But Stefan was looking away, trying to hide a smile. As Hal looked, Stefan's shoulder shook a little as he began to laugh.

'Ingvar,' he called, 'let them go.'

Ingvar was puzzled by the order. 'Let them go, Hal?'

'Let them go,' Hal confirmed. 'Throw Stefan in the harbour instead.'

Stefan half rose to his feet, galvanised with shock. 'Me? What did I do? I didn't do anything!'

But Ingvar had covered the short distance between them and now had his grip locked on Stefan's collar. Ulf and Wulf rolled together in the bottom of the hull, where he had dropped them.

Ingvar climbed over the side of the hull, dropping to the sand, and dragging the struggling Stefan with him.

The smaller boy kept yelling his protests until his words were blotted out by a loud splash as Ingvar, standing knee deep in the water, hoisted him above his head and hurled him several metres out.

'That's impressive,' Stig said. Ingvar's massive strength was a constant source of amazement to them all. 'How did you know it was Stefan?'

'He's an expert mimic, remember,' Hal said. 'And Ulf and Wulf didn't react the way they normally do. They were both saying they didn't do it. Normally, if one of them had done it, they would each blame the other, just to confuse me. And Stefan was looking a little too amused by the whole thing.'

Stig shook his head in mock admiration. 'I guess that's why you're the skirl, and the rest of us are just here to do your bidding.'

Hal shrugged. 'Of course, I could be wrong, in which case, Stefan just got a soaking for nothing.'

Kloof!

'I see you've got a dog,' Stig said.

'That's very observant of you,' Hal said. 'Most people don't notice her.' He looked fondly at his dog, then the fond look gave way to an expression of alarm.

'Hey! Stop that, you great idiot!'

Kloof had found a long-handled brush that Stig had been using to grease the rudder fastenings. She held it now between her forepaws and, with her head tilted to one side, was chewing on it vigorously. Half the handle was gone already and her paws and jowls were thickly coated with grease.

Hal grabbed the brush and tried to drag it from her.

Kloof set her feet in the sand, hindquarters raised, and growled at him, pulling the other way, shaking her head in an attempt to break his grip.

'Let go, you fool!' Hal yelled and she finally did, sending him staggering back, tripping in the sand and falling full length. Kloof stood, wagging her tail, eager for another game.

'Orlog blast you!' Hal shouted. 'You did that on purpose!'

Kloof! said Kloof. Her paws and jowls were covered in the thick grease. Hal grabbed a cleaning rag and wiped most of it off. Kloof tried to pull away from his ministrations.

'Look at you!' he said angrily. 'And I'd just got you cleaned up!'

'Maybe Ingvar could throw her in the water,' Stig suggested, straight-faced. Too straight-faced. Ingvar, who had returned to the ship, leaving Stefan floundering in chest-deep water, cast an appraising eye over Kloof.

'Don't think even I could lift her,' he said, smiling. 'She is a big one.'

'Thorn says she's a mountain dog. They use them to find people lost in the snow,' Hal told them.

'And then, presumably, they ride her home,' Stig said. He held his hand down to Kloof and she whuffled at it, then allowed him to scratch her ears. 'She's a good dog.'

'Trouble is, she chews things,' Hal replied and Stig looked at him in mock disbelief.

'She does? I hadn't noticed. I thought that brush just wore away, I was scrubbing so hard with it.'

Hal ignored the sarcasm. 'She's going to be our ship's dog,' he said. 'She can keep guard when we're in foreign ports.'

'Not a bad idea. Where did you get her?'

'I found her on the mountain yesterday. She was pretty scruffed up and had obviously travelled quite a distance. I took her home and cleaned her up.'

'And your mam let you keep her?' Stig said, his eyebrows rising in surprise.

Hal put his hands on his hips and faced his friend, irritation showing in every line of his body.

'Why do people immediately assume that I need my mam's permission to keep a dog?' he said belligerently.

Stig gave him a thin smile. 'Because I know your mam, remember?'

Hal relaxed, letting the tension drain from his body. 'Yeah, well . . . she said I could keep her. But I think it's best if I keep them apart as much as possible.'

'I would,' Stig said. 'Particularly if she chews things.'

'That's pretty much what I thought,' Hal said. He glanced at the rudder fitting Stig had been working on. 'Are you done with that?'

Stig nodded. 'I was going to give the boys a hand tarring the standing rigging,' he said, but Hal made a negative gesture.

'They can look after that by themselves.' He paused as Stefan squelched his way up the beach past them. The mimic gave Hal an aggrieved look.

'I'm going home to put on dry clothes,' Stefan said. 'If that's all right with you, skirl?'

'Don't be too long. I've got a feeling we need to get this work done as soon as we can.'

Stefan gave a surly wave as he squelched off towards the town.

Stig looked curiously at his skirl. 'Something in the offing?'

Hal nodded. 'I think so. Erak asked me to drop by today — said something about a job for us. Want to come along?'

Stig was already wiping his hands on a spare rag. 'Any idea what he wants?' he said eagerly. Like Hal, he had been chafing with the recent inactivity and the boredom of short patrols. Hal shook his head.

'That's all he said. Let's go and find out what he's got in mind.' He paused, looking uncertainly at Kloof. 'Think I should take her along?'

Stig considered the idea for a few seconds. 'You'd better. If you leave her here, she might eat the ship.'

CHAPTER SIX

'I thought you were up in the mountains, hunting?' Karina said. Lydia was sitting on the workbench in her kitchen, nursing a cup of coffee and watching as Karina deftly boned out a leg of mutton.

'I was. I only stayed one night,' she said.

Karina looked up curiously. 'You usually stay out a bit longer than that, don't you?' She enjoyed Lydia's company and liked the fact that the girl had chosen her as a confidante, often asking her advice about social matters in Hallasholm and, more recently, affairs of the heart.

'I'd planned on being there for four or five days. But a bear started prowling around the cabin and I decided I might make myself scarce.'

'That would seem to be a good idea to me,' Karina agreed. 'So now you have to find another way to avoid Rollond.' She knew about Lydia's problem with the likeable young man. Any other girl in Hallasholm would have fought tooth and nail to get his attention. But not

Lydia. That was one of the things Karina liked about the girl. She was contrary, and Karina liked contrary.

Lydia sighed. 'I saw him coming to the house this morning, with a posy of daisies. I had to sneak out the back window and come over here.'

She had never imagined that she would need her stalking skills, and her ability to use any available cover while moving cross country, to avoid the attentions of a lovestruck young man. Still, she had to admit they came in handy.

Karina turned away to hide a smile. 'You know,' she said, 'it would be best if you just came out and told him you're not interested.'

Lydia pushed herself off the bench and wandered aimlessly around the kitchen, peering into the pots and jars where Karina kept her spices and condiments.

'Yeah, I know,' she said. But she sounded very uncertain about it.

Karina set the first leg of mutton aside. She had trimmed the excess fat from it after she removed the bone, and then spread it out so that it formed a wide, thick slab of meat. After soaking it in a mixture of red wine and oil, fortified by her special mixture of spices, she would grill it over hot coals that evening.

'I just can't seem to find the right time to do it,' Lydia continued.

'There is no right time. It's better to just do it quickly,' Karina told her. 'It's like when a bandage sticks to a wound.' She hefted a second leg of mutton onto her carving board and picked up her boning knife. 'You have to pull it off quickly. It hurts for a second or two. But it's better in the long run.'

'I've tried to tell him three or four times,' Lydia replied. 'But he gets those big puppy dog eyes and I just can't do it. I like him. I don't want to hurt his feelings.'

'You like him. No more than that?'

Lydia shook her head. 'Definitely no more than that. He's a nice person. He's kind and he's amusing and he's very gentle . . .'

'Good-looking, too,' Karina said, eyeing her carefully.

Lydia shrugged. 'Yes. He's good-looking. But looks aren't everything.'

'That's true. You want a boy who's kind and amusing and gentle as well . . . oh, wait a minute, you said he's all those things, didn't you?'

The girl shook her head in frustration. 'Yes! I did! But he still doesn't do it for me. Don't ask me to explain why. I don't know. I wish I did feel more for him. It'd make things a lot simpler. And another thing,' she added, an irritated note creeping into her voice, 'I hate the way people just assume we're an item.'

'Well, tell him you just want to be friends,' Karina said. 'In my experience, boys hate that. Men too,' she added thoughtfully. 'It's usually enough to send them running.'

Lydia pricked up her ears. 'And just who have you sent running?' she asked, a grin forming.

Karina shook her head. 'Never you mind,' she said. 'But I've had my offers since my husband died.'

The grin on Lydia's face widened and she leaned forward expectantly. 'You have?' she said. 'Tell me more.' But Karina dismissed her with a wave of her hand.

'Never mind me. You're going to have to tell Rollond before too much longer.'

'I know,' Lydia said, the grin fading. 'I'll do it after the festival. He's asked me to be his partner. I can hardly hurt his feelings before that. It'd make for a very awkward evening.'

'Good point. But make sure you don't drag it out any longer.'

Lydia nodded. 'You're right. It's time to let him know. It's a pity that *Heron* isn't going on a long cruise. That'd be the best way to distance myself from him.'

'Nothing coming up in that line?' Karina asked, although she knew if there were, Hal would have told her.

'Not that I know of. Just short patrols minding the trading fleet. Out for three days, back for a week. That's not enough time for him to get over me.'

'Maybe something will come up. Hal did mention that Erak wanted to speak to him about something. You never know.'

'That's true,' Lydia agreed. Then, with a devilish smile, she returned to an earlier subject. 'What about you?'

Karina looked up at her. 'What about me?' she said. There was a warning tone in her voice.

'What have you got lined up for the festival? Any of those mysterious suitors planning on dancing the night away with you?'

Karina snorted derisively. 'Me? I'm an old widow. Who'd be interested in me?'

Lydia laughed out loud at that. 'You can't be serious? You're one of the most attractive women in Hallasholm! I've seen how men's heads turn when you're in the market.'

Karina threw the trimmed mutton leg to one side with more than usual vehemence.

'Well, I'm not in the market for any of them,' she said primly, setting to work on a third mutton leg. 'And stop grinning at me like that,' she said, without looking up. Somehow, she knew Lydia was grinning. And somehow, she knew that she hadn't stopped. Finally, Karina set the knife down and looked the girl square in the eyes.

'I have agreed to accompany an old and trusted friend. He will act as my partner. Nothing more than that.'

'And who might that be?' Lydia teased.

Karina straightened her back and said, with great dignity, 'Thorn.'

Lydia's eyes widened. 'Thorn? Our Thorn? I mean . . . Thorn who lives . . .' She gestured in the direction of Thorn's lean-to. 'That Thorn?'

'Do you know another Thorn by any chance?' Karina said stiffly.

Lydia shook her head in wonder. 'No, I don't. Who would ever have thought it? You and Thorn?'

'Nobody would have thought it, because it isn't. And we're not.'

'Not what?' Lydia's grin was as wide as it could be now. 'What are you not?'

'We're not . . . anything,' Karina said. She slashed vigorously at the leg of mutton, removing nearly as much meat as fat.

Lydia couldn't resist it. She crooned softly.

'Karina and Tho-orn, sitting in a tree-ee. Kay-eye-ess-ess-eye-en-gee.'

'This is a very sharp knife I have here,' Karina said evenly.

'I was just leaving.'

'What in the name of chaos is *that*?' Erak asked, pointing at Kloof.

Hal smiled. He was getting used to this reaction.

'She's a mountain dog. They're used to find lost travellers in the snow and lead them to safety.'

'Where did you get her?'

Hal shrugged. 'I found her on the mountain. I think she wandered off from her home and got lost.'

'Hardly what you'd want in a dog whose task is to help people who are also lost,' Erak remarked and Hal acknowledged the truth of the statement.

'She's only young,' he pointed out.

Erak raised his eyebrows. 'I hope she doesn't have any more growing to do. Now come and sit, the two of you.'

They were in the Great Hall of Hallasholm, where Erak conducted official business as the Oberjarl. He gestured to two long benches that flanked his massive oak chair of office. Hal and Stig sat either side of him. Kloof flumped down onto the floor between the three of them, with a massive sigh.

'I asked Stig to come because I assumed that you had something in mind for the *Heron*,' Hal said.

Erak nodded several times. A good skirl usually included his first mate in discussions involving the ship.

'I do indeed.' Then, without further preamble, he said, 'How would you like to go to Araluen?'

Stig and Hal looked at each other in surprise. Whatever they might have expected from Erak, this definitely hadn't been on the list. Stig recovered first.

'What for?' he asked.

Erak shrugged. 'Well, for eight or nine months. That's the usual term.'

'I think he meant why?' Hal said.

'Oh, I see. Well, you know we assign a ship each year as the duty ship in Araluen?'

The two boys nodded. It had been a longstanding practice, since the treaty brokered years before by two Rangers and the royal princess of the western kingdom.

'I've heard about it. I'm not sure what it entails,' Hal said, glancing at Stig, who shrugged.

'Basically, I place a ship at the disposal of King Duncan,' Erak told them. 'If he needs to get people somewhere in a hurry, the duty ship takes them. Our wolfships are faster than anything they have in the Narrow Sea.'

'And *Heron* is faster than any of the other wolfships,' Stig put in.

Erak turned a heavy-browed frown on him.

'With the possible exception of *Wolfwind*, of course,' Stig added diplomatically.

'Exactly,' the Oberjarl agreed. Then the frown disappeared. 'In addition, the duty ship patrols the Narrow Sea for King Duncan and takes care of any smugglers, pirates or slavers in the area.'

'Are there many of those?' Hal asked.

Erak nodded. 'Oh yes. Since we gave up raiding, other countries have swarmed in to fill the gap. Sonderlanders, some Magyarans, of course, and corsairs from the Constant Sea. Iberian slavers are a problem, too. What is your dog doing?' he said, abruptly changing the subject.

Hal looked down. Kloof had wriggled forward and was licking Erak's prized walking staff, where it rested against his chair.

'She appears to be licking your . . . walking stick.'

'Well, tell her to stop,' Erak said. He had considered shoving the dog away with his foot, but she was a very big dog, after all. 'And it's an official staff, not a stick,' he added, with some dignity.

'Cut it out, Kloof!' Hal snapped. She looked at him, a guilty expression on her face, and he gestured for her to get away from Erak's chair.

'Go on! Out of it!'

Reluctantly, she moved back, her tail lowered. She lay on her side again and sighed heavily.

'You were saying?' Hal asked.

Erak nodded and resumed. 'Oh yes. Well, there'll be bags of things to do. Quite a bit of fighting, chasing slavers, catching smugglers, that sort of thing. Should suit your boys down to the ground.'

'Certainly sounds better than playing nanny to the fishing fleet,' Stig said.

'We're right in the middle of re-rigging her,' Hal said. 'That'll take a few days.'

'No rush,' Erak said. 'You can wait until after the festival if you like. That'll still give you time to get round Cape Shelter before the Summer Gales set in.'

'In that case, we'll take the job,' Hal said.

Erak cocked his head. 'Don't want to speak to the others about it?'

Hal paused, but it was Stig who answered.

'Hal's our skirl. We go where he says.'

Erak nodded, impressed. That was the way he had run his ship when he was skirl. He sighed. Sometimes those days seemed so long ago.

'That's settled then. I have some dispatches to send to Duncan. I'll get those to you in the next day or so. Then you can head off after the festival.'

Hal and Stig grinned at each other. They both felt a stirring of anticipation. The prospect of a new mission, a long way from home, appealed to their adventurous spirits. They stood to go, shaking hands with the Oberjarl.

'Speaking of ships,' Erak said, 'have you seen Tursgud's?'

The eager grins faded from the two boys' faces. Tursgud, their nemesis during brotherband training, had turned out badly since losing the brotherband title to the Herons. He had become surly and argumentative, liable to flare up in anger at the slightest reason — real or imagined. His own brotherband members had largely deserted him and he spent his time in the cheap taverns near the waterfront.

His father, hoping to spark some sense of purpose in him, had bought him a ship. But Tursgud had crewed it with a bunch of thugs and petty criminals. The ship itself had been painted midnight blue and he had rechristened her *Nightwolf*.

'She looks fast,' Hal said. She had a long, slender hull and a fine entry. She was rigged in the traditional square sail pattern. 'I'd say she'll be very fast going downwind.'

'Hmmm,' said Erak thoughtfully. 'Just wonder why he painted her that dark colour. Dark ships tend to be that way for a purpose — and it's usually not a good one.'

CHAPTER SEVEN

The main square in front of Hallasholm's Great Hall was awash with light. Lanterns and torches hung from poles and stood in brackets in the walls of buildings and there were three large bonfires set around the edge of the square.

There were also half a dozen fire pits, each one with a spit set over it, where carcasses of bullocks and sheep turned above the red-hot coals, spitting and sizzling as they gradually browned. Cooks moved in from time to time to slice cooked meat from the outer layers of the carcasses, exposing the meat underneath to the heat, so it could grill in its turn. Platters of smoking hot beef and mutton were set out for the revellers to help themselves. Half a dozen large salmon, smoked to a succulent finish in the town's smokehouse, provided a delicious alternative for those who preferred it. In addition, there were bowls of fresh, crusty bread, potatoes baked black in their jackets in the coals, fresh greens and tart pickled cabbage.

The people of Hallasholm were there in force: old, young and everywhere in between. This was, after all, the hay-making festival, the most important night in Hallasholm's social calendar. In addition to just about every inhabitant of the capital, people had travelled from outlying farms and villages to join in the fun. The cleared space directly in front of the Great Hall was packed with couples dancing. A four-piece band consisting of a fiddler and two pipers, accompanied by a tonal drum, kept the music going — jaunty happy country airs for the most part. The musicians were sustained by a constant relay of foaming tankards of ale, deposited in front of them by the dancers. The band seemed to have mastered the art of drinking deep draughts of ale in sequence, so that the music continued, uninterrupted.

Young children ran between the legs of the people thronging the square, shrieking with laughter and excite-ment at being up after their normal bedtime. From time to time, an exasperated parent would yell at his or her off-spring to 'Keep it down! Keep it down, for Thaki's sake!' The children would fall silent for two or three seconds, then the running and shrieking would start all over again.

Erak's great chair had been carried out and set at the top of the stairs in front of the Great Hall, overlooking the square. The Oberjarl sat there, beaming at his people, a tankard in one hand and his magnificent polished staff in the other. At intervals, he drank from the tankard and beat time to the music with his staff. Sometimes, he got the two actions mixed up, but nobody seemed to notice.

Erak looked around the square and, seeing the people enjoying themselves, he felt content. Life in Skandia could be harsh, with its long winters and freezing temperatures.

And the Skandians worked hard most of the year — at sea, fishing or trading, or on land, tending their sheep and cattle and crops. It was a hard life, with not a lot of time for relaxation. On a balmy summer night like this, it was good for his people to let their hair down and enjoy themselves. He smiled, pleased to see that the evening was going well. There had only been a few fights so far, and they had been quickly subdued. And so far, only one girl had been reduced to wailing tears by her boyfriend's dalliance with another girl. All in all, it was a good festival.

Then the smile faded as his gaze fell on a group at one of the side tables.

It was Tursgud, and half a dozen of his unsavoury crew members. They were seated at a table — sprawled would be a better word for it, Erak thought. An ale cask had been broached and was on the table between them. From time to time, they dipped tankards into it and drank deeply. Even across the square, and the background noise of hundreds of happy festival-goers, he could hear their raised voices as they shouted and laughed raucously. People around them drew away, casting disapproving glances in their direction.

'There's trouble about to happen,' Erak said.

Svengal, who was sitting on a stool to one side of Erak's chair, had followed the direction of his gaze. He curled his lip with distaste at the sight of Tursgud and his men.

'Want me to get some of the crew?' he asked.

Erak looked at him. 'Do you seriously think we need help to handle that rabble?' Then he changed the question. 'Do you seriously think *I* need help to handle that rabble?'

Svengal grinned. 'Not really. But I'll tag along for the sheer fun of it, shall I?'

'Suit yourself,' Erak growled. He took up his staff and began to thread his way through the crowd, Svengal following close in his wake. There was no outward sign of Erak's anger, other than the sharper-than-usual *clack! clack! clack!* of the metal-shod staff on the cobblestones.

Tursgud looked up as the Oberjarl approached. His eyes were bleary and he was very much the worse for drinking ale. It was not a law, but it was a generally upheld convention in Hallasholm that young men didn't drink ale until they had turned twenty-one. They might occasionally have a tankard, and people would turn a blind eye. But Tursgud and his crew were all below that age and they had been drinking solidly for some time. Tursgud felt a quick thrill of nervousness as he focused on the Oberjarl's face. Then bravado, courtesy of the ale, kicked in and his lip curled in a sneer.

'I think you've had enough to drink,' Erak said calmly.

Tursgud sniggered. Erak took a deep breath, restraining himself with some difficulty. Behind him, Svengal raised his eyes to heaven. He wondered whether Tursgud knew exactly how much danger he was in at that moment.

'Silly old fool,' said the youth sitting next to Tursgud. His name was Kjord. He was a swarthy-looking young man with long hair that hung in greasy plaits down the side of his head. He'd meant to make his comment in an undertone, but unfortunately it had been louder than he planned. Then he shrugged to himself. There was just the Oberjarl and his former first mate, standing a few paces away, and there were seven of the crew from *Nightwolf* at the table. What could Erak do, after all?

What Erak did was to look at the half-full ale cask on the table before Tursgud. It was about forty centimetres across and sixty centimetres high. The lid had been removed so Tursgud and his cronies could dip their tankards in to fill them. Erak set down his staff, leaning it against the wall behind him, then picked up the cask in both hands and raised it to his lips.

'This your ale?' he asked.

'Well, we bought it,' Kjord said. He maintained his defiant air, yet he felt a qualm of uneasiness. The cask was still quite heavy, yet Erak had raised it without the slightest effort. The Oberjarl tipped the cask and took a long mouthful.

Then, with an expression of disgust, he spat a stream of ale, sending it splattering onto the table in front of them.

'You should get your money back,' he said.

Only Svengal saw what was coming. But then, he'd known Erak for years. The others all had their attention on the foaming ale that was running across the table. As they watched it, Erak raised the cask high, then slammed it down on Kjord's head.

The bottom of the cask gave way and showered the remaining ale down over Kjord's body and shoulders. The outer section of the cask crammed down over his head, encasing it completely. Kjord's startled cry was muffled by the cask and the flood of ale over his face.

He sat upright for a second or two. Then Erak grabbed his collar and jerked him up and back off the bench with one convulsive heave. Luckily for Kjord, the cask protected his head from direct contact with the cobbles as he crashed over. But the impact was too much for the cask and it disintegrated into its component pieces — a handful of staves and two steel hoops that slid down around Kjord's neck.

Tursgud and the other Nightwolves stared at their shipmate in shock and fright. One of them went to rise from his seat but felt a powerful hand pushing him back down.

'Don't,' Svengal told him softly, and he didn't.

Erak leaned down, resting his fists on the table and putting his face close to Tursgud's. 'Now, pick that piece of garbage up.' He jerked his head at Kjord, who was moaning softly. 'And get out of my sight.'

Tursgud met his gaze and felt a blade of fear stab through him. Erak was, for the most part, a cheerful man. It was easy to forget that he'd fought in scores of battles and mortal combats and faced hundreds of enemies in his time. When the affable mask was stripped away, what was left was nothing short of terrifying.

'Yes, Oberjarl,' Tursgud said meekly. He gestured to his crewmen. 'Give me a hand with Kjord.'

Erak turned to Svengal, a satisfied look on his face.

'Well,' said his former first mate, 'it appears that you didn't need me after all.'

'Didn't think I would,' the Oberjarl told him. Then he looked around, missing something. 'Where's my staff? It was right here.'

Svengal shrugged, stooping to look under the table and benches. There was no sign of the staff.

'Beats me,' he said. 'I'm sure it'll turn up. I'll get some of the boys to look for it.'

Reluctantly, looking around him as he went, as if the staff might magically reappear, Erak allowed his friend to lead him back to his chair.

'I just put it down for a minute,' he said ruefully. 'Where can it have gone?'

'Never mind, chief,' Svengal told him. 'We'll find it. And it'll be in the last place we look,' he said comfortingly.

Erak glared at him as if he were half-witted.

'Well, of course it will. Why would we keep looking after we've found it?'

CHAPTER EIGHT

Stig and Hal had watched the confrontation from across the square. In truth, Stig had been on the point of going over himself and telling Tursgud to clear off. He had to admit, however, that Erak had done so with greater aplomb and dispatch than he could have managed.

'Well, that was exciting,' said a familiar voice behind them.

They turned to see Lydia. They had noticed her earlier in the evening, always with Rollond at her side. She looked beautiful, Hal thought, wearing a slender green woollen dress that showed off her slim figure to best advantage, and with flowers twined into her hair. He'd given her an obsidian bracelet on her previous birthday and was pleased to see she was wearing it. She was wearing green open-toed sandals that had semi-precious stones sewn to them. They glittered in the wavering fire and lamplight. He looked at her admiringly. He was more accustomed to seeing Lydia in her leather overjacket, woollen tights and boots, and with her hair pulled back and held by a leather band. He sensed that Stig was gazing at her admiringly as well.

'You look wonderful,' he told her and she reddened slightly, then smiled.

'Thanks. You've brushed up pretty well yourself.'

Hal was wearing a white linen shirt, black trousers and knee-high soft leather boots. Like her outfit, it was a change from his normal rough and ready seagoing clothes.

Lydia glanced at Stig and included him in the smile. 'And how about you? I never knew you were such a dandy.'

Stig was dressed in similar style to Hal. But his linen shirt was embroidered with intricate patterns and he had a silver bracelet on his right wrist.

'Where have you been all evening?' he asked, although he had a pretty good idea what the answer would be.

'Oh, I was dancing with Rollond. Then I had some supper – with Rollond. Then I danced with Rollond some more. And then, for a change, I danced with Rollond. Why didn't either of you ask me to dance?'

Hal frowned. There was an air of resignation in her voice. 'I thought you two were . . . you know . . .' he said uncertainly and was surprised to see the momentary flash of anger in her eyes.

'No, I don't. And no, we're not.'

'Really?' There was a note of keen interest in Stig's voice. Lydia didn't seem to notice it.

'I saw you two carving a swathe through all the pretty girls here,' she said.

Hal shrugged. It was true. Since their triumphant

return from Raguza, all of the Herons had become celebrities in Hallasholm — he and Stig most of all. It irked him slightly that pretty girls, whom he would once have longed to impress, now tended to seek him out, giggling and twittering if he smiled at them or gave them the time of day. I'm still the same person I always was, he thought. Before he could voice the thought, Lydia changed tack.

'I was talking to Jesper earlier. He said something about a mission — a trip to Araluen?' she said. 'Were you going to mention it to me?'

Hal was a little surprised. 'Are you interested in coming along?' he said. 'Of course you'd be welcome,' he added quickly, noticing her eyes narrow.

'I'm still a Heron, aren't I?' she replied. 'At least, I've got the hat to prove it.'

'We sort of thought you'd prefer to stay here with Rollond,' Stig said. He'd obviously missed the undertones in her previous statements.

'Oh please,' she said wearily.

'We'd love to have you with us. You're one of us, after all. It wouldn't be the same without you,' Hal said. Stig nodded enthusiastic agreement.

Lydia heaved a sigh of relief. The mission to Araluen was the answer to her problem with Rollond. And on top of that, she'd enjoy being back in company with the other Herons.

'We're leaving tomorrow, on the afternoon tide,' Hal told her. 'We're taking on last-minute supplies in the morning.'

It was normal practice to load perishables such as fresh milk, fruit, bread and meat as late as possible. Lydia grinned at the two of them.

'I'll see you midmorning then,' she began. Then, as something behind them caught her eye, her jaw dropped in astonishment.

'Will you look at that?' she said.

The boys turned, noticing a stirring in the crowd, and a babble of surprised exclamations from the people around them.

Karina and Thorn were walking across the square, arm in arm, and heading for the dance floor. Karina looked simply beautiful in a blue dress that showed off her perfect figure to full advantage. Her hair was coiled on top of her head and threaded with wildflowers. The style accentuated her graceful, slender neck.

But, stunning as she was, it was Thorn who attracted the most attention.

'He's clean,' Stig whispered in amazement. Thorn was wearing a green jerkin of thin glove-quality leather over a white shirt. His green woollen trousers were carefully pressed and tucked into gleaming, high leather boots. His hair and beard had been trimmed and was brushed till it shone.

As the crowd watched in silence, the pair took up their positions and began to dance. They moved in absolute unison, stepping out the measure of the dance perfectly. A low hum of appreciation rose from the crowd.

'Thorn can dance!' Hal said in surprise. 'Who would have thought it?'

But Stig, even though he watched the pair with some wonder and admiration, shook his head slowly. 'We should have known. Remember how he demonstrated his fighting moves in the net when we were training? Of course he can dance!'

When Thorn had taken over training the Heron Brotherband, he had devised a system to improve their agility and timing, making them perform intricate manoeuvres while stepping inside a large rope mesh net stretched horizontal to the ground. He had shown them what he wanted them to do, stepping forward, backward, sideways at high speed, sometimes with his eyes shut, and never entangling himself.

Hal nodded. If Thorn was light-footed on the battlefield, it followed that he'd be equally so on the dance floor. It had just never occurred to Hal that his friend would dance.

At least when he's dancing, Hal thought, he doesn't have to wave an axe around.

Later that night, Stig and Hal walked home in companionable silence. After some minutes, Stig glanced curiously at his friend, who seemed lost in thought.

'How did it feel, seeing Thorn and your mam dancing?' he asked.

Hal shrugged, then realised he was glad to talk about it.

'I have to admit, I was a little thrown by the whole thing at first,' he said. 'Then I thought, why not? They both deserve a chance to be happy together, if that's what they want. I can think of . . .'

His voice trailed off as he peered into the darkness, towards a thick clump of bushes.

'What's that?' he asked. He could hear a strange growling sound, accompanied by crunching and cracking noises. The growl sounded familiar. He walked a few paces towards the bushes, looked over them and froze in horror.

'Oh no. You idiot of a dog! Erak will kill you.'

In a small clear space behind the bushes, growling and grumbling happily to herself, Kloof was busy chewing on Erak's missing walking staff. She had already reduced it to half its original length and was enthusiastically working on the remaining stump.

Hal swooped and grabbed the free end of the staff, trying to drag it free. Kloof, always looking for a chance to play, clamped her jaws on the other end, setting her rear quarters high in the air and heaving back away from Hal's frantic grasp. She growled playfully and shook her head from side to side as she tried to break his grasp on the staff.

'Drop it, you great hairy fool!' Hal shouted at her. But she only growled and shook the staff harder, her tail lashing from side to side with the fun of it all.

'Let *go*!' Hal commanded. 'If Erak sees you, you're a dead dog! Stig, give me a hand, for pity's sake!'

Stig finally managed to stop laughing long enough to grab Hal by the back of his belt and haul back, adding his strength to the struggle. Even so, Kloof continued to gain on them, dragging them after her as she growled and snarled and rumbled deep in her massive chest.

Finally, unexpectedly, she released her hold on the staff and they tumbled back over each other, rolling on the wet grass. She barked enthusiastically as they disentangled themselves and stood up.

Hal looked at the truncated staff, his face a mask of horror. Half of it was gone — chewed away, leaving only a splintered, raw end. The remaining piece, surmounted by the silver bulb, was dented and scarred in a score of places by Kloof's massive teeth.

'What will we do?' he asked, a note of panic in his voice.

Stig bridled a little. 'What do you mean, "we"?' he asked. 'She's your dog.'

'We . . . I mean, I . . . can't let Erak see it like this. He'll go berserker.'

'Get rid of it,' Stig said succinctly. 'Chuck it in the harbour.'

The harbour was close by and it seemed like an ideal solution. They ran to the quay and Hal drew his arm back, with the staff ready to throw. Then he realised that Kloof was trembling with anticipation, bouncing up and down on her forepaws and rumbling happily.

'Oh no. She's planning to fetch it!' he said. 'Grab her collar, turn her away so she can't see.'

Stig obliged, even though Kloof struggled desperately with him. When he was sure she couldn't see what he was doing, Hal drew back his arm and hurled the ruined staff, spinning end over end, into the sea. The tide was running out and he watched as the staff, floating upright as the weight of the silver knob on one end kept it vertical, slowly drifted out with it, passing through the harbour mouth. Kloof, released by Stig, sniffed busily around them, trying to find some trace of her wonderful toy.

'Thank Orlog for that!' Hal said in a heartfelt tone. Then he and Stig turned to continue their way home, Kloof patrolling happily in front of them, still searching for some trace of the staff and wondering how it had disappeared.

It must be said that it was a mark of Hal's level of panic that he had forgotten, or at least overlooked, one vital fact.

He was a skilled and experienced navigator, and an expert sailor, well versed in the lore of the sea. But in the heat of the moment, and the relief at having got rid of the evidence of Kloof's crime, one vital fact had eluded him.

Tides may go out. But, inevitably, they come back in again.

CHAPTER NINE

The following morning, the crew of the *Heron* were loading last-minute stores, checking equipment and spares, and stowing their own gear in the spaces beside their rowing benches. They would be a long time gone, and Hal wanted to make sure that they had everything they might need for the coming mission.

Stig watched as Hal and Ingvar stowed a full supply of bolts for the Mangler in the locker behind the massive crossbow. He frowned curiously as his friend placed a large canvas roll in the locker. The roll rattled slightly as Hal placed it down.

'What's that?' he asked.

Hal turned to look at him, not understanding the question at first. Then he noticed the direction of Stig's gaze and lifted the roll out again. He unwrapped it and revealed some twenty bolts, lashed together in two bundles. But these were not like the normal bolts the Mangler fired. Instead of the steel-shod sharp point, these were surmounted by a slightly bulbous cylinder.

'It's an idea I thought we might try out,' Hal explained. 'When we were attacking the watch towers at Limmat, I noticed that splinters flying from the balustrade caused a lot of damage.'

Stig nodded. 'I remember. The railings were soft pine and when the bolts hit them they shattered, so that pieces went everywhere.'

'Exactly. So I thought we might try these.' Hal tapped the bulbous end of one of the bolts. Looking more closely, Stig could see that it was made of hardened, baked clay.

'I got Farndl to make them up for me,' he added. Farndl operated the Hallasholm pottery works. 'They're filled with small rocks and shards of broken pottery. I thought if one of these hit a hard surface, the head would break up and throw splinters and rocks in all directions. That way, one bolt might knock over three or four enemy troops.'

Stig was impressed. But then, he thought, ever since he had known Hal, his friend had been coming up with new and ingenious ideas — most of which worked.

They were interrupted by a voice behind them.

'Morning, everyone.' It was Thorn, carrying his kitbag and weapons, stepping lightly down from the quay onto the deck. The crew chorused greetings to him. He looked slightly ill at ease as he met Hal's eye, dumped his gear on the deck and nodded his head towards the steering platform at the stern.

'Can we have a word?' he asked.

Hal nodded and followed the old warrior down the deck, to a spot at the stern where they were a little removed from the crew. He waited expectantly, then realised that Thorn was embarrassed, and not sure how to begin. That was a first, he thought. He sensed he knew what was on Thorn's mind.

'Is this about last night?' he asked.

Thorn reddened, nodding several times. 'Ah . . . yes. Ah . . . ah-ahm. Yes,' he said, clearing his throat nervously.

Hal said nothing, so Thorn continued.

'Just wanted you to know, there's been no . . . funny business between me and your mam. No . . . hanky-panky, if you know what I mean?'

For a second, Hal was tempted to pretend ignorance of what Thorn meant, and tease him for a minute or two, making him explain further. Then he realised how mean-spirited that would be. After all, Thorn was simply trying to explain how things were between him and Karina. Hal put his hand on the well-muscled shoulder in a friendly gesture.

'There's no problem so far as I'm concerned, Thorn,' he said sincerely. 'If you and Mam are —' he hesitated, not sure of a delicate way to phrase the next thought, then settled on an old-fashioned term that Skandians used to describe courtship '— walking out together, I couldn't be happier.'

To his amazement, Thorn blushed a deep red. 'Well . . . not sure that it's come to that. We're friends, is all. Good friends, though,' he added.

Hal nodded reassuringly. 'I'm sure you are. And if you become more than that, then you have my blessing.' He frowned at the words. It seemed odd to be offering Thorn — rambunctious, roistering, unkempt, fearless

Thorn — his blessing. But the grey-haired warrior nodded his gratitude.

'Yes. Well, that's a weight off my mind. Of course, Karina may not feel the same way. We haven't really talked about it.'

'Maybe you could talk about it now,' Hal said, looking over Thorn's shoulder to where his mother's diminutive form was striding along the quay. Come to say goodbye to me, Hal thought, and stepped up onto the shore to greet her. Thorn grunted in surprise, then stepped up behind him, staying back a few paces.

Hal moved forward as his mother approached, prepared for the usual lengthy exhortations to do nothing silly, to take no unnecessary risks, to come back safely, to eat regularly and to keep his socks dry whenever possible. He smiled. It was nice to be fussed over, he thought.

The smile faded as Karina swept past him, barely registering his presence, threw her arms around Thorn's neck and kissed him soundly on the mouth. For a moment, Thorn was caught by surprise. Then he responded eagerly. A muted cry of 'Whoooooo!' came from the crew, who were interested spectators. Finally, Karina broke off the kiss and stepped back, looking up into Thorn's eyes.

'Don't do anything silly. Don't take any unnecessary risks,' she said. 'Eat regularly. And come back safely to me.'

Thorn, still taken aback by the whole thing, nodded sombrely. 'I will,' he said.

'And try to keep your socks dry,' Karina added. Then she turned away from him, seemed to notice Hal for the first time, and patted him absently on the cheek.

'Look after yourself,' she said. Then, chin up and back straight, she swept off down the quay, back the way she had come.

Erak and Svengal were out on their morning walk around Hallasholm. Erak said that a daily walk helped him keep in touch with his subjects, and see what was going on in the town. Svengal knew there was an ulterior motive. Erak walked each morning to keep his waistline down. Life as the Oberjarl was essentially a sedentary one and Erak didn't get the sort of exercise he used to enjoy as a raiding sea wolf. Svengal was content to keep his old friend company. Today, he noticed, Erak was distracted and a little grumpy.

'Beautiful day, chief,' he observed. And it was. There were a few light clouds in the sky, chasing each other from one horizon to the next. Other than that, the sky was a clear, brilliant blue. The sun was warm even though the air itself was always somewhat cool, even in Skandia's summer.

'Hmmmph,' Erak grunted.

'Something wrong?' Svengal asked. He was pretty sure he knew the answer.

'I miss my staff,' Erak grumbled. 'I've got used to it.'

And in fact, he had. He had enjoyed striding along, swinging the long staff out in front of him and planting it solidly to mark each stride, twirling it in the air behind him, then clapping it down once more. It gave a pleasant rhythm to his walk. Now it was gone. They had searched the square thoroughly after the festival had ended, but had found no sign of it.

'Don't know what could have happened to it,' he continued. 'Maybe one of those rabble off *Nightwolf* took it.'

Svengal shook his head. 'Didn't see any of them do it,' he said. 'They were all pretty intent on getting away from you as fast as possible.' He glanced across the inner harbour and noticed that the dark blue ship was missing from its usual mooring. 'Looks like they've gone,' he said.

Erak nodded. 'Tark told me they slipped out of the harbour last night. Good riddance, too.' Tark was the captain of the harbour guard.

But Svengal wasn't listening. His keen eyes had spotted something gleaming in the sand at the water's edge. He jumped down onto the beach and walked towards it. His heart sank as he got closer and recognised the ruined, foreshortened walking staff — one end chewed to splinters and the other still surmounted by its silver knob.

He retrieved it and noted the tooth marks up and down its length.

'Orlog's bad breath,' he muttered. 'This is going to be ugly.'

For a moment, he considered dropping the ruined staff and kicking sand over it to hide it. But Erak had already seen him pick it up.

'What's that?' Erak called.

Svengal tried to hide the staff behind his back. 'Nothing, chief. Just a piece of driftwood.'

But Erak had seen the telltale glint of silver. He walked down the beach suspiciously. 'Driftwood, my backside!' he roared. 'Bring it here! Let me see it!'

Reluctantly, Svengal revealed the ruined walking staff. For a moment, Erak was speechless. Just for a moment. Then he let out an inchoate bellow of rage.

'Chief, don't go . . .' Svengal began. But he was cut off by Erak, now in full voice.

'That demon-blasted dog! I'm going to . . . I'm going to . . .' He glanced around and his eyes lit on a twelve-year-old boy who had been walking along the beach. The boy was staring at the red-faced, apoplectic Oberjarl, fascinated. Erak pointed at him.

'You! Boy! What's your name?'

'Gundal Leifson, Oberjarl,' the boy said nervously.

Erak now swept his arm around to point in the direction of the Great Hall. 'Run to the Great Hall, Gundal Leifson, and bring me my axe. It's leaning against my big chair. Go!'

'Yes, Oberjarl!' The boy took off, running flat out towards the Hall.

Erak stood, arms folded across his massive chest, breathing deeply, muttering dreadful curses.

Svengal eyed him nervously. 'Chief? What are you going to do?'

'I'm going to separate him from his head,' Erak replied calmly, his eyes fixed on the *Heron*. There was a frightening light in his eyes.

Svengal glanced nervously towards the distant ship. 'Hal?' he asked.

'No. The dog. But I'll do for Hal too if he gets in the way,' Erak said.

'The dog's a she, chief,' Svengal told him.

'He, she. Won't matter too much once she doesn't have a head,' Erak said.

On board *Heron*, they heard Erak's wordless bellow. All eyes turned to look at the burly Oberjarl, standing on the beach several hundred metres away.

'What's up with Erak?' Stefan asked.

Stig shaded his eyes with his hands, peering at Erak and Svengal. He saw the Oberjarl was holding something and, as he watched, the sunlight flashed as it reflected from the object. He felt a sinking sensation in his stomach.

'Oh no,' he said. He turned to Hal. 'I think he's found his walking staff.'

Hal turned and looked quickly forward, to where Kloof was curled up in the bow, snoozing. The dog had sneaked away from the house after he had gone to bed, returning just before dawn. Now he had a bad feeling that she had been up to no good. He looked back at Erak.

'Why is he just standing there?' he asked. He noticed that the Herons had unconsciously drawn away, distancing themselves from him. Only Stig and Thorn remained close. As he watched, a young boy came running down the beach road, jumped down onto the beach and handed something to Erak. Sunlight flashed on metal again.

'That looks uncomfortably like an axe,' Stig said.

'Is this the one, Oberjarl?' asked Gundal Leifson. 'It looks a bit . . . short.'

It was Erak's axe and it was short. Half its handle had been chewed away, leaving a ragged, splintered stump of ashwood. Again, Erak bellowed in rage.

'My axe!' he roared. 'My beautiful axe! Look at what that cursed dog has done to it!' He held it out for Svengal to see.

His first mate shrugged deprecatingly. 'It's not too bad, chief. You can always —'

'This was my grandfather's axe!' Erak said, quivering with rage.

Svengal's eyebrows went up in surprise. 'I didn't know that.'

Erak was nodding, as he glared at the ruined weapon.

'My father replaced the handle and I replaced the head,' he said. 'But otherwise, it's completely original.'

Then, with a roar, he took off down the beach towards the quay, brandishing the foreshortened axe in one hand and the equally foreshortened staff in the other.

On board *Heron*, they heard his bloodcurdling cry. Hal glanced nervously to the quay, where a small pile of crates and kegs were waiting to be loaded.

'Get those stores on board and cast off!' he yelled, his voice breaking slightly with nervous tension. The crew of the *Heron* took one look at the bellowing Oberjarl, thrashing his way through the sand towards them, and leapt to obey, pitching the casks and crates onto the deck willy-nilly, then leaping back aboard and running to cast off the mooring lines. Distancing themselves from Hal was all very well, but Erak in his current mood might not recognise such a fine distinction.

Erak had reached the cobblestoned quay as they let the last lines slip. Ingvar had an oar in his hands and was busy fending the ship away from the shore.

Thorn watched with mild interest. 'Thought you were waiting for the tide?' he observed.

Hal turned a fearful glance on him. 'You can wait for the tide if you choose,' he said, mentally urging Stefan and Jesper on to greater speed as they hauled up the starboard sail. The sail flapped, thrashed, then filled with a *whooping* sound as the twins sheeted it home. He felt the tiller come alive in his hands and the ship curved smoothly out into the harbour.

Erak arrived too late, with Svengal close behind him, and Gundal Leifson following on their heels. The Oberjarl let go an inarticulate howl and literally danced in fury on the edge of the quay. To make matters worse, Kloof chose that moment to wake up and stretch. Then, seeing the Oberjarl, she wagged her massive tail and spoke.

Kloof!

Almost blind with anger, Erak drew back the mangled axe, to throw it at the dog. Svengal caught his arm.

'Chief! It's your grandfather's axe, remember?'

Erak glared at him. 'Don't be an idiot!' he snarled and sent the deformed axe sailing end over end across the water. It fell short, splashing into the harbour in the wake of the departing *Heron*.

'You'll have to come back some time!' he roared. The crew on board affected not to have heard him. 'And I'll be waiting when you do!'

On board the ship, Hal said reassuringly to Stig, 'He'll get over it.'

Stig nodded, then said, 'You think so?'

Hal's reply was forestalled by a piercing whistle from the far side of the harbour. A slim figure was standing on the mole, her seabag, weapons and equipment stacked by her feet. On her way to join the ship, she had seen what was happening and run down the opposite sea wall.

'It's Lydia,' Stig said, but Hal was already steering to go alongside the mole.

'Let go the sheets,' he called to the twins, judging the moment precisely. As they did, he turned the ship neatly so that it lost way and slid alongside the wall. Thorn and Ingvar fended off with a pair of oars, while Stig went forward to catch Lydia's seabag and weapons as she tossed them down. Then she leapt across the narrow gap herself, landing light as a cat and dropping into a crouch to absorb the impact. Ingvar offered a hand to help her up.

'Welcome aboard,' he said. She glanced around at the nervous, relieved faces of the crew, took in the jumble of last-minute stores they had thrown aboard, then looked across the harbour to where Erak was still prancing with rage.

'Do you always leave port this way?' she asked.

Ingvar considered the question for a second or two.

'Pretty much,' he said.

CHAPTER TEN

The rain came slanting in from the west, great sheets of it, driven by the wind, striking the oily sea like so many pebbles scattered by a giant hand. *Heron*, with the wind on her starboard beam, was making good time, slicing through the even swell, sending plumes of white spray skyward as she came down into the troughs, then rising like a gull to the next crest. It was a smooth, regular motion, without surprises or sudden, unexpected lurches. Hal stood at the helm, feet braced apart for balance, making continual minute corrections as the constantly varying forces of wind and sea tried to nudge the ship's head away from her course.

Under his orders, the crew had rigged a canvas tarpaulin over a spar placed to run along the centre of the deck from behind the mast. The result was a tent-like shelter. Normally, they only used this as sleeping quarters when they anchored for the night, but Hal had decided that there was no sense in everyone becoming damp and miserable while they were under way. Ulf and Wulf remained in the open, ready to tend the sheets if Hal changed course or the wind shifted. They were huddled in the waist of the ship, wrapped in tarred canvas cloaks that kept most of the rain off. Hal made a mental note to relieve them in another hour, replacing them with Stefan and Jesper. Thorn, who eschewed the comfort of the tent, stating that a real sailor wasn't afraid of a little rain, was stretched out in the rowing well just for'ard of the steering position, wrapped in a rather moth-eaten bearskin and snoring happily.

Hal was wearing sealskin boots and trousers, and a waist-length sheepskin vest with the collar turned up. Naturally, he was wearing the thick woollen watch cap that Edvin had knitted for him when they were pursuing the pirate Zavac. Occasionally, a trickle of cold rain would work its way past the tightly fastened collar and run down the back of his neck. But the discomfort was minor and he enjoyed the cold, fresh air, redolent with the scent of salt water and rain.

Stig emerged from the canvas shelter and made his way aft to join him, balancing easily against the roll of the ship.

'Comfortable?' He grinned, noting the runnels of rain and spray trickling down Hal's face. Drops of water, prevented from soaking in by the natural grease in the wool, clung to his cap like tiny diamonds.

Hal returned the smile. He was at his most content when he was at *Heron*'s tiller, feeling the constant, tiny movements of the ship against his hand, and the pressure as she rose and fell beneath the soles of his feet.

At moments like this, Hal felt totally at one with the ship he had created, exulting in her speed and power and purpose as she surged through the swell.

'Perfectly,' he said. He glanced down at the smooth oak of the tiller, polished by constant contact with his hands. 'I never get tired of this.'

'It must be wonderful to feel something that you've designed and created reacting to your slightest touch,' Stig said. There was a wistful note in his voice. He knew he would never share that feeling with his friend. He was a good helmsman, but Hal was an artist. His judgement of speed, momentum and angles was instinctive. He could sense the interaction between wind and waves and current and simply know where to place *Heron* to best advantage. It was a skill that you had to be born with, Stig realised.

He leaned on the railing, peering down at the grey water rushing past.

'I'm happy to relieve you if you want a spell,' he said, but Hal shook his head.

'No need for that. I'm actually enjoying myself.'

A splash of spray came overside as *Heron* sliced into a slightly larger than normal wave. Stig wiped his face with the sleeve of his jacket, licking his lips and tasting the salt.

'I've been meaning to talk to you about that,' he said. 'I've had an idea.'

Hal smiled. An opening like that was too good to miss. Stig would probably be disappointed if he didn't take advantage of it.

'Wonders may never cease,' he said.

His friend gave him a tolerant smile, and made a circular motion with his hand, as if conducting the expected jibe.

'Yes, yes,' he said. 'Get it all out. But seriously . . .' He paused and Hal gestured for him to go ahead. Now that the moment was here, Stig wasn't sure how to proceed. If Hal took what he was about to say in the wrong spirit, he might be insulted. Then he shrugged. Hal was too intelligent for that. At least, he hoped he was.

'You're a much better helmsman than me,' he began. Always start with a positive, he thought.

'So far, I can't argue with your idea,' Hal said lightly.

'We all know it. I mean, I'm good on the tiller . . .' Stig paused and Hal, knowing he was leading up to something, stopped his teasing.

'You're better than good,' Hal said quietly.

Stig nodded his appreciation of the compliment. 'But you're a complete natural,' he continued. 'You seem to know how the ship will react, what she's going to do. You know how to place her exactly where you want her. It's as if you see her in position before you put her there. It's almost as if she's an extension of yourself.'

Hal shrugged. He knew, without any false vanity, that he was a better helmsman than anyone on board. Better than just about anyone in Hallasholm, in fact. There was an old fisherman who might have a better touch on the tiller than he did. And three or four wolfship captains who were probably as good as he was. He also knew that it was a gift he had been born with — an innate ability to gauge speed, angles, drift and the relative position of other ships. As such, it was nothing for him to feel particularly boastful about. He had this skill through no fault or virtue of his own — although, admittedly, he had practised to develop it to a fine art.

'It probably helps that I designed and built the ship,' he said mildly.

But Stig shook his head. 'You're the same on any ship,' he said. There was a pause as he wondered how to continue.

Hal looked at him shrewdly. 'I take it you didn't come up here simply to praise my unerring skill as a helmsman,' he said. 'I imagine the word *but* is about to make an appearance.'

Stig couldn't help a slight grin forming. 'Ah, you've seen through my skilful verbal gymnastics.'

'Be hard not to. You don't usually shower me with praise and lavish compliments. So let's hear the but.'

Stig took a deep breath. *'But,'* he said deliberately, drawing the word out, 'when we go into battle, you're not at the helm. You're up there —' he gestured towards the bow with his thumb '— shooting the Mangler.'

Hal nodded thoughtfully. Stig had a point, he realised.

'That's because nobody else can shoot it,' he pointed out.

'Only because nobody else has ever tried. You designed it. You built it. So it was only natural that you would be the one who would operate it. The problem is, when we go into battle, that leaves the ship in the hands of someone who is nowhere near as skilled as you.'

Hal said nothing. A slight frown creased his forehead. His first inclination was to disagree. But he realised his friend was right.

Stig noticed his hesitation and continued. 'The thing is, I'm nowhere near as good a helmsman as you are. But I'm just as good a shot. Maybe even better. I could learn to use the Mangler.'

That was true. Stig had borrowed Hal's crossbow on occasions and had proven to be every bit as good a shot as his skirl. And he was much more accurate throwing a spear or a javelin. He had a natural athlete's ability to judge a moving target's speed and direction, and aim his shot so that the projectile arrived in the same spot, and at the same time, as the target.

'This way,' Stig continued, 'we'd be using people where they're best suited. As it stands, you're at the Mangler, yelling instructions to whoever's on the tiller to get us in position, and telling Ingvar where you want him to point the weapon. If you were back here, it would be simpler. You *know* where we need to place the ship to use the Mangler to best advantage.'

Hal nodded. Positioning the ship to give the Mangler the best possible firing angle could be vital in a fight. Then Stig added the clincher.

'Besides, if things go wrong, I'd much rather have you back here in charge of the ship than stuck up in the bows.'

And that was the real point, Hal thought. He had always been torn when he relinquished control of the ship to take over the giant crossbow. He hated leaving the *Heron* in someone else's hands when they were going into danger. In his heart, he knew that this was where he belonged — at the tiller, in control of the ship. This was where he was most comfortable. And this was where he could contribute most to the *Heron*'s success.

'You're making sense,' he told Stig, and he saw his friend's shoulders relax. He realised that Stig had been worried that he might insult Hal with his suggestion and he smiled now to show that this wasn't the case.

'One small problem,' said a deep voice from the rowing well in front of them.

'I thought you were asleep,' Hal said, and grinned at Stig.

'And I thought a smelly old bear had died on the rowing benches,' Stig added.

Thorn grunted as he sat up, throwing back the bearskin. Droplets of water flew in all directions. He turned a disparaging eye on Stig, who shrugged his shoulders unapologetically, then addressed Hal.

'Stig and I are the main fighting party,' Thorn began. 'We're the ones who are first to board if we fight another ship. Can't do that if he's stuck behind the Mangler.'

'That's true,' Hal admitted. 'But he can always join you as we get closer. It'll only take a few seconds.'

'That's not how it worked when we fought those river pirates,' Thorn pointed out. 'Stig and I boarded one and you went off after the others with the Mangler.'

Hal considered the point. What Thorn said was true. He frowned as he tried to think of a solution, but Thorn had one ready.

'Let Stig and Lydia both practise with the Mangler,' he said. The two younger men both reacted with surprise.

'Lydia?' they said in unison.

'Lydia,' Thorn replied. 'She's probably the best marksman on board. You've seen how good she is with those darts. She's an expert when it comes to judging range and deflection. And Ingvar does all the heavy work training the Mangler.'

Stig and Hal exchanged a glance. 'But she's so good at keeping enemy archers occupied while we're approaching,' Hal said.

Thorn made an expansive gesture with both hands. 'Then let Stig handle the big crossbow while we're approaching. Then, once he and I board, Lydia can take over the Mangler. In any case, it makes sense to have more than one person trained to use it.'

Again, Stig and Hal exchanged a glance. 'He's right,' Hal said.

Stig nodded agreement. 'That's brilliant, Thorn.'

'Of course it is,' Thorn grunted. Then he pulled the bearskin up over his head and stretched out again. After a second or two, they heard his voice from under the heavy fur.

'Don't tell her I said she was the best marksman on board.'

'She'll never hear it from me,' Hal said.

The rain eased, then died away midafternoon. The Herons stowed the tarpaulin they had been sheltering under and took their normal sailing stations. Hal turned the helm over to Edvin, showed him the bearing he wanted him to follow on the sun compass and then set to with his tools and some spare wood and canvas. Kloof nosed around him curiously, her head to one side, trying to divine what he was up to.

After an hour or so, Hal sat back and displayed his work.

'A raft?' Stig said. Two casks were joined together, and a framework was mounted about them, with a piece of canvas stretched across it.

'A target,' Hal told him. 'You and Lydia can start practising with the Mangler this afternoon. We'll see how good you are.'

CHAPTER ELEVEN

In the middle of the afternoon, they set the target raft adrift over the side. Then Hal swung the *Heron* into a wide sweeping turn, taking her away from the target. When it was just a small light-coloured dot bobbing on the waves, he swung back, heading to intercept it at a slight angle. The Mangler could not shoot directly over the bows. It had to be aimed a little to either side. Of course, it could traverse to a ninety-degree angle on either beam, but the narrow head-on angle was an easier shot and Hal thought it was wise to start that way.

Lydia, Stig and Ingvar stood beside him as he turned back towards the target.

'We'll do a few dry runs first, to help you get the feel of it. Then we'll let you both try a shot and see how you do.'

They nodded and trooped forward. Ingvar took the training lever from where it was fastened to the mast and fitted it into the back of the Mangler. Stig and Lydia hesitated, not sure who should go first.

'You go,' Lydia said. 'You've been on board longer than I have.'

Stig nodded and climbed onto the small seat behind the Mangler. The rest of the crew members were clustered near the mast, eager to watch. Ulf and Wulf, of course, were at the trimming sheets. They'd be adjusting the sail as Hal brought the ship in to a shooting position.

Stig busied himself getting set behind the huge crossbow. He flicked up the rear sight that Hal had designed. It was marked in fifty-metre increments, from three hundred metres down to one hundred. He crouched and leaned forward, aligning the rear and front sights with the small bobbing target. He noticed how the ship's motion caused the sights to rise and fall on the target.

I'll have to anticipate a second or two so that I shoot when the sights are on line, he thought. He decided he'd wait until the target was a hundred metres away. At that distance, the Mangler shot in an almost flat trajectory.

'Can you call out the range as we get closer?' he asked Lydia.

She nodded. 'When do you want me to start?'

'Start at two-fifty and call it each fifty metres,' he told her. Her years of practice with the atlatl made her an expert when it came to judging range.

She stepped up onto the mast support to get a clearer view past Stig, Ingvar and the huge crossbow. *Heron* swooped on, with the wind over her starboard quarter. As Stig watched, the sights continued to rise and fall over the target. The ship was coming in at a slight angle, travelling from left to right. He decided he'd set the Mangler's point of aim a little to the left, so that the ship's course would bring it onto the line of the target.

'Ingvar?' he said.

'Ready, Stig.' The big boy's barrel of a chest gave him a deep, resonant voice.

'Train a little left . . . more . . . more . . . that's it!'

'Two-fifty,' said Lydia.

Stig checked his sights. The target was gradually coming from right to left. Maybe he needed more angle.

'Left a little more . . . That's it!'

'Two hundred metres.'

Stig smiled to himself. The whole thing was coming together nicely, he thought. Kloof stood close by, her eyes darting from Stig, to the Mangler, to the target bobbing up and down on the waves.

'One-fifty.'

Stig planned to shoot when *Heron* was at the top of her rising and falling action. He could see that the Mangler was trained slightly low. He wound the elevating wheel and watched the front sight rise. The target was drifting faster now.

'Right a little . . . stop!'

He peered down the sights. The line was right. The elevation was right. He waited till *Heron* rose on the crest of a wave and tapped the side of the big weapon to simulate pulling the trigger lanyard.

'And . . . shoot!' he called, at the same instant that Lydia gave the range as one hundred metres. He turned and grinned triumphantly.

'Hit it dead centre,' he told her.

She raised an eyebrow. 'In your mind,' she said sceptically.

They changed positions as Hal took *Heron* back to her starting position. The halyards squealed through the blocks as Jesper and Stefan hauled down the port sail and raised the starboard.

'I'll get you to call the ranges for me too, if you will,' Lydia said.

Stig nodded. With enough practice, he'd be able to judge range as well as the line and the elevation. But for now, the extra assistance had been useful.

They spent the next hour making dummy runs, and gradually, Lydia and Stig became more familiar with the workings of the big crossbow.

'Those sights are an excellent idea,' Lydia said. She was used to estimating direction, elevation and range when she cast an atlatl dart. The sights on the Mangler, graduated for elevation and allowing the shooter to line the target up exactly, were a big improvement.

Finally, Hal hove to and walked down the deck to where the two new shooters stood by the Mangler.

'Ready for a real shot?' he asked.

Stig and Lydia exchanged a glance and both nodded.

'Who's going first?' Hal asked.

This time, Lydia wasn't about to defer to Stig. Both of them were keen to test their new skill with a loaded weapon.

'Rock-paper-knife,' Stig said and Lydia nodded. They faced each other and both counted, 'Ro-sham-bo!' On 'bo', they shot their right hands out. Stig's was clasped in a fist — rock. Lydia's hand extended the first two fingers straight out, the sign for knife. She was crestfallen.

'I was sure you'd go paper,' she said.

Hal shook his head pityingly. 'Stig *always* goes rock,' he told her. 'You should have known. Look at him. He's a rock sort of person.'

Stig raised an eyebrow, not sure if he'd just been handed a compliment or an insult. Then he turned back to the Mangler and straddled the seat.

Ingvar leaned forward and seized the two levers, heaving them back until the heavy cord was latched into the cocked position. As he opened the locker that held the bolts for the Mangler, Kloof came sniffing around, eagerly trying to see what was inside.

'Close that before she chews them all!' Hal ordered immediately. Ingvar grinned. He selected a bolt and closed the locker, much to Kloof's disappointment. Hal shook his head. In the two days they had been at sea, Kloof had managed to chew several items belonging to the crew.

'I'll get back to the tiller,' he said. Hal turned away, then stopped as a thought hit him. 'When you're actually shooting,' he told Stig, 'there's a slight delay between pulling the lanyard and the bow firing. About half a second.'

Stig frowned. 'What causes that?'

Hal shrugged. 'Not sure. Could be the lanyard stretching a little. In any event, remember to allow for it when you shoot.'

He made his way back to the stern and took the tiller. Ulf and Wulf were watching him, ready to bring the sail back under control.

'Sheet home!' he ordered. They hauled on the sheets and the sail filled, shaping itself into a perfect swelling curve. The ship tried to come up head to wind, but Hal heaved on the tiller and she swung nimbly away, gathering speed as she came round.

'Stand by up for'ard!' he called.

Stig raised a hand in acknowledgement, then bent to the sights. Ingvar stepped forward and loaded the bolt into the grooved section on top of the Mangler. Kloof watched him do it, dancing on her toes, rearing back slightly onto her rear legs and letting her front legs come down together on the deck. Her tail lashed from side to side with excitement.

Lydia couldn't help but smile at the dog's prancing. Kloof obviously sensed the anticipation in the small group around the crossbow. Then Lydia shook her head and ignored Kloof, resuming her position on the mast support once more.

'Two-fifty,' she called.

Stig waved a hand to her but said nothing. He was concentrating on his sights.

They came in at speed, the wake hissing down *Heron*'s flanks, spray sheeting back as she occasionally cut deeper than normal into a wave. Stig kept up a muttered string of directions to Ingvar. He wanted this shot to be perfect. This was for real, after all.

Kloof! said Kloof, rising and falling onto her forepaws once more.

'Shut up,' Stig told her, concentrating fiercely. She didn't bark again, but she began to whine in expectation and excitement.

They passed the one-fifty mark, Lydia calling the range as they did. Ingvar was busy, constantly making the tiny corrections that Stig was calling for.

'Ready?' Hal called from the stern.

They all ignored him. Stig peered down the sights, winding the elevation up, watching the target drift from right to left again. He took the firing lanyard in his left hand, took up the tension on it. Mindful of Hal's warning, he smoothly pulled the lanyard just before the target drifted across his sights. There was a slight delay, then . . .

SLAM!

The Mangler bucked with the recoil. The bolt streaked away.

And Kloof, with an excited yelp, hurled herself over the railing, hitting the water with an enormous splash and striking out after the streaking bolt.

For a second, they were all struck dumb by the dog's unexpected action. Jesper and Stefan collapsed with laughter, closely followed by Ulf and Wulf. Stig, who had been concentrating on his sights, hadn't seen the dog leap overboard and was looking around, a bewildered expression on his face. In all the confusion, nobody saw where the shot had gone — except, presumably, Kloof. Hal yelled at his dog to come back — a command that went totally unheeded as Kloof ploughed on determinedly through the water. Lydia and Thorn exchanged puzzled looks, wondering what had come over Kloof. It was Edvin who first realised what had happened.

'She's going to fetch it!' he said. The laughter re-doubled from the twins, Jesper and Stefan.

Ingvar had only seen a blur of movement from behind him and had heard the massive splash as Kloof hit the water. 'What happened?' he said.

Lydia quickly explained the situation and a crooked grin settled over the big boy's features.

Thorn turned a withering look on Hal, who was red-faced with rage as his dog continued to ignore his shouted commands.

'Where did you say you found this dog?' he asked.

Hal shook his head dismissively. 'Never mind that. We'll have to go get her.'

'Why?' Thorn asked. 'She seems perfectly happy out there, swimming off into the distance.'

The ship and the dog were on slightly divergent courses, so that Kloof was moving further and further away.

'We'll have to go round to fetch her,' Hal called. 'Lydia, keep an eye on her so we don't lose her. Stig, get ready to haul her on board. Sail handlers, get ready to go about.'

'Is there anything you'd like me to do?' Thorn asked, smiling sweetly.

Hal glared at him. 'I suppose it'd be too much to ask you to shut up?'

'Absolutely too much,' Thorn said.

They came about, describing a giant circle, then heading back in to intercept the dog, still swimming strongly in the direction she had seen the bolt disappear. Lydia had mounted the bulwark and was standing next to the bowpost, keeping the small black and white shape in sight as Kloof bobbed up and down in the waves. She held the bowpost lightly for balance with one hand, and pointed the direction for Hal to follow with the other.

'I'll bring her alongside the starboard rail,' Hal called to Stig, who moved to the rail and peered ahead. He could see the dog now, still ploughing along determinedly.

'Get ready to grab hold of my legs as we come along-side, Ingvar,' Stig said. 'I'm going to have to lean way over to get her.'

Ingvar nodded and moved to stand just behind him. As they came closer, Hal leaned out as well, measuring the angle and the distance and the speed of the ship. When he judged the moment was right, he yelled.

'Let go the sheets. Down sail!'

The wind spilled from the sail and Jesper and Stefan worked quickly to bring it down, gathering in the bil-lowing folds and stowing them roughly into the rowing well. Hal's forward vision was now unrestricted. He saw the dog close ahead, then saw Stig lean over the rail, sup-ported by Ingvar's powerful grip. He edged the bow to port slightly.

Thorn, watching from alongside Stig's inverted form, turned and waved. 'Hold her at that!' he said. He shook his head in admiration. As ever, Hal had judged the moment exactly.

The speed fell off the ship, and Stig grabbed the swimming dog by the scruff of her neck, hauling her in alongside the hull. Kloof looked up at him, surprised.

A wave broke over Stig, drenching him from head to waist. But he maintained his grip on the dog. Then, as the wave passed, he changed his hold so that he had her under the shoulders.

'Heave away, Ingvar!' he spluttered, spitting out sea water. Ingvar reared back, hauling Stig and the sodden dog up the side of the hull. As Kloof came free of the water, her dead weight doubled and Ingvar grunted with extra effort. Then he felt Thorn's arms around him and the two of them hauled Stig and Kloof on board, sprawling in a heap on the foredeck.

Kloof was first to recover. She bounded to her feet, then crouched. Lydia realised, too late, what was about to happen.

'Look out!' she called, then Kloof shook herself, hurling sheets of sea water from her thick double coat and thoroughly drenching her rescuers. Ingvar and Thorn yelled curses at the dog. Stig, already soaked to the waist, shrugged philosophically.

'A little water never did a true sailor any harm,' he told Thorn, who was glaring at the dog.

'I'm beginning to think Erak had the right idea,' Thorn said grimly.

CHAPTER TWELVE

Hal decided they had spent enough time on target practice. They retrieved the target raft and hauled it aboard. Stig was gratified to see a triangular rent in the canvas.

'I hit it,' he said triumphantly, as he and Thorn stowed the raft in the bow of the ship.

Hal signalled for Lydia to join him at the tiller as they got under way.

'Sorry you missed your chance for a shot. It was starting to take up more time than I'd allowed — what with having to fetch Kloof on board again,' he said.

Lydia shrugged. 'I'm sure I'll get another chance.'

'When we get to Araluen, we'll set up a target onshore and practise on that. That way we won't be losing all our bolts. After all,' Hal added with a wry grin, 'I'm the one who has to make them.'

'Fair point,' she said. 'And in any event, Stig would have been unbearable if I'd missed. He'd have bragging rights for the rest of the journey.'

Hal shook his head. 'Not really,' he said, lowering his voice. 'That hole was already in the canvas when we put the raft over the side.'

An hour later, they sighted a crippled Gallican ship.

Edvin was on the bowpost lookout. 'Ship!' he called, pointing to the south-west.

At first, Hal saw nothing. But as *Heron* rose onto the crest of a wave, he saw a dark shape, low in the water. Stefan, who had the keenest eyesight, had leapt up onto the starboard rail, steadying himself on one of the thick stays.

'She's dismasted!' he called. 'She's in trouble!'

Hal glanced quickly at the wind telltale on the top of the sternpost. The wind was from the north-east. There was no need to tack. He swung the tiller and brought *Heron* round to intercept the other ship. As the wind came further astern, Ulf and Wulf let out the sail to take full advantage of it.

'We'll go aboard if she needs help,' Hal called. 'Stig, Jesper, Stefan, Ulf and Wulf — you come with me. Ingvar, get the boat hook on her and keep us alongside. Edvin, come aft and take the tiller.'

As they came closer, he could see that the other ship was obviously holed. Her bow was low in the water and she rose and fell sluggishly on the swell. She was a trader — a wide-beamed, slow-sailing ship with plenty of room for cargo. Her mast was gone, snapped off a metre from the deck and trailing overside in a tangle of canvas and rope. Hal counted two of her crew struggling ineffectually with it, while another three were for'ard, working on damage to the hull close to her bow.

'Ulf, Wulf, give them a hand to cut that mast loose. Thorn, you can help with that.' Thorn was perfectly capable of wielding an axe with his left hand, Hal knew — in fact, he was far more efficient than most right-handed axemen. He peered more closely at the men for'ard on the ship. There was a ragged, triangular rent smashed in the side of the ship.

'Stefan, Edvin, get out the tent canvas. We'll fother it over that hole in the side.'

Fothering entailed sliding a large piece of canvas, usually a sail, under the ship at the bows and sliding it aft until it sat over the hole. When the canvas was pulled tight, the flow of water into the ship was greatly reduced. It was a technique they had learned during their brotherband training, and which they had used before — when *Wolfwind* had been rammed by the pirate ship *Raven* in the waters off the town of Limmat.

'Can I do anything?' Lydia asked. She understood that this was one of those situations for which she wasn't trained. It was a matter of seamanship and sailing craft. The boys knew what they had to do, and she would only be in the way if she tried to help.

Hal glanced around the horizon before he answered.

'Stay here and keep a lookout,' he told her. 'We want to be sure that whoever did that to her isn't anywhere around.'

'You think they might be?' she asked.

He chewed his lip for a second, then answered. 'To be honest, probably not. But it would be very embarrassing if they came back and sank us while we were trying to save her.'

A faint grin touched her mouth. 'Very embarrassing indeed. I'll make sure it doesn't happen.'

Hal nodded, but he was preoccupied now as they approached the wallowing trader. The men on board had seen them coming and rushed to group together in the waist of the ship. Several of them were shaking their fists, or pieces of wood as makeshift weapons. They gesticulated for *Heron* to keep her distance.

'*Allez-vous en!*' one of them shouted.

'Oh, Gorlog's socks, they think we're going to attack them,' Hal said. 'Anyone speak Gallican?' he asked, recognising the man's language. It was a vain plea. He knew none of the brotherband did.

Lydia stepped to the rail, cupped her hands around her mouth and shouted back. '*Ne paniquez pas! Nous voulons vous aider.*'

Hal looked at her, impressed. 'That sounded good,' he said. 'What did it mean?'

'I told them not to panic, and that we wanted to help them,' Lydia said. Then she frowned. 'At least, I think I did. I'm a bit rusty on my Gallican.'

But it appeared that she had said what she hoped to. That, and the fact that the message was delivered by a girl, seemed to calm the Gallican crew's fears. They lowered their weapons and gestured for the *Heron* to come alongside.

'Let go the sheets! Down sail!' Hal yelled, and swung the *Heron* so that she slid in neatly alongside the wallowing trader. Ingvar snagged the boat hook into the other ship's rail and drew the two ships closer. The hulls ground together, the timbers groaning and squealing as they did.

Kloof barked at the foreign ship. To prevent any more unexpected excursions overboard, Hal had ordered her to be tied firmly to the mast. He was glad now that he had. If she'd gone leaping onto the stricken Gallican ship, she would have caused pandemonium.

He paused to collect his satchel of tools and led the way aboard the other ship. Jesper and Stefan, carrying the bundled canvas tent between them, followed, with Stig bringing up the rear.

Ulf, Wulf and Thorn came after them, heading for the tangle of wreckage and snapped shrouds alongside the starboard rail.

The stocky man who had hailed them stepped aside as they came aboard. The Gallican ship's rail was lower than *Heron*'s, Hal noticed. He gestured towards the bow, and the canvas roll Jesper and Stefan were carrying, sliding one open palm over the other to indicate what they were planning.

'Fother?' he said, hoping the word would be understood. Then, in an attempt to translate the word to Gallic, he said: 'Fother-o? Tent-o? Understand-o?'

'Why do you think that adding *o* to the end of a word turns it into Gallic?' Stig asked, with some interest.

Hal looked at him and shrugged. 'I don't know. I just think it sounds more Gallic that way. Why don't these dopey Gallicans speak the common tongue?'

There was a common tongue that most nations used for communication, in addition to having their own individual languages.

'They've always been a stubborn lot,' Stig said.

'As a matter of fact, we do speak the common tongue,'

the stocky man told them, speaking with a thick Gallican accent and turning a withering glare on them. 'I take it you plan to stretch that canvas over the hole in the hull?'

Hal flushed, realising the man must have understood his comment about 'dopey Gallicans'. No point in apologising, he thought. What's done is done.

'Um . . . yes,' Hal told him. 'My men will help cut away the mast, once the hole is plugged.'

'I appreciate your help – if not your comments,' the Gallican captain said stiffly. Then he led the way for'ard. Jesper and Stefan unrolled the tent and folded it into a double layer. They tied ropes to each corner and slid the canvas around the ship's bow then, with three of the Gallican crew helping, began to work it down under the keel, towards the rent in the hull.

As they did so, Hal opened his tool satchel and took out a heavy hammer. The hole in the hull was a metre high and roughly triangular in shape. The widest part of the triangle was at the top, where the bulwark itself was smashed. He could see the side of the ship flexing around that gap as the hull moved with the action of the sea. If that continued, he thought, there was a chance that the constant flexing would cause the rent in the hull to crack right down to the keel until the ship broke apart. He cast around and saw a broken oar rolling back and forth on the deck. He put it in place across the gap in the rail and quickly hammered nails in at each end to fasten it, bracing the upper side of the hole and stopping that dangerous flexing movement.

Once he had done that, Stig, Jesper and Stefan, assisted by two of the Gallican crew, pulled the canvas into position over the hole and hauled the ropes tight, tying them off when the canvas was as taut as they could make it. The water flowing into the hull slowed to a trickle, seeping slowly through the canvas.

'That should hold it,' Hal told the Gallican captain. 'You'll need to keep baling her out, but she won't sink.' He turned to the group standing ready by the fallen mast. 'Cut it loose!' he called.

They went to it with a will, axes and knives rising and falling in a steady rhythm, cutting through the tangle of stays, shrouds and halyards that held the mast alongside. Finally, there was only the backstay left. It was a heavy tarred rope, about as thick as a man's forearm. Thorn stepped forward and swung his axe.

THUNK!

The rope parted and the shattered mast, sail and tangle of cordage slipped free of the ship, drifting away. As the weight was released, the ship rolled upright, then to port, then settled. Hal watched the makeshift patch carefully. Now that the ship was on an even keel, the rent in the hull was below the waterline for half its depth. Fortunately, that meant that the widest part was above the water. A little more water made its way past the sail, but nothing to worry about, so long as the weather remained good. Hal looked around the horizon, searching for any sign of storm clouds.

The Gallican captain seemed to divine his purpose. 'Weather should be all right for a few days,' he said.

Hal nodded, then studied the ship more closely. The mast and sail were gone, of course, already fifty metres away from the ship and drifting further with each minute.

The stump of the mast was too short to jury-rig a mast, even if there had been timber available to do so. But there was no sign of any spars or timber. Not even any oars — other than the broken one he'd used to repair the bulwark.

The Gallican captain held out a hand. 'Thanks for your help,' he said. 'We were dead men if you hadn't turned up. My name is Jerard. This is my ship, *Hirondelle*.'

Hal clasped the proffered hand. 'Hal Mikkelson.'

Jerard regarded him with suspicion. 'Skandian?' he asked, although the slim young man before him didn't look like the stereotypical bulky, heavily muscled northman.

Hal nodded.

'Then it was your countrymen who did this to us,' Jerard said bitterly.

CHAPTER THIRTEEN

Hal sat down on one of the rowing benches, frowning at Jerard's words. He had a dreadful feeling about who might have been responsible for the attack on *Hirondelle*, but he didn't voice it.

'Tell me what happened here,' he said.

The other Herons clustered around, along with the trader's crew, as Jerard began his tale.

'We were taking a cargo of hides and furs to Gretagne. You know it?' he asked.

'Not well,' Hal said. 'I've been there once, some years ago.'

As a boy, Hal had spent several summers working on trading ships. He remembered Gretagne as a rather noisome, unfriendly little Gallican harbour town on the southern shore of the Stormwhite. The main industry was leathermaking and at least a dozen tanneries lined the harbour foreshores. All of them discharged their unpleasant residue into the harbour itself so that the water was discoloured and foul smelling. He felt it might be untactful to mention that now, particularly in the light of his earlier comment about 'dopey Gallicans'.

'Barely two hours ago, the Skandian ship came up on us — a *vaisseau du loup*, I think you call them?' Jerard continued.

'A wolfship,' Jesper supplied.

Hal looked at him curiously and the former thief shrugged.

'I know a *few* words of Gallican,' he explained.

Hal nodded then signalled for Jerard to proceed.

'We weren't alarmed at first. Everyone knows the Skandians aren't pirates any more.'

'We never were,' Thorn growled. There was a fundamental difference between raiders and pirates. Raiders attacked coastal towns and villages. Sometimes the inhabitants might put up a fight and there would be casualties. More often, they retreated into the countryside and left the raiders to it.

Pirates, on the other hand, preyed on lone ships at sea. They made sure they had overwhelming numbers — most traders had less than a dozen men in their crews — and they took everything of value. Then, since they wanted no word of their presence to be known, they either killed the crews outright or left them to die on their sinking ships.

Jerard shrugged at Thorn's words. To him the distinction was a minor one. 'In any case, we didn't see it coming until it was too late to escape. The ship was dark coloured and it came out of the east.'

Involuntarily, Hal glanced to the horizon. It was late in the day and the eastern sky and sea were almost in darkness. By contrast, the lowering sun blazed brilliantly in the west.

Thorn studied the heavy, wide-beamed lines of the *Hirondelle*.

'Doubt you could have outrun a wolfship anyway, even if you'd seen it coming.'

Jerard nodded morosely. 'True enough. It came straight at us, ramming its bow into us —' he indicated the repaired hole in the bow '— then its men swarmed over us. Two of my crew were killed before I could surrender. There were only eight of us and more than twenty of them.'

Hal and Stig exchanged a glance. Hal could tell that Stig had also guessed the identity of the rogue wolfship. And he was sure Thorn knew as well. He turned his attention back to Jerard.

'They took our strongbox, and our furs. The hides they threw overboard. Then they chopped down our mast and threw all our oars and spars over the side. Our weapons, axes and knives went the same way. They left us sinking, with no way to repair the ship. Their captain even joked about it. "We won't kill you," he said. "We'll leave you for the sharks — and I know sharks." That seemed to be some special joke with him.'

'Tursgud,' Hal said finally and the rest of his crew nodded agreement. Tursgud's brotherband had chosen the shark as their symbol when they had competed with the Herons nearly two years prior.

'You know him?' Jerard asked.

'Oh yes. He's an old friend,' Hal said heavily. Jerard didn't quite understand the sarcasm and Hal had to explain. 'He's not really a friend. But we know him only too well.'

'Looks like he's gone rogue,' Thorn said. 'Just what we need. Another pirate loose on the Stormwhite.'

'You said their ship was dark coloured. Was it dark blue?' Stig asked and Jerard nodded confirmation.

'We need to get after him,' Stig said. 'If one Skandian ship has turned pirate, people are going to think we've all gone that way.' He looked at Jerard. 'Which direction was he heading when you last saw him?'

The Gallican pointed. 'West.'

Stig turned to Hal urgently. 'They can't have too much of a lead on us,' he said. 'We've got to get after them.'

Jerard coughed meaningfully. Stig turned back to him, sensing the Gallican had something to say. But it was Thorn who spoke first.

'I think you're forgetting something. We can't leave these people here. We're going to have to help get them to port.'

Stig subsided, all sense of urgency gone. In truth, he hadn't considered that. They couldn't leave the crew of the *Hirondelle* with their ship damaged and drifting help-lessly. The Herons would be no better than Tursgud and his men if they did that.

'If you could spare us some canvas and a couple of spars, perhaps we could jury-rig something to get us under way?' Jerard suggested. He was less than enthusiastic about the idea, but he hated the thought of the rogue Skandian and his men escaping scot-free.

Hal thought about it but shook his head. 'We're heading out on a long cruise,' he said. 'We'll be away for a year and we're going to need all the supplies we have. I think the best answer is for us to tow you into harbour. Which is the nearest port?'

'Well, Gretagne, of course,' Jerard told him.

Hal sighed. In his imagination, he could smell the vile little harbour already.

'I was afraid of that,' he said. 'Well, we'd better get busy and rig a tow.'

As they climbed back aboard *Heron*, Jesper caught up with Hal and touched his arm.

'What's so bad about Gretagne?' he asked.

'You'll find out,' Hal told him heavily.

With the Gallican ship in tow, *Heron*'s speed was drastically reduced. It took them the rest of that night and halfway through the following day to tow *Hirondelle* in to Gretagne.

As they approached the shore, houses and buildings slowly came into view. Yet the town also made its presence felt in another way. Predictably, Kloof noticed it first. She whined in protest, then lay flat on her belly, rubbing her forepaws over her muzzle in a futile attempt to mask the smell coming from the shore. The rest of the crew took a minute or two longer to sense it. Then cries of protest broke out throughout the ship.

Predictably, Ulf and Wulf blamed each other.

'Why don't you wash your socks occasionally?' Ulf said belligerently. (Or perhaps it was Wulf, Hal was never sure.)

'Why don't you wash your*self* occasionally?' his brother shot back. Then he added, 'Besides, you know what they say. First to smell it usually did it.'

'Yeah? Well, you probably did smell it first, but you just didn't say,' said the other twin. By this time, Hal had lost track of who was who.

'It's neither of you,' Hal said sharply. 'So shut up. It's the tanneries onshore.'

Stig was holding his hand over his nose, unconsciously mimicking Kloof. 'What makes them smell so bad?' he asked.

Hal glanced meaningfully at him.

'It's a combination of the old hides, and what they use to treat them,' he said, adding quickly as he saw the question rising to Stig's lips, 'You don't want to know.'

Thorn was standing by them. He wrinkled his nose in protest. 'Reminds me of me — before Karina took me in hand.'

Hal looked at him. Some years back, Thorn had been a little remiss in his personal hygiene, to put it mildly. Karina had solved the problem by having Hal throw a bucket of water over him as he lay snoring in the snow.

Hal shook his head now. 'Even you were never that bad. Trust me.'

'That's a relief,' Thorn said in a heartfelt tone.

The vile smell became stronger as they approached the town. But they also became more accustomed to it. They plodded heavily through the harbour mouth, with Jerard directing them to a beaching area that was — thankfully — situated away from the row of grim-looking tanneries, and upwind of them.

Two longboats came out from the beach at a signal from Jerard and took over the tow, dragging the crippled *Hirondelle* in to shore and beaching her. Hal, grateful to have lost the nagging dead weight behind *Heron*, ordered the sails down and followed the trader in under oars. The prow grated gently on the shingle beach and they came to rest.

Once his ship was safely beached and propped up to remain level, Jerard walked over to them and climbed aboard *Heron*. He walked back to the command position in the stern, where Hal, Stig, Thorn and Lydia were gathered.

'I owe you my thanks,' Jerard told them sincerely. 'You saved my ship and all our lives and I'm more grateful than you can imagine.'

He shook hands with all of them, then turned back to Hal, an embarrassed expression on his face. 'Unfortunately, that's all I can offer you. Your countryman stole everything I own.'

Hal shrugged off his apologies. 'It's the law of the sea,' he said. 'We don't leave other sailors in danger. You'd do the same for us.'

Jerard nodded his head. 'That's true. But if I can ever do anything for you . . .' he began.

Thorn stepped forward. 'There is one thing,' he said. He jerked a thumb at Kloof, who was watching the proceedings while she chewed on an old boot she had found.

She had found it among Thorn's gear, as a matter of fact.

'You could take the dog — for fifteen silver crowns.'

Hal went to protest, but Thorn held up his hand.

Jerard looked at Kloof, who thumped her tail enthusiastically on the deck as she ripped the upper part of the boot away from the sole. 'I told you. I don't have any money left to pay you,' Jerard said doubtfully.

'I'm not saying you should pay us. I'll pay *you* to take her off our hands,' Thorn told him.

Jerard looked at him uncertainly, then looked at the dog and made a rough estimate of how much she would cost to feed.

'I don't think so,' he said.

Thorn shrugged. 'It was worth a try.'

CHAPTER FOURTEEN

Once they had recovered the canvas tent that had been wrapped around the trader's hull, the Herons wasted little time lingering in Gretagne. The breeze was onshore, coming from the north, so Hal took the ship out of the harbour under oars. When they were half a kilometre from the harbour mouth, he ordered the oars to be stowed and the sail raised. Within minutes, the *Heron* was skimming the waves like her namesake, carving a pure white wake in the grey sea.

'That's better!' he said to no one in particular, exulting in the light, easy movement of the ship after the wallowing, jerking passage with *Hirondelle* under tow.

Gradually, the stench of the tanneries lessened as they moved down the coast. The fresh salt air was a welcome change to all of them.

'Phew!' said Jesper, drawing his first deep lungful of air for some time. 'How do they live with that vile stink?'

'I suppose they get used to it,' Lydia said, but Jesper shook his head doubtfully.

'How could you get used to anything as awful as that?' he asked.

'Oh, it's possible to get used to anything, no matter how annoying it might be. Or anyone,' Stig said, looking meaningfully at the ex-thief. Several of the others grinned. Jesper could be an irritating person at times. He was invariably the one who queried any course of action, always the first to complain about discomfort or difficulty. He noticed the reaction from his shipmates and turned a hurt look on Stig.

'Are you saying I stink?' he asked resentfully.

Stig shook his head. 'No. Just that you're irritating. If you stank as well, that'd be too much.'

Jesper drew breath to reply but Hal was tired of the senseless argument that was developing.

'Let it go,' he said crisply and Jesper subsided, muttering, onto his rowing bench.

Watching and listening, Thorn smiled quietly. He remembered the early days of the brotherband, when Hal had been reluctant to assert his authority. Now it came naturally to him. He was secure in his position as skirl and, as a good captain should be, he was always ready to nip trouble in the bud before it got out of control. Thorn's smile faded as he glanced down into the rowing well. Kloof had another boot in her mouth, and was proceeding to chew it, holding it steady between her forepaws.

His temper flared when he saw that it was the companion of the boot she had destroyed some time earlier.

'Give me that, you numbskull!' he roared, and grabbed at the boot.

As far as Kloof was concerned, this was an excellent game. As Thorn tugged one way, she set her forepaws, raised her backside in the air and tugged in the opposite direction, shaking the boot as she did so in an attempt to break Thorn's grip.

Unfortunately for Thorn, he was leaning over when he first grabbed the boot and Kloof's sudden and violent counteraction dragged him off balance, sending him sprawling. The Herons shouted with laughter — laughter that was quickly silenced as Thorn turned a murderous gaze on them.

He picked himself up. Kloof waited eagerly, tail lashing back and forth, the boot dangling from her jaws, ready for another bout of tug-of-war. It was her favourite game — no doubt because, with a body weight of forty-five kilograms, a low centre of gravity, and four massive paws to grip the ground beneath her, she usually won.

Thorn deliberately climbed to his feet and stood in front of Hal, his hands — one real and one wooden — on his hips.

'If that dog of yours doesn't stop chewing my things, I'm going to brain her with my club-hand,' he threatened. Hal had equipped Thorn with several different devices to replace his lost hand. One was a simple smooth wooden hook. Then there was Thorn's gripping hand, an ingenious split hook that hinged open and closed like a clamp, and allowed Thorn to grip items firmly in place. Finally, there was his club-hand. It was a massive, iron-studded wooden club on the end of an artificial arm. It was a terrifying weapon when wielded by the old warrior and had caused havoc in the streets of Limmat when the Herons had attacked the pirates who had overrun the town.

Hal glared at the dog. He had to admit, Thorn had a point. She seemed to have taken a liking to his belongings. Unfortunately, when she liked something, she showed her affection by chewing it.

'Drop!' he roared at the dog. Obediently, she slid her forepaws out in front of her and dropped to her belly on the deck. The boot was still dangling from her mouth.

'Not you! The boot!' Hal yelled. 'Drop the boot!' Kloof thumped her tail on the deck and he raised his eyes to the heavens in exasperation.

'That's great. One word from you and she does exactly what she wants,' Thorn said sarcastically. 'That's the second boot of mine she's got at! She's already destroyed the other one.'

'Then what's the problem?' Lydia asked sweetly. She had been the butt of many of Thorn's jokes and she revelled in the chance to even the score. He glared at her suspiciously, his bushy eyebrows drawing together like storm clouds gathering.

'The problem is, my lady, that she's *chewing my boots*!' Thorn's voice and volume rose as he said the last few words, pointing angrily at the boot that still dangled from Kloof's jaws. Kloof, aware that they were talking about her, dropped the boot and barked cheerfully. She kept the boot close between her forepaws, however, ready to snatch it up again if Thorn tried to grab for it.

'But you said she's already destroyed the first one,' Lydia pointed out.

Thorn nodded sarcastically. 'Oh, you understood that

part, did you. Yes, she has. She's torn the other one to pieces!'

'Then what good is this one to you?' Lydia asked, maintaining her tone of reason, and smiling angelically at the furious warrior.

'What . . . ?' Thorn hesitated, frowning even more deeply. He had a sense that he'd been outsmarted, but he was so angry he couldn't work out how. 'What good is it? It's my boot! They are both my boots. I have two boots and they are them!'

'That's not grammatically correct,' Edvin said, very careful to maintain a straight face. 'You can't say *they are them*. You have to say *They are they*. *Are* is a reflexive verb.'

'Is that right?' Thorn took a step towards Edvin.

The boy stood his ground and nodded seriously. 'Yes. I'm pretty sure it is.'

Thorn raised his polished wood hook and shook it in front of Edvin's face.

'Well,' he said, 'this is a reflexive hook. How would you like me to shove it up your reflexive nose?'

Edvin considered the comment for about five seconds, then decided that standing his ground wasn't such a good idea. 'I don't think I'd like that at all,' he said, and backed away a few paces.

'Well, that's a very wise decision,' Thorn said. He glared around at the rest of the crew, who were all being very careful not to smile. They were so careful, in fact, that it was blatantly obvious that they were not smiling. 'Anyone else got anything to say?' he demanded.

Heads shook and blank looks were the order of the day.

But Lydia wasn't ready to let him off the hook. 'All I'm

saying is,' she repeated, 'that you said Kloof destroyed your other boot —'

Kloof! barked the dog, hearing her name.

'Shut up!' Thorn snarled at the massive dog. Then he looked back to Lydia, suspicion writ large on his features. He sensed he was being set up for a killer blow here. 'That's right,' he said.

Lydia shrugged disingenuously. 'So what good is this boot?' she asked. He glared at her, then had an inspiration.

'I was planning to repair the other boot,' he said triumphantly.

Lydia had to consider that. His recent appearance at the festival notwithstanding, Thorn was not what might be called a snappy dresser. It was true that he was prone to patching and repairing his clothes until they were more patches than garments. In fact, he had been known to repair and wear clothes until they simply disintegrated around him. But she still had one card up her sleeve.

'So . . . why did you throw it overboard as we left Gretagne?' she asked.

Thorn's face began to grow redder and redder. 'Because that idiot dog destroyed it!' he yelled in frustration.

Lydia smiled at him, content that she had made her point.

The discussion could have gone on for some time. But Hal had noticed a line of dark clouds on the northern horizon. There was a change in the weather coming and a squall was bearing down on them. He glanced quickly to the west, where a long headland jutted out into the Stormwhite. They were going to need sea room to get round it once that squall hit them, he knew. He cursed under his breath. That meant they would have to swing to the north — heading away from the course they needed to follow if they were to catch *Nightwolf*. Still, there was nothing for it.

'Sailing stations!' he snapped. 'We're going to come about!'

They continued beating to the north for the rest of the morning and into the afternoon, until Hal judged that they had enough sea room to clear the headland.

Then he brought the little ship round to port again, holding the wind on her beam as they sped across the rolling waves of the Stormwhite. Lydia, who was standing by Hal and Stig at the steering platform, noticed that the young skirl seemed to be preoccupied, sweeping his gaze around the sea to the west of them.

'Looking for anything in particular?' she asked.

He shrugged disconsolately. 'Tursgud and his ship,' he said. 'Although I'm afraid they have too much of a lead on us now.'

'They'll be long gone,' Stig agreed.

'But aren't we faster than them?' Lydia asked. In her time as a member of the Herons she had come to assume that their ship could outperform any other ship, in any manoeuvre. She was surprised when Hal shook his head.

'Not in these conditions. This is one of our best points of sailing — with the wind coming from abeam. But it's the same for *Nightwolf*. She'll be moving pretty much as fast as us, or even faster.'

'Of course, if we were sailing into the wind, we'd have a big advantage,' Stig said. He didn't like hearing that any other ship could outperform, or even equal, *Heron*. 'We can point much closer to the wind.'

'But we're not,' Lydia pointed out. 'We're sailing across the wind.'

Stig frowned, having to concede that there were some situations where Hal's ingenious design gave them little or no advantage.

'Maybe so,' he said. 'But we'll make less leeway.' He saw she wasn't totally sure what that meant. 'We'll be blown downwind a lot less than he will be. We've got that new fin that Hal designed. *Nightwolf*'s keel is a lot shallower than ours, so she has less grip on the water.'

'But that won't be enough to let us catch her?' Lydia said.

Hal decided he should rescue Stig. He was touched that his friend wanted to show their ship in the best possible light, and didn't enjoy discussing her shortcomings.

'No. I doubt it,' he said. 'We'll just have to keep watching and hope we run across him on the way south, once we round Cape Shelter. Of course,' he added after a pause, 'that's assuming that he is heading that way. He may have turned around and gone east across the Stormwhite.'

But in his heart, he doubted it. Tursgud had been travelling west when he encountered the Gallican trader and Jerard had told them that *Nightwolf* had continued in that direction when Tursgud left the crew of the trader to drown with their ship. It hardly made sense that he would then reverse his course and head back into the Stormwhite.

If they hadn't been sidetracked by the need to help the Gallican ship, and then further delayed by the deteriorating weather, they might have had a chance to catch him. Now that chance was negligible. Hal doubted they would ever set eyes on Tursgud and his dark blue ship again.

CHAPTER FIFTEEN

They rounded Cape Shelter three days later, emerging from the Stormwhite into the Narrow Sea, then
swinging due south for Araluen.

They had sighted half a dozen other ships during that
time, and closed eagerly with all of them. But none of them
were the dark blue *Nightwolf*. Two were fishing trawlers
from Teutlandt and three others were trading ships from
Sonderland — big, clumsy craft with huge lee-boards in
place of keels. It was a design feature that allowed the ships
to traverse the shallow sandbanks that fringed the Sonderland coast with the boards raised and the ships' draught
reduced, then lower them in deep water to act as keels.

There was also one Gallican ship, heading up from the
western coast of Gallica towards the Stormwhite Sea. It
was a small craft, looking too flimsy for the robust conditions in the Stormwhite.

They went south with a steady following breeze, the
kilometres slipping under their keel with each passing

hour. The crew lapsed into the patient, accepting attitude that became the norm on most long trips. The weather was fair. The wind was favourable. They were making good speed and could do nothing to make the ship go faster.

Admittedly, they were sailing in new waters. None of them had come this far west before. But the waters looked the same. The sea was blue on a sunny day, grey when it was overcast. The fresh air smelt of the same salt. There would be no novelty in their lives until they reached new foreign ports. The sea was, after all, the sea.

As a result, they lapsed into a strange, limbo-like feeling of suspended activity and passive acceptance of the passing hours.

Except for Ulf and Wulf.

As ever, with time on their hands, they devoted themselves to endless, and senseless, argument. Watching them, Hal had the feeling that neither of them actually meant what they were saying. They were so accustomed to disagreeing with each other that it was an automatic reaction to not having much to do.

Mindful of Hal's standing orders, which had Ingvar ready and willing to throw them overboard if they bickered too much while they were at sea, they kept their voices lowered. And they kept a surreptitious watch on their skirl, to make sure he wasn't becoming annoyed.

Their current subject of dissent was a boot belonging to one of them — although nobody on board was sure which of them it belonged to. Kloof, barred from touching Thorn's belongings, which Thorn now kept safe in his kit locker, had taken to prowling the rowing benches, searching for unsecured belongings. She was now happily gnawing on the boot, watched by the twins.

'It's your boot,' said Ulf. Or perhaps it was Wulf — nobody was ever sure.

'No. It's definitely yours. She wouldn't chew my boot. She likes me better than you.'

'Then that's why she would chew your boot. And anyway, whoever said she likes you better than me?'

'Are you saying she prefers you?'

'Of course. Everyone does. That's a well-known fact.'

'It's not a fact, and it's certainly not well known. After all, our mam loves me better than you and the dog is simply following her example.'

'You think our mam likes you better than me?' challenged whichever one was the other. (Don't blame me. I've lost track too.)

'Obviously.'

'What makes you say that?' The challenge was couched in a pugnacious tone. The two boys were getting louder, without realising it. The rest of the crew, who had been content to let the argument ride as long as it didn't become too intrusive, were all watching the twins now.

'Ever noticed,' said Lydia to Hal, 'how things get loud and aggressive once a mother's love is invoked?'

'Every time.' Hal sighed. He raised his voice. 'Ingvar?'

The massively built boy was sitting amidships. He looked towards the stern, squinting to see Hal more clearly. He sensed what the skirl had in mind.

'Ready any time you say, Hal,' he called.

The twins looked up nervously, first at Hal, then at Ingvar, who was still sitting peaceably on the deck, his feet hanging down into the rowing well. Ingvar was big and it was easy to equate size with clumsiness. But they knew from bitter experience that he could move as quickly as a cat if the need arose. They lowered their voices. Lydia smiled.

'So . . . what makes you say that Mam loves you more than me?' one of them — let's say it was Wulf — muttered.

'Everyone knows it. Even the dog senses it. She senses it in your reaction.'

'What reaction?' Wulf demanded angrily and his brother made a tut-tutting noise.

'The dog can sense that you're angry, and she senses it's because our mam loves me more than she does you.'

'I'm not angry because of that!' Wulf shouted. 'I'm angry because you're an idiot!'

Ingvar looked questioningly at Hal. Hal held up a hand for him to wait.

'An idiot?' Ulf asked.

Wulf glared at him. 'And a blithering twit. How's that?' He beamed triumphantly, then stopped beaming as his brother grabbed him in a headlock. They struggled together for a few seconds, then Hal signed for Ingvar to intervene.

'All right, Ingvar. Throw one overboard.'

'Which one, Hal?' Ingvar asked.

Hal shrugged. 'Do I look as if I care? Pick one and throw him overboard.'

Ingvar stepped down into the rowing well and grabbed one of the struggling twins by the scruff of his neck. With no apparent effort, he dragged him clear of his brother and hoisted him to his feet. He looked at Hal to make sure. They'd threatened this punishment many times but never actually carried it out at sea.

Hal paused for a second, but then his resolve hardened. Perhaps it was time they did carry through on the threat, he thought. The twins had obviously become a little complacent. It was as well that Hal had ordered all the crew to learn how to swim. It was ridiculous, he thought, to be on board ship and not to have that basic skill. He gestured over the side.

'Throw him,' he said.

Ingvar hoisted the twin — it happened to be Ulf — onto the rail. Instantly, Wulf was on his feet to protect his sibling. Typical, thought Hal. They would fight like cat and dog right up until the point when someone else threatened one of them. Then they would unite against the common foe.

'You leave my brother alone!' Wulf demanded, his fists bunched.

Ingvar regarded him placidly for a second or two.

'All right,' he said. He released his hold on Ulf and the boy tumbled back on board the ship. Wulf grinned triumphantly, then neighed in terror as Ingvar grabbed him instead.

'Hal said he didn't care which one of you went,' Ingvar said, and hurled Wulf into the sea. Kloof barked excitedly and Stig hurried to grab her collar before she could go after Wulf and fetch him.

Wulf surfaced, spluttering and spitting sea water, in the wake astern of *Heron*.

'Jesper, Stefan,' called Hal, 'let the sheets fly.'

As they did and the sail lost power, he swung the tiller to bring *Heron* round one hundred and eighty degrees.

Stig, grinning widely, took the boat hook from its rack against the mast.

'Now I suppose we'd better haul him back aboard,' he said.

PART TWO

ARALUEN

CHAPTER SIXTEEN

Two days after they had rounded Cape Shelter, they saw the dim grey line of the Araluen coast off their starboard bow. Gradually, the country began to take on greater definition as they came closer.

'It's very green,' Stig said, as they began to make out forests and cultivated fields. There was a gentle look to the land — unlike their homeland, with its rocky cliffs, steep, snow-capped mountains and dull green pine forests interspersed with low-lying buildings constructed from massive, rough-hewn logs.

Occasionally, they sighted a village close to the coast and Hal took the ship in for a closer look. The houses were generally wattle and daub — the walls made from thin willow strands woven together over a light timber frame and sealed with liberal applications of mud. The whole structure, once the mud daub dried and hardened, was then sealed with whitewash. The roofs were thatched, with eaves overhanging to below a man's height. Cows and sheep grazed in the lush green fields that lined the coast. None of them took any notice of the small ship speeding past.

They sighted no large ships moored in the many bays they passed. But there was a large number of fishing craft in evidence, usually clustered together in groups of four or five, tied up alongside jetties that snaked their way out into the bays.

The fields were laid out with geometric precision and separated from one another by low stone walls. The countryside of Skandia, by contrast, was far more haphazard in its layout. Skandians did farm and tend flocks, but they weren't as fanatical about it as the Araluans appeared to be.

'What are the people like, Thorn?' Stefan asked. They all knew that Thorn had been on several voyages to Araluen in his time as a sea wolf.

He paused as he thought about it, while they gathered around him, sitting on the deck and waiting for his answer.

'On the whole, they're peaceful enough — and friendly enough. But if you get them riled, they can be very dangerous.'

'They're good fighters?' Stig asked.

Thorn nodded slowly. 'Oh yes, they're good fighters. Each fief maintains a force of mounted knights — they're on permanent duty and they train constantly. Then there's a militia of men at arms — part-time infantry who are farmers and craftsmen most of the time, but are liable to be called up in time of battle.'

'Amateurs then?' Stig asked, in a slightly derogatory tone.

But Thorn shook his head. 'Don't sell them short. They're well trained in all the basics of warfare, and they're well equipped. They may not be full-time soldiers, but they certainly know how to handle themselves on a battlefield. And they're led by professionals. That makes a difference. And then, of course, there are the Rangers.'

'Who are they?' Lydia asked. When Thorn wasn't busy teasing her, she thought, he was a remarkably knowledgeable person — particularly when it came to fighting, and fighting men. He paused for a second or two before he answered her, and Jesper took advantage of the silence to interrupt.

'Didn't two of them come to Skandia a few years back? When the horsemen from the east tried to attack us?'

'The Temujai?' Lydia asked. 'What happened?'

Jesper looked smug. 'Oh, we gave them a good seeing to,' he said, sounding as if he had not only been there, but had been instrumental in their defeat. 'Sent 'em packing with their horses' tails between their legs.'

'It wasn't quite that simple,' Thorn said, with a slight edge in his voice. 'In fact, it was touch and go. If it hadn't been for those two Rangers, we may well have lost that fight.'

Jesper looked suitably chastened.

Lydia moved closer and settled herself more comfortably on the deck. 'So what did they do exactly?'

'Well, Rangers are very skilled tacticians. One of them, the older one, organised our defences. He had us withdraw to a point where the horsemen's numbers weren't an advantage — a narrow plain by the ocean. And he convinced us to fight from behind cover, where the horses weren't anywhere near as effective. The other one was his apprentice. He organised a group of Araluan slaves into an archery unit — took on the horsemen with their own weapon, the bow. And he cut them down in large numbers. Actually turned the battle in our favour.

'All in all,' he continued, 'Rangers are a remarkable group. There are fifty of them and they're all expert archers. Can shoot the eye out of a blowfly at a hundred paces, they say. And they can move without being seen. Some people think they have magical powers.'

'Lots of people can move without my seeing them,' Ingvar put in and the crew chuckled. Then he added, 'But, seriously, how do they do it?'

Thorn shook his head. 'I'm not sure. If I knew, I'd move so you couldn't see me. But they're an incredibly skilled group — and very, very deadly to their enemies.'

'Just as well we're allies these days then,' Hal said. He consulted his chart and sailing notes and pointed to the shoreline. 'I think we're getting close to Cresthaven. That ruined tower on the headland is just a few hundred metres from the bay.'

There was a stirring among the group. Several of them stood to look at the ruined tower, now almost abeam of the ship. Ulf and Wulf began checking their ropes, knowing that Hal might be issuing sail orders soon. Simultaneously, Stefan and Jesper moved to the halyards, in case the ship was going to tack.

They passed the next headland, and Cresthaven Bay opened up before them. It was a relatively narrow bay, with a yellow sand beach and a long, spindly jetty jutting out on the northern shore. Hal assessed it keenly. The bay would be a snug base for them, without concerns about dragging anchors or broken moorings, since the high headland to the north would break the force of any storm. A wolfship was moored alongside the jetty and several figures could be seen moving on the jetty and on board the ship.

'That'll be *Wolfspear*, the current duty ship,' Hal said, and Thorn nodded.

Beyond the jetty, and inland from the beach, there were several long huts, built from logs. The gaps between had been sealed with mud and clay and they were roofed with thick thatching. The logs were weathered and grey but the huts looked solidly built and comfortable.

'Our new home,' Stig murmured. 'All it needs is a lick of paint and it'll be perfect.'

'And a woman's touch,' Thorn said, grinning at Lydia. 'I imagine you'll be putting up lacy curtains before too long, princess.'

'Shut up, old man,' Lydia said. It tended to be her standard reply to Thorn.

To the north of the jetty, the ground rose steeply and was thickly timbered. They could see the beginnings of a track leading into the trees. Beyond, and higher up, they caught glimpses of whitewashed buildings and more thatched roofs. Woodsmoke curled up from several chimneys.

'That'll be Cresthaven village,' Hal said, pointing with his free hand. He checked the wind telltale and the angle to the beach. The port sail was raised, with the wind coming over their starboard quarter.

'We'll take her in on this tack,' he said. 'Be ready to sheet home as we come round to starboard, boys,' he called to Ulf and Wulf. One of them signalled that they had heard him and were ready.

He heaved on the tiller and *Heron*'s bow began to swing to starboard. As it did, Ulf and Wulf hauled in on the sheets to flatten the sail and present it more fully to the wind.

'Wind's going to be blocked once we come inside that northern headland,' Thorn remarked.

Hal nodded. 'There's still enough to bring us into the beach. You can see the catspaws on the water closer in. And we've got plenty of way on.'

Thorn grunted, satisfied that Hal had the situation well in hand. He didn't want *Heron* to suddenly lose the wind halfway into the beach and wallow there while they ran the oars out. Not with another wolfship crew watching them, just as he knew they would be.

But if Hal felt there was enough wind to sail her all the way in, that was good enough for him. In matters of seamanship, he always deferred to the young man.

And, as ever, it turned out he was right to do so.

CHAPTER SEVENTEEN

There was no room to moor at the jetty. The wolfship was taking up all the available space there, so Hal brought the *Heron* curving in to the beach, dropping the sail in the last forty metres and letting the prow grate gently into the sand. As the deck slowly canted to one side, Stefan clambered over the bows and took a sand anchor up the beach, driving it into the ground well above the high water mark.

Now that they were ashore, they became aware of the birds singing in the trees and the distant sound of cattle lowing somewhere on the headland. Strange, thought Hal, how those land-bound noises were masked by the sound of the ship's passage through the water, along with the creaking of the masts and yards, and the constant movement of the sail.

After those first moments of comparative silence, the inlet echoed to the clatter and bustle of sails, oars and spars being stowed. Then the crew had time to look around and take stock of their home for the next eight months.

'I guess those huts are our accommodation,' Edvin said. 'They look comfortable enough.'

He was right. The huts were built to accommodate a normal wolfship crew of twenty to thirty men. The nine Herons, and Lydia, would have plenty of room to spread out. The huts looked to be solidly built and, in spite of Stig's earlier comment, freshly painted. Hal walked slowly forward to the bow as several of the people from the huts approached along the beach. He swung a leg over the rail and dropped lightly onto the firm, wet sand. The rest of the crew, having waited for him to be first ashore, now followed in quick succession. They stood in a semi-circle, a few paces behind him, as the Skandians from the huts came closer. There were three of them in all. The leader, a short, stockily built man with a flaming red beard and hair, stopped before Hal and smiled a welcome.

'Welcome to Cresthaven,' he said, holding out a hand. Hal grasped it and they shook. 'I'm Jurgen Half-Foot, skirl of the *Wolfspear*.' He jerked a thumb towards the graceful, lean-waisted wolfship moored alongside the jetty. Even at rest, wolfships had an air of menace about them.

'Hal Mikkelson,' Hal replied. 'And this is the *Heron*. We're here to relieve you as duty ship.'

Jurgen's smile grew even broader. 'And we're glad to see you,' he said heartily.

Stig frowned. 'Had a rough year?'

Jurgen hastened to shake his head in the negative. 'Not at all! But it'll be good to be heading home again. Three of my men have babies they've never seen — all born since we were stationed here. But it's a pleasant enough duty. The locals are friendly and they look after us well. You won't want for anything while you're here. The food is good. The ale is wonderful . . .' He paused, noticing the youth of the crewmen standing behind Hal. 'Although that probably won't be important to you,' he added, a little uncertainly.

'It'll be important to me,' Thorn growled.

Jurgen studied him, frowning for a moment. Then, as he noticed the missing right hand, recognition dawned.

'Thorn? Is that you?'

'Well, it's not anybody else, Jurgen,' Thorn said pleasantly.

'Hardly recognised you,' Jurgen told him. 'You look kind of . . . tidier than I'm used to seeing you.'

That raised a few eyebrows among the crew of the *Heron*. 'Tidy' was not a word that sprang easily to mind when they thought of Thorn. Hal smiled to himself, wondering how Jurgen would have reacted to the sight of Thorn at the haymaking festival.

'Yes. I'm a regular dandy these days,' Thorn said sarcastically.

Jurgen switched his attention to the *Heron*. He tilted his head thoughtfully. 'So this is the *Heron* we've heard so much about,' he said. 'She's a bit small, isn't she?'

Of course, the *Heron* and her revolutionary sail plan had gained attention in Skandia before Hal and the crew sailed south in pursuit of the Andomal. Her speed, agility and ability to point upwind had all played a role in helping the Herons win the annual brotherband contest.

'She doesn't need to be any bigger,' Hal said. He was used to the comment. 'We don't need as many oars because she sails upwind better than a square-rigger.'

A square-rigged ship like *Wolfspear* had to resort to oars whenever they wanted to travel upwind. That meant they needed a lot of oars, and that meant the ship needed to be big enough to accommodate the oarsmen.

Jurgen considered the answer. 'I suppose that's true,' he said. He was silent for a few seconds, then continued. 'Well, if Erak thinks you're up to the job, who am I to disagree?'

'Exactly,' Thorn said in a tone that indicated no further discussion of the matter would be entertained. It was obvious to the Herons that, in addition to the size of their ship, Jurgen was all too well aware of the youth of their crew — aside from Thorn, that is. As the shaggy-haired warrior had been known to say, he raised the average age of the crew by ten or twelve years, singlehandedly — 'Which is how I do most things these days,' he would add.

There was an awkward pause. Nobody seemed to know where to go next in this conversation. Jesper solved the problem as he often did — by displaying a total lack of tact.

'Jurgen Half-Foot is an odd sort of name, isn't it?' he proclaimed. 'How did you come to be called that?'

Thorn turned away to hide a grin. Even he could remember how Jurgen had been given the name — although there were many things from that time that he couldn't recall with great clarity. Jurgen went red in the face and regarded Jesper, trying to discern whether or not the boy was making sport of him. But Jesper's wide-eyed innocent look convinced him otherwise — although it has to be said that Jesper was a thief and a liar par excellence. The wide-eyed innocent look was a specialty of his.

'Lost three of my toes to an axe,' he said gruffly.

Jesper looked impressed. 'Oh wow! In a battle, was it?'

Jurgen hesitated, then nodded curtly. 'Yes. In a battle.'

All of which was true. But Jurgen, when he told the story, liked to leave the impression that he had been hit in the foot by another warrior. And since Jurgen was still among the living after receiving such a major wound, the assumption was that he had gone on to kill the man who had relieved him of his toes.

The fact was, Jurgen *was* in a battle at the time of the injury. But the axe that caused the wound belonged to him. He was brandishing it — waving it above his head and spinning it in intricate patterns in the air to put the fear of death into the enemy — when his grip slipped and the axe fell from his hand, landing on his foot and neatly removing the toes in question. Jurgen, looking down in horror at the dreadful wound and his ruined foot, promptly keeled over in a faint. Three stretcher bearers had to take him to the rear of the battle, where a surgeon patched him up and bandaged him. From then on, he was known as Jurgen Half-foot. Although his previous *nom de guerre* gave some hint as to how it had all happened. Up until that time, he had been known as Jurgen Drops-a-lot.

For obvious reasons, he preferred his new title. But he disliked having to explain how it came about.

Hal had heard the story some years back. He took pity on his fellow skirl and changed the subject.

'Accommodation,' he said. 'I assume we sleep in the huts?'

Jurgen nodded, glad the subject had moved away from his toes — or lack thereof.

'We've been expecting you, so we made room for you in the smaller hut,' he said. 'But there's only —' he took a quick head count of the young crew '— ten of you, so you'll have plenty of room. Of course, once we're gone you can spread out as much as you like. It'll be sheer luxury.'

Hal grinned, looking at the wattle and daub huts. They were sturdily built and maintained, and they looked as if they would be weatherproof. But luxury was stretching it.

'We can use a little luxury,' he said. 'How long before you head off?'

Jurgen didn't have to think about it. Obviously, he'd been planning *Wolfspear*'s departure for some time.

'Soon as possible,' he said promptly. 'If you're ready now, I can introduce you to the local bigwigs while your crew get set up in the small hut. Then I'll show you round the area and tell you what we've been up to. That way, I can shove off for Hallasholm early tomorrow.'

'No hurry at all then.' Hal smiled. 'Just don't let the door hit you in the backside on the way out.'

Jurgen acknowledged the joke. 'Wait till you've been here eight months,' he said. 'You'll be keen to get home too. And the Summer Gales could start any week now. I want to be round Cape Shelter before they do.'

'Then let's go and meet the local bigwigs,' Hal said. He turned to the crew assembled behind him. 'Thorn, you come with me. Stig, take charge of getting us set up in the small hut. Screen off a separate area for Lydia.'

'I can sleep on board,' Lydia said.

Hal shrugged. 'Maybe. But if we can organise some privacy for you, you'll be more comfortable.' He turned back to Jurgen. 'Shall we meet the locals?'

Jurgen gestured towards the village on the slope above the beach, and stepped to one side, allowing Hal and Thorn to proceed ahead of him. The men who had accompanied him joined Stig and the others as they unloaded their gear and led the way towards the small hut.

The village was a neat affair, and the houses and other buildings looked to be well maintained. They were all single-storey constructions, laid out along one main street, with side alleys running off to access small vegetable plots, worksheds and animal pens behind the houses. There was a common grassed area at the end of the main street, where a handful of sheep and three dairy cows were grazing.

Jurgen led the way to one of the larger houses, in the middle of the village. It was built of the same materials as its neighbours, and to the same general design. But it was nearly half again as big as those either side.

'Headman's house,' Jurgen commented. 'He likes to spread himself out. Thinks it makes him look important.'

'Stands on his dignity, does he?' Thorn asked warily, but Jurgen made a dismissive gesture.

'Not really. He's all right. They're a pretty easy bunch to deal with, as a matter of fact.'

He paused at the door and rapped sharply on the frame. They heard the sound of a chair scraping on a wooden floor inside. Hal raised his eyebrows. A wooden floor was impressive, he thought. He would have expected the floor to be rammed, packed dirt.

The door swung open, hinges squeaking loudly, and an immensely tall man stooped to peer out at them. He regarded Hal and Thorn with a slightly puzzled look, then smiled as he recognised Jurgen, standing to one side. Comprehension dawned on his face.

'Jurgen, come in. And you must be from the new duty ship,' he added, addressing Thorn and Hal. 'Please, come in, all of you.'

'William, I'd like you to meet Hal and Thorn from the *Heron* wolfship. William is the headman here in Cresthaven,' Jurgen added, by way of explanation.

William was well over two metres tall and incredibly thin, which made him seem even taller. He had to stoop to avoid the low beams of the house. He was aged about forty, and bald on top — probably from banging his head on the ceiling beams, Hal thought irreverently. There was a fringe of grey hair ringing his head below the shiny bare pate. He had thoughtful brown eyes and his face was lined with wrinkles — possibly from the strain and responsibility of being headman.

'Welcome to Cresthaven, Captain,' he said, addressing himself to Thorn.

Thorn grinned easily and held up a hand — his only hand, in fact — to stop him before he went any further.

'Hal here is the skirl,' he said. 'I just carry the bags and peel the potatoes.'

William's mistake was a common one. Most people assumed that Hal was too young to be a ship's captain. He and Thorn were used to this and the light-hearted reply helped cover the confusion of people greeting them for the first time. Hal noticed William's eyes widen slightly in surprise. But he recovered quickly enough.

'Oh, of course. Welcome . . . both of you. Please meet my fellow councillors: Gryff Seeder and Sloan Wheelwright.'

The men stepped forward in turn. Seeder was some ten years younger than the headman, and had all his hair. He was blond and blue-eyed and had a muscular build. He was of average height, although alongside William, he looked quite diminutive. Wheelwright was around the same age, possibly one or two years older. He had massive shoulders and muscular arms. Obviously, the labour of making wheels was intense and helped develop the strength of the upper body. His waist was surprisingly narrow and he seemed to taper down from those wide shoulders to a thin pair of legs.

Both men mumbled greetings and Hal and Thorn shook hands with all three. The headman gestured to a table set by a window, to one side of the large parlour. There were several jugs and pottery drinking mugs set out.

'Let's sit and wet our whistles,' he said. 'I've got ale, and wine − oh, and water if anyone wants it.'

'I'll have water,' Hal said.

'Water for me too,' Thorn said. In spite of his earlier comment to Jurgen, he only drank ale sparingly these days − and usually small ale, which had been watered down.

The others opted for ale and William poured the drinks, calling to his wife to come and replenish the ale jug. She was a small grey-haired woman who reminded

Hal of a mouse — scuttling quietly about the room to do her husband's bidding, making eye contact with the newcomers long enough to nod a greeting, then departing again without a word.

'Right,' said William, after a long draught of ale. 'Time to talk business.'

CHAPTER EIGHTEEN

'I suppose you know what your duties are?' William began, with an interrogative glance in Hal's direction.

The young captain nodded. 'In broad terms. Patrol the coast, keeping an eye out for pirates and wreckers —'

'We call them Moondarkers,' Wheelwright put in. 'They operate in the dark periods of the moon, lighting signal fires and false beacons to lure ships onto the rocks.'

'Nice folk,' Thorn said, scowling. 'I'd like to get my hands around their throats.'

'Mmm, quite so,' William agreed. 'Problem is, a lot of ordinary people benefit from their activities, so it's hard to get information about where they're planning to operate.'

'Benefit how?' Hal asked.

This time Seeder answered. 'Moondarkers tend to strip the ships they wreck of anything small and portable and valuable. But the rest of the cargo they leave to rot — or to the tender mercies of folk living near the wreck.

There's a lot of people will help themselves to lumber, cordage, canvas and such if it's left lying around. And a lot of houses along the coast are built in part from the timbers of stranded ships.'

'Fortunately, there aren't a lot of Moondarkers these days.' William took up the lead again. 'The Rangers have pretty well put them out of business.'

Hal and Thorn exchanged a quick glance at the mention of Rangers. There was a tone almost of . . . reverence in William's voice.

The headman went on. 'Our main problems these days are piracy and slavers. There's been an upsurge in the slave trade in recent years. The new slave market in Socorro has seen to that.'

Hal frowned thoughtfully, sifting back through his memory of the navigation notes and updates he had studied.

'Socorro . . . that's in Arrida, isn't it?' he asked.

'On the west coast,' William said. 'Ships sneak across the Narrow Sea from Gallica and Teutlandt – even from Sonderland. They do a quick raid ashore, grab up half a dozen captives, head down the coast and do it all again two or three times, before selling them at the Socorro market.'

'And you're hoping we can stop them?' Hal said carefully.

Jurgen let out an explosive snort. 'Good luck with that. You never know where or when they'll raid. They're here and away within a few hours and by the time news gets to us there's been a raid, they're long gone down the Narrow Sea.'

Hal made a mental note to look into this further. His mother had been a slave and he had a heartfelt dislike for those who participated in the trade. Thankfully, Skandia had abandoned the practice when Erak had been elected Oberjarl. The thought of Erak reminded him of something else that nobody had mentioned so far.

'I was told we'd also be chasing smugglers,' he said. 'Is there a lot of that going on?'

The three councillors exchanged a look before William answered in a dismissive tone.

'Oh, we're not so worried about them. I don't see that they do any real harm. All they do is bring in a little brandy from Gallica. Or the occasional bit of lace and silk from Toscana. Who's any the worse off for that?'

The King, presumably, Hal thought. After all, the smugglers were avoiding taxes charged by the crown for bringing goods into the country. And that meant the goods could be sold at a cheaper price than similar items that were imported officially. He could guess that the people of Cresthaven probably numbered among the smugglers' keenest customers.

Hal surmised that it would not be viewed kindly by the locals if his ship were to become too efficient in catching smugglers. Jurgen caught his eye and obviously guessed what was going through his mind. He gave an almost imperceptible nod, and lowered one eyelid in a wink.

When he thought about it, he decided that his sympathies lay with the smugglers and their customers more than with the King's agents. Skandians always had a healthy disregard for officialdom and its rules. In Hallasholm it was considered unpatriotic to pay the full amount of the tax owed to the Oberjarl. Everyone was expected to cheat a little.

And Erak could hardly complain about the practice. Before he was elected, he was one of the country's more enthusiastic tax avoiders.

Some things are the same in every country, Hal mused. He realised that William was talking again about the tasks the duty ship might be called on to perform.

'. . . that's just the day-to-day stuff, of course. You also have to be ready for special missions that the King needs — transporting diplomats or carrying urgent messages — that sort of thing. But that doesn't happen too often.'

'We only did one of those missions in the eight months we've been here,' Jurgen put in. Hal was a little disappointed at the news. The idea of carrying out secret missions for the King of Araluen had a definite appeal to his young, adventurous spirit.

'Aside from that, you're pretty much at liberty to arrange your own patrolling pattern. Just don't spend too much time tied up alongside the jetty or the villagers will think they're not getting value for their money.'

Hal nodded. 'We wouldn't do that anyway. I don't want my crew getting rusty,' he said. Then he glanced at Thorn. 'Plus we need to give Stig and Lydia more time to practise with the Mangler.'

Seeder looked at him curiously. 'The Mangler?' he said. 'Sounds dangerous.'

'It is,' Hal replied. 'It's a giant crossbow we've mounted in the bows of our ship. It fires a bolt about this long.' He held up his hands, about a metre apart. 'It's proved to be very useful in the past.'

Jurgen showed some interest at that. Prior to Hal, Skandians had never thought to mount a major weapon on board their ships. The wolfships were seen as transport only, getting the sea wolves to the scene of a battle or a raid in the shortest possible time.

'Interesting idea,' he said. 'I'd like to see that later.'

Hal nodded, and then turned back to William. 'What do we do about provisions?' he asked. 'How do I feed my crew?'

'We provide everything you need. You can do your own food preparation for the most part, but you're welcome to eat in our inn one night a week. Just let us know what you like and we'll deliver it each week.'

'Who pays?' Thorn asked. Hal was glad he'd thought of that.

William made a negative hand gesture. 'It's all paid for by the crown,' he said. 'Part of the treaty. Plus we've got a healer in the village who can tend to any injuries your men might sustain. In fact, anything you need, come and see me. We provide what you want and send a bill to Castle Araluen.' He grinned. 'It's quite a lucrative business for us, so don't feel you have to stint yourselves.'

Hal smiled in return. 'I'll try not to,' he said, making a mental note not to chase smugglers and to make lots of demands on the village. William pushed his chair back and stood, although he had to remain stooped over.

'Well, that's about it. Oh, we do have a meeting every week on first-day, to let one another know what's been going on. Aside from that, welcome to Araluen and we're pleased to have you here.' He nodded in Jurgen's direction. 'And sorry to lose you and your men, Jurgen. You've been good guests.'

Jurgen shook his hand as the headman offered it. 'You've looked after us well. But we're all keen to be getting home. I'll take Hal and his crew out to show them the surrounding bays and sandbars. I imagine some of my men will be visiting the village this afternoon, to say goodbye to . . . special friends.' He made his farewells to the other two councillors, then gestured for Hal and Thorn to precede him to the door.

As they reached the steep, winding path to the beach, Jurgen glanced back at the village with a sigh.

'We've had a good year here,' he said. 'They're good people and they'll look after you. Make sure you don't let them down.'

Hal nodded. In spite of Jurgen's claim to be glad to be going home, it was obvious that he would miss Cresthaven and its people. Then the older skirl shook off his momentary melancholy and rubbed his hands briskly together.

'Now let's get going!' he said. 'I want to see if this ship of yours lives up to its reputation!'

Heron certainly did that as they took her to sea and Jurgen familiarised them with local landmarks, sandbanks, narrows, channels and shallows. They cruised several leagues north and south of the bay, getting the feel for the area. He showed them where the tide race built up over semi-submerged reefs, where the bottom rose sharply, ready to strand an unwary navigator. And he pointed out distinguishing features on the land, giving them their local names.

'Handy to know the local names in case someone wants to tell you where they've seen a slave ship,' he said.

'Or a smuggler?' Hal said, keeping a straight face.

Jurgen grinned at him. 'I doubt anyone will want to tell you that,' he said. 'But I think you'd already guessed that.'

For his part, Jurgen was suitably impressed with *Heron*'s upwind performance, and the speed with which she went about from one tack to another. The fin keel fascinated him as he saw how it reduced the ship's downwind drift. Although, like every other wolfship skirl, he raised his eyebrows in disbelief when he saw how the fin passed through the bottom of the ship.

'You cut a hole in her bottom?' he said incredulously, then shook his head. 'Can't say I think that's too smart.'

Like all the others, he was also mystified by the fact that *Heron* didn't simply fill up and sink. 'Luck,' he was heard to mutter. 'Just beginner's luck.'

They ran in close to a long beach that stretched along the coastline and they demonstrated the Mangler for him. Hal took over the big weapon. He wanted to impress *Wolfspear*'s skipper with its power and accuracy, and Stig and Lydia weren't fully trained on the weapon yet.

He shot three bolts at a target set up on the beach and demolished it. Jurgen drew in his breath as he watched the missiles slamming into the wood and canvas target, sending splinters flying. He could obviously imagine the effect those massive bolts would have on a ship.

Finally, as an experiment, Hal shot one of the new pottery-tipped bolts, aiming at a rock at the end of the beach. The result was everything he had hoped for and there was a collective intake of breath from the Herons as the clay head shattered, sending a hail of fragments and shards in all directions, tearing down the small bushes that surrounded the rock, and sending sand fountaining into the air.

'Remind me never to get on the wrong side of you lot in a sea fight,' Jurgen said. He was half joking — but only half. He looked at the youthful crew with new respect. They were young, he thought, but they definitely weren't boys. They had been hardened in battle and they knew how to fight.

Hal offered him the tiller as they cruised back up the coast to Cresthaven. Jurgen had a sure hand on the tiller and he enjoyed the *Heron*'s instant response to his movements of the helm and her speed on a beam reach. He also noted the skill and precision with which her crew handled the sails, bringing one down and sending the other up as they tacked, then sheeting home to send the little ship surging through the water.

'You've got them well trained,' he said to Hal in an aside.

Hal couldn't help feeling a glow of pride at the words. 'They're a good crew,' he replied.

'A crew is only as good as their captain,' Jurgen said, looking at the young man with increased respect. Hal went a little red around the ears, but said nothing.

That night, there was a farewell for *Wolfspear* and her crew in the village. The Herons were invited, but they declined.

'This is your night,' Hal told Jurgen and his crew. 'They want to say goodbye and we'd just be in the way.'

They were rolled up in their blankets when the other crew returned late that night. They were obviously trying to be quiet, but the idea of a Skandian wolfship crew being quiet after an evening of feasting and ale drinking was a totally foreign concept.

As a gesture to their sleeping countrymen, the staggering, stumbling, singing crewmen tried to stagger, stumble and sing in a whisper — with the inevitable result. They fell, they crashed into items of furniture that appeared to move in front of them without warning, and their whispered singing sounded like a chorus of huge snakes hissing and whistling.

The Herons sighed, rolled over and pulled their blankets over their heads.

The following morning, the bleary-eyed crew departed. An equally bleary-eyed group came down from the village to farewell them. Several attractive girls were openly weeping as they waved goodbye. Hal and the Herons stood by on the jetty and cast off the mooring lines, fending the ship away from the jetty with long poles.

The rowing crew raised their oars vertically. It was a manouevre normally done with precision and panache, the oars moving as one. This time, they moved as seventeen or eighteen. They came down to the horizontal jerkily and there was a series of muffled thuds and rattles as the oars were placed in their oarlocks.

Jurgen called the stroke, instantly raising a hand to his forehead in a vain attempt to quell the sudden, lancing pain there, and the ship moved out into the bay. The strokes were uneven, with the ship crabbing awkwardly as several oarsmen missed the water altogether and another dug his oar blade too deep and was promptly catapulted off his bench by the butt end.

As *Wolfspear* rounded the point, the watchers could see several of her crew hanging over the rail, doubled at the waist and peering down at the sea as the first rollers lifted her.

'Looks like they've lost something,' said Edvin.

'Probably their breakfast,' Stefan replied.

CHAPTER NINETEEN

For the next ten days, the *Heron* cruised the waters north and south of Cresthaven, exploring bays and inlets, at times venturing up creeks and small rivers that opened into the Narrow Sea. On more than one occasion, they found old burnt-out fireplaces and scraps of rubbish.

'Someone's camped here,' Lydia said, traversing one of the old camp sites — although her skill at tracking and recognising signs wasn't needed to see the fact.

'How long ago?' Hal asked. Lydia's skills were more valuable in assessing how old the traces were. She shrugged, sucked in her cheeks and reached down to stir the ashes of a long-dead fire with her fingers.

'Not recently,' she said. 'Two weeks, maybe a month ago.'

Thorn had been walking the sandy bank of the small river, searching above the high tide mark.

'They beached a ship here,' he called and the others went to inspect the deep groove cut by a ship's keel in the sand. Hal and Stig assessed the mark.

'Not very big,' Stig said.

'Smugglers don't have to be big,' Hal replied. 'They have to be fast.'

Stefan and Edvin were searching the fringe of the woods that bordered the little river beach. They returned with the remnants of a small keg — missing its top, but virtually intact apart from that. Hal sniffed the inside of the staves and wrinkled his nose.

'Brandy,' he said, passing the broken keg to Thorn for confirmation. 'So I'd say they were smugglers all right, and they sampled some of their own wares.'

Thorn sniffed the cask in his turn and grinned. 'Time was, that smell would have set my pulse racing,' he said. 'More likely they were giving their customers a sample of the goods. It's an old smuggler's trick. You have one cask of superior product and you let them try it. The rest of the cargo is much cheaper stuff.'

Jesper cocked his head to one side curiously. 'And the customers never wise up to the trick?'

Thorn snorted derisively. 'Of course they do. But if they let on, they'll never get to sample the good stuff. They simply adjust the price they pay accordingly. That way, both sides think they're fooling the other.'

'And that's the basis of a good negotiation,' Edvin said seriously.

Thorn looked at him appreciatively. 'Always said you had a head on your shoulders,' he remarked.

'We'll keep an eye on this location,' Hal said. 'If they've used it once, they might well use it again.'

'William did imply that we should leave the smugglers alone,' Stig reminded him.

Hal thrust out his bottom lip. 'Yes. So he did. But if we ignore them completely, they'll get out of control. I think we should nab one of them every so often — just so they know we know what they're up to.'

A smile spread slowly over Stig's face. 'I see what you mean. We've got to keep them honest.'

'As honest as smugglers can be,' Hal agreed. 'Let's get back to the ship.'

They interspersed their cruising with practice sessions on the Mangler for Stig and Lydia. Both of them were highly competitive by nature and Stig, like young men all over the world, had no intention of letting a girl beat him — even a girl as accomplished and capable as Lydia might be.

The two of them sledged each other unmercifully and the crew quickly took sides, betting on their favourite. Jesper held the bets and set the odds, which varied from day to day as either Stig or Lydia moved ahead in the aggregate score.

'It's not a competition!' Hal said in frustration, as Stig crouched behind the Mangler, while Lydia, who was one shot ahead of him on the day, poured a stream of criticism and insults at him. Included were the words 'cross-eyed, hamfisted clod who couldn't hit the side of a barn from inside the barn'.

As Hal spoke, both Stig and Lydia turned to look at him in disbelief.

'Of course it is,' they said in unison. And the crew voiced their agreement. Hal, for once unable to assert his authority, shrugged in defeat.

'All right. It is a competition. But are the rest of you mad?' he continued. 'You're letting Jesper hold the bets and set the odds. You do know that he was a thief, don't you?'

'That's a long way behind me, Hal,' said Jesper, looking suitably aggrieved. 'I'm shocked and deeply hurt that you would throw up my past in my face like that.' All the same, he made a mental note to return half the coins he had been skimming as a commission from the bets left in his care.

He noticed that Hal looked unconvinced and decided he had better return all the coins.

'Honesty,' he sighed to himself. 'It'll be the death of gambling.'

'Can we continue now?' Stig asked sarcastically. Hal gestured for them to go ahead. He guided the *Heron* on a course angling in towards the beach, where a target was set up. As they came within range, Stig began adjusting the Mangler's elevation, and calling corrections to Ingvar, who was training the big crossbow.

'Left ... left a little ... stop ... right a little ... stop ...'

As he saw the target beginning to drift across the sights, he pulled smoothly on the trigger lanyard and the Mangler, after the usual slight pause, slammed back against its restraining straps as the bolt flew on its path.

The bolt missed the left-hand edge of the target by a whisker, then skipped across the beach, sending up successive fountains of sand as it did so. Hal noted the spot where it came to rest so they could retrieve it.

'Miss!' called Jesper, and checked his tally sheet. 'That's twenty-three hits to Lydia, twenty-two to Stig.

Lydia wins. Collect your winnings if you bet on Lydia. Bad luck if you bet on Stig.'

'Just a moment!' Stig protested, going red in the face. 'I want a rematch. That wasn't fair!'

'Looked fair to me,' said Stefan. 'Lydia shot. She hit. You shot. You missed. How could that be unfair?'

Stig looked around wildly, desperately searching for some reason for missing — other than his own lack of proficiency. His gaze landed on Ingvar and he pointed an accusing finger.

'You did it!' he shouted.

Ingvar regarded him with surprise. 'Me? What did I do?'

'You . . . twitched the training lever just as I shot!'

'Why would I do that?' Ingvar asked. He was insulted by the accusation, although he realised that Stig was angry and looking for any excuse for his miss. Still, that was no reason for him to impugn Ingvar's honesty.

'Everyone knows you're sweet on Lydia,' Stig blurted out. 'Remember what you did to Tursgud when he insulted her?'

At their homecoming celebration months earlier, Tursgud had made a sneering remark about Lydia. Ingvar, who was known for his placid, easygoing nature, had punched him in the nose, sending him flying back and knocking several tables down. It had been a sobering demonstration of the big boy's strength and power.

'Maybe you should remember that,' Ingvar said, as he took a pace towards Stig. Stig did remember it all of a sudden, in lurid detail, and he hastily stepped away to place the Mangler between them.

'Well, maybe you didn't do it on purpose,' he said, hoping to placate the giant boy.

'I didn't do it at all,' Ingvar told him.

Lydia stepped forward, hands on her hips as she confronted Stig.

'What makes you think I need Ingvar's help to beat you?' she challenged. 'You're a bumblefooted, hamfisted oaf who couldn't hit a barn door with a bucket of wheat.'

Another interesting barn metaphor, Hal thought. He thought it might be time to nip this disagreement in the bud. But Thorn stepped in.

'That was a pretty comprehensive victory all right,' he said, shaking his head in mock wonder. 'I don't know that I've ever seen such a dominant performance.'

Both Lydia and Stig looked at him suspiciously. They had grown to recognise sarcasm when they heard Thorn utter it.

'What do you mean?' Lydia asked.

Thorn tugged his beard, apparently deep in thought. 'Well, after all, look at the score. You hit the target twenty-three times. *Twenty-three!* That's remarkable. Twenty-three hits out of twenty-seven shots. Incredible! And how many times did Stig score? Fifteen? Sixteen, was it?' He raised an eyebrow and turned his gaze solely on Lydia, who began to flush red in her turn.

She dropped her eyes, becoming intent on a blob of tar on the deck.

'Twenty-two,' she muttered.

Thorn let the message sink in for a few seconds. Then he continued.

'So, after three days, and twenty-seven shots each,

you beat him by the incredible margin of one? That is —'
he looked to the sky, apparently searching his memory
for the right words '— you beat a bumblefooted, hamfisted oaf who couldn't hit a barn door with a bucket of
wheat . . . and you beat him by the magnificent, unprec-
edented margin of . . . how many was it? Oh yes, one.
And you did it at the very last minute?'

'I suppose so,' Lydia said, still not facing him.

Thorn turned to Stig. 'And you, Stig, having lost by
such an enormous score, promptly tried to blame your
friend Ingvar?'

Stig hung his head as well. 'You're right, Thorn. Sorry,
Ingvar,' he said, looking up at the bigger boy.

Ingvar hesitated before he replied. He wasn't angry
so much at being accused of throwing Stig's shot off. But
the first mate's remark that he was 'sweet on Lydia' had
rankled. Mainly because it was true.

Thorn raised his shaggy eyebrows at Ingvar's hesitation. 'Ingvar,' he said softly, 'you're very big and I have
only one hand. But don't think I couldn't throw you overboard if I wanted to. Do you believe that?'

'Yes, Thorn,' Ingvar said meekly. Then he stepped
towards Stig and held out his hand. 'Sorry, Stig.'

The two shook hands. Then Stig held out his hand to
Lydia.

'Lydia?' he said. 'Sorry.'

The slim girl hesitated. She was a member of the
Herons. But sometimes she felt that she was still an
outsider.

'And I could certainly throw *you* overboard, Lydia,'
Thorn told her.

She smiled in spite of herself and shook Stig's hand. 'Yeah. I take back the hamfisted remark, Stig.'

He grinned at her, relieved the bad feeling had been dispelled. 'What about bumblefooted?'

She pretended to consider. 'No. I think that one stays.'

'The thing is,' Thorn said, and they all turned to look at him once more, 'I'm delighted that we now have two crew members who are experts with the Mangler. That makes me feel a lot safer. We're a long way from home, we're all alone and we have to rely on one another. We're not children any more —'

'Well, you're certainly not,' said Jesper, and for once his interruption was well timed. The crew all laughed and Thorn nodded acknowledgement.

'Sad, but true,' he said. 'Just remember, we could be in a fight for our lives any minute. We want the best people available to shoot that monster of a crossbow. And we want to rely on one another and trust one another. If we go into a fight, we'll probably be outnumbered.'

'That's nothing new,' Edvin pointed out, and again Thorn acknowledged the comment.

'Exactly. And we've won in the past because we stuck together and worked together and, most important of all, fought together. So we need to be on top of our game and not squabbling amongst one another like little children at barnskole. We need to work as a team — and a good team doesn't fight among themselves.'

He looked around the assembled faces and was greeted with nods of agreement on all sides.

'So in that case, because the shooting practice was far more than a contest, it was a skill session that all our lives could depend on, and since it could have gone either way, I declare that all bets are off.'

There was a moment of silence then, once more, heads began to nod. That may have been influenced by the fact that more people had bet on Stig than on Lydia. But eventually there was universal agreement.

Almost.

Jesper cast a stricken look at his shipmates. With Stig the loser, he stood to pocket a lot of cash.

'But that's not . . .'

The word 'fair' never made it past his lips. He looked at Thorn, then at Ingvar, then at the cold water surging past the rail of the ship. Then, reluctantly, he began to hand back the money.

As they set course for Cresthaven, Thorn joined Hal at the tiller.

'Hope I didn't step on your toes,' he said quietly.

Hal smiled and shook his head. 'A good skirl knows when to delegate,' he said. 'You did a good job.'

The sun was almost down by the time they arrived back at the jetty in Cresthaven Bay. As Hal brought the ship alongside, and Stefan and Jesper hurried to jump ashore with the mooring lines, a figure stepped from the shadows of the small hut built at the seaward end of the jetty. He was tall and slim and wore a strange cloak, patterned in mottled grey and green. A massive longbow was slung over his shoulder. He waited while Hal and Thorn stepped ashore, leaving Stig to supervise the stowing of sails and lines and other gear. Unlike the majority of strangers who greeted them, he addressed Hal first.

'Good evening,' he said. 'My name is Gilan. The King wants to see you.'

CHAPTER TWENTY

'The King?' Hal repeated, after introductions had been made. His interest was piqued. 'Does this mean there's a mission for us?'

Gilan looked around. There was nobody in sight but the crew of the *Heron*, stowing gear on board the ship. As he hesitated, Hal took the opportunity to study him more closely. This was one of the fabled Rangers Thorn had told them about. He definitely had an aura about him. He was quietly spoken but there was an air of confidence and capability that was unmistakable. He was a man you wouldn't trifle with. Hal couldn't have defined any single attribute that gave him this sense. It was an overall impression gained from Gilan's total demeanour.

After a short pause, the Ranger answered Hal's question. 'Best if we don't discuss details until we're on the way to Araluen.'

Stig, who had stepped ashore to join the small group, frowned. 'I thought we were in Araluen?'

Gilan smiled. 'You are. But Araluen is our principal fief, as well as the name of the country as a whole. Castle Araluen is the royal capital.'

'Any particular reason why we shouldn't talk about the mission here?' Hal was curious to know if Gilan suspected any of the Cresthaven villagers of possible treachery. But the tall Ranger merely shrugged.

'Secrets have a way of getting out when there are people around to hear them,' he said. 'People can be careless. They'll often let slip information, without realising it. A careless word to a wagoner or a fisherman, or even one of the smugglers who frequent this area, could put all our lives at risk.'

'Our lives?' Hal said. 'You're coming too?'

'It's my mission,' Gilan said. 'All you have to do is get me to . . . wherever I'm going . . . as quickly as possible.'

'Sounds fair,' said Hal. He was burning with curiosity but he realised that the Ranger was right. Once a secret got out, there was no recalling it — and no telling who might end up hearing it. The safest solution was to keep it buttoned tight as long as possible, and reveal it to as few people as possible.

'How do we get to this Araluen Fief?' Thorn asked, frowning suspiciously. 'I hope you're not going to tell me we're riding?'

Gilan grinned again. He had an easygoing manner and he seemed to be readily amused. He didn't fit the dark, secretive picture that Thorn had painted of Rangers.

'I know how much you Skandians like to ride,' he said.

Thorn snorted. Hal felt a need to defend his adopted country. 'We can ride,' he said.

Thorn shot him a look with daggers in it. 'No we can't,' he snapped. He had no intention of wearing out his backside sitting astride a fractious, wilful animal that took no notice of his orders and ignored his tugging on the rudder lines — as he called the reins.

'But there'll be no need for that,' Gilan continued. 'There's a river runs from the coast up to Castle Araluen. It's easily navigable and you can sail there, or row if the wind isn't in the right quarter.'

Hal was recalling the tide tables he'd prepared earlier that day. The tide would be running in at ten the following morning.

'Best if we get going in the morning then,' Hal said. 'I've got no wish to navigate a strange river at night. If we reach the river mouth about the tenth hour, we'll have the tide to help us in. That'll make the rowing easier.'

'As I recall, it's about two hours by ship to the river mouth,' Gilan said. 'So we should get moving around the eighth hour.' He glanced critically at the ship. It was smaller than the wolfships he was used to. 'In the past, we've taken our horses on board. The crews built pens for them in the middle of the ship,' he said, a questioning note in his voice.

Hal shook his head. 'We don't have the room,' he said. 'I'm afraid you'll have to either ride back or leave your horse here.'

'I'll ride back,' Gilan decided. 'I'll get going early in the morning. Can you put me up overnight or should I look for somewhere in the village?'

'You'll be fine with us,' Stig told him. 'We've got room for thirty people in the huts and there's just ten of us.'

'That's settled then,' Gilan said. 'Oh, by the way, William invited us all to dinner in the village.' He lowered his voice. 'That's another reason I don't want to discuss what we're up to. Too many people around to hear us up there. And if we don't know the details, we can't discuss them.'

Hal nodded. In the past, he had harboured some reservations about Araluen and its people — principally because none of the people from his mother's village had raised a hand to help her when she was captured on a slaving raid. But he was warming to the Ranger — just as he'd warmed to the villagers of Cresthaven. He wondered whether he had rushed to judgement. That had been known to happen before — on more than one occasion, he admitted ruefully.

For his part, the Ranger continued to observe the young Skandian wolfship skirl — although he looked like no Skandian Gilan had seen before. Whereas his crew were generally tall and heavily built, Hal was relatively slim — although Gilan could see there was plenty of hard muscle on him.

In addition, the skirl was remarkably young. Yet he had a definite air of authority about him. Gilan, who was a keen observer, like all Rangers, had noticed how Hal's crew deferred to him and moved promptly to carry out his orders as they folded and stowed sails and stored loose gear away for the night.

The more he looked, the more he realised how young all the crew members were. None of them would have been older than eighteen, he thought, if that. Then he corrected himself. The bearded, one-handed one called

Thorn was a good deal older and had the look of an experienced warrior about him. He'd be a good man in a fight, Gilan thought, one-handed or not. He noticed the older man's dexterity with the polished wood hook he wore on the end of his right arm. And he noticed how he too deferred to Hal.

For some moments, he had a sense of misgiving about the youth of the captain and crew. Then he shrugged them away. He was not yet thirty himself and people had often thought he was too young for the important duties he carried out. And his friends, Will and Horace, were even younger, yet they had proved that youth didn't imply any lack of ability. Their skill and courage and capability were widely known and admired throughout Araluen.

He sat on a low bollard, waiting for the crew to finish their work on board. He'd noted with surprise earlier that there was a girl member of the crew. Now, as she climbed up onto the rail, prior to stepping across to the jetty, he instinctively rose and offered a hand to help her.

She met his gaze, unsmiling, and ignored his hand, stepping lightly ashore.

He nodded to her. 'My name's Gilan.'

She regarded him for a moment, then replied, still with a lack of expression, 'Lydia.' She had a back quiver that was crammed with curious metre-long darts. A strangely shaped wooden handle hung from her belt and he recognised it as an atlatl, or throwing device. He realised she was staring pointedly at his longbow, which was slung over one shoulder. She nodded towards it.

'You any good with that?' she asked.

He paused thoughtfully before replying. 'I get by,'

he said. 'I'd be interested to see you using that atlatl,' he added.

She glanced down at the handle hanging from her belt. A look of cautious respect came over her face. Lydia, who had grown up as a loner, was uncomfortable around new acquaintances and could be a little prickly with them. But very few people had ever recognised her weapon for what it was, and she felt an instinctive kinship for another weapons expert.

'We should have a contest one day,' she said. 'My atlatl against your bow.'

The tall Ranger smiled at her. 'Good idea. Although I'm sure you'll win.'

I doubt it, Lydia thought. There was an air of confidence about the Ranger that belied his self-deprecating manner. In her experience, people who decried their own ability usually turned out to be very good indeed. And Thorn had told them that Rangers were all expert archers.

A huge boy was preparing to come ashore behind her. Gilan studied his massive shoulders and chest, and the heavily muscled legs. He was a giant, and he appeared to have a giant's strength. But he hesitated as he went to step across to the jetty and Lydia hurried to put out a hand to him.

'Here, Ingvar,' she said, catching hold of his sleeve and steadying him as he gained the firm ground of the jetty. He smiled his thanks.

'This is Ingvar,' Lydia told Gilan. He noticed how her tone had softened. 'Ingvar, meet Gilan.'

'Pleased to meet you. I'm kind of short-sighted,' the giant boy said, obviously to explain why he was leaning forward and peering closely at the Ranger. 'You're a little hard to see.'

'It's the cloak,' Gilan explained. 'It's designed to do that.'

'Well, it's working so far as I'm concerned.' Ingvar smiled. Gilan decided that he liked the huge boy. They shook hands and the Ranger paled at the crushing grip.

'Oh . . . sorry,' said Ingvar, releasing his hand. 'Sometimes I forget myself.'

The rest of the crew came ashore in ones and twos and introduced themselves to Gilan. He mentally filed their names away, matching each to its owner's face. It was a useful skill he had taught himself. If any of them presented himself to Gilan in the next few minutes, he would be able to call him by name.

The crew began to troop up the path to the two huts. Hal fell into step beside Gilan.

'We'll clean up, then go up to the village for dinner,' he said.

'I could use a bit of freshening up myself,' Gilan replied. 'I've been riding all day.'

'A foolish way to get about.' Hal smiled. 'If the gods had meant us to ride horses, they never would have given us ships.'

The dinner was more of a feast, with the central dish being a roast suckling pig, turned on a spit over a bed of glowing coals and basted with oil and juices until the skin was stretched tight and was shining brown.

The meat underneath was little short of heavenly and it was accompanied by potatoes roasted in covered iron pots hung over the glowing coals of the cook fire until their skins were golden and crisp and the interiors were soft and cooked through, soaking up the butter that was melted onto them in large amounts. There were other vegetables, smoked trout from the river, and ducks that were spit roasted after the pig was done and removed from the spit for carving.

William and his two councillors were present, along with their wives and half a dozen other villagers who had been wanting to meet the Skandian crew. It was a pleasant, friendly night, with none of the roisterous, bellowing noise of the farewell for *Wolfspear* and her crew. The Herons politely refused William's offer of ale or wine, but enthusiastically accepted Gilan's offer of coffee. Like all Rangers, he always travelled with a good supply of beans.

Long before midnight, they walked back to their quarters. The half moon was sinking over the hills behind the village, casting a few last moments of silver sheen over the waters of the bay. Within minutes, they were all rolled in their blankets and quiet settled over the two huts, broken only by the soft booming sound of Thorn's snoring. Gilan lay awake for some time, marvelling at the way it carried on the still night air. After all, Thorn was in the next cabin. Obviously, he thought, the Skandians were used to it by now and could sleep through it.

Finally, he dropped off.

Then, just before dawn, when the first birds were beginning to stir in the trees above the bay, there was a thunderous knocking at the door of the larger hut, and a voice shouting for them to rouse themselves.

CHAPTER TWENTY-ONE

Startled out of a deep sleep, Hal made his way to the door and drew the bolt, just as another bout of hammering began. He had his saxe in his right hand and he used his left to throw the door wide open, quickly stepping back out of reach of a possible blow from outside. Behind him, he heard the others stirring from their beds.

There was a lantern burning above the door, and by its dim light he could make out the tall shape of William. The headman was still dressed in his nightshirt, with a heavy cloak pulled over it. There was another man beside him. His face was unfamiliar and he was dressed in farm clothes — a linen smock belted over woollen breeches and heavy work boots.

'What's going on?' Hal demanded.

William, his fist poised to deliver another barrage of knocking at the door, lowered his hand.

'Apologies, Captain Hal. There's an emergency.' William's voice was rushed. He was breathing heavily.

Obviously, he and the other man had run down the steep track from the village. Hal sensed someone behind him and glanced quickly over his shoulder. Stig and Thorn were there, half dressed and both with weapons at the ready. Stig had his axe and Thorn, like Hal, was armed with a saxe knife. Hal gestured for them to lower their weapons and stepped aside, ushering William and the stranger into the cabin.

'Come in,' he said. 'Stig, organise some light, will you?'

The larger of the two buildings contained the main living quarters, with a kitchen and common room. There was a hallway to one side, with four bedrooms opening from it. Hal, Stig, Thorn and Lydia had taken the bedrooms — a matter of seniority for the first three and privacy for Lydia. The other cabin, set some five metres away, was arranged as a large open-plan dormitory, with a fireplace at one end and bunks lining the walls down either side. The rest of the crew were quartered there, along with the Ranger, Gilan. Hal could see lights moving in the windows there. Obviously, William's thunderous knocking had roused the others as well.

As Stig went to work with his flint and steel and lit several lanterns, Hal gestured for the others to sit at the long dining table.

'What's going on?' Lydia emerged from the hallway. She had taken time to dress, although her feet were bare. Like the others, she came armed, with her long dirk in her hand and the belt and scabbard for the weapon looped over her shoulder. Hal motioned for her to join them at the table.

'We're about to find out,' he told her. Then he turned to William, a questioning look on his face.

William gestured to the second man. 'Gough here is from Deaton's Mill,' he said. 'That's a village north of here. They've been raided.'

'Raided? Who raided you?' Hal addressed his question to the man named Gough.

'Slavers,' the man said bitterly. 'They landed in the next cove up from the village and came over the headland before we knew they were there. Hit us after dark and caught us totally by surprise. Killed three and took twelve prisoners. The rest of us ran.'

'How many of them were there?' Thorn asked.

Gough tried to gather his thoughts, but answered uncertainly. It had all happened very quickly and his recall of events was confused.

'A lot. Maybe twenty of them. Maybe more. They came at us from three sides and suddenly it seemed they were everywhere, killing and burning and capturing. Most of the villagers ran for their lives.'

His eyes dropped and Hal guessed that he had been one of those who had run.

William noticed the guilty movement as well and said in an explanatory tone, 'People there are millers and farmers. They're not warriors.'

The door opened abruptly and Gilan entered the cabin. 'What's all the noise about?'

Thorn glanced at him. 'Slavers,' he replied succinctly. 'Hit a village called . . .' He glanced at Gough for the name.

'Deaton's Mill,' the man mumbled.

'Deaton's Mill,' Thorn repeated. 'Three killed. Twelve taken prisoner. The rest of them were run off.'

Gilan uttered a soft curse. He hated slavers and since the Socorran slave market had opened several years previously, they had been preying on small isolated villages along Araluen's east coast.

Hal moved to the wall, where a large chart of the Araluan coastline and the Narrow Sea was displayed. He searched the map for Deaton's Mill, found it and measured the distance with his eye.

'How long ago?' he asked.

This time, Gough answered without hesitation. 'After dark, as I said. But then they didn't leave right away. Drove us off and sat around drinking and feasting on our food and ale — and burning down houses and barns. I managed to sneak back and get a horse. Then I rode here as fast as I could. Took me maybe three hours.'

'But they were still there when you left?' Hal said keenly.

'Aye. Don't know how much longer they stayed, but when I rode south, I saw their ship still at anchor in the cove.'

'What sort of ship was it?' Thorn asked.

Gough screwed up his face in thought. He wasn't terribly familiar with ships but he was pretty sure he knew what this one was — and he wasn't sure how his news would be received by the Skandian crew.

'She was one of yours,' he said. 'A big one, with a wolf-shead on the bow.'

Hal felt a sinking sensation in the pit of his stomach. Suddenly, he was sure he knew what ship it was. 'Could you see what colour she was?' he asked.

Gough pursed his lips uncertainly. 'It were night,'

he said. 'Moon wasn't up so it were hard to tell. But she was dark painted. Maybe black. I'm not sure.'

'Could it have been dark blue?' Lydia asked and Hal realised they were all thinking the same thing.

'Could have been. Wouldn't swear to it, mind. But it could have been blue, right enough. Or black, like I said,' he added.

Hal stood, went to the door and stepped outside, looking up into the treetops to gauge the wind direction. Then he returned to the table.

'Stig, rouse the crew — whoever isn't awake yet — and get them on board. We're going after her.'

Stig hurried to his room to collect the rest of his clothes and his weapons.

Thorn regarded Hal doubtfully. 'You think we can catch her?' he asked. 'They've probably got a couple of hours' head start.'

'Wind is from the west-north-west,' Hal told him. 'If they're going south, they'll be making a lot of leeway.'

'What does that mean?' the Ranger asked.

Hal turned to him. 'They're sailing south but the wind is blowing them to the east for every kilometre they travel. That's called leeway. We don't get blown so far off course, so we can head in a more direct line. That means we're travelling a shorter route, which might just bring us up with her in a few hours.'

Gilan nodded his understanding. It seemed that this young man knew what he was talking about.

'Sorry about the King,' Hal said. 'He'll have to wait.'

'This is more important,' Gilan told him. He decided that it might be worthwhile seeing this young crew in action. 'As a matter of fact, I'd like to tag along if you can fit me in.'

Thorn clapped him on the shoulder, remembering just in time to do it with his left hand, and not the wooden hook he had been strapping on as they spoke. Gilan lurched forward under the impact.

'Always happy to fit in a man with one of those nasty big longbows,' the ragged old warrior said.

Gilan glanced to Hal for confirmation and received a nod. He turned to Cresthaven's headman. 'William, get a messenger off to the King, would you? Let him know we've been delayed by some slavers and we plan to teach them some manners.'

William nodded. 'I'll send a message pigeon at first light,' he said. As the base for the duty ship, Cresthaven kept a flock of pigeons trained to fly home to Castle Araluen.

'Best fetch that bow and your fancy coloured cloak, Ranger,' Thorn told him. 'It's time we were shoving off.'

CHAPTER TWENTY-TWO

Dawn found them three kilometres off the coast, alternately swooping over successive waves, then sliding down into the troughs behind them. Gilan, at Hal's invitation, stood by the steering platform, enjoying the light feeling under his feet as the ship swooped over a crest, then the smooth, gradual deceleration as the prow and keel bit into the resistance of the water in the troughs. He kept his knees flexed to absorb the gradually increasing pressure. He'd been on ships before and he was impressed by the quiet efficiency of the crew as they drove their craft onwards.

The little ship herself was a revelation. She was light as a gull and, as the daylight gradually grew stronger, the sight of the white-flecked water racing past the bulwarks showed how quickly she was moving. The twins were bent to their task in the ship's waist, constantly looking up to check the set of the sail, and making small adjustments to wring the last metre of speed out of the ship.

From time to time, Gilan would glance astern at the white line of disturbed water they were leaving in their wake. It was straight as a sword blade and he nodded silently in appreciation. He knew that an undeviating wake was the sign of a skilful helmsman, and Hal was maintaining the line with minimal effort.

When the sun was a handspan above the eastern horizon, Hal called Stefan and pointed to the lookout position on the bowpost. Stefan swarmed up the foot pegs set either side of the bowpost until he was balanced at the top, his waist level with the heron's head that surmounted the bowpost. He scanned the entire horizon first of all. That was standard procedure. Even though they were looking for *Nightwolf*, it would be foolish to ignore the possibility that another ship – possibly an unfriendly one – might be somewhere in sight.

Satisfied that the rest of the horizon was clear, Stefan made a quick negative signal to Hal, then focused his attention on a thirty-degree quadrant off the port bow. That was where they expected to see Tursgud's ship, if they had made up the lead she had over them.

Stefan shaded his eyes against the glare of the sun as he swept his gaze back and forth across that segment of the horizon. Every eye on the ship was upon him, waiting expectantly for his report. Suddenly, he stiffened, standing a little more upright, his gaze focused on one particular point, although Gilan noted that it was astern of the section of horizon where they were expecting to see the slaver.

'Sail!' he called.

A ripple of excitement ran through the crew. Lydia moved to the port side, took hold of a mast stay, and hauled herself up to stand on the rail. She balanced there easily against the ship's motion, shading her eyes with one hand and maintaining a loose grip on the stay with the other.

'It's not her!' she said after a short pause. 'The hull is yellow.' A few seconds later, Stefan confirmed her judgement.

'Lydia's right. She's not *Nightwolf*. Looks like a trader,' he said. 'She's definitely not a wolfship.'

Obviously, Gilan thought, Lydia's eyesight was keener than Stefan's. He regarded her with some curiosity. He still wasn't sure where she fitted into the crew. She wasn't Skandian, that was clear. She had dark hair and olive skin, whereas the majority of Skandians were blond and blue-eyed. And her slim build indicated that she was from somewhere else.

The rest of the crew relaxed and Lydia stepped down from the rail. Gilan glanced at Hal to see how he was taking the news. The young skirl caught his eye and shrugged fatalistically.

'Didn't really think we'd have caught her this quickly,' he said. Then he grinned and added, 'But you can always hope.'

'I take it you know who this slaver is?' Gilan said.

A frown shadowed Hal's face. 'We're pretty sure it's a renegade named Tursgud,' Hal told him. 'We've had dealings with him before.' There was a grim tone in his voice that told Gilan the previous dealings had been anything but pleasant.

'And he's not your favourite person?' he asked.

Hal paused before he answered. 'Tursgud is a bully,

a liar and a cheat. During our brotherband competition, another ship was sinking, and he left its crew to drown so that he could win a race. Then, a while back, he insulted Lydia and Ingvar broke his nose for him.'

Gilan glanced down the length of the ship to where Ingvar was sharing a joke with Edvin and Stefan. 'Ingvar, the boy mountain?' he asked.

Hal grinned at the description. 'Exactly.'

'I imagine that was quite . . . painful for Tursgud?'

'Extremely, I'm pleased to say. We've always disliked each other but now he's turned renegade. On our passage across the Stormwhite we came across a Gallican ship he'd attacked and left to sink. I don't like him, and I don't like the way he's smearing the reputation of all Skandian sailors. And now, to cap it off, he's taking captives and selling them as slaves. I hate slavers.'

Gilan studied the skirl. Hal's hard expression was at odds with his normal cheerful disposition. 'I'm not fond of them myself,' he replied. Then, studying the empty sea stretching ahead of them, he asked, 'D'you think we've a chance of catching them?'

'Depends on how long they stayed after Gough got away. I'm assuming it was an hour, maybe two. If that's right, it should take us six hours to run them down — give or take half an hour. We might see them late in the afternoon.'

'And if they didn't wait around that long?'

Hal raised his eyebrows. So much of his plan depended on guesswork.

'Then we won't see them before nightfall. And that means we've lost them.'

The day wore on and the *Heron* continued to run south, with the wind over her starboard quarter. The waves rolled through in an endless pattern, rearing up ahead of the little ship, then sliding beneath her as she swooped up the face and slid into each successive trough.

Around midday, Thorn left the spot where he had been snoozing by the base of the mast and joined Hal at the steering platform. Hal had just taken over from Stig, who had been on the tiller for the past three hours.

Gilan, with no duties to attend to, watched the three senior crew members carefully. Now he discerned a change in Thorn's attitude. The older warrior seemed preoccupied, as if something was worrying him. The Ranger sensed that he was expecting something to happen — and his body language indicated that it wasn't going to be something good.

The one-armed warrior was pacing the deck — back and forth, a few metres at a time. His eyes went constantly to the large, curving sail, and the wind telltale — a long ribbon that streamed from the very tip of the yardarm, indicating the wind direction and strength.

Gilan was about to say something when Hal also noticed Thorn's obvious preoccupation.

'Something on your mind?' he asked, a trace of anxiety in his voice. Thorn had spent the greater part of his life at sea. Those years of experience meant that if he sensed trouble, he was probably right.

The bearded sea wolf shook his head doubtfully, as if

worried that voicing his concern might make it become fact.

'Don't like the way the wind feels,' he said finally. He looked up at the yardarm again and, as if on cue, the telltale faltered, a ripple running along its length.

At the same time, the sail flapped, slackening momentarily, then filling again with a loud clap of sound. Ulf and Wulf, caught by surprise after hours of unvarying pressure on the sail, reacted quickly, checking the sheets, hauling in a fraction.

Then the canvas bellied and shook again, with the same thump of noise. This time, everyone on board was craning their heads upwards.

The tension on the sheets eased and the tight, hard curve of the sail slackened again. The canvas shuddered in loose ripples.

'Hal!' one of the twins called in alarm.

Hal nodded grimly. 'I see it. Haul in!'

The twins hauled in on the sheets, hardening the sail as much as possible to the decreasing force of the wind. Hal heaved on the tiller, presenting a broader section of the sail to the breeze. But everyone on board could feel the speed of the ship dropping. The sail flapped again, in spite of the twins' best efforts at trimming.

'Orlog curse it,' Thorn muttered. 'We're losing the wind.'

The telltale began to droop now, as the wind decreased to a point where it wouldn't support the long streamer. The sail flapped and shuddered, and *Heron*'s swooping, soaring progress dropped away. Finally, she lost all way and lay dead in the water, wallowing awkwardly as the waves swept by her, a graceless thing robbed of energy and speed.

Hal cursed quietly. But he was determined to play this game out to the end.

'Down sail,' he ordered. 'Out oars.'

Stefan and Edvin brought the starboard sail down. Ulf and Wulf helped them bundle up the sail and stow it and the yardarm along the length of the deck.

Stig dropped down to his position on the first of the rowing benches. He unstowed the long white oak oar and raised it to the vertical. The other crew members quickly followed suit. Normally, *Heron* used only six oars, but today Edvin and Thorn, in spite of his one hand, were prepared to row.

'Down oars,' Stig ordered and the other seven rowers lowered their oar blades, setting them in the oarlocks until they were resting just above the water.

'Ready!' Stig ordered and they all pushed forward against their oars, cocking the blades.

'Give way! Stroke!' Stig called and the eight blades dipped as one, then heaved backwards against the water. *Heron* surged forward, water chuckling under her bow, and the tiller came alive in Hal's hands once more. Gilan and Lydia moved to stand near him. He looked at them, the bitterness of defeat in his eyes.

'Can we catch them like this?' Gilan asked.

Hal shook his head. 'Assuming they've lost the wind as well, they'll be pulling twenty oars to our eight,' he said. 'There's no way we can match their speed. If they haven't lost the wind, they'll be even faster.'

'Then why continue?'

Hal's eyes flashed in anger now. 'Because I'm not ready to give up just yet,' he snapped.

Gilan made a placating gesture with both hands. That was the problem sailors faced, he thought. If you were a sailor, you grew to depend on the wind, and just when you needed it most, it could desert you.

'I'll take an oar when anyone needs a spell,' he said.

Hal looked at him, sensing the peace offer behind the words.

'Thanks,' he said. 'They can carry on for a while yet.' Edvin could steer if necessary, he thought. Gilan could take over his oar and Hal himself could relieve Jesper. That way, every so often, he could rest two rowers and put in two replacements. Two fresh rowers from time to time could make a difference.

But not enough.

They dragged the *Heron* due south for the next hour, heaving on the oars in a constant rhythm, their minds numbed by the repetitive, mesmeric action of rowing. They were all fit and their muscles were hardened and they kept *Heron* moving through the water at a brisk speed. Even so, Hal knew that *Nightwolf*, with her superior number of oarsmen, would be moving faster than they could hope to.

After another hour, he and Gilan took their places at the oars and Edvin and Jesper rested. It wasn't until they stopped rowing that the two crew members realised how exhausted they were, and how much their muscles were aching. A third hour passed and Edvin and Jesper replaced the twins, with Ulf tending to the tiller. For once, his brother had no derogatory comment to make. All of them were intent on one purpose — to catch the renegade wolfship and recapture the villagers who had been taken prisoner.

And to teach Tursgud a lesson, once and for all.

None of them voiced the thought that their task was a futile one and that, no matter how hard they heaved on their oars, somewhere over the horizon, *Nightwolf* would be moving farther and farther away.

A fourth hour passed. Stefan and Stig were replaced by the twins, with Stig moving to the tiller. Ingvar was offered a rest but doggedly refused, heaving with all his massive strength on his oar.

'Don't break it, Ingvar,' Hal cautioned, grinning in spite of the situation. Ingvar didn't reply, continuing to row.

It was Kloof who sensed the change coming. She had been lying asleep in the bow when, suddenly, she sat up and let out a short, sharp bark, raising her muzzle to sniff the air.

Thorn turned on his rowing bench to look at her, then his eyes flew to the secondary telltale, fastened to the ship's sternpost. The long ribbon fluttered, faltered, then streamed out astern.

'The wind!' he shouted. 'It's veered!'

Even as he said the words, he maintained the steady rhythm of rowing. Hal looked up in his turn and saw the telltale standing parallel to the water's surface.

'It hasn't just veered, it's backed!' Hal shouted exult-antly. 'It's gone round almost one hundred and eighty degrees!'

The others all saw that he was right. The rapidly strengthening wind, which had earlier been blowing from north of north-west, was now coming from the south. A ragged cheer went up.

'In oars!' Hal called crisply, and the long-shafted oars rattled inboard and were hastily stowed. 'Make sail!' He glanced quickly at their heading, came to a decision. 'Up starboard sail!'

The ship was suddenly like a disturbed ants' nest as the crew rushed to their positions for making sail. Stefan and Jesper cast off the bindings on the starboard sail and began to haul on the halyard, sending the yard and sail soaring up the mast in a series of rapid jerks. Edvin and Ingvar joined them, and with the addition of Ingvar's massive strength, the sail positively flew up the mast. Ulf and Wulf were ready as the wind filled it, hauling in on the sheets so that the bow swung to starboard as the sail filled and hardened.

Hal had dashed to the tiller, stumbling in his haste and leaving Stig to stow the oar he had been pulling. *Heron* swung across the eye of the wind, faltered for a second, then surged forward on the port tack.

Gilan could see the exultation on the faces of the Herons. Somehow, this shift of wind had them all excited. The despair of the last four hours was dispelled like morning mist in a rising sun. He made an interrogative gesture to Thorn. The old sea wolf grinned fiercely at him.

'*Nightwolf* can't sail into the wind the way we can,' Thorn explained. 'They'll have to keep rowing, while we can sail. We'll go in a series of zigzags but we'll be moving much faster than they can manage. And we can sustain our speed. Whereas the longer they row, the more exhausted they'll become and the more their speed will drop.'

Gilan felt the blustering south wind on his face, flattening his clothes against his body. The crew's previously forlorn hope was replaced by a firm certainty. The advantage had swung back in their favour — even stronger than it had been before.

They were hot on *Nightwolf*'s trail once more.

CHAPTER TWENTY-THREE

'There she is!'
It was Stefan who called, perched on the lookout
post in the bows. Lydia, who was standing close by, leapt
nimbly onto the starboard bulwark, steadying herself with
one hand on a forestay, and shading her eyes with the
other as she peered south.

'It's *Nightwolf* all right!' The excitement was obvious
in her voice. 'I can see the blue hull and she's rowing for
all she's worth.'

'What's their course and position?' Hal shouted. He
felt a solid thrill of satisfaction. After all the setbacks of
the day, they had finally caught up with their quarry.

'She's off our port bow . . .' Stefan called. Then he
hesitated, as if he was confused.

'What's her course?' Hal asked again. He assumed
she'd be heading due south. Any other course would allow
Heron to catch her all the sooner.

'She's . . . she's going . . . west?' Stefan replied. The

uncertainty was obvious in his voice. It made no sense for the wolfship to be heading west. That way lay the coast of Araluen. Socorro and the open sea lay to the south.

'West?' Hal muttered. He gestured to Edvin to take the tiller, then climbed onto the starboard rail. Leaning out to peer ahead and past the swelling sail, he could make out the dark shape in the distance, rapidly growing in size as they ran down on her. 'What is he doing, going west?' A thought struck him and he called to Stefan. 'Maybe they haven't seen us?'

Stefan turned back to face him, shaking his head to dispel that theory. 'They've seen us. You can see the spray they're kicking up with their oars. They're rowing as hard as they can!'

'He's right!' Lydia called. 'They're really churning up the water.'

Hal could see the other ship, and he could see the rhythmic movement of the oars. But he couldn't make out the spray they were throwing up as they beat at the water. It was too far for him to make out that kind of detail, but he had no doubt that Stefan and Lydia were right. The two of them had eyes like hawks.

Nightwolf, which had initially been off their port bow, was moving slowly across them, crossing their path so that now she was on their starboard bow, moving further and further to their right. Hal had an unobscured view of her now, without the need to crane and peer around the sail. He glanced to the west, where the dark bulk of the Araluan coastline reared up out of the sea.

He stepped down from the rail and took the tiller from Edvin, frowning as he considered the situation. There was nothing for Tursgud to gain by going west as he was. If he had continued to head south, he would have prolonged the chase, and maybe managed to escape them when night fell.

At that thought, Hal glanced quickly to the west again, where the sun was a giant ball of orange, balanced above the rim of the world. They had perhaps an hour of daylight left. He checked the angle between the two ships, measuring with an expert eye. They were currently on the starboard tack. He would hold this direction for another ten minutes, swooping out to the left of their quarry. Then he'd be placed to go about onto the port tack and speed down to intercept her.

Thorn joined him at the steering platform, Gilan a few paces behind him. Even a landsman like Gilan could see the flaw in Tursgud's tactics.

'Maybe he's planning to beach her and escape over-land?' Thorn said.

Hal pursed his lips and considered that alternative. Then he shook his head.

'He won't make it. We're overhauling him too fast. He'll be nowhere near the beach when we come up to him.'

'Tursgud was never a good judge of speed and distance,' Thorn said disparagingly.

Still Hal demurred. 'He isn't that bad,' he said. He called in a louder voice. 'We'll go about in ten minutes.'

Gilan coughed politely. He knew that the crew, and Hal in particular, were busy concentrating on keeping the ship in the best possible position to intercept the slaver. But there was a question he had to ask.

'Have you considered what we should do when we catch up with her?' he asked quietly. 'After all, they out-number us by about three to one.'

Thorn snorted explosively. 'Numbers aren't every-thing,' he said. He had strapped on his club-hand and he swished it experimentally in the air. Gilan just managed not to rear back as the massive, metal-studded club whizzed by, only centimetres from his face. 'We'll soon bring them down to an even fight.'

But Hal realised Gilan was right. It was time to prepare their most important weapon.

'Stig! Ingvar!' he called. They were well forward and they turned to look back at him. He gestured to the Mangler, shrouded in its canvas cover. 'Get the Mangler ready!'

They began unlacing the covers, folding the canvas and laying it aside to reveal the massive crossbow crouched menacingly on its carriage in the bows.

Gilan let out a low whistle of surprise. 'What is that thing?'

Hal grinned at him. 'It's just our little way of equalis-ing the odds.'

Ingvar had opened the locker where the bolts were stowed and he selected one of the massive, metre-long shafts now, laying it ready in the slot along the top of the crossbow. He hadn't cocked the mighty weapon yet. There would be time enough to do that later, and the longer the crossbow was under the enormous tension of the cocked arms, the more chance there was that some-thing might give way. Gilan took in the size of the bolt, and the iron strips that reinforced its point.

'Remind me never to go up against you people in a fight,' he said.

Thorn nodded towards the longbow slung over the Ranger's shoulder.

'Maybe you should string up that peashooter of yours,' he said. 'We might leave something for you to shoot at.'

'Five minutes, Hal,' Edvin said quietly. When Hal had announced his intention to tack, Edvin had turned one of the sandglasses by the steering platform. Now he crouched beside it, peering intently at it and estimating the amount of sand that had trickled through from top to bottom. It was part of his job on board to keep Hal informed of such matters. Hal nodded his thanks, then cupped his hands and called forward, to where Lydia was still perched on the port bulwark.

'Lydia! We'll be tacking soon. Climb down and come aft!'

She waved her understanding. When the ship tacked, she would be in the way of the port sail as it came in. Stefan, perched high up on the bowpost, would be well clear of the lines and canvas as one sail came down and the other went up.

She ran lightly aft and dropped down into her berth, emerging with the quiver of atlatl darts slung over her shoulder. The atlatl itself hung from the heavy leather belt around her waist. She made her way to the small group beside the steering platform and cast a disparaging glance at Gilan's longbow.

'We'll soon see if you can hit anything with that,' she said.

Gilan smiled. He had no wish, or need, to engage in a slanging match with her. He knew how good he was with the bow. She obviously didn't.

Hal frowned at Lydia. Such behaviour was frivolous, he thought. He beckoned Gilan closer.

'You've seen this sort of thing before. Where will they have the prisoners?'

Gilan paused, then answered. 'Usually, they'll build a cage of some sort in the middle of the deck — just behind the mast.'

Hal relayed that information to Stefan, who peered more closely at the fleeing wolfship.

'There's some kind of structure there,' he said. 'I'd say that's what it is.'

'All right,' Hal said to himself, coming to a decision. 'Stig! We'll go about and I'll bring you in astern of her, on her starboard side, at an angle. Place your shot along the line of rowers. But avoid the structure they've built aft of the mast. That's where the prisoners are kept.'

Stig held up a hand to show he understood. A bolt that raked the line of rowing benches, killing or disabling two or three rowers, would throw the other ship into total confusion.

'You'll get time for two shots,' Hal continued. 'Then I'll bear away to the left and we'll turn back in and hit the port side rowers. All right, positions, everyone! We're coming about . . . now!'

Hal swung the bow to the right. *Heron* crossed directly into the wind, faltered slightly, then her momentum kept her turning and she was past the eye of the wind and swinging with increasing speed to the right. The newly raised sail filled with another of those deep *whoomphs*.

'She's turning!' Stefan shouted.

All eyes flew to *Nightwolf*. She had swung ninety degrees to head due south, as if she had been waiting for them to tack before making her move. Hal looked quickly to the west. The Araluan coast was much closer now. He could see breakers smashing white against the cliffs and headlands.

'Realised his mistake,' Thorn said. Then he smiled in fierce satisfaction. 'But it's too late. We've got him. He can't slip away now.'

Hal shook his head, puzzled at the other ship's sudden change in tactics. Nothing that Tursgud had done in the past hour had made any sense — and he knew that the other skirl, while he might be arrogant, cruel and a braggart, was not stupid. So why had he —

'Rocks! Dead ahead! Rocks!'

Stefan's voice rose into a panicked scream as he pointed straight ahead of the ship. Hal cursed and shoved desperately on the tiller. Thorn leapt to his side and pushed as well, adding his strength and weight to Hal's. The bow began to swing to port — slowly, then with increasing speed.

'Let go the sheets!' Hal shouted in the same instant. The twins reacted without hesitation, showing the value of the training for emergencies that the crew carried out over and over again. The sail bellied out instantly as they cast loose the sheets and all the harnessed power that it contained was released. The ship, which had been heeled over under the pressure of the wind in the sails, suddenly came upright, rolled a little the other way, then rolled back, finally losing way and lying rocking in the swell.

Stig had leapt from his seat behind the Mangler and joined Stefan in the bows. He pointed left, then right.

'Rocks! All round us! We're in a shoal! There's another!'

Realisation dawned on Hal and he stared furiously at the dark blue wolfship, barely three hundred metres away.

'Down sail!' he called, and Jesper and the twins lowered the yardarm and gathered in the flapping, thrashing sail. He looked at *Nightwolf* again and saw she was turning once more, swinging to the west as she threaded her way through the rocks and reefs and shallow water.

'He must know a channel through these shoals,' he said bitterly.

'Can't we follow him?' Lydia asked.

He shook his head in exasperation. 'We're too far away to see the exact path he's taking. And it's a pretty tricky path. Look, he's turning again.'

Nightwolf had turned further west, then turned south again. Obviously, somebody on board knew this patch of reefs and shoals intimately.

'But how can he know where to go?' Edvin asked, frowning in puzzlement. 'He's never sailed here before.'

Hal rounded on him, venting his pent-up frustration on the unfortunate youth.

'I don't know how he knows!' he shouted. 'But obviously, he *does*! Maybe he bought a chart from someone. Or maybe one of his crew has been here before. Does it really matter how he knows? He knows!'

'All right,' said the chastened Edvin, backing away a pace. 'He knows.'

Hal took a deep breath and calmed down a little. 'Sorry,' he muttered to Edvin, who shrugged and said nothing. He could understand his skirl's frustration.

'So what do we do now?' Thorn asked.

Hal chewed his lip for a second or two before coming to a decision.

'We row,' he said. 'Two oars only and we'll try to pick our way through. Stig and Stefan, guide us through. Yell out when you see rocks ahead. Ulf and Wulf, you take the oars.'

The twins scrambled into their rowing benches and ran out their oars. They began to row and, slowly, *Heron* began to thread her way through the maze of rocks and shoals that surrounded them.

Stig and Stefan continually called for course corrections. Once, they scraped agonisingly along the jagged edge of a rock, which scored a deep scar in the ship's planks. In this way, they plodded on, several times having to back water and reverse completely as they went up blind alleys in the reefs.

The lookouts were hoarse from their frantic cries warning of rocks up ahead. And all the while, *Nightwolf* was continuing to thread her confident way through the reefs, growing smaller by the minute.

Hal glanced at the western horizon. Night would soon be on them and they couldn't continue like this once it was dark. Already, Stig and Stefan were having trouble making out the runnels of white water and disturbances and whorls on the surface that indicated a rock just below.

They couldn't follow *Nightwolf* any further. And they couldn't pick their way out to open water without risking tearing the bottom out of the ship.

Reluctantly, he faced the inevitable.

'We're going to have to anchor for the night,' he said bitterly. 'Stop rowing, boys.'

Ulf and Wulf shipped their oars. After a quick look at Hal, Jesper and Edvin moved to the bow and heaved the huge stone anchor over the side with a splash. The cable ran out, then came taut as the anchor held, checking them against the tide and current.

They had one last glimpse of *Nightwolf* moving south, mocking them, as the sun sank in a last flare of light, and darkness spread over the water.

CHAPTER TWENTY-FOUR

They spent an anxious night anchored among the rocks and reefs. As the tide turned, *Heron* swung with it, moving in a giant arc. Once, they heard a nerve-rattling grating sound as she brushed against the very top of a rock, and felt a slight jarring sensation in the souls of their feet.

'Haul her in!' Hal ordered, and willing hands sprang to the anchor cable, hauling it in shorter, and moving the ship away from the danger below.

Anxiously, Hal leaned over the side, tying to assess the damage. Edvin leaned with him, holding a blazing torch, and Hal could just make out a deep gouge in the planks by the waterline. He organised a lookout roster in the stern — which was the part that was swinging, as the ship was anchored by the bow. He had the lookouts equipped with shielded torches so that the shields masked the glare from the eyes of the watchers, throwing more light outward.

'Look out for rocks, eddies in the water — anything that might indicate a rock. Yell if you see one and we'll haul in further on the cable.'

He relieved the lookouts every hour. On three occasions, as the tide fell, they had to haul the ship to a new location as it swung close to rocks. Around ten in the evening, Edvin broke out supplies from his limited stocks and they made a frugal meal of bread, cheese and water. He had four apples in his larder as well and they cut them up and shared them around, enjoying the tart bite of the juice and the crunch of the crisp flesh.

Dawn found the crew sleeping fitfully — all except the lookouts and Hal. He was leaning on the bulwark, stony-faced, staring to the south with red-rimmed, sleepless eyes. He'd been in that position hours earlier, when Lydia had left him to turn in for the night. She doubted that he'd moved in the intervening time.

The crew, as they woke, watched him warily, for the most part giving him a wide berth. But Edvin approached him, yawning and knuckling his eyes.

'Sea's calmed down,' he said. 'I could light a fire now and make coffee.'

Hal looked around, as if noticing for the first time that the short, steep waves that had sprung up around midnight, setting *Heron* plunging and rearing at her anchor cable, had died away. She rode the water calmly and evenly.

'Good idea,' he told Edvin. Then he turned away and continued his vigil to the south, as if hoping for some sight of *Nightwolf*.

The heady smell of coffee soon permeated the air and

the crew's spirits rose a little. Thorn took his mug of the hot, sweet beverage, and settled back against the mast, a piece of flat bread balanced on his holding hook. He sipped the coffee and smacked his lips. Then he sighed appreciatively.

'Aaah! That's excellent!' he said. He took a bite of bread, then wiped his mouth with the back of his hand. 'Well,' he said, after a pause of a few seconds, 'I suppose you can't win 'em all.'

He showered those close to him with breadcrumbs and fragments as he spoke. Thorn had never learned the finer points of eating politely — such as keeping one's mouth shut while doing so.

There were a few grunts of agreement from the crew, in spite of the fact that all of them were smarting from having let Tursgud escape in the night. But, as they reasoned, there was nothing that could be done about it. Much as they disliked it, they were prepared to accept the inevitable.

Except for Hal.

He was leaning back against the bulwark, a few metres away from the others, nursing a cup of coffee. Edvin had offered him a piece of bread, but he had waved the food away.

'Who says we've lost?' he asked.

Silence fell at his words. He looked around the surprised faces of his crew members. They had all assumed that Tursgud had given them the slip.

'Who says it's over?' he asked again, challenging them.

Stig made an uncertain gesture and rubbed his chin awkwardly.

'Well, you know, Hal . . . he's gone, hasn't he?' he said finally. A few of the others nodded, although they were loath to meet Hal's gaze. Looking at them, Hal saw that only two people seemed to agree that it wasn't all over: the Ranger, and Lydia.

'And we know where he's gone, don't we?' Hal went on. 'He's given us the slip for the moment, but we know where we can find him again. Am I right?'

Again, Stig hesitated.

'Well, yes. But . . . you know . . .' He stopped again, not sure what it was that Hal should know. He looked at his friend and saw the stubborn set of his mouth and the determination in his eyes.

Thorn intervened. 'Hal, we all understand. You're angry because it was Tursgud who got the better of you. But it might be time to let that go. Don't let the personal side of things cloud your judgement.'

Hal switched his gaze to the older man — his close friend for so many years.

'Yes, I'm angry because it was Tursgud. That goes without saying. But I'm even angrier that I didn't see through his scheme. I put you all in danger by charging in after him. I should have thought, when I saw he was heading west, that he was up to something. But instead of stopping to think about it, I let my personal dislike for Tursgud take over and nearly piled us up on the rocks.'

He looked round at the others, who were standing in a semi-circle, facing him, shifting awkwardly from one foot to another.

'You all heard me!' he said. 'I was so busy telling Stig exactly where I wanted him to shoot, so darn sure I could put him in just the right position, that I nearly sank us.' He nodded his gratitude to Stefan. 'If it hadn't been for Stefan, we'd all be washing ashore, face down, on the next tide.' He looked again at Thorn. 'That's why I'm angry, Thorn. Because my ego and my personal feelings got in the way of my good judgement, and I nearly killed all of us. *That* makes me angry. But with myself, not Tursgud.'

He paused to let that message sink in. He saw that some of the crew were accepting it reluctantly. They were accustomed to looking up to Hal, to trusting his judgement and uncanny instincts as a navigator and helmsman. And it was that trust that made it all the more difficult to bear the fact that he had nearly let them down.

'But let's look at the facts. Tursgud has turned rogue. He nearly killed the crew of the *Hirondelle*, he's taken twelve innocent villagers prisoner and he plans to sell them in the slave market. And we know he's going there. So we know where to find him. If we let this opportunity slip through our fingers, we'll never know where he's got to — until we hear of another village where young men and women have been abducted. Or we find another ship sinking, with its crew left to drown. And by then it might be too late to help them. I say we go after him now. It's the last thing he'll expect us to do.'

For a moment, nobody said anything. They thought about what he said and saw the sense of it. Slowly heads began to nod. It was the Ranger Gilan who broke the silence.

'I think you're right,' he said. 'You know where he's going. He doesn't know that you know. As far as he's concerned, you may well have ended up on the rocks last night. As I see it, you won't get a better chance to go after him. You could wait months before someone gave you a tipoff and told you where he was. But now you know. I say we should go after him.'

The last few words took Hal by surprise. 'We?'

Gilan nodded. 'Of course. He's broken Araluan law. He's taken Araluan citizens prisoner. I've taken an oath to uphold the laws and protect the citizens of my country. Naturally I'm coming with you.'

'But what about the King?' Hal asked.

'He'll just have to wait his turn,' Gilan said. Then he added hastily, 'But don't tell him I put it quite that way, all right?'

'Thorn, what do you think?' Hal asked.

The burly sea wolf shrugged his muscular shoulders and grinned disarmingly.

'When did I ever think about anything?' he asked. 'And if I did, when did people ever take any notice of me? You do the thinking and planning, Hal. That's what you're good at. Just get me close enough to Tursgud so I can part his hair with an axe, or knock his block off with my club-hand. That's what I'm good at.'

'Anyone else got anything to say?' Hal asked. He expected silence and was a little taken aback when Edvin spoke up.

'This Socorro place, how far away is it?'

Hal glanced at the Ranger and raised an eyebrow in a question. Gilan considered for a second.

'Maybe four days' sailing,' he said. 'If the wind holds steady.'

Thorn sniffed the air. 'Let's hope it does. We deserve a little luck.'

Hal moved to the locker in the stern where he kept his charts and sailing notes. He rummaged around and found a chart of the Narrow Sea and the entrance to the Constant Sea. He spread the chart out on top of the locker and traced his finger down the coastline of Arrida, past the opening to the Constant Sea and on south to the Endless Ocean, following the coastline until he came to a large town marked there.

'Here,' he said. He frowned thoughtfully as he estimated the distance from the point where they were now. 'Yes. A good four days. A little more if we have this headwind all the way.' He glanced at Edvin again. 'Why do you ask?' He sensed there was something more than curiosity behind Edvin's question. Edvin was the practical member of the crew.

Edvin twisted his lips together as he thought, then answered. 'I don't have provisions for eight days — four there and four back,' he said. 'I assume you plan on coming back?'

Hal smiled. 'That was my intention.'

'Well, when we left Cresthaven, I only grabbed a few necessities. I'll need to put in to buy supplies if we're going haring off on this trip of yours.'

Hal raised his eyebrows in stunned surprise. 'Haring off?' he said, then repeated, 'Haring off? Is that how you describe it?'

Edvin nodded immediately. 'Yes,' he said simply.

Hal couldn't help grinning at his serious manner. He checked the chart quickly. 'All right, Edvin. We'll put into this little port here — Polperran. The notes say there's a market so you should be able to get everything you want there.'

'That'll do just fine,' Edvin told him.

'Then let's get under way. Ulf and Wulf, on the oars, please. Ingvar and Stig, let's get that anchor up.'

Hal took the tiller and waited until Ingvar and Stig began hauling in the massive stone. Water from the soaked cable puddled on the deck as they brought it in, with Stefan busy coiling the thick jute rope as they recovered it.

Once he felt the anchor break free of the rocky bottom, Stig called, 'Anchor's clear!'

Hal ordered Stefan into the bows again. When he was settled in position, Hal ordered the twins to begin rowing. Slowly, *Heron* crept forward.

'Go left!' Stefan called, pointing with one arm out to port. When the ship was on the right track, he held his other hand up, arm bent at the elbow, and Hal centred the tiller, creeping forward at a snail's pace, waiting tensed for the next helm order.

And so, slowly, painstakingly, they crept out of the shoals until they were in clear water. Then, with a sigh of relief, Hal had the twins ship their oars and hoist the starboard sail.

Eagerly, as if she were glad to be back in her natural element, *Heron* began to slide smoothly through the waters, heading south for Socorro.

CHAPTER TWENTY-FIVE

They sailed south on a series of long, smooth tacks, zigzagging across the south wind and rolling the kilometres under their keel.

On the third day, Hal passed the tiller to Stig and was consulting his chart of Arrida's western coastline, facing the widths of the Endless Ocean, when Gilan stepped close to the chart table — which was actually the lid of the locker where Hal kept his charts and navigation notes.

'Are you free to talk?' Gilan asked. He knew Hal was still thinking about what they would do when they reached Socorro and wanted to see if he could help plan their next move. Hal looked up, smiled and gestured for the Ranger to join him.

Thorn watched from his favoured spot by the mast. He nodded to himself, satisfied with the sight of Hal and Gilan co-operating. Two good minds at work there, he thought.

'What do you have in mind?' Gilan asked. 'We should reach Socorro the day after tomorrow.'

Hal stabbed his finger at the chart. There was a narrow bay approximately five kilometres north of Socorro. The chart showed no sign of any settlement or village there.

'I plan to put in here, make camp, then go overland and reconnoitre,' he said. 'I want to make sure Tursgud is there, and see where *Nightwolf* is moored. Plus I want to check out the layout of Socorro for myself— where the slave markets are, where the slaves are held, what sort of garrison they have there and so on. There's no point in barging in blind and hoping for the best.'

Gilan nodded. 'Socorro is a cosmopolitan city,' he said. 'It's a hodge-podge of different races from around the Constant Sea and the coast of the Endless Ocean. They're all drawn by the slave markets, of course. But even so, your Skandians, with their fair complexions, northern clothing and heavy builds, will stand out in the crowd. Might be best if someone went in ahead of the rest of you and bought local clothing. The Socorrans wear long flowing robes and headdresses that should conceal your men pretty well. Except Ingvar,' he added. 'It'll be pretty hard to conceal him.'

Hal grinned. Ingvar did tend to stand out in a crowd. 'Are you volunteering?'

'I thought maybe Lydia and I could go in and pick up the disguises we'll need. She's olive skinned. She'll pass for a local pretty easily. Plus I imagine she's good in a fight, if that's what it comes to.'

'She's better than good,' Hal told him. 'I'd have her guarding my back any day.'

'That's good enough for me,' Gilan said. Neither of them questioned whether Lydia would be willing to join Gilan on the expedition he was planning. They knew that she would go without hesitation.

'Then,' he continued, 'once you've got some local clothes, you can go into the city yourself and look around. Or, if you like, I could scout the place for you?' He made the offer, but he knew what Hal's reply would be. The young skirl was shaking his head before Gilan finished the sentence.

'No. I said I want to see it for myself,' he said, his eyes riveted on the chart before him. 'If you go on someone else's information, there's always something left out. No offence,' he concluded, looking up to see if Gilan was offended.

The tall Ranger smiled his understanding. 'None taken. I'd feel the same way.'

There were a few seconds' silence before Gilan raised another point that had been on his mind.

'You Skandians, you recognise a ship if you've seen it before, don't you?'

Hal nodded. 'We've been around ships all our lives. It's no special skill. We get to recognise features of a ship the way you recognise a face if you've seen it before – or a person's way of moving and holding himself. Why do you ask?'

'Well, I assume this Tursgud is the same. So what's to stop him recognising this ship when you sail into Socorro harbour? I'm guessing that's what you plan to do?'

'Yes. I don't plan on making my way back to this bay overland,' Hal said, pointing to the inlet they had discussed earlier. 'Once we've got the prisoners free, we want to get away as fast as possible.'

'So my point stands. Won't Tursgud recognise your ship? After all, it's a pretty distinctive sail plan, isn't it?'

'I see what you mean. But I plan to disguise the *Heron*,' Hal replied. Gilan cocked his head to one side in an unspoken question, and Hal pointed to the smooth, swelling shape of the triangular sail. 'We'll take down those yardarms and sails and I'll rig a new extension to make the mast taller, and shape a new yardarm to take a square sail — I can cut that from our canvas weather shelter. Then I'll take down the heron figurehead on the bowpost and replace it with something different.

'If Tursgud is looking for us — and he probably won't be — he'll be looking for that triangular sail. He won't look twice at a small square-rigger. We might even scuff up the paint on the hull a little,' he added thoughtfully.

Gilan pursed his lips, looking up at the graceful, wing-like sail, visualising a clumsy square sail in its place. Hal would be changing the ship's most distinctive feature, he thought. That should throw Tursgud off the scent.

'Will she still handle well with a square sail?'

Hal snorted in sardonic amusement. 'She'll handle, but not well. She'll be clumsy and she won't beat into the wind the way she's doing now. But the important thing is, she'll *look* completely different. Tursgud won't recognise us — particularly if the crew are all in Socorran clothing. We'll look like a small local coaster. On top of that, once I've seen where *Nightwolf* is moored, I'll give her a wide berth. Odds are they won't see us until we've got the prisoners on board and we're heading out to sea. And by then I'll have our normal rig back up again.'

'They'll come after you, of course,' Gilan said.

Hal shrugged. 'I'll face that problem when we get to it. With any luck, the wind will favour us. Otherwise, we'll have to make sure we get a head start on them, so we're out to sea before they have a chance to catch up.'

'Looks like you've thought of everything,' Gilan said.

'No. I know I haven't. There's always something you haven't thought of. But over the next few days, I'll try to fill in as many gaps as I can.'

Gilan clapped him on the shoulder. 'I like the way you think,' he said quietly. 'It never pays to be overconfident and it's always a good idea to assume that something will go wrong.'

There was nothing patronising about his attitude and Hal found himself feeling secretly pleased at the Ranger's words. His self-confidence had taken a beating after his mistake in pursuing Tursgud into the shoal waters several days before. He had spent the previous day thinking over the plan he was formulating, trying to see where he had missed an important point. That was why he had been glad to share his thinking with the Ranger. He had wanted an unbiased opinion and he'd sensed that he would get one from the tall Araluan. His own crew tended to believe that he could do no wrong. It was flattering but, in a situation like this, unhelpful.

'We'll see how things develop,' he said, folding the map and putting it back in the chart locker they had been using as a table.

'Land! Land to the east!' It was Jesper, taking a turn on the lookout position. He was pointing to their left and instinctively the other crew members moved to that side of the ship. On the horizon was a grey, indistinct humped shape rising from the sea. A few seconds later, Jesper called again, pointing to another land mass, south of the first.

'Land! Another cape! South-east of us!'

Hal shaded his eyes, looking at the two masses of solid land, with a gap of some thirty kilometres between them.

'It's the two headlands of the Narrows of Ikbar,' he said. 'That's the entrance to the Constant Sea.' The southern point of Iberion and the northernmost point of the Arridan coast formed the headlands that marked the narrow strait leading into the Constant Sea.

Ulf and Wulf had turned on their benches and were peering, like the others, at the strait. Hal saw a quick look pass between the two of them and made a mental note not to reply to anything they said.

'Who's Ikbar?' Ulf said. His brother turned away to hide a smirk.

Gilan glanced at Hal curiously, saw he wasn't planning to answer, so spoke in his place. 'He was an Arridan demigod, I believe.'

'Oh, don't,' Hal said quietly. But it was too late.

'And what did he do?'

'Well, Ulf, I'm not sure that he did too much of anything,' Gilan said. 'Just paraded round being a demigod.'

'Just a moment,' Hal said, taken aback. 'How did you know that was Ulf?'

It was Gilan's turn to be surprised. He tapped his right forearm. 'He's got a scar, right here,' he said. 'See?'

'You mean like this?' the other twin said, grinning widely and baring his forearm to show an identical scar. Gilan looked from one to the other, not sure what to say.

In the *Heron*'s final duel with the pirate ship *Raven*, Ulf had been wounded on the forearm by one of the pirates when he was boarding. As he fell back, his brother surged forward to avenge him — and received exactly the same injury. It was obviously a favourite tactic of the enemy swordsman to strike at his opponent's forearm — although Hal and Stig sometimes thought Wulf took the wound on purpose so that people couldn't distinguish between them.

'Oh . . .' Gilan said. 'I'm sorry, Wulf. Or is it Ulf?'

'Yes,' they both replied, delighted to have a new victim.

Gilan looked to Hal for assistance.

The skirl shrugged. 'Don't ask me. You brought this on yourself.'

Then Ulf, or possibly Wulf, went back on the offensive. 'So this Ikbar was a demigod. What does a demigod *do* exactly?'

'Not a lot,' Gilan said. 'That's probably why he was only a *demi*god.'

'Yes,' said Ulf/Wulf. 'If he actually did stuff, they'd make him a full-time god, not a semi-demi-deity.'

Gilan's eyes darted from one to the other. Yet in spite of the Ranger Corps' reputation for keen-eyed observation, he couldn't tell the identity of the one who was talking. And he had a suspicion that they'd shifted seats when he'd glanced away for a second. He realised that the rest of the crew were watching with expressions of tolerant sympathy on their faces.

Before he could say anything, one of the twins — and by now he had no idea which one it was — asked a further question.

'Maybe he was thin. Was he thin?' He directed the query to Gilan, who shrugged.

'I'm not sure. Why do you ask?'

'Because it's called the Narrows of Ikbar. Maybe if he was thin, that's why they called it that. Because he was narrow as well.'

'Aaaahm . . .' Gilan began, then stopped. He looked at Hal, who was just too slow wiping the amused look from his face.

Gilan raised an eyebrow. 'Do you put up with this all the time?'

Hal pursed his lips, pretended to consider the question, then shook his head. 'No. I have a foolproof way of dealing with them,' he said.

'And that is?'

'I have Ingvar throw one of them overboard,' Hal said, smiling sweetly.

Gilan looked from one to the other. 'Which one?'

Hal shrugged. 'Doesn't really matter. It usually shuts them both up. You might like to try it. Or, for a change, you could throw them both over the side.'

Gilan shook his head wearily. 'What a truly excellent idea.'

PART THREE

SOCORRO

CHAPTER TWENTY-SIX

It was midafternoon when *Heron* ghosted into the little cove that Hal had selected two days earlier. As they came under the lee of the high cliffs on either side of the bay, the breeze was masked and the sail shivered and flapped loosely.

'Down sail,' Hal ordered. 'Out oars.'

Stig, Ingvar, Thorn and Stefan had their oars ready in the oarlocks, and as Jesper and the twins brought the sail down and stowed it, they began to pull on the oars in a steady rhythm, sending the ship sliding into the cove, creating a perfect V at her bow in the sheltered water. The bow wave spread slowly across the inlet and rippled gently against the rocks at the base of the cliffs.

'Jesper,' Hal said, pointing to the bow. Jesper nodded and moved swiftly forward to take up a position as lookout.

'All clear,' he called, his voice echoing in the confines of the narrow bay.

Hal turned to Gilan and Lydia, who were standing at his side, watching events.

'No rocks or reefs marked on the charts,' he said. 'But it never hurts to make sure.'

The bay was some two hundred metres long, and ended in a narrow, sandy beach. As Jesper called his reports from the bow, it became evident that the sand continued out into the bay, forming a clear bottom. Beyond the beach was a sparsely wooded patch of level ground, which quickly gave way to steep, rocky slopes leading up to the U-shaped ridge that surrounded the bay on three sides. Hal eyed the trees and nodded in satisfaction. There weren't many of them, but there would be enough to provide him with the two new spars he'd need to re-rig *Heron*. And the widely dispersed trees had an advantage. If there were enemies in the immediate neighbourhood, there would be no thick cover to conceal them in the event of a surprise attack. He scanned the hills surrounding the bay and saw no sign of movement or danger.

'We'll beach her,' he said quietly, and the rowers on the benches nodded. If there had been any sign of danger, they would have anchored well out in the bay. But a shore camp would allow them to have a proper cooking fire and camp site. They'd eat and rest well this coming night.

Sitting atop her inverted image, *Heron* slipped quietly down the bay. When they were twenty metres from the shore, Hal called to them to cease rowing and the ship slid smoothly onto the beach, her bow grating in the coarse sand. As she came to a halt, her bow fixed in the sand, her stern swung slowly to the right. Then the keel grated lengthwise against the sand and she stopped completely, heeling over to starboard.

Jesper jumped down over the bow and ran up the beach with the sand anchor, driving its metal flukes deep into the yielding sand to hold the ship fast. He stopped, wiped his hands on his trousers and looked around.

'Nobody home,' he called, his voice echoing faintly off the rocks. The oarsmen drew in their oars and stowed them along the line of the ship, with a series of rattles and bumps that sounded unnaturally loud. Then, once again, there was silence in the cove.

'Set up camp,' Hal ordered and the crew busied themselves unloading the wooden frames and canvas cover they used for a tent on land, as well as a shelter on board their ship.

'May as well make the most of that,' Hal told them. 'I'll be cutting it up for a sail before long.'

Gilan could see that each member of the crew had an assigned task when it came to making camp. Edvin was assembling stones for a cook fire, and laying out his pans and implements. Jesper and Stefan were busy clearing a space for the sleeping tent while Ulf and Wulf lugged blankets and bedding ashore. Ingvar was loaded with the wooden frames and canvas that would form the tent, placing them beside the cleared space while Stig prepared to supervise the building of the tent.

Only Thorn and Lydia seemed to have no assigned tasks, but he noticed they were constantly scanning the ridge above them, their eyes always moving and their hands close to their weapons — an axe in Thorn's case and the quiver of atlatl darts in Lydia's.

'Anything I can do?' Gilan asked Hal.

The young skirl thought briefly. 'You might take Thorn and Lydia and scout the ridge,' he said. 'Make sure there are no locals up there waiting to surprise us.'

Gilan nodded and made his way to the bow, dropping over the side onto the wet sand and trudging to where the one-armed warrior and the slim girl were standing, still scanning the ridge line.

'Let me know if you see anything that frightens you, princess,' said Thorn, grinning at the girl. 'I'll go and chase it away with my axe.'

'What makes you think you could get halfway up that slope without keeling over, old man?' the girl replied crisply. Gilan had the impression he was listening to the latest instalment of a long-standing dialogue. Thorn's soft chuckle at her pithy reply, and her deep frown at the shabby old warrior, confirmed his thoughts.

'Hal wants us to check that ridge,' he said.

They both looked at him and nodded. They had been expecting such an order and they turned and set out up the beach. There was a narrow path that ran up the hill and they headed for it. Gilan unslung his bow from his shoulder and moved his cloak so that he had access to the arrows in his quiver. He noticed that Lydia had withdrawn one of the long darts from her own quiver, fitted the atlatl to the notch in the end and held it ready to throw. Thorn simply rested his axe over his left shoulder.

Sailors, once on land, were notoriously unfit, Gilan knew. But as he led the way up the steep, narrow path, sending showers of pebbles rattling down the hill, he noticed that these two were exceptions to that rule.

Neither of them was breathing hard when they reached the top of the ridge. He might have expected that in Lydia. She was slim and wiry and looked to be in excellent condition. The much bulkier Skandian surprised him, however. He realised that the bulk was pretty well all muscle, with little excess weight being carried in the form of fat.

They paused as they crested the ridge, Lydia and Thorn content to let Gilan lead the way. Before them stretched a panorama of rocks, dusty, uneven ground and low-lying scrub, spreading out in all directions. The sun beat down on them and the rocks shimmered with the heat they had stored for the past eight hours. After the deep shade of the bay, the heat here was oppressive. Gilan shaded his eyes and peered around on all sides. There was no sign of anyone — enemy or otherwise. Although to the south, where Socorro lay, a thin haze of smoke was evident, rising on the hot air, then being stirred by the breeze. Gilan gestured to the northern headland, on the opposite side of the bay.

'Let's make our way round there and take a look,' he said. The others nodded assent and they set off, their boots raising small puffs of dust from the parched ground as they moved around the ridge to explore the far side of the inlet.

On the beach, Hal contented himself that the camp was being put together with the usual dispatch. Then he set off for the trees beyond the beach, calling to Ingvar as he went.

'Ingvar! Come with me, please!'

The big boy had completed the heavy lifting that went

with setting up the sleeping tent. He picked his way over to where Hal was waiting, then fell in step with him as they walked towards the trees.

'What are we looking for, Hal?'

Hal looked sidelong at his friend. 'We?' he asked, smiling gently to make sure Ingvar took no offence.

The huge boy acknowledged the joke. 'All right. What are *you* looking for?'

'We need a couple of new spars,' Hal told him. 'I want to disguise the ship and rig her with a square sail.'

Ingvar thrust out his bottom lip. 'That should do it, all right. I take it I'm along to carry these spars of yours back to camp. I am the beast of burden for this crew, after all.'

'And invaluable you are in that role,' Hal said.

Ingvar gave a soft snort of derision. Then, joking aside, he said, 'Will green timber be all right for spars? Won't you want seasoned wood?'

'I'd prefer it, of course,' said Hal, his eyes scanning the trees around them. 'But new timber should be all right. I only need it for a few days and we're not going to be hitting any heavy weather. That one,' he added, pointing to a straight sapling some ten centimetres in diameter and five metres tall.

They made their way to the sapling and Hal shook it experimentally, then hit the trunk with the back end of the axe, listening to hear how the wood rang. Ingvar watched with some interest.

'Why do you do that?'

Hal shrugged. 'I'm not really sure. It's something Anders always does. But I think if there are flaws in the wood, it won't ring true. It'll sound sort of . . . rattly.'

'Have you ever heard it do that?' Ingvar asked. He had great respect for Hal's technical ability.

'Once or twice,' Hal said.

'And how did it sound?'

Hal paused, not sure how to explain it. Finally, he settled for: 'Sort of rattly.'

Ingvar raised his eyebrows. 'I suppose it's my fault for asking,' he said. 'Do you want me to cut it down for you?'

Hal shook his head, his eyes intent on the tree. There was something about preparing wood for a ship. He knew Ingvar would cut down the sapling in half the time he'd take, but he liked to do it by himself. It made him feel totally in tune with the process, totally involved.

He made his first cut into the sapling and the entire trunk quivered under the impact. Then he cut again, placing the axe blade exactly, so that it deepened the first cut. Then he came at it from the opposite angle, with an overhand cut, and a large wedge of wood flew free from the tree. He made four more cuts, the axe biting deeply into the wood, and the small tree lurched and staggered. He leaned against it, signalling to Ingvar to join him.

'Shove it,' he said and the huge boy added his strength to Hal's so that the sapling quickly keeled over with a rending, cracking noise. It lay parallel to the ground, joined to the stump by a few remaining strands and fibres of wood. Hal measured the distance and placed one more cut into the point where the tree joined the stump. The tree fell free, thudding softly onto the grass.

Hal straddled the tree and moved quickly along its length, deftly trimming the side branches and foliage until the sapling was reduced to a barc pole, five metres long.

'Should do for the mast extension,' he said, satisfied with the result. 'Let's find a new yardarm.'

They left the trimmed sapling lying and trudged a few more metres into the trees, Hal's eyes upwards, checking each new trunk for straightness and strength. Eventually, he found one that suited his requirements. He felled it with a few deft strokes of the axe before trimming off the leaves and branches. There was a slight kink in the trunk, about two-thirds of the way along. He shrugged. It wasn't perfect, but it would serve. He cut off the length he wanted, abandoning the upper third, where the wood tapered, and gestured at it to Ingvar.

'Bring it along,' he said. 'We'll start fitting it tomorrow.'

Ingvar heaved the ungainly piece of wood over his shoulder and they walked back towards the camp, collecting the heavier tree trunk as they went. The extra weight didn't bother Ingvar at all. He balanced the two long spars easily, as if they were featherweights.

On the way back, they intercepted Thorn, Gilan and Lydia, descending from the northern headland. Hal looked a question at them and Thorn shook his head.

'Nobody about,' he said. 'We're all alone.'

But he was wrong. From a hide under a jumble of rocks halfway up the slope at the end of the U-shaped ridge, hostile eyes were watching them, counting their numbers and assessing their ability to defend themselves.

CHAPTER TWENTY-SEVEN

The following morning, Gilan and Lydia climbed to the southern ridge and set out for Socorro. They left Hal frowning thoughtfully over the best way to re-rig the *Heron* with a square sail, while the rest of the crew waited patiently for the tasks they knew he would assign them.

The ground was flat and stony, baked by the sun during the day and frozen at night by the chill desert air. In the distance, to the east, Gilan and Lydia could see a range of massive mountains rearing up from the dry, stony plain, running roughly parallel to the coast. Frequently, their way south was blocked by dry gullies, steep sided and several metres deep. They would have to hunt for an easy way down, where the bank had collapsed, and then find a similar way back up again on the far side. Fortunately, such paths usually corresponded with each other. Obviously, previous travellers had forged a way here. But sometimes, having slipped and slithered down, they had to walk for several hundred metres before they found a place to clamber up again. Lydia voiced her displeasure the third time this happened.

'Who put these darn things here anyway?' she said, kicking at the dry dust in the bed of one of the gullies.

'They're water courses,' Gilan told her.

Lydia studied the rocky, dusty ground around her and sniffed. 'Doesn't look very wet to me.'

'When it rains here, which it doesn't do very often, it comes in an absolute downpour,' the Ranger told her. 'The water collects in those mountains you can see, then comes flooding across the plain in torrents. These gullies — the locals call them *wadis* — are the result. The water finds the path of least resistance and carves its way through, washing everything before it. Over the years, a huge channel forms. If you happened to be in one of these during a flash flood, you'd have no chance of surviving. The water would come through here faster than a horse could gallop, and it would fill the channel up to the banks.'

Lydia glanced around, imagining a wall of surging brown water suddenly erupting round the bend in the channel. At this point, the banks were at least three metres higher than her head and there would be no escape.

'How often does that happen?' she said.

Gilan shrugged. 'Not often. But when it does, there's absolutely no warning. It could be teeming with rain in the mountains right now, with a head of water building up, ready to burst down onto the flatlands and carry everything before it.'

'That's comforting to know,' Lydia said. From their current position, in the bottom of the gully, she couldn't see the mountains in the distance. She had no idea whether or not it was raining over them. She looked along the southern bank. Unfortunately, this was one of the spots where a way out didn't correspond directly with a way in.

'Let's get a move on,' she said, and lengthened her stride.

Gilan smiled and kept pace with her. He noticed that she seemed to relax when they eventually climbed out of the dried water course, some several hundred metres further downstream.

'You seem to know a lot about Socorro,' she said, when they were back at ground level once more. In the near distance, she could see the dark haze of dust and smoke that hung over the slaver city. And she could smell the pungent smoke of hundreds of cooking fires. Gilan nodded acknowledgement of her statement.

'We've been taking a particular interest in the place since the slave market reopened,' he said. 'We may have to do something about it one of these days. That's one reason I decided to tag along with you lot. It was a chance to get some first-hand intelligence on the place.'

She sniffed the air and wrinkled her nose. 'Does your intelligence go as far as telling us what the blazes they're burning in their fires?' she asked. Whatever it was that she smelled, it wasn't woodsmoke.

'Dried camel and goat dung, probably,' Gilan replied. 'They say you haven't eaten until you've eaten a haunch of camel meat roasted over goat dung.'

'And you might never eat again after it,' Lydia replied.

The ground began to rise again as they came closer to the city. At first, they could see only the taller buildings.

Then they crested the rising ground and the sprawl of the city itself came into view, where the houses and other buildings clustered around the roughly oval shape of the main harbour. The buildings were predominantly white, with occasional highlights of bright primary colours — blues and reds — and the sun glared off them. The roofs were flat, and built with a wall around the edges, as was common in this part of the world. In the cool evening air, residents would often eat, relax and sleep on the roof of their house, where they could enjoy the night breeze after the stifling heat of the day. Among the sprawl of one- and two-storey buildings, set at regular intervals, half a dozen tall, elegant spires rose into the sky, their peaks pointed and tiled, each adorned with an ornate balustrade forming a narrow balcony around the entire tower, just below the top.

A high wall ran round the city, extending in a rough circle as far as the two headlands on either side of the narrow harbour mouth. There was a squat castle on the southern headland, obviously designed to defend the entrance.

The quays and jetties bristled with the masts of hundreds of ships moored alongside while the brilliant blue of the ocean sparkled offshore.

'Looks like everybody's here for the slave market,' Gilan commented. They paused and scanned the harbour, looking for some sign of *Nightwolf*. But the ships were too numerous and too tightly packed for them to be able to discern her.

'Hal or Stig could probably pick her out in a few seconds,' Lydia said.

'Let's hope Tursgud doesn't share that ability,' Gilan said, but she shook her head.

'Hal will make sure of that. They all say he's a genius when it comes to rigging and designing a sail plan.'

Gilan looked curiously at her. There was an obvious affection in her voice when she spoke of the *Heron*'s skipper.

'How did you come to team up with them?' he asked, adding, 'You're not Skandian, are you?'

She shook her head. 'No. I'm from a city called Limmat on the Stormwhite's east coast. We were invaded by pirates about a year ago, and Hal and his crew turned up in time to help us kick them out. They saved my life, actually. I'd got away in a small boat but had run out of water. They found me drifting in the Stormwhite and took me aboard.'

She trudged on, her eyes down as she thought of those days when she first met the Herons.

'I stayed with them when they went after the pirate who had led the raid on the town. I liked being around Hal and Stig and Ingvar and the boys.'

'And Thorn?' Gilan asked, teasing her.

She shook her head in exasperation. 'Oh, him! He'll be the end of me one of these days. He's constantly on my back, never lets up.' She paused, then an admiring look came into her eyes. 'But you should see him in battle. He's unstoppable. Gorlog knows what he would have been like with both his hands. He's the battle leader for the crew when we go into action. Stig is his lieutenant. He's pretty fearsome as well.'

'So why did you stay with them after they left Limmat?' he asked.

She hesitated, not sure how to explain the feeling of constriction that had gripped her in her home town.

'My grandfather had died in the fighting and I had no other family. I guess I just felt that I fitted in with the Herons. People in Limmat used to think I was a bit weird because I didn't like to primp and dress up and parade like the other girls. I enjoyed hunting and tracking.'

Gilan smiled. 'We have a royal princess who shares your point of view.'

Lydia thought it wise not to mention the fact that, incensed by the lack of gratitude the people of Limmat had shown to the Herons, she had seen fit to 'liberate' a small sack of emeralds from the town's secret mine and present it to them.

'Speaking of tracking,' Gilan said, his eyes on the ground ahead of them, 'what do you make of that?'

She looked in the direction he was pointing and took a few paces forward, going down on one knee and feeling the marks in the sparse, coarse sand that covered the rock ground.

'A party of maybe fifteen or twenty people went through here,' she said, studying the faint footprints. 'Probably a hunting or raiding party.'

He raised his eyebrows. He'd come to much the same conclusion. 'What makes you say that?' he asked.

She took a few steps along the line of the tracks, which ran at right angles to the path they were following. Once again, she knelt and touched the sand. It was an instinctive gesture, as if she could feel the people who had made those tracks.

'They're all men,' she said finally. 'No women's

footprints here. No children, either. When you see a party of twenty men, it's safe to assume they're either hunting or up to no good.'

He nodded. 'You're right. They're heading east, towards the mountains. At least they are for the moment. Could be an Asaroki raiding party.'

'Asaroki?' she asked.

'Bandits. Brigands. There are tribes of them in this desert. Usually they live in the hills and come down to raid. This bunch were possibly hoping to intercept travellers heading for the slave market. Looks like they're on their way back to the mountains.' He shrugged. 'Still, they don't pose any danger for us. Let's keep going.'

They trudged on. To avoid unwanted attention, Gilan had left his Ranger cloak back at the ship, along with his bow. Similarly, Lydia had been persuaded to leave her atlatl behind. With its metre-long darts slung in a back quiver, it was a conspicuous weapon – particularly if carried by a girl.

The path they were following began to slope down now, and they could see numbers of people making their way into the city through a large double gate, guarded by watch towers on the wall either side. Armed guards were at the gate, checking on those who went through. Occasionally, they would stop a traveller and take him or her aside for questioning. Most of the time, the travellers were allowed to continue. But on two occasions, they saw someone led away to the guard tower.

They made their way down to the gate, having to wait behind a large party of traders leading half a dozen camels and four small donkeys, all laden with goods to sell in the market. Four guards examined the load, jerking the wrappings off the bundles to peer suspiciously at the contents. One of the camels objected to the violent action and reared its head, baring its teeth and roaring. The guard closest to it struck it smartly across the nose with the butt of his spear. The camel objected further and there were a few minutes of confusion before the traders, after paying a substantial bribe, were allowed to continue into the city.

The guard who had hit the camel looked around and saw them. He frowned, assessing them. That was a standard reaction, Gilan thought. These men would be constantly seeking to see how much they could fleece from travellers entering the city.

The guard saw a slim, nondescript man accompanied by an equally unremarkable girl, who kept her gaze down, not making eye contact. He nodded to himself. That was only proper, he thought.

'What do you two want?' he challenged roughly.

Gilan sized up the man quickly. He was dressed in a knee-length leather tunic, oversewn with mail rings. He wore a combination turban and spiked conical helmet with a strip of hammered brass projecting down to protect his nose. He was armed with a heavy thrusting spear and a short sword slung on his belt. His shins were covered with brass greaves and he wore stout leather sandals on his feet.

Gilan could see that he was a bully and a petty thief, accustomed to using his position of power to extract bribes from those he could intimidate. There were two ways to deal with such a man: one was to allow oneself to be cowed, to be submissive and plead for consideration. The other was to adopt the same tone of power and arrogance, and let him know that he was not facing an easy victim.

Since this was a market town, dependent on outsiders entering the city to buy or sell, Gilan knew the man would have no real power to exclude legitimate travellers. The Bey, the official who ruled Socorro, would earn taxes from all transactions carried out in his city. If his guards began excluding traders, his income would suffer. And nothing annoyed an Arridi official more than a drop in income.

Since Gilan felt in no mood to be cowed this morning, he adopted the second approach.

'I'm a trader,' he said, matching his tone with that of the guard. 'Who are you?'

The guard's eyebrows raised at the blunt reply. He looked more closely at the stranger, taking in the unwavering gaze, the air of authority and the long sword at his hip.

'Corporal Jemdal Oran, Third Patrol of the *Dooryeh*,' he replied and, seeing Gilan's questioning look, explained further, 'The Bey's Guards.'

'Well, in that case,' Gilan replied, in a more accommodating tone, 'let me introduce myself, Corporal. I'm Gilan of Cresthaven. I'm a trader and I'm here for the market.'

The corporal nodded, somewhat mollified by Gilan's tone. It was no less than a member of the Bey's *dooryeh* deserved, he thought. But a trader like this could be expected to provide a healthy bribe, so long as he wasn't antagonised.

'Which one? Slave market or gold market? We have both here.'

'I'm looking to buy a few strong slaves,' Gilan told him. 'But I've got some precious stones to trade as well.'

He let his fingers rest on the money purse at his belt, twitching it so that a chink of coins was audible. The corporal's eyes dropped to it, then came back up to meet Gilan's. The Ranger could see the avarice there.

'Slave market opens next week,' the corporal said briskly. 'Only sellers are allowed in at the moment. Buyers have to wait for the market to open. There's a day to view the slaves on sale, then on the next day trading begins.'

'Doesn't give me a lot of time to browse,' Gilan said.

The guard raised his eyebrows. 'The Bey doesn't encourage browsers. If you know what you want, one day is plenty of time to find it.'

One day also adds a sense of urgency to the whole thing, Gilan thought. And that will tend to inflate prices. When people feel rushed, they often spend more freely. But he merely shrugged.

'Fair enough. What about the gold market?'

'We call it the *souk*. That's always open. But no women are allowed in.' He jerked his head at Lydia, who was standing back a few paces, her eyes lowered.

'She's my niece,' Gilan explained.

'I don't care if she's your grandmother's second-best friend,' the guard replied. 'She's not allowed in the gold market. Women, gold and jewels don't mix. They haggle over prices too much and cause bad feeling. Bad feeling causes fights and fights slow up the selling.'

'And that means less tax for the Bey?' Gilan asked.

The man nodded. 'You've put your finger on it. So if you visit the gold market, leave her outside.'

'I'll do that. Where do I find the gold market?' Gilan asked.

The guard pointed. 'In the south-east quarter of the city. You can't miss it. It's roofed over. Biggest enclosed market in Arrida,' he said proudly. 'Slave market is just beyond it,' he added.

'But it's closed to buyers at the moment,' Gilan said.

'That's right. So you stay out of the slave market till next week. And she stays out of the gold market full stop.'

'Whatever you say,' Gilan replied. He moved forward under the gate's massive archway. As he did, his left hand brushed against the guard's right and several coins changed hands. Lydia slipped quietly into the city behind him.

The guard surreptitiously checked the coins that had been passed to him. One gold and two silver. Quite an acceptable amount, but not so much as to cause suspicion.

'Welcome to Socorro,' he said, stepping back to allow them more room to pass through the gate.

CHAPTER TWENTY-EIGHT

Hal spent the morning trimming and shaping the two spars that he had selected for his new mast and yardarm. He set up simple work benches, made from logs supported on twin X-shaped brackets, and laid the timbers across them as he worked with his adze. Thorn watched, admiring his skill and precision. Hal made only the roughest measurements, relying on his eye to shape the timber as he needed it.

The rest of the crew watched idly. Four of them had a ball made from an inflated pig's bladder, and they amused themselves kicking it around the beach, controlling it only with their feet and keeping their hands behind their backs.

Heron's mast was shorter than a standard wolfship's. The long, curving yardarm angled up above the top of the mast when it was raised, providing the height needed for the sails. To rig the ship for a square sail, where the yardarm would be parallel to the deck, Hal would have to extend the mast upwards by at least two metres. He planned to overlap the new spar with the existing mast for its entire length, using the original mast as a support. He would bind it tightly along the entire length of the join.

The spar was almost ready and he was currently curving one side to fit snugly to the rounded shape of the thick, stubby mast. Several times, he and Ingvar would heave the new spar over to the ship and test the fit. He would mark where it wasn't quite right, then go back to work.

Finally satisfied, he and Ingvar carried the new spar to the ship one final time and Ingvar held it in place against the mast. There were still a few small projections that needed trimming, and Hal made the necessary adjustments in place, using a heavy straight-bladed woodworking knife, until the spar sat snugly against the mast, with the curved section of the mast nestled neatly into the groove he had shaped.

'Stig! Ulf! Wulf! Lend us a hand here, will you?' he called.

The three abandoned their ball game and clambered aboard. They lashed the new mast temporarily in place at three points along its length, then Hal began to bind it permanently, using wet rope that would shrink as it dried, tightening the bindings even further. He'd already detached the forestay. Now he climbed the shrouds and reattached it, passing it through a hole he had drilled in the extension mast for that purpose.

He looked up at the new, taller mast and nodded in satisfaction.

'That should do the job,' he told Stig, who was standing beside him.

His friend nodded. Hal had done a neat and efficient job putting the new mast in place. But then, Hal was always neat and efficient with his woodwork.

'Looks just like a bought one,' Stig said, grinning.

Hal raised an eyebrow. 'Never thought I'd go back to square rigging. It just won't feel like the *Heron*. Still, it's only for a day or two.' He replaced the trimming knife and adze in his canvas tool kit and took out the implements he'd need for cutting and shaping the sail.

'If you can rig the stays and halyards for the new yardarm, I'll get on with cutting the sail,' he said.

Stig nodded, and gestured to the others to help him. The new halyards and attachments were a straightforward task, one that could be carried out by any competent seaman — and they all qualified in that regard.

Hal dragged the big canvas weather cover onto the beach and waited while Ingvar spread it out. Using a piece of charcoal, he marked the shape of the new sail into the canvas, drawing extra lines for the places where he would sew in reinforcement and shaping seams.

Edvin approached as he began to cut the sail. 'Did you want to eat before you do that, or wait until you're finished?'

Hal glanced up at the sun. It was past noon and he estimated that it would take several hours to get the sail ready and attached to the yardarm.

'We'll eat now,' he said and Edvin turned back to his cook fire, adding several logs and fanning the hot coals into live flame. He had a fillet of beef still remaining from the stores he'd bought en route. After this, they would be on salted meat and fish and pickled vegetables. But then, he thought, in a day or so they'd be in Socorro.

He sliced the beef, along with several onions, and set them sizzling together in his big black iron frying pan. When the meat was browned, he moved it away from the direct heat and added a measure of wine to the pan, then salt and pepper and some of his spices, and set the savoury contents bubbling gently.

Within a few minutes, Kloof came nosing around, attracted by the smell of the meat cooking. Edvin grinned at her and tossed her a handful of scraps that he'd trimmed from the beef. She snuffled them up in seconds, and wagged her tail hopefully at him. Edvin spread his empty hands out to her.

'That's all, I'm afraid.' She tilted her head in disbelief and settled down, her chin on her paws, watching him closely. When it came to food, Kloof was an eternal optimist.

Leaving the beef mixture to cook, Edvin quickly mixed water and flour together to make a thin batter. He took another frypan, placed it over the fire and, when it was hot, added a pat of butter. Then he spooned a large dollop of the batter into the pan and swirled it to let it spread into a thin layer. When the top began to bubble, he flipped it expertly, revealing the golden pan-fried underside.

He repeated this action until he had a stack of hot, thin pancakes. Then he spooned the beef and onion mixture into them, rolled them and placed them in a pan by the side of the fire to keep them warm.

The rest of the crew, noticing the savoury smells emanating from the cook fire, had abandoned their work and gathered around him, their mouths watering. Thorn approached behind them, glaring at them.

'Did anyone tell you it was time to eat?' he asked fiercely. They looked suitably chastened and shuffled their feet, avoiding his gaze as they moved away from the cook fire.

'No, Thorn,' they mumbled. He looked around the semi-circle of faces, then shoved through them with a huge grin.

''Cause my stomach tells me it's definitely time!' he said. He seized one of the meat and onion stuffed pancakes Edvin had made, taking an enormous bite and smiling beatifically as juice ran down his chin and into his beard. Instantly the boys began to clamour for their share of the food, and before long, the platter of pancakes was empty.

Hal, who had left the partly shaped sail to join them, finished the last of his pancake, sat back and took a long swig of coffee, then sighed rapturously.

'Do you think we should be drinking Gilan's coffee when he's not here?' he asked.

Stig considered the question. 'He'd want us to,' he said gravely.

Hal looked into his cup. It was nearly empty. 'Do you think he'd want us to have a second cup?'

Stig nodded. 'Without a doubt.'

'Keep telling yourselves that,' Edvin told them, shaking his head. But he fetched the pot and poured a fresh cup for Hal. Stig held his cup out and Edvin, rolling his eyes, topped him up as well.

Kloof barked.

'Quiet. Dogs don't drink coffee,' Hal told her, not looking. But the dog barked again, more urgently this time. Hal glanced up and suddenly leapt to his feet.

'Arm yourselves!' he shouted to his startled crew. 'Now!'

A party of armed men was making its way down the eastern slope of the ridge that surrounded the bay.

CHAPTER TWENTY-NINE

As they strode through the narrow, winding streets of the town, jostled by the crowds moving around them, Lydia moved up beside Gilan, abandoning the subservient position she had adopted at the gate.

'How do we find the bazaar?' she asked.

Gilan gestured to the milling throng around them. At least half the people were carrying bundles of goods to trade, usually by the simple expedient of balancing them on their heads, tied up in giant rolls. Others were leading donkeys laden with nets of fruit and vegetables.

'Follow the crowd,' he said. 'That's where they'll be heading.'

They allowed themselves to be carried along with the human tide. It was, Lydia thought, a little like floating downstream in a strong river current. Eventually, they arrived at the market. Stalls were laid out in neat, ordered rows, most of them with green or brown awnings to keep the heat of the sun off the goods and the traders themselves. Fruit, vegetables, meat and livestock were all on display, usually laid out on blankets spread over the cobblestones. The air was alive with voices shouting, arguing, laughing and bargaining in half a dozen different languages, the common tongue being the most prevalent.

Gilan took her elbow and guided her past a row of stalls selling melons, oranges, onions and assorted vegetables. 'This is the food section. Let's find the clothing stalls,' he said. 'You do the buying — say you're buying for your older brothers.'

'Won't it look suspicious if we buy ten sets of clothes?' Lydia asked.

He nodded. 'Decidedly. So we won't buy them all in one place. The robes are pretty much one size for all.'

'Except Ingvar,' Lydia said with a smile.

'Except Ingvar. He is a size, isn't he?'

They crossed over three aisles, moving from the food section of the market to the section where clothing and fabrics were on sale. Gilan stopped at a money changer and exchanged some of his Araluan money for dirum, the local currency.

He frowned as he studied the purseful of coins he had been handed. 'I think he might have taken advantage of me,' he said.

Lydia raised an eyebrow at him and looked from him to the money changer. He was an overweight, swarthy man, whose eyes were constantly darting about him and whose hands made continual small movements.

'I'm sure he did,' she said.

'Nobody ever got the better of a money changer,' Gilan said.

He gestured at a stall where a trestle table displayed a variety of garments, ranging from the voluminous trousers that the locals wore, to brocaded and garishly decorated waistcoats, to the simple, flowing robes and headdresses they were after.

'Off you go,' he said, handing her a fistful of dirum. 'Remember to haggle a little.'

She gave him a pitying look, dropping the coins into a side pocket on her vest. 'I'm a Limmatan,' she said. 'I was born haggling.'

A faint smile crossed Gilan's face. 'Interesting picture that conjures up,' he said. 'Just don't argue too much or you'll have women banned from this market as well.'

She looked around. The market was predominantly filled with women of all ages and sizes. They were gesticulating, throwing their hands in the air, uttering shrieks of apparent despair at the prices quoted. From time to time, one of them would throw the goods they were inspecting back on the trader's table and walk off indignantly, only agreeing to return to the negotiation when the seller agreed to a cut in price.

'If they were to ban women here,' she said, 'the market wouldn't survive.'

She approached the stall and began fingering one of the long white linen robes, a look of distaste on her features. The trader at first pretended not to notice her, then, as she held up one of the robes to inspect it more carefully, he casually came closer and muttered a price.

Lydia laughed and tossed the garment back onto the table, shaking her head disdainfully. She began to turn away but the trader picked the garment up and called her back, with an impassioned plea for her to consider the superior quality, and so the inflated price, of the garment in question. Gilan watched with interest as the charade continued. At first, Lydia offered a figure less than half the amount the trader was asking. The trader's eyes rolled to heaven and he clutched his chest over his heart in a 'you're killing me' gesture. Then he offered an infinitesimal reduction on his previous price. Lydia countered with an equally infinitesimal increase in her offer and so the bargaining continued, the trader constantly asking slightly less, Lydia constantly offering slightly more.

After three minutes, they had reached a reasonable area of negotiation, where the difference between what was offered and what was quoted was becoming smaller and smaller. Then Lydia played her trump card.

'I want three,' she said. 'I have three brothers and I'm buying one for each of them.'

The trader fingered the narrow beard on his chin and thought deeply.

'For three you will pay less,' he said magnanimously. 'Eight dirum each one.'

'Six,' she said firmly. 'No more.'

'Seven,' he said.

'Done,' she replied. The dialogue was rapid fire, with neither one of them having time or inclination to consider the other's offer.

The trader deftly folded three of the robes for her, placing them on the table while she counted out the money. Then they began again as she indicated that she wanted three *kheffiyehs* — the simple but effective linen headdress, held in place by a double loop of twisted horsehair, that would shield the wearer from sun, wind and dust.

By now, each had a sense of the other's skill and determination, and the negotiations were much quicker. A few minutes later, she moved away, the new clothes folded in a sack. Gilan took charge of it and they walked through to the next aisle, where another trader and another store awaited them.

'We could have got a better price if I'd bought all ten there,' she pointed out.

Gilan shrugged. 'The objective isn't to get a better bargain,' he said. 'And he might remember a girl buying ten robes and headdresses. We don't want people asking questions. Markets like this are crawling with spies and agents on the lookout for anything unusual.'

She nodded and repeated the process at a second and third stall. Interestingly, all of them charged the same amount at the end of the haggling, which made her feel that she had struck a reasonable bargain. Either that or they recognised her as an easy mark, she thought.

They took a break and sat at a stall selling coffee and sweet pastries. The coffee was delicious — thick and grainy and heavily sweetened. Gilan rolled it around his tongue appreciatively.

'They know their coffee in this country,' he said.

Lydia pulled a face. There were too many grounds in the cup for her taste.

'Now what?' she asked as he drained his cup. The look on his face told her that he was considering ordering a second. 'We do need to get back to the ship sometime this week.'

He nodded reluctantly. 'True. Then perhaps we should have a look at the gold market.'

She frowned. 'What's the fascination with the gold market?'

'We're planning to liberate the captives,' he told her. 'And that means we'll be raiding the slave market. We might have to stage some sort of diversion and I figure the gold market might be the best place to do it.'

'What kind of diversion do you have in mind?' Lydia asked.

He smiled. 'A fire's always good. Nothing gets an Arridan trader's attention better than a threat to his gold. And it'll probably draw the patrols away from the slave market while they try to put it out. So I'd like to have a look at it and get an idea of the layout.'

'What about me?' she asked.

He smiled again. 'You're a woman,' he said. 'You aren't allowed in the gold market.'

'The heck I'm not,' she said. She gestured to the sack of clothes they had purchased. 'With one of those robes and a headdress, who's going to know the difference?'

'You don't think your overwhelming femininity will give you away?' he teased.

She gave him a pitying look. 'You know, you're starting to make Thorn look agreeable.'

She found a secluded spot behind the coffee stall and donned one of the robes and *kheffiyehs*. Gilan gave the stall owner a small coin to take care of the clothes for them and studied her as she emerged, now wrapped in the flowing robe and with the *kheffiyeh* arranged over her head. It was an effective disguise and with her olive skin, dark eyes and slim build, she would pass easily for a young boy.

'Let's take a look at this gold market,' she said.

CHAPTER THIRTY

The attackers wore black and white striped robes over baggy linen trousers that were gathered at the ankles. Their feet were clad in stout leather sandals and they wore cone-shaped brass helmets on their heads, over long linen turbans whose tails hung down their backs. Each of them carried a small, round metal shield, shaped like an oversized bowl. As they reached the bottom of the slope, there was a series of rasping metal on leather sounds as each man drew a long-bladed curved sword.

'Move it!' Thorn barked.

The crew scrambled to gather swords, axes and shields. As they formed up around him, he was busy shedding his grasping hook from the end of his right arm. Stig passed him the huge, bone-crushing war club Hal had fashioned for him and he strapped it in place, using his teeth to pull the straps tight. He nodded his thanks to Stig, picked up a shield — a large round one in place of the small metal shield he often used — and the two of them stepped forward, shoulder to shoulder.

'Shield wall,' Thorn said, then quickly called, 'Shields up!'

The warning came just in time. He'd spotted movement at the fringe of the approaching group of armed men. Three of them had short but powerful bows. The arrows rattled against the raised shields. Two deflected off the metal bosses. The third thudded directly into the wood of Stefan's shield and stayed there, quivering.

Hal took the situation in at a glance. So far, he hadn't joined the shield wall, which had formed rapidly in a semi-circle. Instinctively, the crew had placed themselves in position to defend the ship. Moving behind them, Hal heaved himself up over the bulwark and ran aft to where his crossbow and quiver of bolts were hanging beside the tiller.

He stepped his foot into the stirrup at the front of the crossbow, grabbed the cord in two hands and heaved it back until he heard it clack into the restraint. He fed a bolt into the groove on top of the crossbow and ran forward to the bow again, the quiver of bolts, slung hurriedly over one shoulder, banging loosely against his side.

There was a man in the centre of the approaching line who was obviously in command. He gestured to the archers, placed at either end of the line, and pointed his sword at the waiting Skandians. The bows came up again and Hal could hear the creak of straining cord, hide and wood as they drew back.

He flipped up the rear sight on the crossbow, estimating the range at less than a hundred metres. He centred the foresight on one of the archers and, as the man released his arrow, Hal squeezed the trigger lever of his crossbow.

There was the usual ugly slamming sound, then the bolt sped on its way. He'd hurried the shot and it went low, taking the man in the thigh. The force of the shot jerked the man's leg out from under him and he fell, dropping the bow and clutching at his injured leg. The arrow that he'd shot, along with the other two, thudded harmlessly into the Herons' big circular shields.

Then the leader of the group yelled a command, raised his sword, lowered it to point at the waiting Skandians, and led his men in a wild, screaming charge.

'Brace!' shouted Thorn and the Herons set their feet, leaning their weight into the big wooden shields, overlapping them so that their combined strength was ready to resist the charge.

The attackers crashed into the unyielding shield wall, rebounding and staggering with the shock of contact. Their normal victims were traders and travellers, not used to fighting and more inclined to flee at the sight of the charging, sword-wielding Asaroki. This time they had come up against trained, expert warriors, fully armed and ready for their attack. Four of the attackers went down in that first impact, as the Skandian axes, and Thorn's mighty club-hand, smashed into them. Thorn himself took care of two of the attackers, with a blindingly fast forehand and backhand sweep that sent them flying off their feet. Stig's vertical axe stroke dropped another where he stood and Edvin accounted for the fourth with a swift, expertly placed sword thrust. As the bandit sank to his knees, a surprised look on his face, clutching at the wound in his side, Edvin grimly recalled Thorn's teaching:

Three centimetres of point is as good as thirty of edge.

Instinctively, the surviving attackers withdrew from that implacable wall of shields and deadly weapons. The leader looked back in an attempt to rally his men and, as he did, another crossbow bolt buzzed over the heads of the Skandians and hit him squarely in the chest. The impact hurled him backwards and he crashed into two of his men, dead before he hit the sand.

But if the defenders thought his death might discourage the remaining raiders, they were quickly disabused of that notion. The second in command of the band screamed an order and they hurled themselves forward again. This time, they had a little more success. They concentrated their attack at one end of the line, reasoning that the most capable fighters would be at its centre. Seven of them drove Ulf, Wulf and Edvin back, and began to spill round the flank of the line to encircle the defenders. One of them avoided Edvin's darting sword by mere centimetres, then moved behind the smallest of the Skandians while another attacker took his attention. The first bandit drew back his sword, ready to plunge it into Edvin's unprotected back, when a snarling black and white hurricane smashed into him.

Forty-five kilograms of enraged dog slammed into the Asaroki, sending him sprawling. Desperately, he raised his sword arm to protect himself, but Kloof's mighty jaws crunched shut on his forearm and the weapon fell to the sand while its owner screamed in pain and fright.

'Good dog, Kloof!' Edvin said, realising the threat

a few seconds too late. Without the dog's intervention, he would be dead by now. Kloof released the terrified bandit's arm, wagging his tail at Edvin. 'I'll make a note to feed you more often,' Edvin told her.

The man she had attacked crept away, sobbing, dragging himself on his stomach with his left arm, his ruined sword arm dragging behind him.

As Kloof foiled the flanking movement, Thorn saw the time was right for a counterattack. He felled the bandit facing him with a side sweep of his club-hand into the man's ribs, caught Stig's eye and nodded forward.

'Let's get 'em, Stig!' he yelled, in the traditional battle cry of Skandian warriors.

The two of them surged forward, their terrible weapons rising and falling with blinding speed. By their side, and a little behind them, Jesper and Stefan added their share of mayhem as they drove a wedge into the confused attackers. More of the bandits went down. The others held for a few seconds, then, as if at a signal, broke and retreated up the beach.

'Hold!' Thorn shouted. They had accounted for more than half of the band that had attacked them, but they were still outnumbered and their safety lay in their cohesive formation. If they broke ranks now to pursue them, the bandits could possibly turn the tables on them.

The raiders retreated up the beach. Then, seeing they were not being pursued, they stopped and re-formed. The two groups faced each other, neither willing to move. The bandits' new commander harangued them, shouting insults and exhortations. But they hesitated. None of them wanted to be the next one to go down before the Skandian axes.

Ingvar had spent the battle behind the Skandian line. His poor eyesight put him at a disadvantage in a fight like this. Uncertain as to whom he was facing, not sure if it was a friend or an enemy, he would hesitate, and that could be fatal. But there was one task at which he was the consummate expert.

'Ingvar! Load for me!' Hal yelled. He had cast the wrappings off the Mangler and was sitting behind it, training it round by shoving with his feet against the deck to line up with the reduced group of attackers. Ingvar peered around, realised what was happening, and ran for the ship, hauling himself up over the bulwark and making his way forward. Leaning past Hal, he seized the two cocking levers and heaved them back in one swift, powerful motion, cocking the crossbow's massive arms. He turned to the locker where the bolts were stored, but Hal already had one selected. He dropped it into the loading groove and Ingvar saw that it was one of the new pottery-headed bolts.

By sheer chance, the bandits had grouped around a rock outcrop at the end of the beach. Hal lined the sights up on it now, adjusted the elevation slightly and pulled the lanyard.

SLAM!

The bolt streaked away and smashed into the rock, its warhead shattering and releasing a storm of sharp pottery shards and small rocks. They sliced into the grouped bandits. Two of them went down, lacerated and bleeding. A third had his arm torn open by a whirring chunk of shattered pottery. Most of the others were struck by smaller fragments or stones.

Coming on top of the beating they had already taken, this was too much. With one accord, they turned and ran for the ridge, slipping and falling in their haste, staggering to their feet and continuing to climb the steep slope, conscious all the time that another of those frightful missiles might shatter to pieces among them.

Thorn lowered his shield to the ground beside his feet and looked around at his small band of fighters.

'Everyone all right?' he asked and received a chorus of affirmative answers. Only Ulf had sustained an injury — a long, shallow gash above his left eye. Edvin put down his weapons and went to fetch his medical kit. He quickly wound a bandage around Ulf's head.

Thorn smiled contentedly at the sight. At last, he thought, they had a way to distinguish between the identical twins — if only in the short term.

'And which one are you?' he asked.

Ulf, always ready to exploit a situation like this, smiled back.

'I'm Wulf,' he said innocently.

CHAPTER THIRTY-ONE

The gold market, or *souk*, was an immense rectangular space that stretched for several city blocks in all directions, surrounded by a continuous wall built from massive sandstone blocks. There were four entrances, one in the middle of each side. A spreading roof of flat tiles covered the rectangle, which contained a labyrinth of narrow alleys, each one lined with stalls selling gold, precious stones, silver, brassware and, incongruously, musical instruments. The term 'gold market' was obviously a loose one, as there were also a large number of stalls dealing in ornate carpets and heavy fabrics.

With its network of narrow cross streets, twisting and turning away from a broad central thoroughfare, it resembled a city in miniature. The ground followed the natural contours of the land, so that the alleys ran up and downhill in a random pattern, at times rising quite steeply, then plunging down once more, adding to the impression that one was traversing a vast indoor city.

Light was provided by hundreds of oil lamps, creating moving shadows and reflecting garishly from the gold and brass that was on display on all sides. In addition, the roof was pierced at regular intervals by large skylights, and broad, glaring shafts of sunlight pierced down into the dim interior, sending more golden reflections dancing and shimmering, and making the areas where direct sunlight didn't reach seem dimmer by comparison.

The market was crowded with people, all bargaining intensely with the stall holders. Competition between the different stalls was fierce, so that if a buyer wasn't satisfied with the price on offer, he could move on to another stall and another trader.

While the bargaining was nonstop, it was nowhere near as raucous as that in the outdoor general market. Voices were restrained and negotiations were conducted in lowered tones, albeit forceful ones. Possibly, thought Gilan, the traders didn't want other potential customers to hear the prices they were offering to their current client. That way, each customer had to negotiate his own best price, without benefiting from someone else's ability to haggle.

The alleys were crammed. People moved in both directions, hurrying and jostling one another heedlessly in their attempt to get where they were going. Gilan and Lydia had to force their way through, at times bumping shoulders with those coming in the opposite direction.

Several times, Lydia muttered, 'Sorry,' as she brushed against people. After the fourth such occasion, Gilan, who had been watching carefully, led to her one side, out of the flow of traffic.

'Don't apologise,' he said quietly. 'They don't. It's all part and parcel of being here. If you bump someone out of the way, that's simply the done thing. Just keep your eyes down, don't make eye contact, and don't stop walking when you bump someone.'

Lydia nodded. 'Sorry,' she muttered. He patted her on the shoulder, then led the way out into the milling human tide again.

They stopped at a crossroads set at the top of a steep hill, looking down on all four sides to where the alleys twisted and wound through the golden, glittering light. The low roof accentuated the narrowness of the alleys. They seemed to wind and stretch far into the distance. There was a tea stall at the summit of the hill, serving tea, sweet cakes and savoury snacks. Gilan led the way to a table and they sat, looking around them, taking note of the surrounding mass of stalls, traders, shops and people.

'It's like an ants' nest,' Lydia said.

Gilan nodded. 'Could be the perfect place to stir things up,' he said. 'I'm thinking if we started a fire somewhere like this, where's there's a kitchen and lots of cooking oil, it would give Hal and the others a free hand to break into the slave market and get the prisoners out.'

A waiter approached them and Gilan ordered mint tea and savoury potato cakes stuffed with spiced mutton for the two of them.

'Of course,' he said, 'they'll probably have to contend with a few locked doors to get in and out of the slave quarters. That might be tricky.'

Lydia shook her head. 'Locks mean nothing to Jesper,' she told him. 'He can open the strongest lock in a matter of seconds, and pick your pocket while he's doing it.'

Gilan's eyebrows shot up. 'Sounds like a valuable skill,' he said. 'We should try to get a closer look at the slave market — at least from the outside — before we head back. I'm still trying to figure a way we can get a look inside. Be a bit difficult breaking the prisoners out if we don't know what we're walking into.'

'I'm sure Hal will come up with something,' Lydia said complacently.

Gilan pursed his lips. 'Let's hope so.'

They finished their meal and he paid the bill, then stood and began to lead the way downhill. They had entered via the gate in the north wall and he knew the slave market lay on the south-west corner of the gold market. He stopped at a crossroad, got his bearings — not easy in a place where cross streets ran at irregular angles and directions — and pointed south.

'We'll go out the south gate, and have a look.'

Lydia nodded and followed him downhill. The street was too congested to allow them to walk side by side and they threaded their way through the crowd in single file. Although they were on one of the wider main thorough-fares, the fact that it was wider didn't make the going any easier. It simply accommodated more people pushing and shoving in opposing directions. The hill was quite steep and the cobblestones were slick with the passage of thousands of feet. Lydia found she had to pick her way carefully to avoid slipping.

They heard shouting coming from downhill and to their left. It was subdued at first, and masked by the stalls and shops. Then, some thirty metres below them, a man emerged from a side alley onto the main street, running flat out and looking back fearfully over his shoulder.

The shouting intensified as three members of the *dooryeh* burst out of the same alley, in hot pursuit of the running man.

He was fifteen metres ahead of them, running like a hare. But he slowed as he hit the steep upward slope, leaning forward, driving his legs to greater effort. Before the *dooryeh* reached the slope, they had narrowed the gap. One of them was still shouting, but he was the one bringing up the rear. The others were saving their breath to tackle the steep climb. They were burdened by their armour and the weapons they carried and their quarry gradually began to pull away from them again as they encountered the sloping ground.

As the running man drew near, Lydia could see he was dressed in filthy, tattered rags. He was thin to the point of emaciation, and his beard and hair were wild and stringy. His eyes were haunted, wide with fear. That fear seemed to lend extra wings to his feet as he put on a spurt and began to widen his lead over his pursuers. Lydia noticed a heavy gold chain clutched in his right fist. Obviously, he had stolen it from a stall down one of the side alleys and had been seen doing so.

Gilan put an arm back and drew her to one side. There was no future in getting involved — to do so would only draw attention to them and then Lydia's male disguise, flimsy as it was, would probably be pierced.

Then everything went wrong, all at once.

A waiter from the tea stall they had just left was walking ahead of them, carrying a tray of glasses of tea to one of the stalls. He held it in one hand, hanging from a swivelling handle, so he could hold it above the jostling crowd. He managed to sidestep the careering thief just in time, avoiding spilling the hot tea with the skill of long practice. He fired an angry epithet after the fleeing man.

At almost the same moment, a gold trader from one of the stalls lining the thoroughfare decided to lend a hand in the pursuit. He was a fat, elderly man, dressed in a knee-length sleeveless brocaded vest worn over the ubiquitous billowing trousers. His feet were shod in soft felt slippers, worked with golden threads.

'Thief! Thief! Stop him, someone!' he shouted indignantly, placing his bulky self in the path of the running man and bracing for the inevitable impact.

The thin escapee sidestepped him easily. The trader's clutching hands caught hold of his ragged shirt and held him for an instant. But the thief spun around, swinging the other man in a half circle, and breaking free of his grasping hands. The material of his shirt tore, leaving a strip in the gold trader's fist.

The trader went staggering off balance down the slope and crashed into the waiter, sending him and his tea glasses flying. The two men crashed to the cobblestones in a tangle of arms and legs as the first of the patrol arrived, running full tilt. He assessed the situation instantly, and hurdled the two fallen men in his stride. But his hobnailed sandals landed in the puddle of spilt tea that had been left on the slick cobblestones and his feet shot out from underneath him. He crashed down onto the cobbles, his mail shirt ringing with the impact, his spear clattering on the stones as it fell from his grasp. He rolled over onto his hands and knees, preparing to regain his feet, when one of his comrades arrived and, unable to avoid him, tripped over him and fell as well.

The third man, swerving desperately to avoid his fallen companions, sidestepped wildly, felt himself slipping and regained his balance by rebounding from the nearest bystander — who happened to be Lydia.

He shoved clear of her, resuming his headlong pursuit of the thief. Unfortunately, she was caught unawares and was sent flying into the display counter of a jewellery store, sending gold chains, necklaces and trays of rings showering into the air, bouncing and clattering off the cobbles. She lost her footing and sprawled on the floor of the stall, winded and disoriented. The stall owner screamed insults at her as he dropped to his knees, frantically gathering up his scattered goods.

'Sorry,' she gasped but, panicking as he thought she was trying to steal some of his goods, he swung an open-handed blow at her. She ducked, but a little too late, so that it caught her a glancing blow on the top of her head and knocked off her headdress, revealing her long hair.

The stall keeper gaped at her, recognising her as female. Such a thing was unheard of in the gold market. The last time a woman had infiltrated here had been several years ago. He pointed at her, his scattered goods forgotten for the moment.

'You're a woman!' he screeched, his voice breaking with surprise. Lydia scrambled for her lost *kheffiyeh* in a belated and useless attempt to resume her disguise. The trader turned, looking for the patrolmen who had caused the accident.

Fortunately, they were intent on resuming their pursuit of the ragged thief they had been chasing, pounding off up the hill after him. He was now a distant figure, twisting and turning through the crowd, most of whom turned to stare after him.

The merchant saw that they were going to be of no help and turned to his neighbouring traders, ready to raise the alarm.

'It's a woman!' he shrieked. But before any of the surrounding Arridi could pay any attention, Gilan grabbed a heavy carpet from one of the stall's other display tables and quickly threw it over the man's head, muffling his high-pitched cries of alarm so they were nothing but a vague mumble.

'Get your hat on!' he ordered Lydia and, as she hurriedly wound the *kheffiyeh* around her head, hiding her hair and obscuring half her face, he pulled a corner of the carpet away from the stall keeper. The man, red faced and spluttering after being confined under the heavy material, drew breath for another cry of alarm.

'Oh shut up,' Gilan told him and hit him on the point of the jaw with a perfectly placed left hook. The man's eyes glazed then rolled up and he sank back, as limp as a roll of carpet himself. Gilan flipped the corner of the carpet back over the stall owner to conceal him, grabbed Lydia by the arm and hustled her out of the stall, hurrying away downhill.

Several of the bystanders sensed that something was amiss. But events had moved so quickly and the situation was so confused that they weren't completely sure what had taken place. There had been a lot of running and shouting and falling and tables being knocked over and nobody had a clear picture of anything.

One of them took a pace towards Gilan, saw the dangerous look in the stranger's eyes and the way his hand dropped to the hilt of his long sword, and hurriedly backed off.

Then the confusion increased as a group of urchins, following the excitement of the chase, caught sight of the gold chains and precious stones scattered on the floor of the stall and rushed to help themselves, shouting excitedly. Several of the stall keeper's neighbours, in a surprising show of solidarity, stepped in to stop them and began cuffing and cursing the young boys, grabbing the chains and jewels from their grasping hands and sending them on their way. In the resultant confusion and bustle of activity, nobody paid any further attention to the two foreigners as they hurried away, disappearing into the milling crowds.

'Well, that *was* exciting,' Gilan said. He looked at her and added, 'Your hat's not straight.'

Lydia adjusted the *kheffiyeh*. Her heartbeat was only just returning to somewhere near normal.

'D'you still want to look at the slave market?' she asked.

Gilan turned a stony stare on her. 'Let's get the heck out of here. I think we've pushed our luck far enough.'

CHAPTER THIRTY-TWO

When they returned to the small cove north of Socorro, Gilan and Lydia stood at the top of the ridge surrounding the bay, momentarily puzzled.

The ship moored in the cove bore little resemblance to the *Heron*. She had a tall mast with a yardarm mounted at right angles, and a square sail furled loosely along it. In addition, the distinctive heron figurehead on the bowpost had been replaced by a circular piece of timber carved to resemble a watching eye. The eye motif was repeated on each bow, daubed there in blue paint. The hull of the ship was streaked with dirt and grime.

For a moment, the two hesitated.

'Is this the right cove?' Gilan asked, although he knew he couldn't have made an error as grave as coming back to the wrong place. But that definitely wasn't their ship, and it definitely wasn't where their ship had been when they had left that morning. The thought struck him that perhaps this new ship had arrived during the day and Hal and the others had sought to avoid it, putting to sea and sailing down the coast.

Then Lydia spotted Ingvar's massive bulk among the crew members moving on deck. 'That's them,' she said. As she looked she recognised more of the crew. 'Hal's re-rigged the ship to make her look different.'

Gilan raised an eyebrow. 'He certainly succeeded. I wouldn't have recognised her.'

'But why aren't they still on the beach?' Lydia asked.

Gilan was studying the beach where *Heron* had been run aground. Looking up towards the treeline, he could see a neat line of mounds in the sand — mounds where the earth had been freshly turned, so that the damper under-soil contrasted with the dry surface sand.

'Those are graves,' he said, pointing to the row of mounds. 'There's been a fight here. Hal must have decided to anchor out in the bay in case whoever attacked them decides to come back.'

As he spoke, he loosened his sword in its scabbard. The action was purely a reflex, performed without any conscious thought. If there had been hostile forces here earlier in the day, there was nothing to say that they weren't still somewhere in the vicinity. Lydia, noticing the gesture, touched her hand against the hilt of her dirk, reassuring herself that it was still there.

They both scanned the slopes surrounding the bay.

'Can't see anyone,' Lydia said.

'Doesn't mean there's no one here,' Gilan warned her and they began to make their cautious way down the slope to the beach.

'Who would have attacked them?' Lydia asked. She was scanning the deck of the ship, trying to count heads to make sure nobody was missing. But the Herons kept moving around, making it impossible for her to keep count. She saw Stig, Hal and Thorn, and thought she recognised Stefan. Eventually, she was satisfied that everyone was on board.

'Could have been anyone,' Gilan said. 'These plains are swarming with bandits. Could even have been those Asaroki who crossed our path this morning.'

'But they weren't heading this way,' she pointed out.

Gilan made a noncommittal gesture. 'They would have had scouts out to either side. They could well have spotted the ship beached here and decided she'd be easy prey.'

'Big mistake,' she said grimly, glancing at the row of graves once more.

They were halfway down the rocky path when they heard a cry from the ship. Stig was balanced on the starboard bulwark near the bow, waving to them. Lydia returned the wave and they picked up the pace, hurrying down the last of the path to the level ground at the bottom.

Knowing he would have to row back in to pick them up, Hal had attached a short hawser to the anchor and buoyed the upper end with a float. Now he could simply untie the ship from the floating buoy, without having to bring in the full anchor rope, and row in to collect the two missing members of the party. Then, once they were aboard, the ship could be quickly moored to the buoy once more.

In the calm waters of the bay, Edvin had lit his stove, set in a large pan of sand for safety. The crew gathered round while he served Gilan and Lydia coffee.

'There's not a lot of this left,' the cook observed as he poured Gilan's cup.

The Ranger tilted his head quizzically. 'Really? There was plenty when I left this morning.' He looked suspiciously at Hal, who assumed an expression of total innocence that was an immediate giveaway.

'It's the sea air,' he said, by way of explanation. 'It tends to evaporate coffee.'

'I've noticed that too,' Stig put in. He too had adopted an ingenuous expression.

Gilan snorted. 'Well, there's plenty in Socorro,' he said. 'We can restock there. Why are you out in the bay?'

They told him of the attack that morning, and how Kloof had given the alarm just in time. Gilan looked at the big dog, who was lying in the bow, happily destroying someone's boot. He made sure it wasn't one of his before he commented.

'She's a handy beast to have around.'

'Very handy,' Edvin agreed. 'She saved my bacon when one of the raiders got behind me. Made a right mess of him, too,' he added, with a satisfied smile.

Gilan gestured towards the line of graves. 'Who buried the dead raiders?'

'We did,' Thorn said. 'Their friends didn't seem inclined to and we thought it was better to bury them than leave them lying around in this heat.'

Gilan nodded his agreement. Then he and Lydia described events in Socorro. Hal frowned as he heard the news that they couldn't spot *Nightwolf* in the harbour.

'I'll need to know where she is before we sail in,' he said. 'Don't want to end up mooring alongside her.'

Gilan shrugged. 'Sorry. The harbour is pretty crowded, and neither of us is very good at telling one ship from another. By the way, you've done a great job disguising *Heron*. We couldn't recognise her when we came back.'

'Unfortunately, the first of those statements tends to negate the value of the second,' Hal said. He chewed his lip thoughtfully. 'I'll need to go and look for myself tomorrow,' he said finally.

Gilan nodded. He had expected as much. 'I'll come with you,' he offered.

Lydia looked up from her coffee. 'Do you want me along too?'

Hal shook his head. 'You've pushed your luck enough,' he said. 'Gilan and I will go. The fewer of us, the better.' He looked back to the Ranger. 'You say there's a spot overlooking the city where I can see the harbour?'

'That's right,' Gilan told him. 'With any luck, we won't even need to go into the city itself.'

But luck wasn't with them. The following morning, they stood on the rocky outcrop overlooking the harbour while Hal peered closely at the ships anchored and moored there. He searched one section of the harbour at a time, using his cupped hands to screen out the surrounding areas, searching for that dark blue hull.

But to no avail. He breathed out heavily, dropping his hands to his sides.

'Can't see her,' he said. Then he pointed to a section of the harbour obscured by a group of taller buildings set close to the waterfront — warehouses, he assumed.

'But those buildings are blocking my view. We'll have to get closer — or higher.'

He indicated one of the tall towers that Lydia had noticed the day before.

'Should be able to see from there,' he said. 'What is it — some kind of lighthouse?'

'It's a prayer tower — a minaret,' Gilan explained. 'The Socorrans worship a trio of gods — Hahmet, Jahmet and Kaif.'

'Not Kahmet?' Hal asked.

Gilan gave him a withering look. 'Hahmet is the god of war, Jahmet is the god of love and Kaif is the god of good harvests, fair weather, business success and family matters.'

'Kaif's got a pretty full plate, hasn't he?' Hal observed. 'Hardly seems fair.'

'I guess they thought war and love would keep the other two busy. In any event, the prayer callers lead prayers to one of the three, three times a day. Hahmet at the sixth hour, Jahmet at midday and Kaif at the sixth hour in the evening. They climb up inside the tower to the balcony you can see at the top and call the prayers from there.'

'Apart from that, are the towers occupied?' Hal asked.

Gilan shook his head. 'There's no other use for them. They're so narrow you couldn't use them as living space. Basically, they're an enclosed spiral staircase.'

'So it's the tenth hour now. I figure we've got two hours before the midday prayer session begins?' Hal said.

'Plenty of time,' Gilan agreed, and they began to make their way down the slope to the city. Gilan decided to enter by a different gate from the one he had chosen the day before. Both of them were dressed in the long white robes and *kheffiyehs* that he and Lydia had purchased and they entered without incident — choosing to follow a family group with baskets and nets of produce to sell, who occupied the gate guards as they calculated how big a bribe they could levy. Hal simply held up a gold five-dirum piece and the guards waved them through.

They threaded their way through the narrow, flag-stoned streets to the prayer tower. The surrounding square was virtually deserted. One elderly beggar was dozing in the sunshine, his back leaning against a wall. Other than that, a few people passed by, none of them paying attention to the two white-robed figures.

There was no door at the base of the prayer tower — just an open arch-topped doorway. Inside, they could see the first few risers of a metal grid staircase winding round the interior walls.

'Trusting folk,' Hal observed.

'Why not?' Gilan replied. 'There's nothing here to steal.'

Gilan and Hal glanced both ways up and down the street and, picking a moment when nobody was looking in their direction, they plunged into the dim coolness at the bottom of the tower.

The metal stairs rang and vibrated under their feet as they made their way upwards, winding round and round in the darkness. There was no handrail on the inside of the stairs, so Hal and Gilan kept their right hands brushing against the outer wall of the tower.

The stairs seemed endless and the darkness became blacker the higher they climbed from the entryway. Then, as they approached the top of the stairs, the light began to grow again until they eventually emerged onto the narrow balcony with its ornate carved railing, at the very top.

They took a few seconds to catch their breath. They were both fit and in excellent condition, but it had been a long climb. Then Hal stared out over the city, spread out below them.

'Spectacular!' he said. They could see the massive gold market roof off to the south, and beyond that, a wooden amphitheatre that was the site of the slave market. The houses, shops, manufactories and other buildings sprawled far below them. People moved on the busy streets, looking for all the world like small insects scurrying back and forth.

And finally, to the south-west was an unrestricted view of the harbour and the ships moored there. Hal turned his attention to the section he had been unable to see from the hill outside the city. He scanned it for some time, working slowly over each section, then gave a satisfied grunt.

'There she is,' he said quietly.

Nightwolf was moored alongside a wharf on the south-east, or inland, side of the harbour. The long, lean hull stood out among the smaller, wide-beamed trading vessels that surrounded her. He studied the layout of the harbour, noting that there were plenty of unoccupied berths in the northern arm of the bay, where the harbour narrowed and a river fed into it. Glancing from *Nightwolf* to the less occupied reach of water, he satisfied himself that a mooring there would be hidden from the wolfship's view. He'd simply have to bribe the harbour master to make sure of securing a berth in that northern arm.

'One small problem,' he muttered to himself. 'We'll have to sail out past her when we leave.'

He pondered that problem. He planned to re-rig *Heron* with her normal sails and yardarms once they were in the harbour. They'd need every ounce of speed they could get out of her when they made their escape. The city would be alerted and undoubtedly any ship trying to leave harbour would arouse suspicion. And, even with *Heron*'s normal rig, *Nightwolf* was probably the only ship in harbour that would be able to match her speed.

'We have another small problem,' Gilan said quietly. 'Someone is coming up the stairs.'

CHAPTER THIRTY-THREE

They could hear footsteps shaking the metal stairs, far below them. Hal glanced around desperately, looking for some way to escape. If they went down the stairs, they would run into the person who was coming up.

Of course, they could wait by the doorway that led to the balcony and overpower whoever it was — so long as it was only one person. He listened again and could hear only one set of footsteps labouring upwards — growing slower the further they came.

He was loath to do this, however, as he didn't want to attract any attention, or raise any sort of alarm in the town. It was more than possible that someone had seen them enter the tower. If the prayer leader were found unconscious, the word might go out that two foreigners in long robes had been seen here. That could lead to a hue and cry and might alert Tursgud to the fact that he had been followed.

He looked at the Ranger and saw that he was obviously

thinking along the same lines, looking for a way to escape.

Except there was none.

'Maybe we can hide round the far side of the balcony?' Hal suggested.

But Gilan shook his head. 'They move around the balconies, calling the prayers to all points of the compass. We could try moving around ahead of him but the balcony is too small and the tower too narrow. He'd spot us for sure.'

'What's he doing here anyway?' Hal demanded angrily. 'You said he didn't lead any prayers until midday.'

Gilan shrugged apologetically. 'I may have got the times a little wrong,' he admitted.

Hal glared at him. 'Well, this is one heck of a time to find that out!' he fumed. 'What are we going to do?'

In reply, Gilan gestured upwards. 'The roof,' he said. 'We'll climb up there. Chances are he'll never look up.'

The roof was a steep conical affair, covered in smooth, flat tiles. It projected out a little further than the balcony, providing vestigial shade to the prayer caller – although close to midday as it was, any shadow it cast was virtually nonexistent. The tiles were covered in the dust and dirt of many years in the desert air. They looked slippery, Hal thought. He didn't like that.

But Gilan had already climbed onto the balcony. Reaching out and a little backwards, he seized the edge of the tiled roof and heaved himself up. For a moment, his legs dangled over empty space as he got a firm hold. Then he clambered onto the roof, one hand grasping the pointed spike that surmounted it.

'Come on!' he hissed urgently. The footsteps were closer now. Closer, but even slower.

Hal hesitated. He was used to swarming up and down the masts of ships without a second's thought. But a mast was nowhere near as high as this. He glanced over the balcony rail and his head swam.

'Don't look down!' Gilan warned him, a second too late.

'You could have mentioned that earlier,' Hal said through gritted teeth.

The footsteps on the stairs were growing ominously closer. He stepped one leg up onto the balustrade, leaning in to support himself with his hands on the tower wall. Then he stepped the other leg up as well, half turning so that he was facing the tower.

He gripped the edge of the roof. A small gutter ran round the circumference. It provided a handhold, but it was frighteningly small. He hesitated. To gain the roof, he'd have to swing himself up and out over the yawning drop below him.

'Hurry it up! I've got a friend in Araluen who'd be up here in seconds,' Gilan said in a loud whisper. He seemed to think that would encourage Hal to move faster.

'Maybe you should have brought him,' Hal snarled. Then, taking a deep breath, he heaved himself up and over the edge of the roof, his hands scrabbling for purchase on the smooth, dust-covered tiles. He hung in the balance for a second or two, then Gilan seized him by the scruff of his neck and hauled him up.

His legs were still dangling over the edge of the roof when they heard the prayer leader arrive on the balcony — fortunately a little way around the tower from where they were. Hal drew them up quickly and half crouched, half lay on the steeply sloped tiles. He could feel his hands and body slipping, ever so slowly. Gilan strengthened his grip on Hal and stopped him from sliding further. They crouched on the roof, their faces only centimetres apart.

Below them, Hal could see the back of a turban-clad head as the prayer leader moved to begin his call. His voice rang out with amazing power, ululating and wavering in a strange singsong chant. In the first few words, Hal caught the name 'Kaif'. Obviously, these prayers were for the god of harvests, family life, business success and two or three other categories that he couldn't recall at the moment.

'What if he looks up?' he whispered.

'He won't,' Gilan said definitively. When Hal looked at him, he shrugged — as well as he could in their current position.

'Who climbs all this way and then looks up?' Gilan whispered. Then he added, 'Now shut up before he hears you.'

There was little chance of that happening. The prayer caller's deep baritone voice rang out over the city, booming out his requests for a happy family, a good harvest and a profitable year. Or at least, Hal supposed that was what he was praying for. The prayers, naturally, were in the Arridan language.

He felt himself slipping again and pressed his flattened hands as hard as he could against the dusty, slick tiles. There was little resistance there. Gilan, with his grip on the spire giving him an anchor, heaved him back up a few centimetres. But he was in a bad position, with little leverage.

The caller stopped and Hal breathed a sigh of relief.

He's finished, he thought, and none too soon. Maybe he'll go down now.

But to his horror, he heard an echoing prayer ringing out from the next tower in line. And then the next after that. Once all five had finished, the caller below them began another prayer, his rich voice booming and echoing over the city.

'Does he have to cover off all his categories?' Hal asked desperately.

Gilan nodded, biting his lip with the effort of holding Hal steady. 'Probably,' he replied.

Fortunately, this prayer was shorter. But they still had to wait until it was repeated from the other five towers, the voices growing progressively fainter as the distance increased with each one.

The caller moved to the other side of the tower and began his next chant. He was out of their sight now and Hal took advantage of the fact, and the noise that the caller was making, to place his feet further apart, pressing hard against the tiles of the roof to get better purchase. For a moment, as he moved, he began to slide again and his heart shot into his mouth.

At this point in proceedings, he realised, if he tumbled back down onto the balcony and overpowered the prayer caller, people would immediately sense that something was wrong. The prayer sequence would be broken and the callers in the other five towers would be waiting for their tower to continue the prayer. It wouldn't take long for someone to come and investigate.

Perspiration sprang out on his forehead. And, worse still, on his hands.

'Hold on!' Gilan hissed.

'Try saying something useful!' Hal snapped back at him. He removed one hand from its tenuous grip on the tiles, wiped it desperately on his robe, then pressed it flat against the tiles once more. He repeated the gesture with his other hand.

Thorn would have fun up here, he thought, and resisted a hysterical urge to giggle.

The prayer rang out across the city as the other towers repeated it. Then their caller was chanting once more. As he came to the end of this chant, Hal was sure he detected a note of finality in the man's voice.

Oh please, just finish it and go, he pleaded silently. His right leg was beginning to cramp with the effort of holding his weight against the inexorable force of gravity pulling him towards the edge of the roof.

Again, the other towers repeated the prayer. Then the man appeared on the balcony below them again, close to the doorway. He threw back his head and called something that sounded like:

Haiyaaahali!

This had a definite note of finality to it. And the other towers repeated it in order, the series of *Haiyaaahalis!* echoing across the sprawling buildings below.

Hal watched the top of the turbaned head turn towards the doorway leading to the stairs, then disappear from sight. He groaned with relief as he heard the man's footsteps receding down the metal stairway. Then he allowed himself to slide over the edge of the roof, swinging his legs back in to the balcony and letting go.

He misjudged slightly, catching his ribs on the balcony

edge as he tumbled down, then landing heavily on one knee. But those two pains were nothing to the agony in his thigh as the cramp suddenly knotted and took hold of the large muscle there.

He rolled onto his back, his knee raised, grasping the tightened muscle and groaning. Gilan dropped lightly down and knelt beside him.

'Are you all right?' he asked.

Hal glared at him through the agony of the cramp. Why do people ask that when you're lying on your back groaning, Hal wondered. Instead, he simply shook his head and said through gritted teeth, 'Cramp.'

He experimented desperately, trying to find a position to ease the knots in his thigh. But, as always happens with a cramp, there was no way he could move his leg without exacerbating the problem. He kneaded his fingers into the tightened muscle, trying to loosen it. For a moment, it eased, then constricted again, worse than before.

'Aaaaaah!' he cried.

Gilan knelt by him, unable to help, watching anxiously.

Hal clenched his fist and pounded it repeatedly into the offending, tight-knotted muscle. I'll have the mother of all bruises there tomorrow, he thought. But the action loosened the taut muscle a little. He put a hand up to Gilan.

'Help me up,' he gasped. Gilan drew him to his feet. Or rather, to his foot, as he stood on his left leg, unwilling to put weight on his right. He bent over, breathing heavily.

Gilan looked at him apologetically. 'Sorry about that,' he said. 'I really thought the prayer call wasn't until midday. And I thought it would be for one of the other gods — not Kaif. The prayers to them are a lot shorter. They have less to do, after all.'

Hal glared at him, busily kneading his thigh muscle and wincing with the pain that caused.

'In future, try to get your times and your gods right,' he said.

Gilan looked suitably chastened. He gestured to Hal's leg. 'Can you put weight on it?'

Hal tried, then shook his head as he felt the movement of his leg about to trigger another savage cramp.

'Not yet,' he said. 'Give me a minute.'

Gilan nodded sympathetically. 'Take your time,' he said. 'Remember, you've got to make it back down those stairs.'

Hal glared at him through pain-wracked eyes.

'Thank you so much for reminding me of that,' he said.

CHAPTER THIRTY-FOUR

There was a fresh, steady breeze blowing out of the north-west the following morning. The crew rowed *Heron* out of the narrow inlet where they'd been anchored, then hoisted the new mast.

Ulf and Wulf wrinkled their noses in distaste as they sheeted the square sail home. By now, they were used to the smooth, powerful curve of their usual rig, reminiscent of a bird's wing. The square sail, like all sails of its kind, tended to surge and flap in the breeze. It wasn't possible to sheet it home as firmly as their triangular sail. It billowed and relaxed alternately, causing the ship to move forward in a series of surging, lurching swoops.

'How does she handle?' Stig asked, standing beside Hal and watching his friend's lips move in a silent curse at yet another lurch.

'Like a log,' Hal said bitterly. He'd forgotten how clumsy a square sail could be.

The square sail notwithstanding, they made good time

down the coast. In under two hours, they were off the entrance to Socorro harbour. The pungent smell of smoke that Lydia had commented on two days previously mixed with dust and spices and a slight taint of decaying matter to overlay the fresh sea air.

'Furl the sail,' Hal ordered. 'We'll row in.'

He wasn't about to negotiate the harbour entrance under sail. It was a narrow channel with shoals and mudflats on either side, and a sharp, almost ninety-degree turn to starboard halfway along its length, to prevent raiders dashing into the harbour and seizing any of the ships moored there.

'Leave the yardarm up,' he called, seeing that the crew were preparing to lower it and stow the sail properly.

'Just furl the sail on the yard and leave it in place,' he said. 'I want us to continue to look like a square-rigger, even if we're rowing.'

The normal six rowers took their places on the benches and began to stroke smoothly, sending the slim ship speeding across the long, lazy swell towards the harbour entrance. There was none of their previous surging, stop-and-go movement now. The oar strokes were steady and powerful and the hull was graceful and well shaped, cutting through the water easily.

The fort on the southern headland, which had appeared squat and stocky when viewed from the hill above the town, took on a different aspect from sea level. It towered over them as they entered the harbour mouth, dominating the narrow entry channel. Its walls were formed from massive sandstone blocks that glowed with the colour of honey in the sun. A yellow flag, emblazoned with a red lightning shape, flapped lazily from its battlements. Hal could see helmeted heads lining the ramparts, and could make out the pale ovals of faces turned towards them. No ship would enter this harbour without undergoing a thorough inspection, he thought.

He noticed the angular forms of several catapults on the battlements — clumsy throwing machines that could hurl large boulders over a long distance. He guessed that their range was at least equal to the distance between the two promontories.

No ship could leave harbour, either, he realised, without risking a rain of jagged rocks plunging down on it from those catapults. In a few days, they might be facing such a threat.

Thorn, standing by him, seemed to share the same idea. 'They're not terribly accurate,' he said, nodding towards the crane-like arms of the catapults. 'But if they let go in a salvo, things could be interesting.'

Hal shrugged. He was confident in *Heron*'s agility and speed of manoeuvre. Avoiding the clumsy machines, slow to shoot and inaccurate, would be relatively simple.

'It'd take a lucky shot to hit us,' he said.

Thorn looked at him, head tilted to one side, for some seconds. 'Sometimes people get lucky,' he replied.

'Nothing we can do about that,' Hal told him.

Thorn nodded fatalistically. 'True enough.'

They had slid past the fort now and the channel took a sharp turn to the right. Hal steered through the bend and the harbour opened up beyond it.

To the south there was a forest of masts, all bobbing and rocking on the remnants of the swell that forced its way through the narrow channel. He was relieved to see that the northern arm of the harbour was still relatively unoccupied.

Lydia was in the bow, keeping a lookout. She turned now and called to him, pointing to starboard.

'There's the harbour master's wharf.'

He followed the line of her pointing arm and saw the universal sign for the harbour master's wharf — the symbol of the local currency — indicating that this was where visiting ships paid harbour and mooring fees. And bribes, he added cynically. In this case, it was an ornate letter *D*, signifying dirum, with two slanting bars through it.

He steered the *Heron* towards it. There were two men on the wharf, relaxing in the shade of a canvas awning. They rose lethargically and moved to the wharf's edge as *Heron* came alongside. Thorn, who had moved to the bow, tossed them a mooring rope.

Once the ship was secure, and wicker fenders had been hung over the side to protect the hull from the rough timbers, Hal and Thorn stepped up onto the wharf.

Gilan raised an eyebrow in question. Did they want him along?

Hal shook his head curtly. As a young skirl, he was used to harbour officials trying to browbeat him and take advantage of his apparent lack of experience. Thorn's weathered face and grey beard more than compensated, and they were accustomed to letting officials assume he was the captain of the ship. Adding the Ranger's presence might be overkill. And it might make the harbour master wonder whether they had something to hide.

The boards of the wharf vibrated under their boots as

they strode in step to the small wooden shack at the base of the wharf. The line handlers, their work done, returned to their relaxed positions in the shade.

They pushed open the door of the harbour master's shack and went in. For a few moments, they were virtually unsighted, until their eyes, used to the bright glare of the sun outside, became accustomed to the shady interior.

The shack was divided into two rooms, with the larger one serving as an antechamber to what Hal assumed was the harbour master's office. The door to that section was closed, and inscribed with Arridan script that he couldn't read.

The larger room was furnished with wooden cabinets along one wall, a rather threadbare carpet in the middle of the floor and a large table with one wooden chair behind it, where a clerk was seated. The surface of the table was chaotic. Sheaves of paper and rolled scrolls were scattered across it. Some were overflowing from file trays. Others simply littered the table top. A small work area had been cleared in the mess, in front of the seated clerk.

The clerk was dressed in the local fashion, in the same sort of flowing robe that they wore, and with a *kheffiyeh* on his head. His headdress was arranged in a different style from theirs, so that the sides were folded upright, away from his face, and gathered on top of his head. It seemed a more practical style for someone who was working indoors, hunched over papers.

The man's robe was grey rather than white, with several unidentifiable stains on it, most of them down the front, where food had spilled. His person showed the same lamentable lack of cleanliness. His skin was oily and his cheeks were fat — as was the rest of him. He filled the flowing grey robe quite substantially. He didn't rise as they entered but, glancing beneath the table, Hal could see that his feet dangled several centimetres above floor level.

'Yes?' he said. His tone was neutral, neither friendly nor dismissive. He looked at them with dark eyes, his gaze switching from one to the other. Then he took a sip from the glass of tea on his table. He grimaced and turned to a side door, bellowing angrily.

'Ullur!'

'Yes, *effendi*!' came the instant reply. The door opened to admit one of the line handlers from the wharf outside.

The clerk gestured to his tea. 'This is cold. Get me a fresh one!'

'At once, *effendi*!' Ullur replied. His words were submissive but his tone wasn't. He obviously had little respect for the other man's authority. As he reached for the tea glass, the clerk aimed a swipe at his head with the back of his hand. Ullur obviously was expecting such a move and swayed backwards, avoiding the blow. Then he seized the glass and scuttled out of the room.

The clerk, now obviously in a much worse mood than before, turned to them again, frowning.

'Yes?' he repeated. His tone was sharper this time.

'We want a mooring for ten days,' Hal told him.

The man's eyes, which had been trained on Thorn, switched to the younger man, a slightly surprised expression showing in them. Hal unhitched his money purse from his belt and began to loosen the drawstring that closed it. They would actually be out of here in less than a week if all went well, but it didn't hurt to confuse the issue.

'It's ten dirum a day,' the man told him, pulling a ledger towards him and dipping his quill in an inkwell.

'I was told five,' Hal said.

The eyes flicked from the ledger up to his face. 'You were told incorrectly,' the man said.

Hal shrugged slightly and began to re-tie the fastenings of his purse.

'But there is a weekly rate,' the man said. 'Eight dirum a day.'

'We're staying more than a week,' Hal pointed out. 'Six would be fair.'

The clerk's face showed what might almost have been taken for mild respect. 'I'm not in the fair business. Seven.'

'Seven it is,' Hal agreed and reopened the purse, extracting a fifty and a twenty and placing them before the man. The man's hand swept out like a pudgy cobra and the money disappeared into a drawer in front of him. He took up the pen once more, head bent over the ledger. Bureaucracy thrived on paper forms and reports and records, Hal thought.

'Ship's name?'

'Ariadne,' Hal told him. Ariadne was a goddess of the Hellenese, a race from the north-east corner of the Constant Sea. In consultation with Gilan, he had decided that the Herons' fair complexions would be suited to that race, and this way, there was no likelihood that Tursgud would be alerted to the arrival of a shipful of his countrymen.

The pen scratched as the man wrote laboriously, flecks of ink spattering from its frayed point onto the ledger page. 'Hellenese, are you?'

He didn't seem too interested one way or the other, so Hal declined to answer.

The man finished writing and closed the ledger with a slam, pushing it to one side. That'll have smeared the ink, Hal thought. The clerk slid open a drawer in the table and produced a larger sheet, scanning it swiftly. Viewing it upside down, Hal could see it was a chart of the harbour, with berths and moorings marked and numbered. He glanced at Thorn, who had another purse ready in the side pocket of his vest. It contained a hundred dirum, in case they needed to bribe the man to assign them their preferred position for a mooring. But Thorn relaxed as he saw the man jab a stubby finger at the north-west arm of the harbour.

'Mooring forty-three, north-west,' he said, shoving the map towards them and turning it so they could study it more easily. 'Numbers are on the jetties,' he added.

Hal nodded. That was standard practice. He slid a further ten dirum across the table. 'For your kind assist-ance,' he said. That was standard practice too.

The man grunted. This time, the money wasn't swept into a drawer, but disappeared inside his grey robe.

As they turned to go, the man yelled towards the side door once more.

'Ullur, you lazy oaf! Where's my tea?'

Hal and Thorn exchanged a glance. They had both seen the surly expression on Ullur's face and an unspoken agreement passed between them. If they were the clerk, they wouldn't be drinking anything that Ullur prepared.

They cast off and rowed up harbour, finding their mooring in a relatively uncrowded inlet. As they stowed the yardarm and sail properly, Edvin set up his stove and began preparing a meal, using the last of Gilan's coffee to make a final pot.

'I'll buy more ashore,' he reassured the Ranger.

Gilan raised his eyebrows at the somewhat cavalier treatment of his coffee beans. Then he shrugged mentally. He was eating their provisions, he thought, and Edvin's cooking was good. Sharing his coffee was a small price to pay.

Particularly when he knew they would be able to buy much better coffee ashore in Socorro. The Arridans, after all, had introduced coffee drinking to the rest of the world.

The crew lounged on the deck, relaxing after their meal. Only Hal seemed preoccupied. He stood and paced back and forth, deep in thought.

'Something on your mind?' Gilan asked him.

'I'm still trying to work out a way to get into the slave market. We can't plan a rescue if we don't know what we're facing.'

'Buyers are allowed in the day before the sale begins,' Lydia told him.

He nodded distractedly. 'That's cutting it too fine. That means we'd have to do a reconnaissance, then plan the rescue, all within a few hours.'

'Well, only sellers are allowed in before the sale,' Gilan pointed out.

Hal's mouth set in a tight line as he tried to find a way around the problem.

Thorn's face lit up with a beatific smile.

'Why don't we sell Ingvar?' he suggested.

CHAPTER THIRTY-FIVE

The reaction from the crew was mixed. The majority looked shocked. Ulf and Wulf were obviously amused by the idea of having their nemesis sold off to the highest bidder. Jesper fingered his chin thoughtfully, trying to assess how much they might get for the massively built boy. Lydia was outraged.

'Sell Ingvar?' she said, her voice rising into a higher register than normal. 'You really are too much, old man! How could you suggest such a thing?'

Ingvar's reaction was the most interesting. He nodded thoughtfully.

'You know, that's not a bad idea,' he said.

Lydia rounded on him furiously. 'Not a bad idea? It's a terrible idea! Have you taken leave of your senses?'

Ingvar shook his head, grinning at her. 'Not that I'm aware of.' He switched his gaze to Thorn. 'I assume you don't mean to leave me to the tender mercies of whoever buys me?'

Thorn pushed his bottom lip out and tilted his head to one side.

'Not necessarily,' he said. 'Depends on how much we get for you.' Ingvar regarded him steadily for a few seconds and he added, 'Actually, I thought we'd rescue you along with the others.'

'No need to take it as far as that,' Hal said, catching on to the idea. 'We can simply take Ingvar along to the market, pretending we want to sell him. That way, we can get a look at what we're up against, how many guards there are, what sort of locks are on the doors . . .' He glanced at Jesper as he said this.

The former thief nodded. Unconsciously, his hand dropped to touch the canvas wallet that he always kept handy. It contained his lock-picking tools.

'Then,' Hal continued, 'I could ask for a valuation on him.' He smiled at Ingvar. 'Should get plenty for a big hulk like you.'

Ingvar replied, without smiling, 'Although I do cost a lot to feed.'

Stig made a disclaiming gesture. 'Gruel is cheap,' he said. 'That's what they'll feed you. Gruel,' he repeated the word, savouring its sound.

Ingvar's top lip wrinkled at the thought. 'I'd want more than gruel,' he said. 'You should stipulate that, Hal.'

'I'll definitely do that, Ingvar. Point is, whatever they tell me you're worth, I'll get on my high horse and say it's not enough. Then we'll leave in a huff, taking you with us.'

'I've always wanted to travel in a huff,' Ingvar mused. 'It sounds very comfortable. I imagine they're well padded.'

'Lined with feathers, in fact,' Gilan put in.

'So who goes to the slave market with you?' Stig asked. Hal considered his answer.

'You and Thorn,' he said. 'I'll need some muscle to contain this big bruiser, even if he is chained up.' He slapped Ingvar affectionately on the shoulder. Ingvar raised one eyebrow in response. 'And Jesper, of course. He'll need to get a look at the locks they're using in there.'

Jesper nodded.

'I want to be in on it too!' protested Ulf.

'And if he's going, I need to be along to look after him,' Wulf added. 'He's a little slow on the uptake, after all.'

Ulf turned on him indignantly. 'Me? Slow on the uptake? Then why did our mam tell me, "Take care of your brother. He's not too bright?"'

'She was talking to me,' Wulf said placidly.

But Ulf was shaking his head. 'She was looking at me!'

Wulf spread his hands in a 'that proves it' sort of gesture. 'She's cross-eyed,' he said, which was the truth. Their mother did have a definite cast in one eye and it did tend to wander through a wide arc from time to time. Ulf tried to think of a reply, but Ingvar interrupted in a cautionary tone.

'Wouldn't care to be thrown overboard in this harbour,' he said. 'That water is very badly polluted.' Ulf's protest died unspoken on his lips. He and his brother resumed their seats on the rowing benches. They had risen to their feet in the passion of the moment. Ulf looked from Ingvar to Hal.

'Are you sure you couldn't sell him for real?' he asked plaintively.

'When do you want us to drag him along to the slave market?' Thorn asked.

'Tomorrow,' Hal said decisively. 'No point in wasting time — and we may find that we need to get special equipment ready for the rescue.'

'What sort of special equipment?' Stefan asked.

Hal shrugged. 'I have no idea,' he admitted. 'Maybe nothing. It'll depend on what we find at the market. In the meantime, there's something I want to attend to tonight. I'll need Stig, Thorn and Ingvar to help me with that.'

'Are you sure you need me?' Ingvar said, surprised. Stig and Thorn were the two best warriors in the crew. Usually, Ingvar's short-sightedness precluded him from being included in any fighting.

'Definitely,' Hal told him. 'They'll be along in case we run into any trouble. I need you for some heavy lifting.'

'When do we do this . . . whatever it is?' Stig asked. The prospect of action cheered him immensely.

'After midnight,' Hal replied. 'So get some sleep early, all of you.'

It was well after midnight when the four of them padded silently through the deserted streets of Socorro's waterfront district. A few blocks back from the water, the night was alive with the sound of carousing and arguing from dozens of taverns. But here, the buildings were mainly warehouses and storage sheds — busy during the day but deserted by night.

Here and there, a solitary lantern burned high on the wall of a building, casting a dim, uncertain light over the area.

Ships were moored alongside the wharf. Their halyards made a low rattling sound against the masts as the wind stirred them, and there was a constant slap of water against the hulls as they rose and fell gently.

For the most part, the ships were dark and silent, their crews either asleep or absent onshore. Occasionally, the four silently moving Skandians would see a night watchman leaning on the rail, staring over the side at the black harbour.

'Left here,' Hal whispered. He had scouted their route at sundown, when the light was uncertain and there was less chance of his being recognised in the event that he ran into Tursgud or one of his crew. They were in the south reach of the harbour, heading for the spot where *Nightwolf* was moored.

They followed, moving in single file, staying in the deep shadows left by the scattered lanterns. Ingvar stayed close behind Hal. In this dim light, he was at less of a disadvantage than normal. None of them could see clearly, and at least he was accustomed to that condition. He was burdened by an immense coil of heavy rope slung over his left shoulder.

It consisted of half of *Heron*'s anchor cable. Stig and Thorn carried the other half, in two pieces, between them. Hal was unburdened, aside from his own tool bag and two of the inflated bladders that the crew used for their football game.

Stefan had frowned when he saw his skirl inflating them. 'Planning on challenging Tursgud to a game?'

Hal had grinned. 'Something like that.'

He stopped now, in the shadow cast by a storage shed at the harbour's edge, holding up his hand for the others to do likewise. They moved around him and he pointed to a large wooden wharf twenty metres away.

'*Nightwolf*'s moored over there,' he told them. They all craned around the edge of the shed to look at her. Sure enough, the long wolfship was moored on the far side of the wharf. Her yardarm was hoisted, and the sail was furled loosely on it. Obviously, Tursgud liked to be ready to make a fast getaway if necessary.

'I'm going to go into the water on this side, and swim under the wharf to reach her,' he told them. 'You get busy splicing the anchor cable. I'll come back this side when I need it.'

Stig nodded his understanding. But so far, Hal hadn't explained exactly what he was planning to do, or why.

'What's the plan?' he asked.

'Insurance,' Hal told him. 'When we leave, the alarm's sure to go up and people will come after us. The only ship I'm concerned with is *Nightwolf*. None of the local ships will have the speed to catch us. But she might, if the wind's in the right direction. So I plan to slow her down.'

While he had been speaking, he had opened his tool bag and taken out a hand auger and a large bit.

'I'm going to bore a hole in her sternpost, just below the waterline, and pass the anchor cable through it. Then I'll fasten the other end to one of the wharf pilings. That way, if they take off after us, they'll get a very nasty surprise by the time they've gone one hundred metres.'

'What if the rope floats up in the meantime and they

see it?' Thorn said, frowning. Sometimes, Hal was known to forget small details like that.

'There's plenty of scrap pieces of metal on the wharf here. Tie some of them to the line before you pass it down to me. That'll keep the rope below the surface and out of sight.'

Thorn grinned approvingly. Hal did seem to have thought of everything this time. One thing puzzled him, however.

'What are you going to do with those bladders?' he asked.

'They're to keep me afloat while I'm boring the hole,' Hal told him. 'After all, I'll need to use two hands.'

As he spoke, he was tying a short length of cord between the two bladders. Then he stripped down to his underwear and placed the rope across his chest and under his armpits, so the bladders were held at shoulder height behind his back.

Thorn studied the arrangement and could see how, once in the water, the bladders would float up, pulling the cord tight under his arms and across his chest. He whistled softly.

'Good thinking,' he said. He never failed to be impressed by Hal's ingenuity.

But Stig had a problem with the plan. 'You're really going to swim in this water?' he asked, pointing down to the black, glossy surface of the harbour.

Hal's teeth showed in a quick grin. 'I'm swimming in it, not drinking it,' he said. 'Now let's go.'

And, bending double, he led the way across the darkened wharf to the edge.

The task was completed in a little over two hours.

The thick cable, weighed down by several iron shackles and chain links, was securely fastened to *Nightwolf*'s sternpost, just below the waterline. The other end passed round one of the thick wharf pilings, also below the surface. Hal had fastened the rope to a point well underneath the stern of the ship, so that the likelihood of anyone looking overboard and seeing it was low.

'What if they decide to move the ship before we leave?' Stig asked, as Hal dried himself off and re-donned his clothing.

Hal shrugged. 'It won't really matter. They'll damage her and that's the important thing. Either way, they won't be able to follow us when we sail out.'

The four friends ghosted back through the now deserted streets of the city to the northern arm of the harbour. As they stepped aboard *Heron*, seven anxious pairs of eyes focused on them.

'Any problems?' Gilan asked.

'All as smooth as silk,' Hal said. '*Nightwolf* is now securely tethered to her wharf, although her crew are completely unaware of the fact.'

'Let's hope she tries to leave in a hurry,' Stefan said. 'What do you think is likely to happen when she does get under way, Hal?'

Hal thought about his answer for a few moments. 'Well, the least that will happen is that she'll do her sternpost some damage — maybe pull it out of alignment.

Or even dislodge the backstay and weaken the mast. And since all the planks are attached to the sternpost, she might spring a few of them.'

'I hope we're around to see it,' Stefan replied, smiling at the thought of the disaster waiting for Tursgud and his crew.

'I hope we're a long way down harbour from her if it does happen,' Hal said. He yawned. 'Let's get some sleep. We've got a big day tomorrow. We have to sell Ingvar.'

'If only that were true,' muttered Wulf.

CHAPTER THIRTY-SIX

They dressed Ingvar in a torn, sleeveless shirt and tattered knee-length shorts. Thorn wound a length of grubby linen around Ingvar's head, like a makeshift turban, leaving one end hanging down over his shoulder. He stood back and surveyed his work.

'Perfect,' he said. 'You look just like a slave!'

Ingvar looked sidelong at the strip of cloth hanging beside his face. 'Why would a slave have a dirty piece of linen tied round his head?'

Thorn shrugged. 'No idea. But it does make you look the part. It gives you a sort of . . . melancholy look.'

'I'll give you a melancholy look when we get back,' Ingvar threatened jokingly.

They tied Ingvar's hands securely in front of him, then fastened a length of old chain around his neck. Jesper had bought the chain and several old padlocks earlier in the bazaar.

Ulf and Wulf regarded their giant shipmate quizzically.

'He does look a little like a trained bear,' Ulf said and Wulf nodded. For once, they were reasonably sure that Ingvar, burdened as he was, couldn't throw either of them overboard.

'And you two look like a pair of chattering monkeys,' Lydia said acidly. She liked Ingvar and she didn't enjoy seeing him being teased by the twins.

They both looked suitably taken aback by her comment. They were never entirely sure about Lydia. She didn't seem to have a strong sense of humour and her hand was always hovering by the long dirk she wore at her side. The long, *sharp* dirk she wore at her side.

Ingvar smiled tolerantly. 'It's all right, Lydia. When I get back I'll knock their heads together.'

She patted his arm. 'I'll look forward to that,' she told him. Even though she knew it was play acting, the sight of Ingvar trussed and chained and ready to be sold as a slave upset her. The sooner this was all over, the better, she thought. She looked up, surprised, as Hal gave voice to the thought that had just run through her mind.

'Sooner we get this done, the better,' he said. 'Jesper, take the lead.'

The plan was for Jesper to precede them through the streets of Socorro by thirty or forty metres. He could slip unobtrusively through the crowds, while they would obviously draw attention. If Jesper caught sight of Tursgud or any of his crew, he would hurry back and warn them. After all, the massive Ingvar and the shaggy, bearded, one-armed Thorn were a distinctive pair and Hal didn't wish the renegade skirl to have any warning of their presence in the city.

'Are you sure you'll recognise Tursgud's men if you see them?' Hal asked.

Jesper nodded confidently. 'I've seen them often enough, lounging around the tavern in Hallasholm as if they own it,' he said. 'Besides, they all have a distinctive rat-like manner that's hard to miss.'

They set out, with Jesper scouting on ahead, Hal leading Ingvar by the chain around his neck and Stig and Thorn, fully armed and weapons ready, pacing either side of him, as if guarding him. Stig carried his battleaxe. Thorn elected not to wear his club-hand. Instead, he wore a small shield on his right hook and carried a sword slung on his right hip, ready to be drawn left-handed.

Hal was unarmed, save for his saxe knife, which actually meant that he was more than adequately armed.

They walked in a large arc to the east, giving a wide berth to the arm of the harbour where *Nightwolf* was moored. Hal reasoned that her crew would most likely contain their movements to the taverns and inns closer to the waterfront. There was no reason why they should venture further inland.

But still, you never could be sure, which was why Jesper preceded them. The streets were narrow and winding, crammed with people moving in both directions. The little procession drew curious glances from passers-by. Ingvar was enough to draw a second glance. He towered over most people in the street and his massive shoulders and arms were thick and hard with muscle. Seeing his size and the rope and chain bindings that contained him, most people drew aside as the group passed them.

They emerged from one of the narrow streets into an

open plaza. Ahead of them, and on the opposite side, was the sprawling mass of the gold market. The high walls were built from blocks of sandstone. There was an entryway a few metres to their right. The gates were massive, made of blackwood, studded with iron bolts and reinforced with heavy strips of the same material.

Stig whistled quietly. 'Pretty impressive,' he said. 'Are they all like that?'

'According to Gilan, yes,' Hal said.

Jesper, who had waited for them at the beginning of the plaza, curled his lip at the sight of the lock on the gate.

'I'd have that open in twenty seconds,' he said disparagingly. The gate might look massive, but the lock was old-fashioned and, in Jesper's view, barely more efficient than a loop of rope over a post. A stream of people moved into the market, hurrying and jostling one another as they went.

'When does it close?' Thorn asked.

Hal looked round at him. 'According to Gilan, it doesn't. They trade twenty-four hours a day. Of course, things slow down a little late at night.' He signalled for Jesper to take the lead once more, heading left.

They passed the corner and headed around the eastern side of the market. Stig craned his head as he turned back to look the way they had come, then at the distance remaining before them.

'This place is huge!' he said.

Thorn nodded. 'Gilan said it's like a town within a town.' Earlier, Gilan had apprised them of this plan to stage a diversion by lighting a fire in the gold market.

Eventually, they reached the end of the eastern wall

and turned the corner. The slave market stood before them, fifty metres away.

It was a huge wooden amphitheatre, a circle of high timber walls, unpainted and faded to grey by the desert sun and wind.

The walls were four metres high and, from where the Skandians stood, offered no way of entry. They were featureless and unwelcoming, stretching away in a curve on both sides and presenting a blank face to the world outside. It was a sobering sight, totally in keeping with the nature of the place.

For a moment, they stood uncertainly, baffled by the uncompromising nature of those grim, grey walls that seemed to offer no way of entering or leaving. Then Hal gathered his wits and pointed to the right.

'There must be a gate somewhere,' he said. 'Let's go.'

Following his lead, they began circumnavigating the massive circular structure. But as they did, they continued to be faced by blank walls until they began to half believe that there was no way in, that they would complete a full circle back to where they had begun without discovering a way into the slave market. Even Jesper was discouraged.

'How can I break in if I can't find a lock?' he muttered.

And then they came to the gateway.

It was built under a high timber entryway, consisting of a massive beam that was supported above an opening in the wall — an opening that was five metres wide and barred by double gates built in the same grey timber as the walls. Above the gates, the walls extended upwards for another two metres and there was obviously a walkway behind them. Hal could see half a dozen guards staring down at them, armoured in the customary chain mail and leather, and with conical spiked helmets incorporated in a turban-like headdress. One of them turned away and called off to the side, where a small enclosed structure was situated. A door opened in response to the call and an officer emerged. He was more expensively equipped than the guards on the rampart. His helmet was silver plated, as was the chain mail vest he wore. Both helmet and mail gleamed in the sun. Unlike the other guards, he didn't carry a spear, although Hal was sure that there would be a curved sword belted round his waist.

The guard who had summoned him pointed down to the small party waiting outside the gate. The officer leaned over the timber balustrade and shouted down to them.

'No entry until the eve of the sale!' he said. He sounded angry, as if this was a call that he made all too often to foreigners. 'Come back then. Sellers only until then!'

Hal glanced at Thorn, who cupped his hands and bellowed back, in a voice that was trained to carry above the roar of storm winds and waves.

'We're selling!' he shouted, jerking a thumb towards the tethered Ingvar. 'What do you think this is — a side of mutton?'

'Not very flattering, Thorn,' Ingvar muttered.

Thorn shrugged and grinned at him. 'We're not here to flatter you, just to sell you,' he said.

There was a quick consultation on the walls above them. The officer shouted down again.

'All right. Stand back while we open up. And you'll leave your weapons at the guardhouse inside.'

They heard feet descending a timber stairway inside the walls. Then, a few moments later, the massive gates began to creak open, a gap forming between them, then growing to twice the width of a man's shoulders. At that point, the gates stopped moving. Obviously, the guards weren't about to open up too wide, in case there were other men lurking somewhere to the sides, ready to rush in.

'Come on in!' shouted the officer. 'And no tricks or we'll skewer you!'

'Charming,' Thorn said in a low voice. Then he bowed and gestured for Hal and Ingvar to precede him through the gate and into whatever lay beyond.

CHAPTER THIRTY-SEVEN

What lay beyond was a vast, circular arena, with a floor of thick, grey sand.

In the centre was a raised platform — presumably where the slaves to be sold would be put on display. Wooden steps led up to it on either side. Around the arena were rows and rows of benches, rising in tiers. Hal counted quickly. There were eight rows of benches, rising steeply from the arena floor. This would be where the buyers and spectators sat, calling their bids to the auctioneer and his assistants on that central platform. At a quick guess, he estimated the benches would hold between one thousand and fifteen hundred customers.

On the far side, directly opposite the entrance they had just passed through, the rows of benches were interrupted by another massive opening. This one led to a recessed gate, level with the rear row of seats. The tiers of seats formed a slope-sided tunnel either side of the entry, with timber railing preventing those in the seats from falling into the gap.

Level with the back wall of the arena, there was another heavily fortified gate.

As they stepped onto the sand-covered floor of the arena, they were met by half a dozen guards, all armed with swords and spears and wearing leather and mail armour. They wore the now familiar turban/helmet combination. The guards formed a loose cordon around them, watching them warily, ready for any sign of aggression.

Hal held up his hands in a gesture of peace.

'Relax,' he told them. 'We're here to sell, not to fight.'

One of them, obviously the senior, gestured to the sand at his feet.

'Weapons,' he said. 'Drop your weapons.'

Hal turned to his companions. 'Do as he says,' he told them. He could see that neither Stig nor Jesper liked the idea of surrendering their weapons. Thorn appeared more philosophical about the whole thing.

'You'll get them back when you leave,' the guard told them. 'But no weapons are allowed in the slave quarters.'

That was reasonable enough, Hal thought. There were dull thuds as Stig's axe, then Jesper's and Thorn's swords, fell to the sand. One of the guards handed his spear to his neighbour and moved forward, stooping quickly to gather the weapons. He carried them to one side, and deposited them on a table.

'Knives too,' said the man in charge. All of the Skandians were wearing saxe knives. At his urging, they unbuckled them and handed the belts and sheathed weapons to the same guard. The saxes joined the other weapons on the table. Hal's waist felt unnaturally light without the reassuring weight of the knife nestled there.

Satisfied that they posed no threat, the guard in command beckoned them to follow, heading for the opposite gateway. They fell in behind him, Hal leading the way with Ingvar, then Jesper, Thorn and Stig in a tight knot. Jesper's eyes darted quickly about him, taking in the size of the gates and any other detail that might be important when they came to break in. So far, he could see nothing that would delay him more than a few seconds.

They trudged through the thick sand to the gateway. The guards kept pace with them, forming a screen around them. They stepped into the shade of the entry tunnel and the commander of their escort produced a ring of keys and proceeded to unlock the gate that faced them.

Jesper's lip twitched derisively as he looked at the key, and the massive lock it fitted.

The guard shoved one of the double gates open and gestured for them to enter. They trooped in, their escorts following them, and found themselves in a large, well-lit room.

It was bare of furniture, apart from a rectangular table set facing the entry. A man sat at the table, looking up at them as they entered. He was small and dapper, with olive skin and a thin black moustache. He was dressed in the usual long white robe but, instead of a *kheffiyeh*, he wore a green turban. His dark, quick-moving eyes assessed them, lingering for a moment on Ingvar's massive frame. He quickly categorised Stig and Thorn, marking them down as guards — muscle tasked with keeping the massive slave in line. Hal, he could see, was in charge. Jesper was another matter altogether. He frowned and pointed at him, addressing himself to Hal.

'Who is this?'

'My secretary,' Hal replied without hesitation. 'My assistant,' he added, when the man seemed puzzled. The dark eyes checked Jesper again and seemed satisfied with the answer. Probably, he thought cynically, the 'assistant' was the only one among them who could count or calculate.

'I'm Mahmel,' the man said, making no movement to rise or to shake hands with them. He wasn't introducing himself so much as identifying himself to them, and that required no ceremony. 'I'm the market co-ordinator. You're looking to sell this slave, I take it?'

Hal prevaricated. 'Well, I could be,' he said. 'It depends on the price I get. What's he worth?'

Mahmel looked at him with world-weary eyes. He wasn't about to start haggling.

'Where are you from?' he asked, changing tack. Hal wondered what that had to do with the price but he answered readily enough.

'We're Hellenese,' he said. 'You know our country?'

'Yes. I know it,' Mahmel said in a bored tone. 'And I know the people of Helleno love to haggle. You'll do it all day if you get the chance. But we don't do it here in this slave market. Your slave here —' he jerked a thumb at Ingvar '— is worth whatever the highest bidder is willing to pay for him. No more. No less.'

'That might not be acceptable to me,' Hal said, a trace of righteous indignation in his voice.

Mahmel shrugged. He made it an expressive, graceful movement.

'Then that will be a pity, because you will take what

is offered. That's the rule of this market. Once you bring a slave here for sale, you accept our terms and conditions. You can't beat around the bush and waste everyone's time with your Hellenese-style bargaining. He's here. He's for sale. You take what you get — less our commission.'

'Nobody told me that,' Hal began.

Mahmel raised a hand to stop him. 'Did you ask anyone?'

Hal hesitated. 'Well . . . no. But I —'

'Then that was your mistake,' the manager said, with a tone that said no further discussion was invited. 'If you bring him here to sell him, you automatically accept the rules and conditions of the market.'

'That's not fair! I —'

'You assumed that you could set your own rules? Well, you can't. He's here. He's in the auction in three days' time. And he'll stay here until then.'

Hal glanced desperately at Thorn and Stig. Thorn gave the slightest shrug of his shoulders. They couldn't really argue too strongly. They were unarmed and out-numbered. Mahmel had obviously done this before. Yet they hadn't considered the possibility that Ingvar might be held here and forbidden to leave.

Ingvar stepped forward, his hands joined in a pleading gesture towards Mahmel. The instant he moved, there was a multiple rasp of steel on leather and their escort all drew their swords. He stepped back a pace immediately, but spoke in a pitiful whine.

'Please, sir,' he said, 'may I talk to my master?'

Up until now, the discussion had been carried on in the common tongue. But now Ingvar spoke in Skandian.

Mahmel frowned, obviously not understanding. 'I don't speak Hellenese,' he snapped. Then he looked at Hal. 'Tell him to speak the universal tongue if he speaks to me. Better still, tell him not to speak to me.'

But before Hal could say anything, Ingvar turned to him and dropped to his knees, sobbing as he spoke. He had spoken Skandian to see if Mahmel could understand the language. Now, seeing that he obviously couldn't, Ingvar spoke urgently to Hal. His words, however, were completely at variance to the tone of submissive pleading that he adopted.

'This is a good thing, Hal. If I'm kept prisoner here, I can contact the Araluan captives and get them ready for the breakout.'

Hal glanced at him, working overtime to keep the look of admiration from his face. People all too often thought of Ingvar as slow, because of his size and his poor vision. But his mind was as sharp as a sword and he'd instantly seen the advantage that would come from having someone on the inside at the slave market.

'Good point, Ingvar. I hadn't thought of that,' he said, making his words sound harsh and commanding. He looked back at Mahmel. 'I've told him that if he doesn't obey you, you'll beat him with whips.'

Mahmel shrugged. 'Of course I will. Someone that size needs to be kept in line.'

'Exactly. And that raises another matter. If you're planning to keep him prisoner here . . .' He paused.

'And I am.'

'Then I want reassurance that you're capable of holding him. He's my property, he's a valuable slave and

I want to know that your arrangements here are secure. After all, as you point out, he's big and powerful and he could be a handful for your men.'

Mahmel considered the request. It was perfectly reasonable, he thought. After all, the young Hellenese had deemed it necessary to have two brawny armed men to control the slave. The request simply showed that he had a good head for business, and that was something Mahmel respected.

'That's logical,' he said. 'You can inspect our arrangements while we take him down to the holding pen.'

He clicked his fingers at the guard commander, who stepped forward, his hand out to take the chain from Hal. Hal passed him the chain and the guard started towards a door at the rear of the room.

Ingvar baulked. 'I'll see you in two days, Hal,' he said in Skandian, making his voice sound like a submissive whimper.

'Trust me, Ingvar. We won't leave you here,' Hal replied in the same language. Then, to Mahmel, he said: 'Right. Let's see how secure this prison is.' Sensing that Mahmel was about to order his companions to stay behind, he pre-empted the man and pointed to Stig and Thorn.

'You two stay here,' he said brusquely. 'Jesper, come with me.'

Mahmel had, in fact, been on the point of restricting access to Hal alone. But he decided to let the matter ride. The assistant was nowhere near as large or as muscular as the other two and seemed harmless enough.

'Very well,' he said. Then he indicated for Hal and

Jesper to follow the guards as they led Ingvar through to the slave pen.

They descended a flight of eight stone steps, then the stairway turned ninety degrees to the left and a heavy iron gate barred further progress. The senior guard handed Ingvar's chain to one of his followers and produced a large key ring from an inner pocket. There were only two keys on it and he used one of them to open the gate. Jesper watched, lynx-eyed. The key turned easily, evidence that the lock was in constant use. Jesper studied the pattern of the wards — the notches cut into the blade of the large key — as the guard withdrew it from the lock. It was a simple enough design and he suppressed a smile. A loop of rope over a post might take him longer to crack, if it was knotted tightly.

They trooped down the stairs and took another right-angle turn to the left. A wooden door, set in an arched opening and reinforced with brass strips, faced them. The area was dimly lit by two lanterns high in the wall beside them. The guard now produced the second key, a smaller one this time. He pounded on the timber door twice in quick succession, then once more after a pause. Then he inserted the key and unlocked the door. Again, the lock turned smoothly and they heard a slight click as it opened.

'Why knock if you have a key?' Hal asked.

Mahmel glanced round at him. 'There are eight guards on the other side of that door. If they hear it opening without that knock, they'll be ready to cut down anyone who enters.'

Hal nodded. 'Impressive. How often do you change the signal?'

'Every week,' Mahmel told him. 'We have six patterns and we rotate them at random.'

Hal pursed his lips thoughtfully. It was the second day of the week and they planned to let the slaves loose on the fifth day. He'd wager that the coded knock changed every week on the first day. That meant the knock they had just heard should still be valid when they broke in.

The guardroom was a large square, with flagstone walls and floor. Rush matting was laid over the floor to provide a modicum of comfort. The room was furnished with a table and eight comfortable-looking wooden chairs — all with curved backs and arms. There was an iron stove in the centre of the room, with a pipe chimney that went out through the ceiling. The grate glowed red with flames now. Hal guessed that it was kept burning constantly. In spite of the outside heat, the air in the room was damp and chill. Four bunks were ranged along a second wall and each was occupied by a guard. The other guards were grouped around the table, playing dice. The dice players wore their armour and their weapons were stacked close to hand. The four in the bunks were in various stages of undress. Hal studied them keenly, although he appeared to be uninterested in them. None of them were young. Three were grey haired and all of them appeared to be either overweight or in poor condition. They were guards, used to dominating unarmed, submissive prisoners, not fighting men, he assessed. One of them yawned. There were several lanterns in the room, and light also came in through a high skylight.

The men at the table looked up curiously as the group entered. Seeing Mahmel, one of them made to rise, calling the others to attention. But Mahmel waved them down again.

'Relax,' he told them. 'We're bringing in a new prisoner.'

There was another heavy wooden door on the wall to the right of the point where they had entered. This one, Jesper noted, was locked with a simple draw bolt. The guard commander drew the bolt and they followed him through into a small antechamber, where once more, they encountered an iron grille gate. This led into a huge, low-ceilinged room. As they approached it, there was a murmur of voices and a rustle of movement from within. Hal could make out the pale shape of faces peering at them through the gloom. This was the slave pen, he realised.

'How many have you got in here?' he asked.

'At the moment, seventy-three. Your man makes seventy-four. We can fit ninety at a pinch but we rarely get that many,' he said.

Hal looked doubtful. 'Seventy prisoners and you've only got eight guards?' he said. 'That hardly seems adequate to me.'

Mahmel smiled confidently. 'It's adequate. The prisoners are chained in strings of ten or twelve. They're manacled to the main chain by the wrist, so they find it hard to move. And the guards are armed, of course. Besides, there are also the guards from the gatehouse.' He indicated the man who was leading Ingvar. 'There are twenty of them. And there's a garrison building thirty metres from the main entrance, tasked with keeping order in the gold market. They're *dooryeh* — fifty fully armed and trained fighting men — not your normal prison guard. They can be in here within minutes if there's trouble.'

Hal nodded, maintaining an absent, careless look on his face. But his brain was racing as he added the figures. Seventy-eight guards, he thought. That was going to take some handling.

The guard commander turned to Hal now, fingering the padlock that fastened the heavy chain around Ingvar's neck.

'Got the key?' he asked. 'We won't need this any longer. I'll chain him with one of the strings inside.'

Hal glanced at Jesper, who produced the key. The guard unlocked the chain from Ingvar's neck and passed it to Jesper, then inserted his own key into the iron gate. It swung open easily, like the others, and he shoved Ingvar inside. Two of the other guards stood by him, swords drawn and ready for any trouble. But Ingvar submitted meekly. The commander led Ingvar to where a line of slaves were slouched on the damp flagstone floor of the slave pen. They were all manacled to a heavy chain that stretched between them. The commander found an unused manacle and snapped it onto Ingvar's right wrist. Jesper frowned. In the dim light, he couldn't make out the lock on the manacle. Then he shrugged. Most likely it would be as primitive as the other locks he had seen.

'Seen enough?' Mahmel asked.

Jesper started guiltily. Then he realised the question had been addressed to Hal and he calmed down.

Hal nodded. 'Certainly looks secure.'

Privately, he was thinking: Seventy or eighty guards only minutes away — we're going to need Gilan's diversion in the gold market.

CHAPTER THIRTY-EIGHT

Ingvar stooped under the low ceiling as the guards led him into the dim recesses of the dungeon. He cast furtive glances to either side as he was led past the rows of slaves.

Some of them looked up to study this new addition to their numbers. Others ignored his arrival. It seemed that their incarceration had dulled their interest in the goings on around them. A new slave had been added to their numbers. So what? His arrival wouldn't change the routine of the prison. They wouldn't receive any more or any less food. The term of their captivity wouldn't be lengthened or shortened. Consequently, they paid him no mind, staring straight ahead.

For his part, Ingvar's heart was hammering inside his ribs. He had no real idea what he was getting himself into. He'd appeared calm enough when he suggested to Hal that he should remain behind in the prison, and pointed out that he would have the opportunity to make contact with the Araluan slaves. But he had suggested it because he saw only one alternative. Had Hal and the others refused to leave him here, there would have been a fight. Mahmel struck him as a despot, who wouldn't listen to reasoned arguments against what he wished to be done.

And the Skandians were unarmed and outnumbered. There could have been only one outcome to such an uneven battle.

Better, he thought, to forestall any resistance and trust his friends to secure his release at a later date. But now, he wasn't sure that he'd acted wisely.

They'd committed a serious error of judgement by bringing him in chains to the slave market. Had they checked, as Mahmel pointed out, they could have learned that slaves delivered to the market were immediately imprisoned to await the sale day. But they had acted precipitately — he as much as the others — by presenting him for sale. Now he was imprisoned, with secure gates, locks, chains and guards between him and freedom. And he wasn't sure if the Herons would be able to set him free again. Much as he admired Hal's ingenuity, he was all too aware that sometimes the young skirl overlooked import-ant details in a situation. And this appeared to be one of those times.

Ingvar felt suddenly alone and vulnerable. For the past two years, he had been an integral part of the close-knit community that was the Heron Brotherband. The brotherband members watched out for one another, and provided help, advice and support to their brothers whenever needed. He had grown to depend on that support, and it had been in stark contrast to his early years, when his poor eyesight had made him an outcast who was left to his own devices, to blunder through as best he could.

Now, suddenly, he was on his own once more, and if the crew of the Heron couldn't release him when the time came, he faced a lifetime of slavery — and a lifetime of being alone. For all his size and power, Ingvar was little more than a boy, and the very real prospect of a life where he never saw his friends or his home again made tears of doubt and fear prickle his eyes.

Angrily, he shook his head to clear them.

That's all I need, he thought, to be seen crying for my mam.

His sudden movement caused the guards to draw back from him. One of them half raised the heavy club he was carrying, thinking that the new slave was about to rebel.

Ingvar brought his shackled hands up in front of him in a submissive gesture.

'Sorry,' he muttered. 'I had something in my eye.'

The guards relaxed. The one without the club jerked on the chain attached to his manacles, pulling his hands back below waist level once more.

'Just watch yourself,' he ordered gruffly. 'No sudden movements or Tarik will bust your brains for you.'

'Yes, sir,' Ingvar said meekly. His worried state of mind made it all the easier to act submissively. 'Sorry, sir.'

The guard called Tarik spotted a small gap between two of the slaves. He gestured with the club.

'You two. Make some room,' he ordered, and they began to shuffle apart. But a voice from further down the line of chained prisoners interrupted them.

'Tarik! Bring him here. I've got loads of room by me!'

The guard looked towards the voice. Almost as an afterthought, he made a gesture for the slaves to stop making room for Ingvar.

'That's you, is it, Bernardo?' he called. There was a note of distaste in his voice that Ingvar didn't like.

The voice out of the shadows replied. 'Yes. It's me. You know I like to make all the new arrivals welcome. Bring him here.'

The guards exchanged a glance and shrugged. They really didn't care one way or the other where Ingvar ended up and past experience told them that the prisoner called Bernardo could make trouble if he didn't get what he wanted.

'Come on, you,' said the guard holding Ingvar's chain. He tugged on it and dragged the big Skandian further into the dungeon, leading him towards a spot on the opposite wall.

Ingvar peered shortsightedly at his new companion. Bernardo was swarthy, with a mass of black hair and a bushy black beard. He was around thirty years of age, heavily built and well muscled. Ingvar estimated that they were about the same height and with the same breadth of shoulder. But where Ingvar had the classic Skandinavian physique — broad and burly — Bernardo had a more athletic appearance, like a boxer or a wrestler.

From his accent, appearance and name, Ingvar took him to be Iberian. The guards shoved Ingvar down onto the damp stone floor beside him. As the prisoner had claimed, there was plenty of space there, although Ingvar noticed that the neighbouring slaves were crammed closely together. It was apparent that Bernardo had forced them to make room.

The Iberian smiled widely as Ingvar settled awkwardly on the cold stone floor beside him, but the smile never reached his eyes. They were black and cruel as a hawk's.

'There, my friend. Make yourself comfortable. Bernardo is here to look after you.'

The guard who had been leading Ingvar now produced a metre-long piece of chain with a manacle at each end. One of these he quickly secured around Ingvar's left wrist. The other he attached to a longer, heavier chain stapled to the wall. Ingvar noted that there were up to a dozen other slaves attached to this main chain — including, of course, Bernardo. Once he was secured, the guard undid the manacles that he had been wearing up till now.

Ingvar wriggled his buttocks on the rough stone, trying to make himself as comfortable as possible. He felt a quick stab of fear as the Iberian continued to stare at him, still smiling. He dropped his gaze. He had no wish for any confrontation.

Bernardo was one of those domineering types who could often be found in a prison. Bigger and stronger than the others, they would prey on their fellow captives, exploiting their weaknesses and asserting their own authority over those around them. While Ingvar wasn't aware that Bernardo conformed to this type, he sensed the malice in the man. Once the guards left, there would be trouble — but it would be slow building. Bernardo wouldn't come straight out and attack him. He would prod and goad him until they reached a flash point.

Ingvar sighed to himself. He didn't want trouble. He was big and strong, but he wasn't an aggressive type, choosing to react physically only when there was no other choice. Bernardo, he concluded, was exactly the opposite.

In fact, Ingvar appeared to the Iberian to be the perfect choice for a demonstration of his dominance. He was big, so the other slaves would recognise the object lesson when Bernardo gave him a beating and reduced him to a cringing wreck, pleading for mercy.

In this, Bernardo made one important mistake. As has been noted, Ingvar was built in the classic Skandian mould. He was wide and bulky. Bernardo mistook the bulk for fat. He assumed Ingvar would be an easy target. In his experience, big, fat boys were easily cowed into submission, and Bernardo enjoyed easy targets.

He looked sidelong at Ingvar, who sat with his head bowed and his eyes down, not making eye contact. Bernardo nudged him with an elbow.

'You're taking up too much room,' he declared.

Ingvar shuffled a little to his right. 'Sorry,' he muttered.

The elbow nudged him again, harder this time, jarring into his ribs.

'Come on, fat boy. You can't take up more than your share of room.'

Ingvar moved again. The prisoner on his right, emboldened by his submission to Bernardo, snarled a curse at him and shoved him back. This resulted in another elbow jab from Bernardo. Ingvar shuffled himself again and tried to find a compromise position. This was going to become unpleasant before too long, he thought.

This time, Bernardo seemed content to leave him be. But he continued to stare fixedly at Ingvar. This wasn't over. In fact, it was only just beginning.

CHAPTER THIRTY-NINE

'We're going to have to make sure the garrison and the gatehouse guards are fully occupied,' Hal said. 'There's nearly eighty men in those two groups and we can't fight that many.'

He was sitting on the edge of the steering platform at the stern of the ship. The crew were gathered round him in a half circle, seated on the deck, as he explained his plans. He looked now at Gilan.

'That means you'll have to get that fire started before we break in.'

The Ranger thought for a few seconds. 'We'll start the ball rolling about half an hour before you want to make your move,' he said. He glanced quickly at Lydia for concurrence and she nodded. 'That'll give us time for the fire to take hold and the alarm to be raised. And that'll bring the *dooryeh* running.'

'We could add to the confusion,' Jesper suggested. 'If we started yelling the alarm that the gold market was on fire and being attacked, we could stir things up a little faster.'

Hal considered it but ended up shaking his head. 'It's a good idea,' he admitted. 'But I'd rather we kept out of sight at that point. If we start yelling the alarm, there's a chance someone might wonder who we are and what we're up to. We can't risk that.'

'What time are you thinking of breaking in?' Thorn asked.

'Two hours after midnight,' Hal replied promptly. 'That way, the prison guards will have relaxed. And the streets will be clearer. We don't want to find ourselves fighting through crowds as we're making our escape.'

'That makes sense,' Stig said. 'And who do you want in the raiding party?'

'You and Thorn. Jesper, of course. And me.' He paused, waiting for the protests from those he had left out. He didn't have long to wait.

'What about me?' Ulf and Wulf spoke at exactly the same time and in exactly the same tone of wounded indignation.

Stefan added his objection a second or so later. 'You're leaving me out? What for?'

Only Edvin accepted the statement without protest. He'd been half expecting it. He was the smallest member of the crew, and the least effective in a fight.

'I need you on board,' Hal told them. 'While we're getting the prisoners out, I want you to re-rig *Heron* with her normal mast and sails. You're the sail handlers and trimmers, so you can do it faster and better than anyone else.'

'You're going to take on eight guards with just four of you? Don't you think you'll be a little outnumbered?' Ulf asked. And for once, his brother was in total agreement. He nodded emphatically.

In truth, Hal was concerned about the imbalance of numbers. After Stig and Thorn, Ulf and Wulf were the two most capable warriors on board. But they were the sail handlers, and so were totally familiar with the rigging for the mast and sails. He was tempted to split the difference — leave one on board to help re-rig the ship and take the other along on the raid. He hesitated, and glanced at Thorn, who seemed to read what was in his mind.

'Four of us will be more than enough,' he said firmly. 'Any more and we'll be getting in our own way. And besides, if we hit them two hours after midnight, you can bet that at least half of them will be snoring in those bunks.' He looked at Jesper. 'I assume you can get that door open without making any noise?'

Jesper nodded confidently. 'The lock is easy,' he said. 'And you saw how well maintained it was. They'll never know we're there until we come bursting in.'

Thorn ran his left hand idly over the smooth wood of the massive club-hand that was resting on the deck between his feet.

'You just get the door open and Stig and I will do any bursting that's necessary,' he said. 'We'll clean them up in jig time.'

Stig grinned in fierce agreement. 'Couldn't have put it better myself, Thorn.'

The old warrior looked at him with a raised eyebrow. 'I know,' he said, and the others laughed as Stig flushed, realising he'd left himself wide open for that retort.

But Wulf wasn't prepared to give in so easily. He hated the thought of being left out of the coming fight.

'Hal, we've got two days. Why can't we re-rig the ship now — get it done before the raid? Then I could come with you.'

Instantly, Ulf turned on him. '*You* could go with him?' he said indignantly. 'Why not me? What makes you special?'

'It was my idea,' Wulf told him.

Ulf shook his head vehemently. 'No! You just said it. I'd already thought it!'

'Then you should have said it when you did,' Wulf retorted.

'I was going to. But you interrupted!'

'How could I interrupt you when you weren't saying anything?' Wulf challenged.

Hal looked round for Ingvar, remembered where he was and sighed.

'Just shut up, the two of you, please,' he said. He was tired and worried about Ingvar, and his mild tone came as a surprise to the twins. They promptly stopped their bickering, sensing his mood and the reason behind it.

'Sorry, Hal,' Wulf said.

'Yes. Sorry,' his brother echoed.

The rest of the crew exchanged surprised looks. They had never heard either of the twins apologise for their behaviour in the past — unless they were being threatened with being tossed overboard by Ingvar.

Truth be told, Ulf and Wulf missed their massive shipmate. They found a perverse enjoyment in the brink-manship they practised with him — arguing and bickering

up to the point where he threatened to heave them overboard, then quickly pulling back before he acted. So far,
they had only misjudged once.

'We can't re-rig the ship any earlier,' Hal told them
now, in a patient tone. 'If we're seen setting up new masts
and yards, it'll cause comment — particularly with such a
distinctive and different sail rig. People will start talking
and there's a chance that word might get to Tursgud.

'We simply can't risk that. If he hears about a foreign
ship with a triangular sail, he'll know it's us. And from
there, it won't take him long to figure out why we're here.
He'll warn Mahmel that we're planning to rescue the
Araluan slaves, and if that happens, our chances are zero.
The guards will be on the alert and we won't get within a
hundred metres of the slave market without being spotted
and stopped. Surprise is our best ally and we can't take
any chances that it might be compromised. We need to
wait till the last minute to replace the yardarm and sail.
And we need to do it in darkness.'

He paused before adding his final argument. 'And
remember, if our plan to break into the market is ruined,
we'll be leaving Ingvar in there, as well as the twelve
Araluans.'

Ulf and Wulf looked at the deck as that final thought
sank in.

'I suppose you're right,' Ulf said.

'We can't leave Ingvar behind,' Wulf said.

Hal studied them both for a few seconds, then nodded
his appreciation of their attitude.

'Thanks, boys,' he said. 'I know you'd love to come
along on the raid, but you'll be doing something just as

important back here. If we don't get our normal sail and mast replaced, we'll never make it out of the harbour.'

He glanced around the rest of the crew and took in the serious expressions on their faces. Up until now, none of them had thought about the consequence of failure — the fact that they would be leaving Ingvar to be sold as a slave. In the time they had known Hal and sailed with him, they had never seen one of his battle plans go wrong. Now, when they saw the obvious tension in their skirl and the strain on his face, they realised how finely balanced their chances were.

'Anyone got any other questions?' he asked and there was a general chorus in the negative. The group began to break up, with Stig and Thorn moving to check and sharpen their weapons, while the twins and Stefan made sure they had all the halyards, shackles, stays and spars they would need when the time came to replace the sails. At least, they thought, they could get some of the preparatory work done in advance. Edvin lit his fire and began preparing lunch. Jesper checked through the items in his lock-picking kit, selecting the picks he would need, having checked out the keys and locks in use at the slave market.

As this more or less normal shipboard routine began, Lydia made eye contact with Hal and, with a jerk of her head, beckoned him towards the stern, where they could speak privately.

He followed her slim, erect figure. He could see that she was angry. It was obvious in every line of her body. And it was obvious whom she was angry at, he thought wearily. He really wasn't in the mood for a confrontation with Lydia. He was tense and nervous about the coming attack on the slave market. There were so many things that could go wrong, so many indefinables and unforeseeables. Consequently, when Lydia launched her verbal attack on him, he was more than ready to reply.

'I don't know how you could do that,' she said bitterly.

He knew what she was talking about, but asked, nevertheless, 'Do what?'

'How you could leave Ingvar — desert him in that slave pen while the rest of you all came back safe and sound.'

'We didn't have a lot of choice,' he pointed out. He resented having to explain his actions to her. But he knew that she and Ingvar had a special relationship and he thought he owed her that much. 'We were outnumbered and unarmed. And it wasn't as if Mahmel suggested we leave him there. He told us flat out. Those are the rules here.'

She shook her head angrily. 'Then you should have known that and not taken him there in the first place. Trust Thorn to come up with such a ridiculous plan!'

'It wasn't a ridiculous plan,' Hal said evenly. 'And if you recall, Ingvar was all in favour of it when it was suggested.' She opened her mouth to reply but he continued, raising his voice and overriding her.

'And, if you'd listened to what I said earlier, you'd remember that Ingvar himself said that it was a good idea for him to remain in the slave pen. He said he'd have a chance to get the Araluans ready for an escape.'

'Well, of course he'd say that! He idolises you. He'd do anything to win your respect and admiration! You'd better make sure you get him out of there in one piece!'

Hal's eyes narrowed. 'I think you're selling Ingvar short,' he said. 'He didn't choose to do it so I'd admire him. He chose to do it because he could see immediately that it was a good idea. Ingvar is much smarter than most people give him credit for.'

Lydia flushed. She'd made the statement out of spite, in an attempt to make Hal feel guilty, to feel that it was somehow his fault. She certainly hadn't meant to denigrate Ingvar's intelligence or ability to think independently.

'Well, maybe not . . .' she faltered.

Hal seized the initiative. He took a half pace closer to her, keeping his voice lowered. But it was still full of intensity.

'Remember one thing, Lydia. Ingvar has been my friend, my good friend, for years. Far longer than the short time you've known him. We share a special bond as members of the Heron Brotherband that perhaps you don't quite appreciate. I like him. I admire him. He's brave. He's honest. He's loyal. And he's smart enough to see an opportunity like this and take advantage of it. He doesn't do things to win my favour or approval. He does them because they're the right thing to do. I'm surprised I have to tell you that, of all people.'

She dropped her eyes, realising that what he said was true. But Hal had more to say. He was angry now and he wanted to vent that anger a little.

'What's more, I don't need you telling me that I'd better get him out of there in one piece. I plan to do just that — or die trying. So do Thorn, and Stig and Jesper and every last one of us. Ingvar's a Heron, and we don't leave our brothers behind.'

Lydia looked away across the harbour, unwilling to

meet his gaze. She knew he was right. She knew she was out of line. But, proud and independent as she was, she couldn't quite bring herself to admit it.

'Well . . . all right then,' she said, grudgingly. 'But let me tell you this: if anything happens to Ingvar, I will never forgive you.'

Hal held her gaze for several moments in silence.

'Let me tell you,' he said finally. 'If anything happens to Ingvar, I'll never forgive myself.'

CHAPTER FORTY

As the day went on, Bernardo continued to goad and torment Ingvar — both physically and verbally.

'Come on, fat boy,' he would sneer. 'Make a little room for those of us around you.' This accusation, and variations on it, would be accompanied by painful jabs with his elbow or fist, usually aimed into Ingvar's ribs.

He would vary this theme from time to time, querying why Ingvar continued to accept such treatment.

'Are you a coward?' he would ask. 'A big fat coward? Yes. I think you are. Otherwise you wouldn't let me do this. Or this!'

The last few words were accompanied by a punch or an elbow. Sometimes, he would punch Ingvar on the point of his shoulder. He invariably did this without warning, catching Ingvar by surprise and making him grunt with pain. When he heard this involuntary reaction, Bernardo would sneer and repeat the punishment.

But still Ingvar refused to react or retaliate. He knew

that any such action would lead to an all-in brawl with the Iberian, and he had no wish for that.

After several hours, Ingvar found himself struggling with another problem. He had blithely told Hal that if he was in the prison, he would be able to contact the Araluan captives and prepare them for the rescue attempt. Now that he was here, he could see no way he could accomplish this. There seemed to be no way he could speak privately with the Araluan captives, assuming he could determine who they were. And he could hardly announce the rescue mission to the prison at large. He had no idea how many informants might be among the other potential slaves, ready to betray his secret for better treatment from the guards.

But he was sure there would be several such people. Bernardo himself was a prime candidate. His heart sank as he realised he had placed himself in this hazardous position for no good purpose.

Finally, after Bernardo had ignored him for half an hour, he decided he would have to make some sort of attempt to make contact with the Araluans. Once he had done so, he could try to figure out how to alert them without warning the rest of the prisoners of the upcoming rescue attempt.

He raised his head and called out in the common tongue. 'Are there any Araluans here?'

A voice responded promptly from the other side of the dungeon, five metres further along. 'Yes! There are twelve of us here. Who's that?'

Before he could respond, however, Bernardo, roused from his malevolent silence, rounded upon him.

'What do you care? Who are you to start shouting questions in my prison? Who asked you to raise your voice?'

Each of these questions was accompanied by a vicious elbow jab into his ribs. As he winced from the blows, Ingvar began to experience a slow-burning anger. It built within him, yet still he contrived to keep the peace.

'I'm sorry,' he said. 'I have a friend who's an Araluan.'

'Who is that? Are you Araluan too?' the voice from across the passageway called. But now Bernardo rounded upon the unseen speaker.

'You shut up!' he shouted. 'It's no concern of yours who he is.' He turned back to Ingvar, his eyes glittering with anger. 'Where are you from? You don't look Araluan. What's your name?'

'I'm Hellenese,' Ingvar replied. Then, reasoning that Ingvar didn't sound very Hellenese, he adjusted his name to suit his professed nationality. 'My name is Ingvos.'

'Hellenese?' sneered Bernardo. 'That's a barbarous country full of ignorant swineherds. Say something in your barbarous language if you're Hellenese.'

In point of fact, Bernardo didn't want to hear Ingvar speak Hellenese. He was simply looking for a way to belittle and browbeat the young man and this was as good as any. But, unwittingly, he had presented Ingvar with the solution to his problem. The Hellenic Islands were a remote archipelago at the eastern end of the Constant Sea. The odds were that an Iberian like Bernardo would have no knowledge of their language. It had no commonality with the Iberian tongue. He decided to adopt the ruse he had used earlier with Mahmel, and spoke in Skandian

— an equally remote language. But his growing anger led him to pepper his words liberally with insults.

'All right, you overgrown oaf. Hear this: you have an unpleasant nature and you smell like a swamp.'

There was a brief cry of laughter from one of the Araluans and Ingvar swung quickly towards the sound, even though he could not see the man who had laughed.

'Do you speak Skandian?' he asked.

A different voice replied, in broken Skandian. 'I speak. I worked with Skandian duty ship at Cresthaven. Sold them fish.'

'Shut up!' Bernardo shouted, his gaze switching from Ingvar to the Araluans and then back again. 'Shut up! I run this prison and I decide who speaks!'

'Really?' said Ingvar, reverting to the common tongue. His growing anger had wiped out the doubts he had felt earlier. At least now he could see a course of action presenting itself. 'I rather thought the guards did that.'

Several of the other prisoners around them snickered briefly. Bernardo glared round at them, silencing them, then grabbed the front of Ingvar's tunic and pulled him close, so that their faces were only centimetres apart. Flecks of spittle landed on Ingvar as the Iberian raged at him.

'You don't make jokes! Understand? You do as I tell you!'

And finally, Ingvar decided enough was enough. The anger, up until now a glowing ember, roared into full flame. He was a Skandian warrior, he thought. He was a member of the Heron Brotherband, after all. And the Herons had triumphed over Tursgud in their brotherband contest, then recaptured the stolen Andomal, sinking Zavac's pirate ship and killing Zavac himself into the bargain. Ingvar's pride surged. A Heron could do anything he set his mind to, and it was time this pathetic, posturing Iberian bully was made aware of the fact.

Turning towards Bernardo, he hit the Iberian full in the face with three rapid-fire left jabs. The punches travelled less than twenty centimetres, but they had all the strength of Ingvar's powerful arm and shoulder behind them.

Bernardo's head jerked back with the first punch, then came forward in time to meet the second and third. Ingvar heard the sound of bones cracking as the man's nose broke. Bernardo uttered a choked cry, dazed from the rapid sequence of devastating punches. Then Ingvar whipped the metre-long chain that attached him to the wall into a loop around the Iberian's neck and pulled it tight.

Bernardo tried to fight against the constricting chain cutting off his breath. But to no avail. Ingvar had him securely and he leaned back to tighten the loop. Bernardo scrabbled at the Skandian's arms and hands with his nails, kicked his feet ineffectually against the stone floor, then, after a short struggle, he slumped unconscious.

Only then did Ingvar release the pressure on the chain. Bernardo took one enormous, shuddering breath and fell to one side.

'Nice work,' said the slave to Ingvar's left — the one who had previously cursed him for crowding against him. Now, seeing how easily Ingvar had dispatched the prison bully, he thought it might be a good idea to show there were no hard feelings. Ingvar looked at him, his eyes hard.

'He had it coming,' he said.

The other prisoner nodded enthusiastically. 'He did indeed!'

And suddenly, Ingvar felt a whole lot better. The black mood of doubt and despair lifted from him and a sense of triumphant pride flooded through him. Bernardo had just learned the hard way that it didn't pay to treat a Heron with contempt. Furthermore, as a member of the Heron Brotherband, Ingvar had the support and backing of invincible warriors like Thorn and Stig.

Most of all, he realised that he could count on the ingenuity of his skirl. And in that second, he knew he would escape from this situation. Hal and his shipmates would never let him down. No matter what difficulties or dangers presented themselves, Hal would find a way to overcome them.

He shoved the unconscious figure of Bernardo contemptuously, then spoke in Skandian again.

'You Araluans take heart! My shipmates are coming to rescue you and take you back to Araluen. But keep it quiet, understand?'

There was a pause while the Skandian-speaking Araluan translated to his comrades. Then he called out again. 'When? When are they coming?'

Ingvar hesitated. There might well be other Skandian speakers in the dungeon and he didn't want to reveal too much detail. 'Sometime in the next few days,' he said vaguely. 'Just be quiet and be ready to follow my lead when the time comes.'

Beside him, Bernardo stirred groggily, his breathing snuffling wetly through his broken, flattened nose. Ingvar regarded him for a few seconds then, remembering the hours of taunting and goading that he had endured, he jabbed his elbow into the man's ribs.

Hard.

CHAPTER FORTY-ONE

Gilan strung his longbow, then slung it diagonally over his back, so that it stretched from just above his left shoulder to the back of his right boot. Slinging it at an angle like that allowed him to fit it under the voluminous white robes, with only a small section of the upper end protruding above his shoulder and making a slight hump under the robe — and even that was hidden by the tail of his *kheffiyeh*.

He had adapted his quiver — normally slung over his shoulder — to hang from his belt. He clipped it into place now and pulled the robe around him. Aside from that one small peak at his shoulder, there was no sign that he was carrying a longbow.

He wore his sword, of course, in a scabbard that hung from his waistbelt. The peculiar double knife scabbard, holding a saxe knife and a smaller throwing knife, balanced the weight of the sword on the opposite side.

'Nearly time to be off,' he said quietly.

Hal nodded. He looked around to where Lydia was donning her robe and *kheffiyeh*. She had her quiver of atlatl darts concealed under the robe, hanging diagonally across her back like Gilan's bow. But they were shorter than the bow and the robe hid them completely.

She glanced up, caught Hal's eye and nodded. Since their heated discussion the day before, relations between the two of them had returned to normal. Hal knew she was too proud to ever apologise to him or admit that she was in the wrong. But she had gone out of her way to be pleasant and friendly in a dozen small ways, doing small favours for him or sharing the occasional joke — usually at her own expense. He smiled at her now. He was glad they were back on speaking terms — particularly with both of them heading off into uncertain and dangerous situations. He realised that there was a possibility that they might never see each other again and he would have hated the bad blood between them to have continued.

He turned back to Gilan. 'What time are you heading out?'

'Around the eleventh hour. That'll give us time to get into the market, scout out a good place to start the fire and have it well and truly burning by a quarter hour to two. We'll try to make it as far from the slave market as possible. That way, we'll draw the *dooryeh* further away from you and leave you with a free hand.'

Hal nodded several times. He was nervous and tense. His stomach was set in tight knots and his mouth was dry.

It wasn't fear, he knew. Once the action started, once things were under way, he would be fine. But it was the waiting that always got to him. The hours beforehand, thinking over the plan, trying to foresee problems — and there would always be problems — and plan for every eventuality.

He wished he were going with Gilan and Lydia. At least then he'd be doing something, and not having to put up with this seemingly interminable waiting.

The bell in the city watch tower clanged suddenly. All eyes on the ship instantly turned in the direction of the tower, even though they couldn't actually see it from deck level. Unconsciously, Hal's lips moved as he counted the clangs, mouthing the numbers from one to eleven.

The bell sounded out each hour, then sounded a single stroke to mark the quarter hours.

'We'll be going,' Gilan said. He glanced at Lydia. 'Ready?'

She nodded, making a final check of her belt to be sure her atlatl and her long dirk were both in place. Gilan and Hal shook hands, then Lydia embraced him quickly.

The rest of the crew gathered round to farewell them, murmuring good wishes as the two white-robed figures prepared to climb up onto the wharf.

'Remember,' Hal said, 'once you've got the fire going, head straight back here. Don't come looking for us. Just get back here and be ready to sail when we arrive.'

'Got it,' Gilan said. He didn't see any need to point out that Hal had given them those instructions at least ten times during the day. The young skipper was anxious, he realised. A burly figure loomed up beside them and he turned to shake hands with Thorn, doing so left-handed.

'Mind yourself in that guardroom,' Gilan told him.

Thorn grinned cheerfully. He never had any stomach butterflies before a fight.

'I plan to be subtle,' he said.

Gilan looked at him, his head tilted curiously. 'How's that?'

'Once we go through that door, I'll bash anything that moves. And if they don't move, Stig will bash them.'

'You have a strange concept of subtle,' Gilan said.

Thorn's grin grew wider. 'So I've been told.' Then he became serious. 'Take care out there. And take care of the girl too. Sometimes, she can be a little impulsive.'

Being Thorn, he made no effort to lower his voice when he added the second instruction. Lydia's temper flared. 'Impulsive! I'll give you impulsive, old man!'

'See what I mean?' Thorn said to Gilan.

Gilan grinned back. 'I don't think Lydia needs anyone to look after her.'

'Maybe not. But do it anyway,' Thorn told him. 'Or you'll answer to me.'

'I'll bear it in mind,' Gilan said. Thorn was constantly teasing and infuriating Lydia. It was obvious, however, that he felt a strong regard for her — obvious to everyone but Lydia.

'Are we going or not?' she said impatiently.

Gilan winked at Thorn and turned away. 'We're going,' he said. 'Let's get this done, shall we?'

He clambered up onto the wharf, Lydia close on his heels. They looked back to the ship, raised their arms in farewell, then turned and hurried off into the narrow entrance of an alley leading away from the waterfront.

As they travelled further into the city, the narrow, winding streets that took them under dark archways and past silent doorways gave way to wider thoroughfares that were well lit and bustling with noise and people. Taverns and eating houses predominated here. There were stalls as well, selling all kinds of merchandise, and lit by flaring oil lamps to show off their goods.

Lydia and Gilan, walking in single file with Gilan leading the way, threaded a path through the slow moving tide of eaters, drinkers and shoppers. On all sides, the spruikers for restaurants and bars called out to them, promising the *tastiest* food, the *finest* wine and ale and the most *convivial* company in the city. They ignored all these entreaties and pressed on.

Gradually, the streets became darker and quieter again, as they reached a residential area of the city. Here the walls were high and windowless, maintaining the privacy of those inside. The roofs were flat and covered with awnings, so that the residents could relax and enjoy the evening breeze high above the streets. As they walked quickly past the darkened fronts of the houses, through the occasional pool of light thrown by an oil light mounted high on the plastered walls, Lydia had the uncomfortable and unwelcome feeling that dozens of eyes were watching her from above.

Her softly shod feet made little noise on the uneven cobbles. To Lydia, however, each footfall sounded deafening. And she was convinced that anyone seeing them as they hurried along would immediately divine their purpose and raise the alarm.

They passed through a small square where a fountain splashed invitingly and trees were set about benches to provide shelter during the heat of day. By night, they provided deep shadows and Lydia's overworked imagination peopled those shadows with enemies. Lydia didn't like cities — particularly a city as big and extensive as Socorro. She had grown up spending most of her time in the forests and fields around her home town. She knew the sounds of a forest and could identify potential danger easily. In a large city like this, with its tortuous alleyways, high walls and shadowy archways, every noise she heard and every movement she saw was enough to set her teeth on edge.

Even the pleasant splashing of the fountain bothered her. It could be masking other sounds, less benevolent.

She glanced sideways at Gilan. As the crowds died away, she moved up to walk beside him. She wondered whether he was feeling the same nervous tension that she was. But the hanging sides of the *kheffiyeh* masked his face.

'Not long now,' he said. His voice was calm and encouraging, as if he had sensed her doubts. He turned and smiled at her, and she became aware that she had been gripping the handle of her dirk beneath her cloak in an iron grasp. Lydia relaxed her fingers as she and Gilan plunged through another archway, followed a curving, narrow alley, then emerged into the clear square that faced the gold market.

The marketplace itself loomed above them, a dark mass pierced only by a gateway opposite where yellow light shone, spilling out onto the cobblestones of the square.

They had travelled via a circuitous route that brought them to the south-western gate — the one furthest removed from the neighbouring slave market. Fortuitously, it was a gate by which they hadn't previously accessed the gold *souk*. That way, there was less chance of encountering a guard they might have seen previously, one who might remember them and ask awkward questions.

Even at this late hour, there was a crowd milling outside the gate, waiting to gain entrance. As they crossed the square, Gilan pulled one of the tails of his *kheffiyeh* across his face to obscure part of it. He knew that if he covered his face completely, it would only arouse suspicion. But the partial concealment was nearly as effective, and far less noticeable or memorable. Lydia took her cue from him, doing likewise.

They tagged onto the end of the queue waiting to enter, moving slowly forward. Before long, they were no longer the end of the queue, as other keen traders joined on behind them. On this occasion, the guard seemed to be merely going through the motions of checking people as they entered. There was little talk and each group or individual received only the most perfunctory inspection before being waved through.

Lydia and Gilan were no different. The yawning guard glanced quickly at them, then waved them forward with a complete show of indifference.

As they stepped through the gateway, then went through an arched entrance, the darkness disappeared in a blaze of lantern and candle light reflecting off the gold and brass displays that lined the streets. The smell of grilling meat filled the air and Lydia's stomach rumbled. She realised she hadn't eaten since the afternoon. Gilan looked at her, amused.

'I take it from that thunderous noise that you're feeling peckish?' he said.

She shook her head. 'Forget pecking. Put some food in front of me and I'll tear it to pieces.'

'Might not be a bad idea to do that while we get our bearings,' he said. They were in a part of the market they hadn't visited before and, while there was nothing essentially different from the parts they had already seen, they could use a little time to check out the surroundings and pick a likely place where they could start their diversion.

He led the way to one of the many tea houses in the market and they sat at a small table on spindly chairs. The waiter brought them mint tea, grilled mutton still sizzling on skewers, and flat bread with a salad of chopped parsley and mint.

They ate and drank, and the Ranger's eyes were never still, darting from one stall to another, from one side street to another as he studied the lay of the land. Once again, they had selected a spot at the top of a natural hill, where the streets and side alleys fell away on all sides. Finally, he casually pointed to a spot halfway down and on their left, at the junction of the main street and a narrow alley.

'That looks like the place,' he said. 'Finish your tea and we'll take a closer look.'

CHAPTER FORTY-TWO

The rescue party left an hour after Gilan and Lydia had slipped away to the gold *souk*.

Hal spent the intervening time pacing the deck, from bow to stern and back again. From time to time, he would stop and inspect the work being carried out by Ulf, Wulf, Edvin and Stefan. They had the halyard and stays rigged and ready and were now refitting the triangular sails to the long, slender yardarms.

At one stage, Stig began to rise to his feet as Hal paced past him. Thorn laid his left arm on Stig's forearm. 'Where are you off to?' he asked, although he knew full well.

Stig glanced after his friend, pacing with his head down. 'Thought I'd keep him company.'

Thorn shook his head. 'He doesn't need company right now. He needs to be alone.'

Stig studied Hal more closely as he turned and began to pace his way forward once more. He could see the frown of concentration creasing his friend's forehead, the set of his mouth and the distant look in his eyes and he realised Thorn was right. He sat down and began honing the blade of his axe once more. The axe was already sharp enough to shave the hairs on his forearm, but all Skandians knew an axe could never be *too* sharp.

For his part, Thorn had already strapped on the fearsome club-hand that Hal had made for him. In addition, he was wearing a sword on his right hip and his saxe in a scabbard on his left. A small, bowl-shaped metal shield lay on the deck beside him.

Jesper, the fourth member of the raiding party, and in some ways the most important, sat in the well where the rowing benches were situated. He had his lock-picking wallet open before him, and a selection of half a dozen old and new padlocks arranged on the bench. Some he had had for years. Others he had bought as recently as that afternoon in the bazaar.

Now, as he sat, humming quietly to himself, he would pick up a padlock at random, inspect it quickly, then select the correct lock-pick from his kit and proceed to open the lock. The succession of smooth clicks were audible throughout the ship as he practised his craft. It was a strangely soothing sound. The locks were well oiled and well maintained and it took only seconds for him to manipulate the pick in each of them and have the jaws spring open.

Finally, satisfied that his fingers were sufficiently nimble and sensitive enough to assess the resistance of each lock as he manipulated it, he packed the padlocks away, rolled his lock-picks back into the canvas wallet, and slung it around his neck, over his shoulder.

In the distance, the watch tower bell chimed, its peals ringing steadily out over the city. As before, Hal's lips moved unconsciously as he counted the strokes, although once the bell had sounded twice, indicating that it wasn't sounding a quarter-hour signal, it was inevitable what the end result would be.

'Eight, nine, ten, eleven, twelve,' he said quietly.

His sword belt was leaning against the steering platform and he moved towards it now, swinging it round his waist and buckling it on in a smooth movement borne of long practice. He donned his white robe and *kheffiyeh* then, as an afterthought, shoved his Heron watch cap through his belt. Once they were at the slave market, they planned to abandon the white cloaks — they would only stand out in the darkness. When that happened, he was going to lose the *kheffiyeh* as well, and don the watch cap — the Herons' uniform headgear. He noticed the other three picking up their caps and shoving them inside jackets or through belts. Obviously, everyone had the same idea.

Kloof had watched him donning the sword belt and cloak. Now she reared up on her hind legs, straining against the length of rope that kept her tethered to the mast. He stepped to her and ruffled her ears as she whined expectantly.

'Not tonight, girl,' he said. 'You stay here and keep an eye on Ulf and Wulf.'

The twins grinned up at him and Kloof subsided, disappointment evident in every line of her body. She let her front legs slide out from under her on the decking and slumped down on her belly, chin resting on her paws, her eyes following Hal's every move.

'Keep her tied up,' he said to Edvin. 'She's liable to take off after me and we won't have time to find her later.'

'I'll take care of it,' Edvin said. 'Good luck, Hal.'

'Take care, boys!' Ulf called softly.

'Brain a *dooryeh* for me, Thorn,' Wulf added.

The raiding party climbed up the short boarding ladder to the wharf.

'Who's got the grapnel?' Hal asked. His voice seemed unnaturally loud.

Thorn tapped his shoulder. 'It's here.'

They planned to scale the high wooden wall of the arena, at a point level with the office and the slave pen. For that purpose, Thorn was carrying a coil of light, strong rope, with a grappling hook attached to one end. They would throw the hook over the wall, heave on it until it set, then swarm up the rope to gain entrance.

'Jes, do you have the booster?' he asked.

Jesper nodded and held up a metre-long piece of wood — the butt of an old oar. They would use it to help get over the wall.

Hal paused for a moment, taking a quick inventory. They had their weapons and the grapnel. And Jesper had his lock-picks. There was nothing else they needed, other than a decent measure of good luck, he thought grimly.

'Let's go then,' he said.

CHAPTER FORTY-THREE

The four raiders crouched in the shadows. Above them, the massive wall of the slave market blocked out the night sky. Hal looked at Thorn, standing ready with the rope and grapnel Jesper had handed him. 'Let it go,' he said.

Thorn had the coil of rope looped over his club-hand. He held the end, with the triple-hooked grapnel in place, in his left, letting it swing easily back and forth. The hooks were wound with canvas to reduce the sound they would make when the grapnel hit the timber benches inside the arena.

Now Thorn stepped away from the wall, swung the weighted line back and forth a few times, and cast it underhand up the wall.

It was a task he had performed hundreds of times in his career as a raider, so it was not surprising that his cast was perfect. The grapnel sailed upwards, trailing the length of knotted rope behind it. As it cleared the lip of the wall, it lost momentum and began to fall back. But Thorn had cast it on an angle, so that it was slightly inside the lip of the wall. There was a dull thud as it made contact with the timber, then Thorn pulled the rope tight, setting the padded hook against the edge of the wall before it could rattle and clatter across the benches.

'You've done this before,' Hal said softly and he saw the gleam of Thorn's teeth in the moonlight.

'Once or twice,' the old sea wolf agreed. Then he handed the end of the taut rope to Stig and took a position alongside Hal, their backs to the wall, facing Stig, with the metre-long piece of oak held between them at waist height. Thorn held it in his left hand, bracing it with the wooden club-hand for extra purchase.

It had been agreed that Stig would be the first one to go over the wall. Jesper was more stealthy, but if there was potential trouble on the other side, Stig was the best equipped to deal with it. Thorn would go last. This was one situation where his lost hand put him at a disadvantage. The others could scramble quickly up and over the wall. He would have to be pulled up.

'On my count,' Stig said, holding the knotted rope in his hands, not letting it sag. 'One, two, three!'

On three, he dashed forward, his hands hauling in the rope as he went so that it retained its tension. Then he leapt up, stepping onto the piece of timber held by his friends. As they felt his weight come down on the wood, they heaved him upwards, boosting him for the first two or three metres of his upward journey. As he flew up, he continued to reel in the rope.

It was a movement that required a lot of co-ordination

and hours of practice. But it was almost second nature to anyone who had trained in a brotherband or served on board a raiding wolfship in the old days. When the momentum of the upward boost died, Stig was in position with the soles of his feet against the timber wall. He continued to haul in on the knotted rope, retrieving it hand over hand and walking his feet up the wall as he did so.

As a result, what would have been an awkward, time-consuming climb was accomplished in less than twenty seconds. Stig transferred his grip from the rope to the parapet and vaulted over the top of the wall, landing soft-footed on the top bench of the arena.

As soon as he landed, Stig drew his axe from the belt loop that held it and turned — knees flexed, weight on his toes — to face the interior, and any enemy who might have been waiting.

There was no one. Slowly, he straightened and laid the axe down. He peered over the parapet, looking down on the three pale ovals that marked the upturned faces of his friends.

'All clear,' he called softly. 'Give me a second to tie off the rope.'

As he had released his grip on the rope, the grapnel had fallen to the timber floor, with another muffled thud. It was a small enough noise, but no noise at all would've been better. He hastily tied the rope off now, looping it round the support for one of the benches. Then he twitched it violently, sending a message to his friends that all was ready.

He didn't watch Jesper's ascent. He was there to make sure no danger threatened from the interior. But he heard the scrambling, sliding impact of his boots against the wall as Thorn and Hal boosted him up, and he completed the climb under his own power. Stig heard the grunt of exertion as Jesper rolled over the parapet and landed beside him. He slapped Jesper on the back. Jesper grinned at him, then drew his sword and took up a position on watch.

It took longer for Hal to negotiate the wall. Thorn couldn't provide any upward thrust for him, so he had to climb the entire way unaided. But he was fit and his muscles were hardened from years of hard work and weapons practice and he swarmed up the wall like a giant, dark spider.

'Any problems?' he whispered to Stig as he crouched below the parapet.

Stig shook his head. 'All clear so far,' he said. 'Let's get Thorn up here.'

Thorn had set about tying a loop in the end of the knotted rope. Now he placed one foot in the loop, seized the rope with his left hand, and waited. He heard a low whistle from above, then the rope tightened and began to move as Stig and Hal started hauling it up.

Thorn rose, fending himself off from the wall with his free foot, ascending in a series of smooth jerks as his two friends reeled him in like a giant fish. As he came level with the wooden parapet, ready hands reached out to help him up the last metre or so and he rolled over the edge and crouched beside them.

'You're going to have to cut down on your intake of ale,' Stig whispered indignantly. 'You weigh a ton.'

Thorn eyed him balefully. 'It's the weight of responsibility I feel, looking after careless fools like you,' he said.

Jesper sniggered quietly while he re-coiled the rope.

The four of them crouched on the timbers of the benches. To their right, halfway round the circular structure, they could see the dim lanterns that marked the main entrance and the guardhouse. They waited several minutes but there was no movement from that direction.

The tunnel that led to the slave quarters was to their left. It was in complete darkness, and from this vantage point, they could see that above the gates, spanning the tunnel itself, was a roofed structure similar to a gatehouse. There were several chairs in place under the roof. Presumably that was the point where important guests watched proceedings while a slave auction was in progress.

Hal gestured to it with his thumb. 'Let's get under cover there while we're waiting.'

Moving in single file, they ghosted around the top row of benches until they were safely in the shadows under the roof.

Hal indicated the chairs. 'May as well make ourselves comfortable,' he said. 'Now all we have to do is wait till someone yells, "Fire!"'

CHAPTER FORTY-FOUR

The spot Gilan had selected was a small, closed room — apparently a store room of some kind — set between two of the gold stores in a narrow alley off the larger main thoroughfare.

The stores themselves were ablaze with lamplight, reflecting brilliantly from the chains, pendants, rings, bangles and other gold jewellery laid out in intricate patterns on the counters. A few shoppers browsed the glittering arrangements, occasionally pointing to a piece so that the merchant could hand it to them for closer appraisal.

Gilan nudged her and they ambled slowly past the nearer jewellery store. As they came level with the blank door between the two stores, Gilan stopped and made a pretence of removing a stone from his boot, hopping on one foot as he did so. His eyes scanned the wooden door. It was old wood, without much remaining strength. The door was fastened by a simple metal hasp that closed over a loop of iron. A padlock was set through the iron loop.

'We could use Jesper here,' Lydia muttered.

But Gilan shook his head. 'Don't need him. That wood is dried out and weak. The screws holding the hasp in place will hardly have any purchase at all. There's obviously nothing of value behind the door.'

He looked back at the store they had just passed. There were three potential customers browsing the goods, and inspecting individual items. The merchant and his bodyguard were completely occupied, watching the shoppers and keeping track of the items that they asked to inspect. They had no eyes for anything outside the shop.

By contrast, the second store was empty. The merchant sat on a high stool behind the counter. His eyes roamed the alley, alighting on the two newcomers. The heavy-set guard sat a few metres away on another stool. His eyes scanned the alley as well.

Gilan nudged Lydia. 'Go and look at the jewellery,' he said in a low voice. 'Ask to see a couple of pieces at once. That should get them concentrating on you so I can open the door.'

Lydia nodded.

'Don't speak,' he added as an afterthought. 'Just point at the pieces you want to see.'

She stepped into the store, stooping to look at the items on one of the lower shelves of the counter. Inevitably, the merchant's eyes went down as well, trying to see which piece had caught the new customer's fancy. The guard stood up and moved closer to his employer, a heavy blackwood club dangling on a leather thong from his wrist.

As their attention focused on Lydia, Gilan drifted back to stand beside the wooden door. He slipped his saxe from its scabbard and, leaning against the door, worked the blade under the brass hasp.

Lydia pointed to a ruby pendant on a chain of heavy gold links. The merchant retrieved it from its display stand and handed it to her, letting the chain drape over her hand and hang down either side.

All the better for him to keep an eye on it, Lydia thought. She studied the pendant for several seconds, pursing her lips thoughtfully. Then, without returning it, she pointed to another — this one a ball of gold filigree work on a finer chain.

The merchant held up his forefinger, shaking it from side to side in an unmistakable sign of disapproval. He pointed to the ruby pendant in Lydia's hand.

'One piece at a time.' His voice was guttural but his use of the common tongue was clear enough. Lydia shrugged, pretending not to understand. She held the ruby pendant away from his outstretched hand and pointed more insistently at the gold filigree piece.

Again, the merchant's reply was in the negative. His voice rose in pitch as his annoyance grew. He reached for the ruby, seizing the chain before Lydia could move it out of reach. She retained her grip on the pendant and frowned at him, then pointed to the filigree pendant again.

'One at a time!' the merchant repeated. Why couldn't this ignorant foreigner understand the most basic rule of the gold *souk*?

Lydia allowed a look of comprehension to cross her face. She nodded and held out the ruby pendant. The merchant snatched it from her grasp and held it close to his nose to inspect it. Satisfied that it was the original article, he nodded. His manner relaxed and he replaced the ruby and chain on their stand, handing her the gold filigree item in its stead.

'Aaah!' said Lydia, in as deep a voice as she could manage. She pointed to the new pendant and smiled, pointing to the original pendant, then herself.

The merchant smiled in return. His bodyguard, in response to Lydia's pantomime, laughed as well.

Gilan jerked the saxe knife away from the wood. The screws were pulled loose from their hold and the hasp came away into his waiting hand. The sound of cracking wood was faint, and the guard's laughter covered most of it.

Released from the lock's hold, the door swung inwards. Gilan shoved it open further with his shoulder and stepped inside the small room, pushing the door shut behind him.

As Lydia took the filigree pendant, she pretended to drop it. The store keeper reacted like lightning, catching the piece before it reached the ground and frowning at her. Out of the corner of her eye, she saw Gilan slip inside the store room and close the door behind him.

Nobody else seemed to notice, and she breathed a sigh of relief. She studied the filigree work, shook her head and pointed to the ruby. Once again, she delayed matters by not handing the filigree back to the merchant before he could pass her the ruby. Then she smiled and seemed to comprehend his gestures. She glanced quickly at the store on the far side of the small room Gilan had just entered. One of the customers had left, but the merchant was fully occupied with the other two. It occurred to her that the best way to rob one of these stores would be to work as a pair and split the store keeper's attention.

Inside the dim store room, lit only by shafts of light breaking through the warped timbers of the door, Gilan took stock of his surroundings. As he'd surmised when he saw the state of the door, there was nothing of value kept here. It was a store room for cleaning materials. There were three wooden buckets with mops standing in them in one corner. Cloth cleaning rags hung from shelves and several small casks gave off an eye-watering smell. Solvents, he thought. Just the thing for cleaning tarnished jewellery and renewing the sparkle.

And just the thing for starting a fire.

He began to tear some of the rags into strips and pile them under a carton full of other cloths. He jammed his saxe into the bung of one of the solvent casks and let the volatile liquid spill over the torn cloth he had prepared. There was a crate of glass bottles nearby, packed with straw to prevent their shattering. He added handfuls of straw to the pile of drenched cloth.

There were several bundles of old linen curtains stacked to one side. He seized one and slashed at it with his saxe, sending clouds of dust and dry material fragments flying, and added it to the pile he'd already created. The first cask was empty so he broached another, checked that it had the same pungent contents, and spilled some of it over the cloth.

The inside of the store room was beginning to reek with the sharp-smelling solvent. He hoped the door would prevent the smell reaching the merchants on either side.

He moved to the door and peered out through one of the cracks between the planks. Lydia was still engaging the merchant. He couldn't see what was happening in the other stall.

Too late to worry about that, he thought. He took out his flint and steel and struck a spark into a small handful of tinder. The little spark grew into a flame as he breathed gently on it. Once it was well alight, he thrust the burning tinder into the pile of soaked cloths.

There was a slight delay, then the pile ignited with a soft *WHOOF*. Flames leapt up eagerly, licking at the support timbers that held the shelving and ceiling in place. Satisfied that the fire wouldn't go out, he stepped quickly out through the door, leaning against the door jamb casually as he pulled it shut behind him.

Again, nobody noticed.

Mahmel awoke suddenly from a dreamless sleep. One moment he was relaxed, breathing deeply, limbs limp. The next his eyes were open and he was wide awake. Beside him, his wife remained asleep, her breathing making a little sighing noise at the end of each intake.

He had no idea what had woken him. He sensed something was amiss. He lay still, staring at the fluttering awning over his head, trying to recall if he had heard or felt anything in the second before he woke.

But there was no memory of any disturbance.

As was the custom, he and his wife, Saleema, were sleeping on the flat roof of their house, with a canvas awning stretched over them to provide shelter in the unlikely event of bad weather. He swung his legs over the side of the bed and stood. Saleema stirred but didn't wake, turning over and settling again.

He walked to the edge of the roof, where a waist-high parapet ran round the edge, and peered out into the night. The black bulk of the slave market arena was a few blocks away. As the market co-ordinator, he was granted a house and servants within easy reach of the market — but far enough away so that the sometimes pungent body odour of the slaves didn't reach his home.

Nothing stirred there. There were a few lanterns lit on the perimeter of the wooden wall, and over the main entrance gate. One shone dimly in the guardhouse by the main gate.

He sniffed the air. There was a faint scent of woodsmoke on the breeze, and the usual acrid smell of camel and goat dung fires. But the land breeze was wafting them out to sea.

He turned his attention to the massive gold *souk* — a huge structure that sprawled over half a dozen city blocks. He could see the bright lights of two of the entrances but, once again, nothing seemed amiss.

He yawned. Odds were, there was nothing to worry about. But he had learned over the years not to ignore premonitions like this. Sometimes, they turned out to mean nothing. But at others, they had provided forewarning of potential disaster. He walked soft-footed back to the bed and began to don his striped robe over the loose linen trousers and vest he wore to sleep.

Saleema sensed his movement and sat up, her hair tousled and her eyes bleary.

'What's the matter?' she said.

'Probably nothing. Go back to sleep. I'm just going to the market to check on things.' He quickly donned his green turban — the symbol of his authority — and pulled a green cloak over his shoulders against the night's chill.

'At this time of night?' she protested, but he leaned down and patted her hand.

'Go back to sleep,' he repeated. 'I won't be long.'

She slumped back, grumbling muffled words that he knew related to his overactive sense of duty. He smiled and buckled on his long scimitar in its scabbard, then went down the stairs to the ground level, where his two bodyguards slept on cots beside the door, fully dressed. One of them had his foot hanging over the side of the cot. Mahmel kicked it gently and the man instantly sprang awake.

'Get up,' he said. 'We're going to the arena.'

Flanked by the two heavily built guards, Mahmel made his way through the dark, silent streets. They hadn't gone more than fifty metres before he heard the shouts in the distance, warning of fire in the gold *souk*. Then an alarm bell began clanging stridently.

'I knew it!' Mahmel muttered. He began to run.

CHAPTER FORTY-FIVE

Thin tendrils of smoke were beginning to curl through the cracks in the door to the store room. Gilan tugged the door shut against the warped frame, then nodded to Lydia as she emerged from the jewellery store.

The store keeper stared after her with a sour expression. She had wasted ten minutes of his time and he realised now she had never meant to buy — a merchant came to know those things about potential customers after a few years. But you could never simply tell such people to move on. If you were mistaken, you could lose a valuable sale.

Casually, the two interlopers began to stroll back towards the main thoroughfare, where they'd planned their escape. Lydia glanced back and jogged Gilan with her elbow.

'I can see smoke coming under the door,' she whispered.

'Shut up and don't look,' Gilan ordered.

They were almost back to the intersection with the

main thoroughfare when disaster struck. A party of half a dozen Socorrans entered from the main street, jamming the narrow alley, and there were several moments of milling confusion as Lydia and Gilan tried to find a way past them. Gilan, conscious that at any moment the smoke might be spotted and the alarm raised, began to shove his way through more forcibly, using his shoulders and jostling the Socorrans out of his way. He came face to face with one of them and stepped back in surprise.

It was the merchant he had knocked out the previous time they were in the *souk* — the one who had unmasked Lydia as a girl. His jaw was marked with an ugly blue and yellow bruise where Gilan had hit him.

For a moment, the man merely regarded him angrily, annoyed that the stranger had jostled him. Then Gilan saw recognition dawning in his eyes.

'You were here before!' the man said. 'When that thief tried to escape!' Then he pointed an accusing finger at Lydia. 'She's a female!' he yelled. 'There's a woman in the *souk*!'

Instantly all his companions were yelling. Inevitably, hearing the word 'thief' in the gold market, someone got the wrong end of it all and began shouting that there was a thief trying to escape. The men formed a solid wall in front of Gilan, preventing him from shoving through. Several of them were trying to draw their scimitars, but the close quarters and the crowding prevented them.

'*Dooryeh! Dooryeh!* Thieves in the market! Call the *dooryeh!*' one of the men shouted.

'You're already doing that,' Gilan told the Socorran through gritted teeth. He had one of his strikers in his left hand and he used it now — a short, hooking punch that nevertheless had the power of his shoulder and his turning upper body behind it.

He caught the man on the side of the jaw and the Socorran's eyes glazed over. He collapsed like a rag doll, bringing down the man behind him.

Then Lydia heard the rhythmic tramp of hobnailed sandals running in step, and a detachment of eight *dooryeh* rounded the corner. The corporal in charge looked at the milling group in front of him and called a brief order.

'Swords!'

Eight scimitars rasped from their scabbards and the armoured men began to move forward in a wedge formation. They hit the back of the men grouped around Lydia and Gilan and began shoving them out of the way. The merchants and their servants reacted instinctively, shoving back and turning to berate the new arrivals. Gilan looked back over his shoulder, down the alley. There was another narrow roadway intersecting it about twenty metres away. He pointed his sword at it and yelled to Lydia.

'Back! Back to the next corner!'

At that moment, one of the *dooryeh* broke through the melee that had formed between them. Seeing Gilan and Lydia, and recognising them as foreigners, he aimed a cut with his scimitar at the taller of the two figures facing him.

Gilan parried the blow easily, and as the scimitar came to a ringing, arm-jarring stop, Lydia took a pace forward and punched her dirk into the soldier's upper arm.

The heavy blade sliced through the man's chain mail shirt like a hot knife through butter. He felt a sudden burning pain in his arm. His fingers opened involuntarily and his sword dropped on the cobbles, bouncing and ringing off the stone.

'Run!' Gilan shouted at her. But now they found themselves facing the bodyguard from the store Lydia had entered. The store keeper, no man of action, had wisely retreated behind a display counter. But he added his voice to the growing clamour.

'He's a thief!' he yelled, pointing to Lydia. 'He stole a pendant!'

He had no way of knowing if that was true. But he'd heard someone call the word 'thief' and this person had been looking at his pendants and handling them, so he decided to take no risks.

'She's a girl!' the trader they had encountered the day before yelled, as if this were somehow worse than being a thief. Maybe it is in this part of the world, Lydia thought grimly.

The bodyguard, a big Arridan from the southern forests, with skin almost as black as coal, barred their way with his massive bulk, his club raised threateningly. Gilan assessed him quickly. The man was no skilled fighter. His stance was clumsy and unbalanced and the Ranger had no wish to kill him for merely doing his job. Gilan raised one booted foot and planted it into the man's solar plexus, then straightened his knee rapidly, sending him flying back.

The bodyguard crashed into one of the original six men who had rounded the corner and started all the trouble. This man staggered in his turn and crashed against the old door to the store room. The door, secured only by the jamming of its warped frame, offered virtually no resistance. It flew open and he stumbled inside. As the door opened and admitted a draught of air, flames and smoke billowed out into the alley.

Now a new cry joined the confused chorus of 'Thief' and 'Female!' and 'Call the *dooryeh*!'

'FIRE! FIRE IN THE MARKET! HELP!'

Thick, choking smoke filled the narrow alleyway and cries of alarm went up from the other store keepers on either side. For the moment, the *dooryeh* were unsighted and baffled. The flames and smoke were unexpected additions to the rapidly growing confusion in the little alley. Gilan seized Lydia's arm and began to drag her towards the junction to their left.

They ran with their arms up over their noses and eyes to ward off the stinging, stinking smoke. They reached the turnoff to the new alley and stopped in despair. A party of *dooryeh* were advancing along the cross street towards them. There were at least a dozen of them. Lydia and Gilan were cut off from their planned retreat route. Gilan cast wildly around. Several of the first group of *dooryeh* were emerging from the clouds of smoke behind them.

'Come on!' he said, and dragged Lydia down the alley, moving away from the main thoroughfare and their planned escape route. The second party of *dooryeh* saw them hesitate, then turn and run. Instantly, the warriors doubled their pace. A person who was running was a person who was guilty, they all knew.

As they moved further into the alley, the air cleared a little. Gilan, whose eyes were stinging and running with tears, took stock of their position and felt his heart sink. They had run into a blind alley. Ahead of them was a curving row of stalls and store houses, with no way out. One of the store keepers ran out to shout at them, grabbing at Gilan's left arm. Quickly, the Ranger stunned him with a blow from his sword hilt and the man crashed down on the cobbles. Seeing the ease with which the Ranger had dealt with him, the others drew back. Then, staying well clear of the glittering sword, they ran for it, pushing one another in their haste to get clear, and tangling with the *dooryeh* who had just rounded the last bend.

Gilan turned to face the oncoming guardsmen. Quickly, he tossed aside the hampering white robe and *kheffiyeh*. He unslung the huge longbow and passed it to Lydia.

'String this,' he ordered. Then he added, 'Do you know how?'

She nodded and took the bow, while he continued to face the oncoming *dooryeh*. Stepping her right foot in between the bow and the string, she locked the back of the bow against her left ankle. Then, grunting with the effort, and using all the strength of her body, thigh and back muscles, she bent the bow and forced the string up its length until the loop at the end of the bowstring slipped into the notch at the bow's tip and held fast.

'Done,' she announced.

'Good. Keep it ready,' Gilan told her. He didn't look at her. His eyes were locked on three of the *dooryeh* who were advancing, shoulder to shoulder, along the alley towards him. They eyed the long, straight-bladed sword in his hand warily. It weaved and flickered from side to side as he kept it moving constantly, the tip of the blade low, threatening them, warning them against coming closer.

Then he heard a grunt of exertion from the girl behind him, and a hissing sound as something flew past his ear.

The *dooryeh* on the left of the slowly advancing line suddenly staggered back, spun around by the force of a speeding metre-long dart that seemed to come out of nowhere and transfixed his right shoulder. He screamed in pain as he fell on his side. His companions looked at him in horror, looked up and saw Lydia preparing to cast another dart.

They turned and ran back around the bend, leaving their comrade, sobbing with pain, to drag himself awkwardly after them.

'Good work!' Gilan said, turning to look admiringly at Lydia. Like him, she had discarded her robe and *kheffiyeh*. She held the second atlatl dart ready in its thrower.

She grinned at him. 'Might make them respect women a little more.'

'I should think it will. But I doubt they'll be in any hurry to admit women into the markets.' He sheathed his sword and took the bow from where she had set it resting against one of the store counters. An arrow seemed to appear on the string and Lydia looked impressed in her turn.

A head came round the bend in the alley, twenty-five metres away from them. Before Lydia could move, Gilan had drawn, aimed and shot, sending an arrow thudding into the fabric-covered store front half a metre from the curious face. The face disappeared immediately, with a yelp of fright.

'What now?' Lydia asked. 'I assume we have a plan B?'

He shook his head. 'We're way past plan B,' he told her. 'And we've gone past plan C as well. We're up to plan D now.'

'And what's plan D?'

He jerked his head down the alley to the corner. 'Anyone comes round that corner, we shoot them.'

She pursed her lips critically. 'Doesn't sound too ingenious,' she said.

He shrugged. 'I'm not good at ingenious. I'm good at dangerous.'

As he spoke, the head appeared again and he shot again. But it had jerked back almost as soon as it was exposed and his shot missed. Almost instantaneously, one of the *dooryeh* broke cover and dashed for a stall five metres down the alley and on the left-hand side. He disappeared into cover as Gilan shot again. Another guardsman tried to follow, seeing Gilan's bow was empty. But he reckoned without the speed and accuracy of the Ranger's shooting and a fourth arrow hit him in the side as he was halfway across the alley.

The first head appeared again, bobbing rapidly in and out. But Gilan was wise to this trick now and he held his shot.

A dark mass flew across the open space by the bend in the alley and Gilan's arrow hit it before it had gone two metres. He cursed as he realised he had been tricked. The *dooryeh* had thrown a cloak across the gap and he'd shot it. While he did so, two more of them dashed across the gap and made it to the cover of the stall.

'Feel free to take a hand any time you like,' Gilan said mildly.

But Lydia shook her head. 'I'm not as fast as you. I'd be wasting darts.'

He smiled. 'It's a wise person who knows their limitations,' he said.

There was a cracking noise of splintering wood from the stall where the *dooryeh* had gone to ground. Lydia frowned.

'What was that?' she asked.

'I'd say they're breaking through to the next stall,' he said. 'They'll work their way down from stall to stall until they reach us.'

There were five stalls between the one they were sheltering in and the one where the *dooryeh* were concealed, each one only a few metres wide. Gilan cursed. While they were talking, another two *dooryeh* had darted across the alley, diving into cover in the stall.

'I'd better keep my eye on things,' he said. 'If you have any ideas, remember to speak up.'

There was a short pause. Then Lydia replied:

'What about the roof?'

CHAPTER FORTY-SIX

From their vantage point at the top of the tiers of benches, Hal and the others had a clear view of the dark bulk that was the slave market. They had been crouching in the shadows of the roofed structure over the gateway tunnel, waiting for something to happen.

For what seemed like an age, the slave market remained dark and depressingly silent. Then they heard the faint sound of shouting, followed by the clanging of an alarm bell. As the warning was passed along from one person to the next, they made out the word, 'Fire!'

More shouting followed — indistinct and muffled. The words couldn't be made out but the tone of alarm was all too obvious.

Another bell began clanging. This one was closer and Hal realised it was in the guard area of the arena itself. Lights began to show in the windows of the guardroom opposite them, and orders were being shouted. After a few seconds, a stream of half-dressed, half-armed men began to make their way out of the ground-floor doors. The massive gates creaked open and the men formed into squads and headed at a jog for the gold market.

The main garrison building was thirty metres away and lights were coming on there now as well. Hal realised that the time was right. The level of confusion would be at its highest now, as men asked what was happening and ran to take up their stations.

He tapped Jesper on the shoulder. 'Let's go.'

Jesper had the rope ready, tied to the base of one of the fixed benches. He tossed it over the edge, letting it fall into the sand-floored tunnel leading away between the tiers. He wriggled over the edge and went down the rope hand over hand. Stig followed, then Thorn. The old sea wolf could manage the downward climb easily enough. He wrapped one end of the rope round his upper right arm, above the club-hand, taking up the tension in the bight of rope around his arm. Then he seized the rope with his left hand, clamped his feet together over one of the knots, and lowered himself over the edge of the railing, sliding down rapidly to the sand below.

Hal was close behind him and they grouped together before the large wooden door that led into Mahmel's office. Jesper sorted through his supply of keys and picks and finally settled on one. He inserted it into the lock and turned slightly. Then he inserted a pick with a rounded protrusion on it and ran it gently into the lock, his eyes closed in concentration. He felt the tumblers of the lock as his curved pick slid over, depressing them.

Then there was a distinct click and he opened his eyes and grinned at Hal.

'After you,' he said, making a bowing gesture.

Hal drew his sword. The sound of the steel rasping gently against the leather and brass of the scabbard was reassuring. Holding it down by his side, he turned the door handle and pushed the door inwards, flattening himself against it to allow Stig and Thorn past him, as they had arranged.

The two Skandians leapt into the room, their soft boots making barely any noise as they moved lightly and stayed on their toes. Seeing the way clear straight ahead, they fanned out left and right, advancing into the room with their weapons ready.

The room was empty.

Mahmel's table, the main piece of furniture in the room, was neatly covered with a light piece of cloth. His chair was pushed in against the table. There was no lamp and the only light came through the large open door behind them. Hal pointed to a lantern on the table.

'Get that lit,' he ordered and Stig moved quickly to comply. The wick caught and the yellow light flared up, casting giant, wavering shadows of the four Skandians against the walls in the room.

'Nobody home,' Stig said, relaxing. He lowered his battleaxe to rest its head on the floor as he surveyed the empty room.

'There'll be plenty downstairs,' Thorn said.

Jesper was already moving to the second locked door, sorting through his picks again. Dimly, through the open door, they could hear the cries of alarm and the strident clanging of the two bells.

'I'm surprised nobody's come up to see what that's about,' Stig said, but Hal shook his head.

'They probably can't hear it down there. They're quite a way below ground.'

It also occurred to Hal that the dungeon guards were probably briefed not to react to alarms heard outside the slave market. Their job was to contain the slaves in the vast prison pen below the arena, nothing more.

'Are you two going to stand there nattering all night?' Jesper asked. He had the door to the top of the stairs open. Once again, he gestured for the others to go before him and, once again, Stig and Thorn led the way, weapons ready to greet any guard who might be on his way up the stairs.

But the stairs were deserted. They crept quietly down to the first turn and paused. Stig leaned around the wall and peered down. The stairway was lit by torches set in the walls, as they had seen on their first visit. The flickering yellow light showed the stairs were empty. Stig gestured for the others to follow and they went down. As Hal had surmised, the thick walls cut off all sound from above. The only noise evident was the soft pattering of their sealskin boots on the stone.

Thorn and Stig reached the bottom of the stairs, facing the massive wooden door set in the arched opening in the stone wall. Jesper moved forward, his lock-picks ready. But Thorn put out his left hand to restrain him. Jesper looked at him, puzzled, then Thorn gestured for Hal to move up to them. They could see a thin line of light underneath the door.

'Lights are on,' Thorn said. 'Where's the table?'

Hal closed his eyes, visualising the layout of the room. Thorn, of course, hadn't accompanied him and Jesper on their previous visit. He pointed ahead and a little to the right.

'There,' he said. Thorn stared in the direction he had indicated, fixing it in his mind, then asked in the same quiet voice:

'Is it end on to the door or set crossways?'

'Crossways,' Hal said promptly.

Thorn nodded in satisfaction. That would make things easier, he thought. 'And the bunks?'

Again Hal pointed. 'To the left of the door, ranged along the left-hand wall. And about three metres from the door,' he added, before Thorn could ask.

'Good.' Thorn paused, setting the positions in his mind, preparing himself for sudden, blindingly fast action. He glanced at Stig. 'You got that, Stig?'

Stig nodded confirmation.

'I'll go for the table first,' Thorn told him. 'You go left and take care of anyone who's trying to get out of the bunks.'

'Got it,' Stig said. His voice was calm and matter of fact. But Hal could see his hand clenching and unclench-ing on the haft of his battleaxe.

Thorn turned to Jesper.

'Jes, can you get that lock open without making too much noise about it?' he asked.

Jesper smiled. 'Trust me.'

Thorn rolled his eyes to heaven. 'Why do I never trust people who say that to me?' he asked. Then, before Jesper could answer, he motioned towards the door with his club-hand.

'Open it and get out of the way,' he said. Jesper stooped over the lock, his two picks sliding into the keyhole and his sensitive fingers feeling the movements of the tumblers inside the lock's mechanism as he teased them open. He took a little longer over this lock, as he wanted to avoid any unnecessary noise.

Then a soft *click!* was audible to them all. He glanced at Thorn, making sure the old warrior was ready, then turned the door handle and threw the double doors wide open.

He felt Stig and Thorn sweep past him like a hurricane as he moved to his right to stay clear. Hal, sword in one hand, saxe in the other, moved in behind them to provide support wherever necessary.

The guardroom was lit by three lanterns and a brace of candles on the table. After the dimness of the stairwell, the light inside was positively brilliant. Four of the guards were seated at the table, directly in front of Thorn. They looked up from their dice game, frozen with shock at the terrible sight of Thorn, massively built and his wild hair flying out underneath his black watch cap, storming towards them. For a moment, all any of them could see was the massive club that formed his right hand.

Then, one of them, slightly faster on the uptake than the others, began to rise, just as Thorn kicked the heavy table over. The two guards on the far side went down under it. The two on the side nearest Thorn were caught by a quick back and forth sweep of his club, thudding into their skulls and sending them sprawling to either side.

Stig went round the table at a run. There were three men dozing in the bunks. They'd taken off their chain mail and leather armour and were wearing undershirts and trousers. Drowsily, they came awake, trying to work out what was happening.

Before they could, Stig's axe had done its work, sweeping backwards and forwards to send two of them back to sleep. Like Gilan earlier in the evening, Stig drew the line at actually killing the men, unarmed and defenceless as they were. He used the flat of his axe blade to hit them and knocked them senseless. The third man actually made it out of bed. He was on Stig's left and the young Skandian drove into him with his shield, the heavy metal boss in the centre crashing into the man's ribs and the force of the impact hurling him back against the stone wall. His head hit the stone and he too resumed his all-too-briefly interrupted slumber.

One of the two men pinned under the table finally disentangled himself and shoved himself back along the floor, away from Thorn's terrifying club. He scrambled on hands and knees to reach the rack where the guards' weapons were stored. He'd just got his hands on a sword when Thorn's small shield swung in a wide arc and hit him on the side of the jaw. He went down, limp as a rag. The other man pinned under the table wisely made no move to extricate himself. He lay back on the floor, hands raised in a gesture of surrender.

'Where's the eighth man?' Thorn demanded harshly. Four men at the table and three asleep. There should have been eight in the room, according to what Mahmel had told them.

'Maybe he called in sick,' Jesper said.

Then, from an inconspicuous door behind Thorn that

had so far gone unnoticed, the eighth man erupted into the room, charging straight at Thorn, an iron-studded club in his hand.

Thorn whirled to face him, but trod on the unconscious body of one of the men from the table. He staggered and lurched awkwardly, desperately trying to recover his balance as the club began its forward arc, aiming to shatter his skull.

CHAPTER FORTY-SEVEN

'The roof?' Gilan said, puzzled. 'What about it?'

Lydia gestured up to the ceiling in the stall where they had taken shelter.

'That bit doesn't look too substantial,' she said.

Gilan looked up and agreed. The ceiling was made up of thin sheets of wood supported on battens. It was more for appearance than strength.

'If we break through there, we can get to the outer roof, smash through a few tiles and run for it. I noticed the other day that there are walkways set along the roof — presumably so workmen can walk on them without breaking the tiles.'

'Do it,' Gilan told her. 'Break through the ceiling and then get some of the tiles out of the way. I'll keep our friends busy.'

They could hear more timber shattering and cracking as the *dooryeh* broke through to another stall. Without another word, Lydia ran to the back of the stall they were in. She looked around, saw the display counter standing empty and dragged it under the spot she had selected. Cat-like, she leapt onto it, and found she had to stoop under the ceiling. In this part of the stall, rich brocaded material hung in folds from the ceiling, creating an exotic tent-like appearance. She ripped it down with her dirk, then sank the point of the blade between the ceiling material and the thin batten it was fastened to. She levered upwards and there was a rending noise — though not as penetrating as the ones the *dooryeh* were making — and the ceiling panel fell free, opening the way into a low, dark space above.

The lightweight battens wouldn't support her. She stood upright, with her head through the gap she had created, and felt around in the darkness for something more substantial. Her hand touched a thick, hardwood rafter. That would do, she thought. Gilan had discarded his bow in favour of his sword. She stooped, grabbed it and tossed it up into the roof space. She reached through the hole, found the rafter again and heaved herself up after the bow, lying across the rafter at first, then gradually coming up into a crouch, balanced on it. She heard a rending crack from below, followed by a sharp cry of pain. She hoped it wasn't the Ranger.

The thin wall Gilan was facing suddenly bulged inwards, then split. A huge crack appeared in it and one of the *dooryeh* was forcing his way through, a scimitar in his hand. His eyes widened in alarm as he saw Gilan ready and facing him. He tried to extricate himself from the tangle of split wood and hessian but before he could, Gilan's sword darted out and ran him through.

The Ranger's previous reservations about not killing a man who was simply doing his job were gone now. These men were soldiers, trained fighters. And Gilan and Lydia were outnumbered and fighting for their lives.

As the man went down, another guard tried to force his way past, kicking flat-footed at the rent in the wall to widen it. Behind him, Gilan could see other faces — dark skinned and bearded — and the gleam of weapons. In the constricted space of the stall, it was difficult to swing the sword, a fact that put the scimitar-bearing *dooryeh* at a disadvantage. The scimitar was designed to cut and hack at an enemy, not to thrust. Gilan's straight-bladed Araluan sword was more suited to the conditions. As a second guard forced his way through the wall, Gilan parried a clumsy, off balance thrust and darted his own sword forward like a striking snake.

The *dooryeh* was wearing a chain mail vest. It would protect him against a dagger thrust, but against Gilan's specially hardened blade, with the strength of his body, shoulder and arm behind it, it was of little use. The point smashed the chain links aside after the briefest pause, then went on into the man's body. He gave a great shout and sank to his knees, effectively blocking the path of the men behind him.

'Hurry up!' Gilan yelled. He could see a sword blade smashing through another part of the light wall that separated the two stalls. Any moment now, he'd be defending two breaches.

Crouched in near darkness, balanced on the rafter, Lydia shoved against the underside of the tiles above her. She'd always assumed that tiles were simply laid on a roof, without any fastening. But these ones seemed impossible to shift. She felt with her fingers for a join between two of them, then drew her dirk and inserted it in the tiny crack.

Nothing moved. She tried levering the dirk back and forth, to no avail. Then, shoving the point hard up against the break between the two tiles, she hammered her free hand against the pommel, forcing it up into the gap. It was airless and hot in the narrow roof space and perspiration ran down into her eyes.

She hammered again and felt something give. Again! And the left-hand tile actually moved a few centimetres upwards. Once more, she thrust up at it, straightening her bent knees to use the big muscles in her body, and the tile flew clear, clattering loudly down the sloping roof as it did.

With one tile missing and the structural integrity of that part of the roof gone, it was relatively easy to smash and heave others out of the way. She rapidly widened the gap, hurling the loosened tiles down the shallow slope of the roof. When she felt she had enlarged the hole sufficiently, she ducked back into the ceiling space and hung head-down from the rafter.

As her head emerged through the rent in the ceiling, Gilan was dealing with another *dooryeh* who had broken through. They faced each other, scimitar and sword touching, then moving apart, then touching again as they tested each other, the tips moving in small circles, each duellist's eyes intent on the other.

The guard was a capable swordsman, Gilan could see. He was nowhere near Gilan's level of skill, but he was an opponent worthy of respect. One mistake, and no matter how skilful you might be, you could find yourself dead, the other man's blade sliding between your ribs and the blood and life flowing out of your body. You didn't toy with an opponent like this. You didn't try to be fancy or tricky or to wound him or disarm him. When the opportunity came, you killed him.

Or you died yourself.

The moment came.

The *dooryeh* lunged the scimitar forward, the blade inverted so that the tip pointed down. It was a move calculated to test Gilan's speed and reflexes, but the *dooryeh* mistimed it slightly and was a fraction of a second slow in withdrawing the blade and recovering his guard position.

Gilan's sword shot forward, flicking the scimitar aside a few centimetres, slid past, struck, then withdrew. The guard felt the impact, felt the point penetrate his chest, and almost immediately withdraw. Then he felt the hot gush of blood that spelled the end. He looked up at Gilan, shock and surprise in his eyes.

They were always surprised, Gilan thought. They always thought it couldn't happen to them.

The man sank to his knees, his lips moving as he tried to speak. But no words came.

'Come on!' It was Lydia, her voice cracking with tension as she leaned down through the hole in the ceiling, her hands stretched out to help him. He turned back momentarily to where another guard was stepping through the ragged hole, shoving his recent opponent to one side as he came. Gilan drew back his arm and sent his sword spinning, end over end, at the man.

The unexpected tactic caught the *dooryeh* by surprise. He flung up his scimitar to deflect the spinning sword, stepped to one side and slipped, falling across the dead body of the man who had preceded him. As he went down, he saw the foreigner leap up, hang for a few moments, then draw himself up through a hole in the ceiling.

'They're going through the roof!' he yelled.

But it was too late. The foreigners were gone.

Lydia, the moment Gilan turned away from the rent in the store wall, wasted no time getting out of his way. She tossed his bow up through the hole in the tiles, then seized both sides of the hole and jackknifed herself up onto the roof. One of the tiles was lying close by and she retrieved it, holding it ready. A few seconds later, Gilan heaved himself up onto the roof beside her.

'Damn,' he said angrily. 'I was quite fond of that sword.'

She had no idea what he was talking about, but she gestured to where his bow lay a few metres away. As he moved to retrieve it, she leaned back over the hole. She could see a pale face peering up from below the gap in the ceiling.

'This way!' she heard the man yell. Then, aiming carefully, she dropped the tile through the two gaps. She heard a dull thud, followed by a cry of pain. She looked again and the face had gone. Gilan touched her arm, pointing up the shallow slope of the roof. The raised plank walkway along the apex was ten metres away and the Ranger started out towards it, the tiles beneath his feet groaning and cracking as he ran. She followed him, stepping gingerly as she felt the tiles give beneath her feet, expecting any moment to go plummeting through them, back into the gold market. Then she was on the firm footing of the walkway.

She looked back. Smoke was beginning to seep out through the narrow cracks between the tiles. Then a head and shoulders emerged through the hole she had smashed in the roof. A guardsman clambered out, looked around and saw them.

'This way! They're going this —'

He got no further. Lydia's dart flashed across the roof and hit him in the chest. He staggered back under the impact, then went crashing through the hole, back the way he had come. They heard muffled cries of alarm as he fell, presumably landing on top of his comrades.

'Nice shot,' Gilan said, the admiration obvious in his voice. 'That'll make them think twice about poking their heads out through that hole.'

'Let's get going,' Lydia said. Her heart was pounding with the tension of the last few minutes. Adrenaline was surging through her system and her hands were shaking. Under these conditions, she knew that the shot had been more of a fluke than anything else. But fluke or not, it would do as Gilan said and delay their pursuers.

'Which way?' she asked.

Gilan pointed and ran, heading north-west. The walkway ran along the spine of the roof, which was oriented south-east to north-west. This way had them heading back towards the harbour.

'Shortest way's best,' he said. 'We'll find a way down once we're closer to the north-west wall, then get back to the boat.'

'It's a ship,' she said.

He shrugged. 'Whatever. We'll get back to it. I get the feeling this is not going to be a good place to be in the next hour or so.'

Behind them, to their left, they heard a smashing sound. Turning to look, they saw several tiles being flung aside as someone made another exit through the roof. Smoke roiled up out of this hole and a dim figure was just visible, climbing up, crouching on the roof and searching for them. He saw them and threw up a hand to point at them, just as Gilan's arrow hit him. He flung out his arms and fell back without a sound, sliding a few metres down the slope of the roof.

'It's not a good place to be right now,' said Lydia. Once more, she was astounded by the Ranger's speed and accuracy. They had both seen the guard emerge. Yet she hadn't managed to draw a dart from her quiver before Gilan nocked an arrow, drew back, aimed and shot.

And hit his target.

'Save your breath,' he told her and they set off again, running, crouched low. The moon had risen while they had been in the *souk*. It seemed to flood the broad, shallow-sloped roof with light so that they felt totally exposed to view. Fortunately, the feeling was an illusion, as there was nobody to see them.

They were almost to the north-west wall of the *souk* when Gilan paused, holding up an arm for her to stop. He looked behind them. There was no sign of any pursuit on the roof. But that didn't mean that the alarm wasn't being raised in the market below them.

'We could break back through the tiles,' Lydia suggested. 'We're well away from the fire now.'

But Gilan shook his head. 'If we go back in, we'll have to go out through one of the gates, and they'll all be secured by now.' He gestured at their clothes. 'And without our robes and *kheffiyehs*, we do tend to stand out. We'll have to find a way down the wall.'

He stepped off the walkway and began to edge carefully down the sloping tiles to the edge of the roof. Lydia followed tentatively, once again feeling the tiles bending and cracking under her feet. This roof will leak like a sieve if it ever rains here, she thought. As Gilan reached the edge of the roof, he went down on hands and knees to spread his weight, and moved to look over the edge.

She joined him, also crawling, feeling the roof's movement under her lessening as she did so. He pointed to a spot ten metres back from where they crouched.

'There,' he said. There was an arched gateway between the wall of the *souk* and the building adjacent. The top of the arch was two metres below the roof. From there, it was another two or three metres to the ground. But there were plenty of footholds and handholds in the rough stone of the arch and they could scramble down it. Or they could hang at arm's length from the arch and drop to the road below.

The trick would be getting down to the arch from where they were. They would have to jump and the top of the arch was less than a metre wide. Gilan knew he could manage it without losing his balance, but he wasn't sure if Lydia could.

'Are you up for it?' he asked her.

She didn't reply, but ran lightly to a spot above the arch, slid her feet over the edge of the roof and dropped without hesitation. She landed light as a cat on top of the stone arch, absorbed the shock of the fall with her flexed knees, and kept her balance with her hands spread wide. From there, she stooped and let herself hang by the arms. There was a drop of less than a metre beneath her feet and she let go, landed with barely a noise, looked up at him and nodded.

'Apparently, I am,' she said.

CHAPTER FORTY-EIGHT

Hal moved instinctively, faster than conscious thought. In a fraction of a second, he sensed that, even if he ran his sword through the attacking Socorran, the wicked club would undoubtedly complete its arc. The guard would be dead. But so would Thorn.

Instead, he swung backhanded with his sword at the wooden head of the club itself. The sword struck home with a loud *THOCK!* The razor-sharp edge bit into the hardwood and locked there, stopping the club in mid-stroke. Then he jerked the sword to one side. The blade, sunk deep in the wood, dragged the club with it, pulling the guard to his left as he held onto the shaft of the club.

Thorn quickly swung his small shield in a vicious left hook and hit the man flush on the nose. Blood spurted and, almost masked by the thud of connection, Hal heard a small cracking noise as the bones in the nose gave way. The guard gave one long sigh of pent-up breath and fell on his side, his face now a mask of blood. The club fell from his hand, dragging Hal's sword blade down with it.

Thorn looked round at his young friend. 'Thanks,' he said. 'He nearly had me.'

Hal nodded. He put one foot on the club and jerked his sword free. There was no need for either of them to say more. They were shipmates and brotherband members and that was the way things were between them. Any of the Herons would have done the same thing — although possibly not with the instinctive speed and lightning reflexes Hal had shown. In fact, Thorn realised, had it been anyone other than Hal, or possibly Stig, standing behind him, the odds were that his brains would be splattered over the floor by now.

'Where in the name of Perlins and Gertz did he spring from?' Jesper said, eyeing the previously unnoticed door through which Thorn's attacker had sprung.

Thorn wrinkled his nose in distaste. 'I'd say that's the privy,' he said. 'For Orlog's sake, someone shut that door.'

Stig obliged while Hal gestured for Jesper to open the door leading to the slave pen.

'Now that they're all accounted for, let's do what we came to do,' Hal said.

Jesper had the door unbolted in a second and they filed through.

As they entered the stone-lined passageway that led to the cell, they heard the sound of bodies stirring and an undertone of whispered comment. They also noticed the strong smell of nearly seventy unwashed bodies and the unpleasant odour of overfull latrine buckets.

Hal was second in line after Jesper. There was no need for Stig and Thorn to lead the way now that all the guards were incapacitated. He turned back to Stig, who was bringing up the rear.

'Pass me one of those lanterns, will you?'

Stig did so, and the extra light flooded the passageway, exposing the first few metres of the huge cell beyond the grille gate. Now the voices behind the gate were louder and more insistent as the prisoners realised that the new-comers weren't the soldiers who had been guarding them for the past weeks. A dozen voices were raised, crying out to ask who they were and did they have any water, and demanding that they be set free.

Hal took the lantern from Stig's hand and stepped closer to the grille.

'Quiet!' he shouted. As the noise continued, he repeated the order, even louder. Gradually, the hubbub of frantic voices died away and the slaves waited expectantly for his next words.

'Ingvar!' he called. 'Are you there?'

'I'm here, Hal,' Ingvar's deep voice replied from the gloomy interior. Peering in its direction, Hal saw a movement in the shadows at the rear of the room as Ingvar raised his hand.

'Have you located the Araluans?' Hal asked.

Jesper was moving to open the grille but Hal stopped him, saying in an aside, 'Just wait till we see how things are here, Jesper.'

Jesper, who was stooped over to access the lock with his picks, looked up at him in surprise. Hal had a sudden premonition that there might be trouble with the other captives if he rescued only the Araluans.

'We're here, Captain,' came a voice from the opposite

side of the cell to where Ingvar was chained. 'Your man says you've come to release us.'

Instantly, the chorus of voices broke out again, as the other slaves all shouted and pleaded to be released as well. Deciding it was safe to proceed, Hal motioned for Jesper to open the door. When he did, Hal stepped through into the cell, holding the lantern high to throw its light further. Stig and Thorn stood ready by the gate, in case he needed help.

As Mahmel had told them, the slaves were chained together in gangs of ten or twelve. They were shackled by one wrist to long chains that ran through iron rings set into the walls either side, leaving a narrow open space down the centre of the room. Presumably, the guards used this to feed the prisoners, or to take one gang from the cell without coming into the reach of the others. Hal moved in now, looking at the faces lining either side of the long, low-ceilinged room.

There was a wide mixture of racial types represented here. He saw swarthy Arridans, black-skinned tribesmen, and pale-skinned Gallicans. There were olive-skinned men and women from the half a dozen countries that bordered the Constant Sea.

They were all confined here, men and women alike, with no vestige of privacy between the genders. Perhaps, he thought, after losing your liberty and dignity, that was no longer an issue. Hands stretched out to him as he moved through the cell, and voices pleaded with him to be released, the chains rattling and clanking as the prisoners moved.

He saw Ingvar sitting quietly, chained to a group of prisoners. The big lad smiled as he saw the dim figure in the lantern light.

'Is that you, Hal?' he said. 'I wondered when you might get here.'

First things first, Hal thought. He turned and called back to Jesper.

'Jesper! Come and unlock Ingvar!' He glanced curiously at the prisoner next to Ingvar. He was a big man with a black beard, and an ugly bruise that spread across his nose and cheek. He seemed intent on staying as far from Ingvar as possible.

As Jesper made his way down the central cleared area, the calls from the prisoners were renewed. They realised that this was the man who could set them free. Jesper reached the spot where Ingvar was sitting and moved towards him. Instantly, prisoners from either side moved to intercept him and Hal drew his sword, stepping in among them.

'Get back!' he warned. 'We'll get to you in good time!'

Perhaps it was the tone of command in his voice. Or perhaps it was the fact that, after weeks or even months of imprisonment, they were conditioned to obey orders, but they pulled back and allowed Jesper room to release Ingvar.

As Jesper unlocked the padlock, and ran the long chain back through the wrist cuffs of the slaves shackled to him, the others in the group rose to their feet and began to surge towards the open grille. Hal blocked their way, his sword raised so that the point was at chest level.

'Stop!' he said.

They eyed the gleaming blade doubtfully. Stig and Thorn advanced into the cell, shoulder to shoulder, blocking the narrow access way. Silence fell as the cries died away and the captives eyed these newcomers suspiciously.

'Unchain the Araluans, Jesper,' Hal ordered quietly. Ingvar, rubbing his wrist where the shackle had rubbed against it, showed him to the group of twelve Araluans shackled together on the opposite side of the room. Hal heard the rattle and clank of shackles falling free onto the stone floor. Again, a murmur ran through the room. He held the lantern high and raised his voice so that it carried to every corner of the cell.

'Now look, I can release all of you. Or none of you, if that's what you choose.' A wary, expectant silence fell as he said the last words. He continued. 'I'm taking these Araluans out of here on my ship.'

'Take us all!' shouted a swarthy man a few metres away, chained to a group who were obviously his countrymen. But Hal shook his head.

'I don't have room for you all,' he said. 'I barely have room for these twelve.' He indicated the Araluans, who were now unchained. Jesper ushered them past him, towards the gate. Again, there were angry cries from those waiting to be released.

One of the men who had been chained with Ingvar stepped closer to Hal.

'We could make you take us,' he threatened. 'How would you stop us?'

The man felt a large hand on his shirt, turning him away from Hal. As he turned, he found himself facing Ingvar, less than a metre away. 'Do you want some of what Bernardo got?' Ingvar asked quietly.

The man looked at the cowed figure of the bully,

huddled against the wall, then looked back at Ingvar and saw the steely determination in his eyes. Hurriedly, he dropped his own gaze and shook his head.

'No. No. Carry on,' he muttered.

Ingvar nodded, then addressed the others nearby. 'Anyone else have any silly questions?'

The newly released slaves muttered and shuffled their feet. Nobody wanted to contend with the massive Skandian. Hal made a mental note to ask Ingvar what had gone on in the dungeon. He realised that the bearded man's injuries probably had nothing to do with the guards. But time was pressing and he didn't have time to pursue the matter now.

'I can't take you with us,' he repeated. 'But if you want to try to make your own way, we'll release you.'

Again, voices cried out for him to do this, but he held up his hand, the sword still in it.

'I've got to warn you, the Socorrans might not take it too kindly if you try to escape. If they recapture you, you could be in a lot of trouble.'

'We'll take our chances.' It was one of the black-skinned group from the south. He was tall and well muscled and obviously a warrior. His group comprised eight men and four women. All of them looked fit and able to fight. Hal nodded to him.

'If that's your choice, we'll let you go,' he said. 'But wait till we have everyone released. If a dozen of you run for it now, you'll alert the guards. The chances will be better if everyone goes at once.'

The man considered what he had said and nodded briefly. It made sense. If fifty or sixty of them ran at once, the guards would have their hands full.

'All right,' he said. 'We'll wait. But get these blasted chains off us!'

Hal looked towards the entrance and saw the last of the Araluans passing through the gate. Hal and Stig mustered them through the guardroom. Jesper waited by the gate, awaiting instructions.

'All right, Jes!' Hal called. 'Unlock any who want to go.' He gestured to the man who had spoken. 'Do this group first,' he said, then spoke to the man in an undertone. 'We'll set your group free first. But you'll have to help us control the others, in case someone decides to make a run for it.'

'That's agreed,' the man said. He held out his wrists as Jesper hurried through the cell to where they stood. Again, the clicking sound of shackles being released echoed off the stone walls. Hal noted that Jesper had found a key that fitted the shackles and padlocks. Whether it was from his own kit or he had taken it from the guardroom, he had no idea. But it was certainly faster than using his lock-picks.

On Hal's orders, he released those closest to the rear of the cell first, working his way back towards the gate. At least a third of those imprisoned declined the offer of release. They knew they would have little chance of escape once they made it out of Socorro itself and into the desert surrounding the city. Looking at the state of their clothes and their long, unkempt hair and grimy bodies, Hal surmised that they were the prisoners who had been held captive longest and whose spirits had been broken by their confinement. The newer captives still held some hope, and the idea of escape burned like a beacon for them.

They made their way back to the gate, with Jesper

releasing those who wanted to go, and a growing crowd of liberated prisoners shuffling behind them in the dim light. Once they were in the guardroom at the base of the stairs, Hal turned to the southerner, who was still close to him.

'What's your name?' he asked.

'Jimpani,' the man replied.

'Very well, Jimpani, here's what we're going to do. We go upstairs to the slave market office and wait there. The main gate is opposite, across the arena. My group will go first — any argument with that?'

Jimpani shook his head. 'That's fair. You got us out.'

'All right. Hold the rest of them back here. Jesper will open the main gates. Odds are the guards quartered there are all busy fighting a fire in the gold market. But there may be a few left behind. We'll deal with them if there are. Once we're through the gate, the way's open for the rest of you. Get across the arena as fast as you can and out the gate. Split up and head in whatever direction you want to. And good luck. I hope you make it home.'

He saw Jimpani's teeth flash white in a fierce grin. 'We'll make it,' he said confidently. 'And thanks.'

'My pleasure,' Hal told him. Then he started up the stairs to the slave market office, followed by his four crewmen and the twelve Araluans. He heard the patter of dozens of feet on the stone steps behind him. A hand dropped onto his shoulder and he looked around into Ingvar's eyes.

'I knew you'd be back for me,' the huge youth said.

Hal shrugged. 'Couldn't leave you here. I need someone to control Ulf and Wulf.' He paused, then added in a more serious tone, 'Now all we have to do is get back to the ship, and get out of here.'

CHAPTER FORTY-NINE

Mahmel hurried through the near empty streets towards the gold *souk*. Now that he was at ground level, moving through the twisting narrow streets, he could no longer see the massive, sprawling building. But he could hear the shouts and the insistent clanging of the alarm bell.

After several minutes, he came to the western gate of the *souk*. There was a milling crowd outside. People were rushing this way and that, some carrying buckets and barrels of water, others laden down with the gold and jewellery they had planned to sell in the market. Obviously, Mahmel thought, they were merchants who had stripped their stalls bare before they escaped, taking their valuables with them so they wouldn't be lost in the fire.

He sniffed the air. He could smell woodsmoke — and the more acrid smell of burning fabric — hessian and canvas.

There was a hubbub of voices around him — shouting,

incoherent voices, some calling out orders, others seemingly just calling out, all of them adding to the confusion. The way to the western gate was blocked by a crowd three or four deep. Most of them didn't seem to know where they were going or what they were doing. He turned to his two bodyguards and jerked a thumb at the crowd in front of him.

'Clear a path,' he said briefly.

The bodyguards didn't hesitate. They drove forward into the crowd, shoulder to shoulder, shoving people aside, striking out with the thick, metal-shod staffs they carried, kicking and elbowing anyone who was slow to move. People shouted and cried out in pain. But as they turned angrily to confront those responsible for the sudden assault, they recognised the men's uniforms and armour — and the turban of the smaller figure striding behind them. Mahmel's green turban marked him as a senior administrator in the city's hierarchy — the sort of person you didn't antagonise if you were wise. Such men had vast power, long memories and short tempers. The wise move in this situation was to accept the blows and kicks and get out of the way in a hurry.

The guards on duty at the gate saw Mahmel and came to attention.

'What's going on here?' he snapped.

The senior of the two cleared his throat nervously. He wasn't used to talking to such an important figure.

'A fire, sir. There's a fire in the *souk.*'

'I can see that, you imbecile!' snapped Mahmel. He went to speak further but was drowned out by the clanging of the alarm bell, which had begun once more.

He glared at the vacant-faced guard standing off to one side, who was tugging on the bell pull.

'What are you doing?' he demanded, then had to repeat the question in a louder voice. The bell ringer started out of his trancelike state, pausing momentarily.

'Sounding the alarm, lord,' he said.

'I think that's been taken care of by now,' Mahmel said in an acid tone. He turned back to the first guard. 'Are the *dooryeh* here?'

The man nodded. 'Yes, lord. The men from the garrison, and the men from the slave market guardhouse as well. They're all here. And the fire monitors.'

The fire monitors were the official fire brigade for the city. Mahmel stepped to one side to peer down the long main thoroughfare of the *souk*. There was plenty of smoke evident, but he could see no flames, no sign of fire leaping from one stall to the next.

'Have they got it under control?' he asked.

The guard hesitated. 'I . . . don't know, lord. I think maybe they have.'

'Where did the fire start?'

'Um . . . in the south-eastern quarter . . . I think.'

'Then go and find out. And find out if it's under control.'

'Yes, lord. At once.' The guard started to back away, nervously bobbing his head in a truncated attempt to bow.

'RUN!' shouted Mahmel and the man turned and ran, grasping at his helmet as it threatened to fall from his head. Mahmel turned to the man who had been mindlessly ringing the bell. His hand still grasped the rope bellcord, as if he were ready to start again, any minute.

'As for you, do something useful. Come and take charge here at the gate,' he ordered.

The man saluted nervously, then moved to take up a position by the table set across the gateway. Mahmel shook his head in disgust. Some of these men couldn't think for themselves. He beckoned his senior bodyguard, who stepped forward, waiting for orders.

'Find the commander of the *dooryeh*,' Mahmel told him. 'He'll most likely be in the south-eastern quarter of the *souk*. Tell him to report to me here.'

'Yes, lord.' The bodyguard slapped his palm to his chest in salute, turned and ran into the smoky interior of the *souk*. Mahmel beckoned the other bodyguard forward.

'See if you can find me a glass of tea,' he said. 'One of the tea houses must still be open.'

'Yes, Lord Mahmel,' the man replied and he hurried off into the *souk* as well.

All very well for you, the guard thought to himself. The *souk*'s on fire, people are panicking in all directions, and you expect me to find a tea house still serving.

It took him ten minutes and he was rewarded by an angry scowl from his master as he handed him the glass of hot mint tea. A few minutes later, the other bodyguard returned, accompanied by a colonel of the *dooryeh*. Close behind the colonel strode a corporal in a blue tunic. A signal horn hung from his belt. The colonel saw Mahmel sitting on a straight-backed wooden chair sipping his tea, noted the significance of the green turban and strode forward, coming to attention.

'Colonel Bekara, lord. Commander of the gold market garrison.'

'What's been going on here, Colonel?' Mahmel asked. Then, before the man could respond, he added sarcastically, 'And don't tell me there's been a fire. I can see that. I want details. How did it start? Who was responsible? What damage has been done?'

The colonel paused, gathering his thoughts.

'The fire was started by two foreigners, sir, in the south-east quarter. One of them distracted the merchants there while the other broke into a store room and lit the fire. Apparently, one of them was a woman. They were recognised. They were seen in the market yesterday.'

Mahmel frowned, stroking his chin thoughtfully. 'What did they steal?'

The colonel shrugged. 'I don't think they stole anything, sir. They lit the fire, then they were recognised and a detachment of the patrol gave chase. They escaped by breaking through the roof.'

'And your men simply let them go?' Mahmel's voice was dangerously soft.

The colonel drew himself up angrily. 'I lost two men and three others were badly wounded, sir.'

'To a man and a *woman*?' Mahmel asked.

The colonel took a deep breath. He was about to answer angrily. But he recognised Mahmel and he knew the man had a vindictive streak. He was not a good person to get on the wrong side of.

'They were apparently skilled fighters, sir,' he explained.

Mahmel snorted disgustedly. 'So it seems. In any event, what did you do?'

'When the alarm went up, I mustered the garrison and

- 406 -

led them here — along with the guard detachment from the slave market. I thought we might need as many men as possible to get the fire under control. I sent a runner for the fire monitors as well.'

'And is the fire under control?'

'Yes, sir. It hadn't spread too far and we managed to localise the danger. Mind you, if we hadn't got here when we did, it might be a different story,' he added.

Mahmel nodded distractedly. 'Yes, yes. I'm sure all your men were very brave and very efficient, Colonel.' He frowned as a thought struck him. 'You say you brought the entire garrison, and the detachment from the slave market?'

'As I say, I had no idea how big the fire was. I thought we might need a lot of men.'

'So the slave market is currently unguarded?'

'No, sir. The eight duty guards in the dungeon guard-house are still there.'

'But nobody else?'

The colonel shuffled his feet uncomfortably. 'Um . . . no, sir. But I'm sure they —'

'Let me summarise, Colonel.' Mahmel had no wish to hear what the colonel was sure about. 'Two foreigners, a man and a woman, come in here, set a small fire, steal nothing, create all sorts of confusion, then escape over the roof, after killing several of your men. Why do you think they would do that?'

'I . . . um . . . I'm not sure, sir.' The colonel was begin-ning to perspire. He had a good idea what the administrator was getting at, but he didn't want to voice the thought.

'It doesn't occur to you that perhaps they wanted

to draw you and your men here — away from the slave market? That this was all an elaborate diversion while someone else broke in and set the slaves free?'

'That could be the case, sir . . . I suppose,' the colonel replied.

Mahmel's eyes narrowed as he recalled the four Hellenese men who had brought the big slave into the market two days previously. They hadn't been happy about leaving him there, he remembered. And he recalled that two of them made sure they had a good look at the security arrangements in the cellar.

And now two foreigners had broken into the market, set a fire and escaped.

'Get your men back here immediately!' Mahmel snapped. 'Form them into squads and throw a cordon around the city. Send a runner to the harbour fortress and get more men from there to block off the streets. I want ten men to come with me to the slave market.'

'Yes, sir!' The colonel snapped his fingers to the signaller who had accompanied him. 'Sound the withdrawal, then the assembly,' he ordered. 'Do it now!'

As the horn began sounding its wailing summons through the streets of the *souk*, the colonel looked round to find Mahmel's angry stare fixed on him.

'Squads of ten. Send them out through the city. Tell them to recapture the slaves if they can. If not, kill them.'

'You think there's really been an escape, sir?' the colonel asked. His blood ran cold with the thought. If any slaves were killed or made their escape, someone would have to pay for it and he had an uncomfortable feeling who that person might be.

'You'd better hope there hasn't been, Captain,' Mahmel told him.

The colonel cleared his throat awkwardly as the first of his troops came running out of the *souk* in answer to the horn's call.

'I'm a colonel, sir,' he said.

'Not any more,' Mahmel told him.

CHAPTER FIFTY

Thorn and Stig led the way across the arena, weapons at the ready. Jesper was close behind them, then Ingvar and Hal shepherded the twelve Araluans across. There were nine men and three women in the Araluan party. Their clothes were all rags and several of them were injured — with wounds roughly bandaged in dirty scraps of cloth.

'They're in pretty bad shape,' Hal observed to Ingvar.

The big youth shrugged. 'They're half starved,' he said. 'Tursgud fed them barely anything, and since they've been here it hasn't been much better. Plus some of them have been badly beaten.' He scowled angrily. 'The Socorrans seem to think that if they mistreat slaves and starve them, they'll be weak and easier to control. Apparently they feed them up just before the sale to put some condition on them.'

Hal could see that Ingvar was right. 'Doubt they'll be much use if we have to fight our way out,' he said.

Ingvar shook his head. 'They're not warriors anyway, Hal,' he replied. 'They're farmhands and house servants. Most of them wouldn't know one end of a sword from another.'

'Well, if we run into a patrol, keep them back behind us and we'll let Thorn and Stig take care of the fighting.'

Ingvar grinned. 'I imagine they're more than capable of handling that.'

Thorn, Stig and Jesper were at the main gate now. Thorn and Stig took up positions either side of Jesper while he applied himself to the lock. After a few seconds' work, the gate swung open, making no sound on its well-oiled hinges. Stig and Thorn went through, weapons ready for trouble. But there was no sign of any guards on the other side and they beckoned for the others to follow.

As he went through the massive gates, Hal turned back to the tunnel they had recently vacated. He saw movement there and waved his arm. Instantly Jimpani and his countrymen began to sprint across the sand in a tight group, followed by a raggle-taggle band of the other slaves who had chosen to take the chance of escaping.

Thorn turned to Hal as he emerged from the arena. 'Which way?'

Hal pointed across the open parkland and to the right. 'Back the way we came,' he said. 'Keep to the side streets.' The main roads would be the first to be blocked off once word of the escape got out.

They set out across the open ground, with Hal and Ingvar working to keep the Araluans in a cohesive group. It wasn't easy. Some of them were weaker than others and those who were wounded found it hard to keep up.

'Keep going!' Hal ordered. 'Run! If they recapture you, you'll be in big trouble!'

It was a race against time now, to get clear of the slave market before the Socorrans had a chance to throw a cordon around the city streets. The former slaves did their best to obey him, but the pace was still painfully slow — restricted as it was to that of the weakest. Hal glanced back and saw Jimpani and his band emerge from the gates, look around, and head off in the opposite direction to the one the Skandians had taken. Then more figures appeared, running haphazardly, without any sense of co-ordination or organisation.

As he reached the concealment of a narrow alleyway beyond the park, Hal heard a shout and the ringing clash of weapons being drawn. He looked back, peering around the corner of the alley. A group of *dooryeh* had appeared, running from the direction of the gold market. Their leader was the green-turbaned Mahmel and, as Hal watched, he yelled a command for the slaves to stop, and for his men to advance on them.

Some of the escapees, alarmed by the sudden appearance of the soldiers, threw up their hands in surrender, blocking the exit of others behind them through the gate. About a dozen of those already outside chose to run.

It was a fatal mistake.

The *dooryeh* were carrying short, powerful bows and, at a command from Mahmel, they began shooting at the fleeing slaves. At such short range, they couldn't miss and the would-be escapees began to fall, some crying out in pain, others ominously silent.

Almost immediately, the survivors stopped in place, hands raised in surrender.

'Let's get out of here,' Hal said, and Thorn and Stig began to lead the way through the winding streets, keeping up a steady jog.

The prisoners couldn't maintain the pace, however. One of the women among the Araluans was in particularly bad shape. She limped painfully after Stig and Thorn, but fell behind, even with two of her countrymen trying to support her. Two others were nursing injuries as well and gradually the group became strung out over a fifty-metre distance until Hal called for Stig and Thorn to stop. One of the Araluan men, a former ploughman named Walton, seemed to be their leader. He shook his head apologetically to Hal as the skirl tried to exhort the Araluans to greater speed.

'Ophelia can't manage it,' he said. 'She's weak from starvation, and two of the guards beat her yesterday until she was unconscious. And both Ambrose and Silas were wounded when we were first captured.' He nodded his head to two of his other countrymen who had taken the opportunity to sink to the cobblestones. Hal noticed both of them had severe leg wounds. It would be impossible for them to run in such a condition.

'Can we let them rest for a few minutes?' the Araluan pleaded.

Hal bit his lip, then nodded. There was no point coming all this way to rescue them, he thought, only to leave them behind once they were free.

'Just a quick rest,' he said. He walked to where the woman was sitting leaning against the stone wall of a building that fronted the alley. She was young – he guessed she was in her mid-twenties. She was small and looked quite frail. She was gasping with pain and exhaustion and he could see the dark bruises on her face and legs. There was fresh blood showing through an improvised bandage around her waist. He dropped to one knee beside her and her eyes opened. She reached out a hand and seized his wrist in a weak grip.

'May the gods bless you for coming,' she said, wincing with pain as she spoke. 'Ingvar told us you'd come for us. Thank you.'

Hal waved her thanks aside. 'Never mind that,' he said gently. 'But we have to keep moving. Can you make one more effort? Just for a short while?'

She nodded, but he could see that even that small movement caused her pain.

'I'll try,' she whispered. 'Just give me another minute.'

He squeezed her hand. 'I'll give you two,' he said and she smiled weakly at him. He glanced up at her companions, one of the other women and a young man.

'Do all you can to keep her moving,' he said and they nodded. Then he moved to the two wounded men. One of them had a gaping wound in his thigh. It had been bandaged, but the exertion of running across the park had opened the wound so that it was bleeding heavily once more. The other was nursing his right ankle, which was hugely swollen and black with a terrible bruise – or worse. Hal wondered briefly whether the ankle was broken. If so, it would be enormously painful to walk on.

He looked around at the other Araluans, who were all watching him with a mixture of hope and despair on their faces — hope that they were being rescued. Despair because they were moving so slowly. He appealed to two of them who seemed to be in better condition than the others.

'Can you help him?' he asked, indicating the man with the injured ankle. 'We have to get to our ship, and then you can all rest. But the patrols will be sent out shortly to block our way — and we have to keep ahead of them.'

The two men shifted their feet and lowered their eyes, unwilling to meet his gaze. He felt a surge of anger.

'Do you want to leave him here?' he demanded sharply. 'Is that the way you care for your friends?'

'All right. We'll take him,' one of the two said. But the reluctance in his voice was all too obvious and Hal shook his head in disgust.

'You do or I'll leave you here with him,' he snapped. 'Now get him on his feet and help him!' He glanced around and saw Ingvar's huge bulk silhouetted against the light from the end of the alley. 'Ingvar, can you carry the one with the leg wound? If he tries to walk, it'll just keep bleeding and it could kill him.'

'Not a problem, Hal,' Ingvar said.

Hal felt a surge of affection for the big youth. No questions, no complaints. Hal smiled his gratitude.

'See if you can bandage that wound a little tighter,' he said. 'Anything you can do to stop the blood.'

Ingvar moved to the wounded man and checked the bandage on his leg. It was totally inadequate for the huge wound. Ingvar took off his shirt, tore out one sleeve, and began to bind it tightly around the man's leg. In a few seconds, the new bandage was red with blood, but it seemed to stem the flow a little.

'Let's get you up,' Ingvar said and, without any apparent effort, he swung the man up, carrying him piggyback like a child. He glanced at his skipper. 'Ready when you are, Hal.'

'All right,' Hal called softly. 'Let's get the injured ones on their feet and let's move out.' He gestured for Thorn and Stig to go ahead. 'Jesper,' he said, 'stay with me and we'll bring up the rear.'

Slowly, painfully, the party recommenced its journey towards the harbour.

Tursgud had spent the evening in a tavern. He'd been forced to go further afield than normal, as several of the drinking places he'd frequented in the past week had banned him and his crew. They'd caused too many fights and too many disagreements. And while dockside tavern keepers expected, and tolerated, a certain amount of violence, too much was bad for trade. When people were fighting, they weren't drinking.

So on this night, he'd ventured ashore alone. He tried to gain entry to several places close to the docks, but he was recognised and rejected. He considered objecting. He was a big, well-muscled youth and he carried a saxe at his side, like all Skandians. But the taverns were well supplied with even bigger, more heavily muscled, guards, whose job it was to enforce the tavern keepers' edicts, and so he rejected the idea.

Grumbling to himself, he moved further away from the familiar streets close to the docks until he found a small, rather dingy bar where he wasn't known. He spent the night there, hunched over a table in the corner, repeatedly calling for his ale cup to be refilled, and becoming more and more unpleasant each time he did so.

He was angry about the way things had worked out in Socorro. He had assumed he could bring his cargo of slaves to the city, sell them to the people who organised the slave market, and move on. But he discovered, as Hal had, that the market didn't buy slaves directly. The auctioneers acted as middlemen, organising the auctions and paying only when the slaves were sold — and keeping a hefty commission of thirty per cent for themselves.

Which meant if Tursgud and his crew wanted to be paid, they had to wait until the auction, which wasn't due for another day. And in the meantime, they were being stung for harbour dues and mooring fees. Hence his current bad mood.

That mood hadn't been improved when the owner of the bar he'd been drinking in had abruptly told him to leave several minutes ago. He was the last remaining customer and the barkeeper had approached his table and seized the empty tankard from in front of him.

'Get me another,' Tursgud demanded, his words slurring a little.

The barkeeper snorted derisively. 'That's all you get,' he said. 'We're closing. Take a look around you. There's no one else here.'

In fact, there was one other person. He was a big, heavily muscled southerner who worked for the bar, and he was casually swinging a heavy blackthorn club from side to side, smacking it into his left palm. Tursgud studied him through hooded eyes. He'll be slow, he thought. I could easily take him with my saxe before he could swing that club at me.

Then good sense prevailed. There was no logical reason to suppose that the other man would be slow in his reactions. Big men often moved as fast as a small man could — and very few men survived as guards in a bar if they were slow. On the other hand, Tursgud had the intelligence to realise that *he'd* been drinking all evening, and his reactions would almost certainly be impaired.

Snarling to himself, he rose and shambled out of the bar. He hadn't gone more than two metres before he heard the door slam behind him, and the noise of the bolts being shot home. He turned back and made an obscene gesture at the closed door, then, reeling a little, he began heading back along the narrow street towards his ship.

At the intersection with the next alley, he paused, hearing the sound of running feet. He drew back into the shadows. There seemed to be a large party of people coming his way.

He was startled when the first of them appeared, and he recognised Thorn and Stig, both armed and both scanning the streets to either side. Even though he knew he was in shadow, Tursgud drew back even further, watching as a group of a dozen people followed the two Skandians. His eyes widened as he recognised the dozen Araluans he had delivered to the slave market. Then he cursed silently as he saw Hal and Jesper bringing up the rear, both with weapons drawn and ready.

What are they doing here? he asked himself, and the answer was almost immediately apparent. They had pursued him off the Araluan coast. But when he had led them into the maze of shoals and reefs, he assumed they had either given up the chase or, better still, been wrecked on the reefs.

Now, he realised, they had followed him here and released the Araluan slaves. At the same moment, he realised where they would be heading. Their ship, that cursed *Heron*, must be somewhere in the harbour. His mind worked overtime as he tried to overcome the fog of alcohol. He hadn't seen it in the outer harbour, so they must have found a mooring in the north-eastern arm, where they would be out of his sight.

That meant that when they tried to escape, they'd have to sail past the point where *Nightwolf* was moored.

And that meant he could be ready and waiting for them.

CHAPTER FIFTY-ONE

Ulf stood back and surveyed their handiwork with satisfaction. The ship was re-rigged with its two fore and aft yardarms and triangular sails. They had unfastened the forestay when they took down the temporary square-rigged yardarm, then reattached it in its original position once the twin yardarms were in place. He tested the tension on the thick rope. It felt bar-taut and he nodded to himself.

Stefan beckoned to Wulf.

'Give us a hand running the starboard sail up,' he said. 'I thought I felt that block catch a little before.'

Stefan, Edvin and Wulf heaved on the halyard and the sail slid smoothly up the mast — until it reached a point halfway up. Then, as Stefan had predicted, the rope jammed in the block and the yardarm stopped moving up. Annoyed, they released the halyard and let the yardarm and sail slide down again. Stefan moved to smear grease into the block — a large wooden pulley that gave them extra purchase when they were hoisting the mast and sail — to make it run more smoothly. As he did so, Kloof, who was tethered to the mast, leaned forward eagerly, sniffing at the grease and getting in Stefan's way. He took a half-hearted swipe at her with the brush he was using. She wagged her tail and tried to catch the brush in her teeth.

'Move her away, will you?' he appealed to Ulf. After all, Ulf had been doing nothing in the last few minutes but watching and Stefan thought it was time for him to lend a hand. Ulf obligingly stepped across the deck and unfastened the length of cord that held Kloof in place.

With the instinctive cunning of all tethered dogs once they feel the tether loosened, Kloof jerked suddenly away, putting all her forty-five kilograms of weight behind a lunge for freedom. The thin cord slipped through Ulf's hand and she was free. She darted aft, easily evading Edvin's desperate clutching dive, and crouched, backside high, forefeet and nose low, waiting for Ulf to make a move to recapture her.

'Bad dog!' he said. 'Come back here!'

He crept carefully towards her. The loose end of the cord was barely two metres away, lying on the deck. At the last moment, he made a dive for it, as quickly as he could.

But, fast as he was, Kloof was even faster. She hurled herself to one side and the cord whipped away from Ulf's clutching fingers.

'Stop cackling and give me a hand!' Ulf snarled at the other three. The sight of Ulf blundering after the nimble-footed dog had set them laughing helplessly. Now they gathered themselves and moved to help him, planning to hem the dog in between them.

But Kloof wasn't in any mood to be hemmed. Assessing the relative sizes of Stefan and Wulf, she darted towards Stefan, pulling loose from his hands as they clutched briefly at the scruff of her neck, then cannoning into him and sending him crashing into Edvin so that they both went sprawling into the rowing well.

The way to the wharf was now clear. In a series of great bounds, she crossed the deck, leapt to the top of the bulwark, then onto the timber planking of the wharf. Once there, she set off at high speed and disappeared into the maze of narrow alleys at the end of the wharf.

'Kloof! Come back! Good dog! Here, Kloof!' Wulf shouted desperately. Then, in despair, he added, 'Oh, Gorlog take you! Bad dog!'

Stefan put two fingers into the corners of his mouth and let out a piercing whistle. But there was no sign of the massive dog.

Ulf rounded on his brother in a fury. 'Why didn't you catch her?' he demanded. 'She was right in front of you!'

'Don't blame me!' Wulf retorted angrily. 'You were the idiot who untied her from the mast!'

'Because he told me to!' Ulf shouted, pointing an accusing finger at Stefan.

'I didn't tell you to untie her and then let go of the rope!' Stefan replied with considerable spirit. 'That was your own bright idea. What did you think she was going to do?'

They glared at each other. Then Ulf calmed down a little.

'Do you think we should go after her?' he asked. The others considered the idea, then both shook their heads.

'We'd never catch up with her now. She's gone looking for Hal,' Edvin said.

'Let's hope she finds him.' But Stefan's tone of voice indicated that he didn't hold out any great hope for such a thing. Ulf sighed, then tried to put a positive face on the event.

'She'll find her way back,' he said. 'She's a smart dog.'

Stefan looked at him morosely. 'What is there about that dog that makes you think she is in any way smart?'

Ulf considered the question for a few seconds. Then his shoulders slumped. 'You're right. She's an idiot. Maybe we're well rid of her.'

'Tell that to Hal,' Wulf said heavily and the three of them exchanged worried glances. They looked up hopefully as they heard footsteps approaching on the wharf — for a moment harbouring the ridiculous hope that someone had caught the dog and was bringing her back. But it was only Gilan and Lydia. The two dropped lightly down onto the deck and surveyed their disconsolate shipmates.

'What's going on here?' Gilan asked.

Edvin pointed down the wharf in the direction in which Kloof had escaped.

'Kloof got away,' he said. 'Ulf untied him.'

'Because Stefan told me to!' Ulf protested violently.

'All right, all right!' said Stefan, holding up his hands to calm down the angry outbursts that were threatening from all sides. 'It was an accident. Nobody did it on purpose. The fact is, she's gone. How did it go at the gold market?'

Gilan shrugged. 'We got the fire started, and nearly got caught by the *dooryeh*. Then Lydia broke us out through the roof and we got away.'

Lydia glanced at him. He made it all sound so simple and uneventful, she thought, remembering the rising sense of panic she had felt as she tried to break an exit through the roof tiles while Gilan had held the *dooryeh* at bay below her.

'Did you see if Hal and the others got the prisoners out?' Ulf asked but the Ranger shook his head.

'We didn't stay around to watch. There were guards all over the place, so we headed back here to the ship. I'm sure they'll be here before long.'

Lydia looked along the wharf to where a dark alley led off into the town. 'Hal's not going to be too happy when he finds his dog is missing,' she said.

'You can go and look for her if you like,' Stefan told her. 'But I suspect Hal is going to be in a hurry to get out of here when he gets back — dog or no dog.'

Mahmel led a group of twelve *dooryeh* at a steady run down the main thoroughfare to the harbour. The thud of feet on the cobbles mixed with the jingle of chain mail and the slap of sword scabbards as they ran.

He knew for certain now who had instigated the escape. One of the guards on duty had been present when Hal and the others had delivered Ingvar to the market two days ago. He recognised the Hellenese men — as he thought they were — as the group who had charged into the guardroom, clubs and axes swinging.

'They came by ship,' Mahmel muttered to himself. 'They'll be heading back to it.'

'They took the twelve Araluans with them, lord,' the guard told him. 'They won't be able to move quickly. Three of them were badly wounded.'

Mahmel thought quickly. Chances were, the escapees would avoid the main streets, reasoning that they would be patrolled. If they took to the back alleys, they would have to wind their way back to the harbour. And if they were further delayed by the wounded Araluans, there was a good chance he could get in front of them and block their path.

The majority of the escaped slaves had been rounded up, or in some cases killed. Only the Araluans and a group of Zambazi warriors from the southern jungles were still on the loose. He decided he'd take care of the Zambazi another day. For now, he wanted to apprehend those Araluans and their cursed Hellenese rescuers.

Quickly, he ordered a lieutenant and a half platoon to follow him and set out on the direct main route to the harbour.

'We're going to have to stop again,' the spokesman for the Araluans told Hal.

Hal cursed quietly. They were making terribly slow progress, hampered by the wounded Araluans, and the girl Ophelia in particular. She slumped against the rough stone wall of a house now, her breath coming in ragged, desperate gasps. None of the other Araluans were in sufficiently good shape to carry her. He considered having Thorn or Stig take on the job. But he needed both of them unhampered and ready to fight if they were ambushed. And he was realistic enough to know that if he tried to carry the woman, he'd be exhausted before they went a hundred metres.

He knelt beside Ophelia. She looked up and recognised him. The fear she was feeling was all too evident in her eyes.

'Don't leave me behind,' she pleaded.

He smiled at her and shook his head. Truth be told, he had considered the idea. But almost immediately, he had rejected it.

'We came here to take twelve of you home,' he told her. 'That's still my plan.'

Behind them, the city was ominously silent now. Previously, they had heard distant shouting and occasional cries of pain and alarm, presumably as the patrols gathered in groups of escaping slaves. Now there was no noise at all, only the normal night sounds. That indicated that the other escapees had been re-taken or killed. And that meant the patrols would be able to concentrate on their little group.

He wondered briefly how Jimpani and his party had fared. He had a feeling that they would have got away successfully. The dark-skinned warrior had struck him as a capable sort of leader.

He looked around. The slaves were slumped against the white plastered walls of the houses that lined the alley. Ingvar stood with the wounded man still firmly in place on his back. He'd decided it was easier to continue to carry him while they stopped, rather than set him down and then have to lift him into place once more.

'How are you managing, Ingvar?' he asked.

Ingvar nodded, unsmiling. 'I'm fine, Hal. Give the word and I'm ready to go again.' It wasn't a boast. It was a simple statement of fact. Ingvar had been starved and probably ill treated for two days in the slave cell. But his strength was undiminished.

He's indefatigable, Hal thought. Then he gestured to the two Araluans who were helping Ophelia.

'Time to go,' he said. 'Get her on her feet.'

She groaned as they raised her, putting her arms around their shoulders and standing either side of her. The two escapees helping the man with the badly damaged ankle looked rebellious for a moment. Hal met their gaze and let his hand fall to the hilt of his sword. No words were needed. The two men stooped and hauled their compatriot to his feet.

'Lead on, Thorn,' Hal called. He sensed that they must be close to the broad, straight main thoroughfare that led to the harbour. They'd been twisting and winding through the back alleys and narrow side streets for some time now.

'Not long to go now,' he called encouragingly to the Araluans.

Heads down, exhausted, they shambled behind Thorn and Stig as the two Skandians led them out of the back alley and onto the broad main road.

And stopped.

Hal emerged at the rear of the column, wondering what was holding them up. Then he saw.

A dozen armed guards, under the command of the green-turbaned Mahmel, were forming a line, swords drawn, and blocking the way to the harbour.

CHAPTER FIFTY-TWO

'Oh dear, oh deary me!' Thorn said in a ridiculous falsetto voice. 'What *are* we going to do? It's twelve big hairy guardsmen and Mahmel in a natty green hat.'

It was all very well to joke about it, Hal thought, but the situation was serious. They were well and truly out-numbered and the *dooryeh* were professional soldiers and trained fighters. Stig and Thorn were good, he knew. But against these odds, they'd have to be better than good.

'What *are* we going to do?' he asked quietly, in Skandian. 'It's twelve to four — thirteen to four if you count Mahmel.'

'Oh, I never count Mahmel,' Thorn said breezily.

Ingvar spoke up, a little annoyed. 'Twelve against five,' he corrected. 'Don't forget I'm here, Hal.'

'You stay back, Ingvar, unless we really need you,' Hal told him briskly. Ingvar, with his huge size and massive muscles, could be devastating in attack. But his poor eyesight made him vulnerable to any counterattack an enemy might launch. Usually, in battle, Lydia stood back a little, armed with her darts and ready to drop anyone who tried to take him by surprise. But Lydia wasn't here, and against these odds, Ingvar's companions would be too occupied to keep an eye out for him.

Ingvar said nothing, but gave an ill-tempered grunt. He hated being a passenger in a fight, even though he knew Hal was right.

'I'll tell you what we're going to do,' Thorn said, also speaking in Skandian. 'On my command, we're going to charge these jumped-up prison guards.'

'You have noticed that they outnumber us three to one,' Jesper pointed out.

Thorn nodded. 'I have. That's why they won't be expecting us to charge them.'

'I certainly wasn't until you mentioned it,' Jesper said.

Thorn spared him a quick, fierce grin. 'Always do the unexpected, Jesper,' he said. 'Particularly if you're in a tight spot.'

'Are we in a tight spot?' Jesper wanted to know.

'I think it's about as tight as I'd like it to be, so let's loosen it a little,' Thorn said. 'Are we all ready to surprise our friend in the green hat?'

The others chorused their assent. Thorn drew in a breath to call the charge when suddenly, a snarling, snapping, tan and black hurricane erupted out of an alleyway beside the line of *dooryeh* facing them.

Kloof hit the left end of the line like a battering ram, knocking two of the guardsmen over. They, in turn, crashed into a third. The third man staggered, and turned to face the horrifying sight of forty-five kilograms of enraged dog. All he could see were red eyes and huge, snapping teeth. He yelped in fear as Kloof's jaws clamped shut on his sword arm with all the force of a bear trap. The sword fell from his fingers and he dropped to his knees. Instantly, Kloof released him and leapt at the next man in line, who shouted in terror and fled, with Kloof hot on his heels, barking nonstop.

Seeing the enemy so disorganised and in utter confusion, Thorn yelled the time-honoured Skandian battle command.

'Let's get 'em, boys!'

The four Herons charged forward in a tight group, axe, swords and the mighty war club on Thorn's right arm ready to wreak havoc.

Thorn was the first to make contact. His club smashed down on the *dooryeh* commander's scimitar, smashing it out of the soldier's hand. Before the man had time to react, Thorn's small shield slammed full into his face, breaking his nose and cheekbone. The sergeant stumbled backwards, blinded by blood and tears, his hands to his face, sinking to the cobblestones, huddled over in agony.

Seeing he was well and truly out of the fight, Thorn wasted no further time on him. He swept the club backhanded in a sideways rising arc at the next man in line. It was an unexpected attack. The soldier was expecting an overhand strike — most people did when they faced a club. The club smashed into his hip and there was an ugly crunching sound as bones gave way. Like his commander, the soldier fell to the ground, desperately trying to drag himself away from further harm, whimpering in agony.

Now Stig was in the fight, his mighty axe stroke thundering down onto a *dooryeh*'s raised shield. The metal-reinforced wood might have stood up to a sword, but Stig's axe, with all of Stig's strength behind it, was no mere sword. The shield split in half and the horrified soldier watched as the gleaming axehead continued its downward arc with barely a pause. It was the last thing the unfortunate guardsman saw.

Almost instantaneously, and with the reflexes of a cat, Stig deflected a scimitar thrust from his left with his shield, then stepped left and slammed the metal boss of the shield into his attacker's body.

There was a *whoof* of exhaled breath mixed with a grunt of pain from several cracked ribs. The soldier went down — luckily for him as it turned out, as Stig's horizontal axe stroke came whistling just centimetres above his head.

Hal crossed swords with another guardsman. They struck and parried at each other. Then he became aware of a second man coming at him from his left. He stopped the scimitar blade with the saxe in his left hand. Then parried a cut from the first man with his sword. Almost immediately, he had to leap to his right as the man on the left disentangled his scimitar and lunged at him. Hal felt the thick taste of fear in his mouth as he realised he couldn't continue fighting the two of them for much longer. Sooner or later, one of them would penetrate his guard while he was occupied with the other. He swept his saxe sideways, deflecting another scimitar thrust. Then he sensed movement on his left, coming from behind him, and Jesper's sword flashed past him, taking the left-hand attacker in the centre of his body, flicking in and out like a striking snake. The guardsman fell sideways, staring in horrified disbelief at the blood welling from the wound. His chain mail and sword clattered as he crashed onto the cobbles.

'Thanks, Jes,' Hal called. Now that he was able to concentrate on his original opponent, he drove the man back with a series of blindingly fast slashes, forehand and backhand, battering at the man's guard until, as it faltered, he saw his opportunity and lunged the point of his sword through an opening. He hit the man in the thigh and the soldier staggered, then fell, dropping his scimitar to clench his hands around the wound, trying to stem the flow of blood.

As Thorn had told them repeatedly, *You don't have to kill a man to put him out of the fight.*

And in the space of a few violent, fast-moving seconds, the entire tenor of the encounter had changed. Seven of the *dooryeh* were dead or wounded, and two more were only just staggering to their feet after Kloof's enraged charge out of the alley.

While all four of the Herons were untouched.

The surviving Socorrans looked around in horror. Their three to one advantage had evaporated to little more than parity. They looked for Mahmel, their leader, and saw the green-turbaned figure sprawled across the body of a guardsman, both men covered in blood.

Thorn smiled at them. Somehow, the smile was more reminiscent of a shark baring its teeth than an expression of good humour.

'Shall we continue?' he asked, and they began to back away — first one, then others following his example.

Then, to clinch matters, Kloof returned from her pursuit. She charged back into the main street, barking and snarling. There were ominous red stains about her muzzle.

That tipped the balance. The surviving *dooryeh* scattered and ran, leaving their dead and wounded behind them. Kloof set off after them, but they had run in several different directions and she couldn't quite decide who to follow.

'Kloof! Here, girl! Good girl! Here!' Hal called and her hackles went down and she trotted obediently to him, her tail sweeping heavily, grumbling and growling deep in her chest still. She flumped down and sat beside him, looking up at him. Carefully, he wiped the blood from her muzzle with a piece of cloak he had taken from one of the fallen guardsmen. Then he wiped his sword and re-sheathed it.

'By Ergon's tears,' Walton said, invoking an obscure Araluan god in an almost reverent tone. 'I'm glad you're on our side.'

They surveyed the crumpled bodies lying on the cobbles. Several of the wounded were still trying to drag themselves away. Jesper pointed to them.

'What do we do about them?' he asked.

Hal shook his head wearily. 'Leave them be,' he said. 'We don't want them.'

Stig was standing over the bloodstained figure of Mahmel, his axe dangling loosely from his hand.

'Don't remember seeing him in the fight,' he said curiously. 'Who settled his hash for him?'

The others exchanged glances and shrugged. Nobody could remember striking down the slave market manager.

- 433 -

'Not sure,' Jesper said. 'It all got a little confused there for a few minutes.'

'That's true,' Stig said. 'Orlog's breath, have you ever seen anything like Kloof here when she charged into them?' He moved over and fondled the big dog's ears. She grinned at him. 'Good dog, Kloofy. Good, *good* dog!'

Kloof lolled her tongue at him. There was no sign now of the terrifying, snapping, snarling monster that she had become when she charged into the Socorrans. Hal looked around at the huddled group of Araluan slaves.

'Well, at least you've had a chance to rest up for a few minutes,' he said. 'Now let's get back to the ship.'

As the sound of their footsteps died away, there was a rustle of movement among the dead and wounded guardsmen and Mahmel slowly raised his head. Satisfied that the Herons had gone, he lurched to his knees, then to his feet. His tunic and cloak were drenched with blood, but none of it was his.

In fact, Mahmel had taken no part in the brief and bloody fight. Seeing how it was shaping, he had dropped his scimitar and thrown himself across one of the fallen guardsmen, smearing himself with the man's blood and lying still until the enemy had left.

He looked around the bloodstained cobblestones for his scimitar, retrieved it and slid it back into its scabbard. There was no need to clean the blade. It hadn't drawn blood at all. In fact, it hadn't been *used* at all.

The foreigners were heading north-east. He turned

now and began running to the west. His guess had been right. Hal's final words had confirmed that they had a ship somewhere in the harbour, and they were heading for it now. They had taken the road leading to the north-eastern reach, so they still had some distance to go. The harbour fort, with its battery of catapults, was much closer.

That's where Mahmel was heading. To get out of Socorro, they'd have to run the gauntlet of those fearsome machines. He couldn't wait to see the jagged rocks raining down on their helpless ship as they tried to make their way out through the narrow channel.

CHAPTER FIFTY-THREE

The sail rigging crew, and Gilan and Lydia, looked up in relief as their five comrades, accompanied by a dozen Araluans, emerged from the alleys onto the broad surface of the wharf. Kloof gambolled cheerfully along ahead of them, occasionally barking as if to say, 'Follow me! I know the way!'

'Lend a hand here! We've got wounded!' Hal called.

Stefan, Edvin and Gilan all leapt up onto the wharf and ran to help. Ulf and Wulf, knowing they would soon be departing, busied themselves making sure their newly rigged sheets were clear of any obstruction. The wind was out of the north-west, blowing steadily as the desert cooled. They knew they'd be using the port side sail, so they prepared it for hoisting.

'Who's injured?' Edvin asked urgently. He was the trained healer in the crew.

Hal calmed his worst fears. 'None of us. Some of the Araluans need help — particularly one of the women.'

He indicated Ophelia with a jerk of his head and Edvin moved to her, gesturing for her companions to set her down. He examined her quickly, feeling her side, probing gently to see if any of her ribs were fractured. She smiled weakly at him as he patted her hand.

'You'll be fine,' he said, then looked up to her companions. 'Get her aboard.'

He moved to the other injured ex-slaves, nodding his head as he saw the tight bandage wound neatly round one man's thigh.

'Who did this?' he asked. He noticed that Ingvar's shirt was missing a sleeve. The huge youth pointed a thumb at his own chest.

'I did,' he said.

Edvin nodded approvingly. 'Nice job. But we'd better loosen it for a few minutes to let the blood flow back into the limb. Otherwise, he could lose it.'

He saw that the third injury was a man with a severe ankle sprain — perhaps even a break. But there was no immediate danger and he could wait till last. His two companions, who were supporting him, looked at Edvin with sour faces as he straightened after examining the man's ankle.

'Carry him aboard,' he said.

'Can someone else do it?' one of them complained. 'We've been carrying him for hours!'

Hal's hand on his shoulder jerked him round so that he found himself facing the skirl's angry glare. The Araluan shrank back a pace or two. Hal was young — he wasn't yet twenty. But there was something in his eyes that demanded instant obedience.

'Yes. Someone else can do it!' Hal snapped. 'But if they do, you're not setting foot on my ship. In fact, I'll tie you both up and leave you here for the *dooryeh* to find. I'm sure they'll be glad to see you. Are we clear on that?'

The Araluan's eyes slid off to one side, unwilling to meet Hal's furious gaze. He nodded and mumbled something incoherent.

'I said, are we clear?' Hal shouted at him.

He shuffled his feet. 'Yes, yes, whatever you say,' he mumbled.

Then he and his friend lifted their countryman and moved to the edge of the wharf, where Ulf and Wulf, finished checking their equipment, were waiting to lift him down into the ship. Hal met Thorn's gaze and shook his head.

'Honestly!' he said. 'Some people think only about themselves! Those two have been nothing but trouble. We should have left them behind.'

'I see you found Kloof,' Wulf said cheerfully, as the dog bounded down onto the deck.

'Yes. We did,' Hal said, a note of suspicion in his voice. 'I was wondering how she got loose.'

'I sent her to find you,' Wulf said easily. 'Thought you might need guiding back to the ship.'

Hal noticed that neither Edvin nor Stefan would meet his gaze as Wulf made that statement. Ulf looked away as well, as if something across the harbour had suddenly claimed his attention. There was more to this than Wulf was saying, Hal realised. But his thoughts were interrupted by Stig's cheerful rejoinder.

'Just as well you did! She really saved our bacon. Went charging into a platoon of *dooryeh*, scattering them like ninepins! They didn't know what hit them.'

'Yeah. I thought she might come in handy,' Wulf said airily.

Again, the others seemed unwilling to meet Hal's gaze and now he was sure there was more to this than he was being told. Still, he had more pressing matters to attend to right now. He resolved to quiz Edvin and Stefan later. Ulf, he knew, would lie for the sheer sake of it. Worse, he might tell the truth so that Hal would assume he was lying. That had happened before.

Hal walked quickly aft, unlashing the fastening on the tiller, which kept it from banging back and forth with the movement of the water while they were moored.

Stig had marshalled the twelve Araluans into the centre of the ship where they were out of the way. He looked curiously at Hal.

'Oars?'

Hal shook his head, after checking the sternpost wind telltale. For the first leg of their course, the wind would be from astern.

'We'll run down harbour on port tack, then turn starboard so we're on a reach for the first leg of the channel,' he said. 'Unless the wind shifts, we can make it out of here on one tack.'

Stig nodded. 'Makes sense to me.'

'And besides. I don't want people tied up rowing. I want you and Ingvar on the Mangler when we're running past those catapults at the fort,' Hal said. Then added, 'Gilan and Lydia too.'

They looked up as they heard their names mentioned and he beckoned them closer.

'When we're in that narrow channel, opposite the fort, we'll be sitting ducks for those catapults. I want you two to keep up a constant barrage on them. Pick off the crews. Make them nervous. Nervous men don't take time to aim,' he said.

They both nodded. In a reflex action, Gilan's hand went up to touch the feathered ends of the arrows in his quiver, now back in their normal place over his right shoulder.

Hal looked at the Araluans and made a downward gesture with the flat of his hand.

'Lie down,' he said to them. 'You'll be out of the way and you may be a little safer.'

The Araluans began to comply, but before they did, Walton, their spokesman, stepped closer to the steering platform.

'We haven't thanked you yet,' he said. 'Everything's been in a rush, but we haven't thanked you properly. We owe you our lives and our freedom — even George and Abel.'

From the direction of his quick glance, Hal realised that George and Abel were the reluctant pair who had carried the wounded man back to the ship. They looked suitably ashamed of themselves and reddened, while the other Araluans chorused their enthusiastic agreement to Walton's words. Hal waved a dismissive hand.

'Time enough to thank us later,' he said. 'We're not out of here yet.' He looked around his expectant crew, standing ready to get under way.

'Stig, get the bow and stern lines. Ingvar, shove us off. Stefan and Edvin, as soon as we're clear of the wharf, get the port sail up.'

Lydia watched the usual scene of organised and efficient chaos as the crew members went through their drill for leaving port. Stig ran along the wharf, casting off the bow line, then the stern line as the bow started to swing away from the wharf's side. He dropped lightly back onto the deck as Ingvar set an oar against one of the wharf's pilings and set the *Heron* moving out into the fairway with a powerful shove. The halyards ran squealing through the blocks as the port yardarm and sail rose quickly up the mast. Then there was the now familiar *whoomph* of captured air as Ulf and Wulf sheeted home and set the sail.

Heron accelerated away from the wharf, the port side sail almost at right angles to catch the steady breeze that was blowing over their stern quarter. The water hissed under her forefoot and chuckled down her sides as she gathered way. Hal felt an enormous sense of relief. He was back in control of things here at the tiller. They might have to face Tursgud yet, and they would certainly have to run the gauntlet of those catapults. But his ship was fast and manoeuvrable and he was confident he could cope with anything the Socorrans threw at him. He smiled grimly as he realised how appropriate that expression was in this circumstance. That was exactly what they would be doing.

The bow wave peeled away from the ship in a giant V on the placid harbour waters. As it reached the shore, it set moored ships bobbing and rocking.

Ahead of them, the narrow north-eastern arm opened into the wider expanse of the harbour proper.

That was where Tursgud would be, if he was going to be anywhere.

'Jesper,' he ordered quietly, 'get onto the bow lookout. Keep an eye out for Tursgud and *Nightwolf*.'

Jesper looked surprised. 'Do you think he'll try to stop us?'

Hal met his gaze steadily. 'If he sees us, he'll try to sink us,' he said. He glanced at Lydia and Gilan. 'Get ready. We may need you any minute.'

Stig caught his eye and gestured to the Mangler in the bow, shrouded in its canvas covers. 'What about Ingvar and me?' he asked.

Hal nodded. 'Get her ready to shoot. But I don't think we'll need you against *Nightwolf*. We'll save our ammunition for the catapults at the fort.'

Stig grunted agreement and, calling to Ingvar to accompany him, went forward and began removing the covers from the Mangler. A few of the Araluans uttered expressions of surprise at the sight of the massive crossbow.

'What on earth is that?' one of them said.

Thorn favoured him with a wolfish grin. 'That's a little surprise for anyone who tries to stop us,' he said.

'They're coming, skirl!'

Tursgud had posted a lookout on the higher ground of the wharf alongside them. Now, as he followed the direction that the man was pointing, his lips curled in a satisfied sneer.

The familiar, and hated, triangular sail was visible as

the *Heron* slipped out of the narrow north-eastern reach into the more open waters of the main harbour. He beckoned the lookout back on board, and checked to see that his crew were ready.

Two men stood by the bow and stern lines — he'd replaced the normal heavy hawsers with light ropes. When the time came, they would hack through them, untethering the ship from the shore.

Six others were crouched, ready to haul the big square sail aloft. The wind was on their beam and that was their best and fastest point of sailing. Tursgud crouched by the tiller — as if his crouching would somehow delay the *Heron*'s spotting them. He planned to let the smaller ship sail down the middle of the fairway. Then, at the right moment, he'd cut the bow and stern lines and hoist the sail. *Nightwolf* would go from dead stop to full speed in the space of about thirty metres. The wind was strong enough to let them power out across the harbour and intercept the *Heron*. When they did, the cruel, iron-tipped ram set under *Nightwolf*'s bow would smash into the other ship's frail sides, rending and tearing the planks, shattering the ribs and letting the cold harbour water surge in.

The tide was running out. That meant that any survivors from the sinking ship would have little chance of reaching shore. They'd be swept out to sea, moving ever faster as the outgoing tide was constricted by the narrow exit channel and accelerated as a result. And good riddance to them, Tursgud thought savagely.

It had been a long time since Hal and his crew of misfits had heaped scorn and shame on Tursgud's head.

But today, he would finally have his revenge.

CHAPTER FIFTY-FOUR

'Any sign of *Nightwolf*?' Hal called to Jesper.

'Not so far,' came the reply. It wasn't surprising. Even though they knew Tursgud's ship was moored on the western side of the harbour, the chance of picking one ship out among the forest of masts would be slim. But Hal knew they were close to where the dark blue ship was moored.

'Keep your eyes peeled,' he called, and regretted it immediately. There was no point in telling Jesper to keep a good lookout. He'd do that without being told. Gilan and Lydia had moved to the waist of the ship, clear of the port sail, their weapons ready.

All eyes were fastened on the harbour shore sliding past them on their left.

Tursgud watched the graceful little ship cruising smoothly down the outbound channel in the middle of the harbour. His eyes narrowed as he judged distances and speed. He would let *Heron* come almost level with him, then he'd bring *Nightwolf* surging out from the wharf. He gauged the distance to *Heron*. She was about a hundred metres from the western shore, where *Nightwolf* lurked, ready. He smiled. That would give him plenty of time to reach maximum speed before he smashed into that hated little ship.

He remembered how she had bested him in the final race in the brotherband contest two years ago. Just when he thought he had beaten her, she had spun on her heel and accelerated into Hallasholm harbour to deny him his victory.

Today would be a different story.

'Raise the sail and sheet home!' he ordered.

His first mate stared at him in surprise. 'But we're still tied up —'

Tursgud rounded on him in a fury. 'Get that sail up!' he snarled.

Hastily, the first mate gave the order to the waiting sail crew. The huge square sail went up the mast, swelling out in the wind, then hardening into a perfect curve as the sail handlers sheeted home. *Nightwolf* began to surge forward under the massive thrust, then was brought up short as the hawsers tautened.

For a few seconds, there was an ominous creaking from the rigging and the mast as the wind tried to tear her loose from the shore and the hawsers held her tight.

'Axes!' yelled Tursgud, leaving it until the last possible

minute before something broke loose. The two thuds came close together, almost merging into one, and the bow and stern lines were severed, the ends springing high into the air as the strain was suddenly released.

Nightwolf shot forward, like an arrow leaving a bow.

On board *Heron*, Jesper saw something unusual. He was looking for a ship moving out into the harbour — presumably under oars, as that was the way most ships departed. In his peripheral vision, he saw a movement on the western shore of the harbour. Something rose up, then suddenly blossomed into a long, dark rectangular shape.

He peered more closely, confused, not sure what he was seeing. Then he realised it was the square sail of a wolfship filling with the wind.

'Here he comes!' he yelled, pointing to port.

Hal heard two dull thuds echo across the water — the sound of the two axes cutting *Nightwolf*'s light hawsers, although he didn't know it at the time. Then the dark hull shot away from the wharf, her big square yard braced around to catch the wind at the best angle, the sail already full and powering the wolfship towards them at a prodigious rate. He could see the white beard of a bow wave at her waterline as she continued to gather speed. Tursgud's tactic, while risky, had achieved his aim. She had gone from a dead stop to almost top speed in a matter of thirty metres. Hal gauged the distance to *Nightwolf*, then to the wharf she had left. A little over a hundred metres, he thought.

He hoped.

'How long was that hawser we tied to her?' he asked Thorn, who was standing beside him. Like everyone on board, Thorn had his eyes glued on the rapidly approaching wolfship.

Several of the Araluans, seeing *Nightwolf* bearing down on them, and recognising her as the slaver who had brought them here, cried out in alarm. They looked at Hal, wondering why he was taking no evasive action. Perhaps he thought they could outrun the blue ship. But it was obvious that they wouldn't.

'About a hundred metres — more or less,' Thorn replied calmly.

Hal snatched his eyes from the onrushing wolfship to look at Thorn in alarm. 'Well, which is it? More or less?' he asked. 'That could make one great big difference here!'

Thorn shrugged fatalistically. 'Soon find out.'

Hal nudged the tiller and edged *Heron* a little further away from the western shore. *Nightwolf* was terribly close now. Dimly, he registered the twang of Gilan's bow, heard the *whooshing* release of Lydia's atlatl as they began to shoot at the ship bearing down on them.

Might kill a few of the crew, he thought. But it won't slow the ship at all.

A horrified thought struck him. What if, sometime in the past few days, Tursgud had discovered the hawser attached to his sternpost and removed it? He pictured the tall skirl laughing at Hal's childish stratagem, waiting for his chance to smash *Heron* into splinters of driftwood.

Nightwolf continued to bear down on them, moving faster and faster with every metre she travelled. Hal's grip on the tiller tightened until his knuckles were white. She was only fifteen metres away and he could see the disturbance under her prow where the savage ram was sliding, just below the surface of the harbour.

His mouth was dry with fear as he realised he'd outsmarted himself. The hawser had been discovered. Or had broken loose somehow. Any minute now the renegade wolfship would —

There was a terrible *CRACK!* and *Nightwolf*'s bow reared up out of the water like a startled horse as she came to a dead stop. The water around her seemed to boil.

The tall mast whiplashed forward, snapped at its halfway point, and came crashing down over the bow of the ship, bringing the sail and yardarm with it.

Then they heard a dreadful rending noise that tore at Hal's shipwright's heart as *Nightwolf*'s sternpost was torn clear of her keel. The hawser stood up bar-taut behind it for a second, water squeezing from the weave of the rope, then whiplashed away as the sternpost was ripped clear.

The sternpost was the anchor point for all the ship's longitudinal planks. They curved round the carefully shaped frames and were fastened to the thick timber of the sternpost, forming the curved, narrow counter of the ship.

With the sternpost gone, the planks sprang apart, leaving an enormous gap and opening the entire stern of the ship to the hungry seawater. The stern simply ceased to exist. The water rushed in and the boat filled and sank.

It all happened in seconds.

For a short time, a bubble of air trapped under the sail kept it floating on the surface of the harbour. Then the plunging weight of the sinking hull dragged it down after it and there was no sign of *Nightwolf* on the black water. A few bits and pieces of equipment floated there. Hal saw a bucket and a round shield drifting on the fast-running current towards the narrow channel that led out of the harbour. One or two heads bobbed on the surface and they could hear their desperate cries. Then they fell silent.

Those on board the *Heron* were shocked to silence for a few seconds. Stig finally spoke.

'By the gods of the Vallas,' he said. 'I've never seen anything like that.'

'I never want to again,' said Lydia. The sudden destruction of the other ship was so violent, so fast, it had horrified her. One minute, the ship and its twenty crewmen were plunging towards them.

The next, they were gone.

'Can Tursgud swim?' Hal asked of no one in particular.

Stig, his eyes still riveted on the spot in the harbour where *Nightwolf* had disappeared, shook his head.

'I don't think so,' he said.

'Who cares?' said Thorn gruffly. 'He was a pirate and a slaver and a renegade. And he was doing his best to kill us. I say good riddance.'

Hal shook his head, numbed by what he had just seen. He hadn't expected *Nightwolf*'s fate to be so sudden or so brutal.

'I suppose so,' he said.

Thorn shoved him on the shoulder.

'I know so! Now pull yourself together!' he snapped. 'We've still got to get out of this hellhole.'

CHAPTER FIFTY-FIVE

They were bearing down fast on the narrow exit channel. They'd keep the wind on their starboard side as they turned up into the first leg of the channel, then turn left for the final leg — the part that was guarded by the fort.

And its battery of catapults.

Hal swung the bow to starboard as they entered the first part of the channel, Ulf and Wulf hauling in the sail as he did so to keep it taut and powering them along.

The moon was in the final stage of its movement across the heavens, enormous and orange as it sat just above the horizon, flooding the harbour with a soft light that was almost as bright as an overcast day. Hal could see the bristling line of beams that marked the trebuchets and catapults. They were hauled back, fully cocked, ready to throw the massive boulders loaded into their buckets.

'The fort's signalling,' Stig said.

Hal saw he was right. Just below the flagpole on the

squat turret beside the channel, a signal hoist had been raised — three yellow lanterns, arranged in the form of an inverted triangle. He had no idea what that meant and he glanced at Thorn for an explanation.

'It means *lower your sail and bring your ship alongside the wharf*,' Thorn told him. 'In other words, *surrender or we'll start shooting.*'

'How accurate are those things?' Hal asked. He had no experience with the massive weapons the Socorrans were about to use.

Thorn shrugged. 'Not terribly,' he said. 'If I were in charge of them, I'd —'

He was interrupted by a thundering, rolling crash of timber on timber, and the five machines all launched their huge missiles at once. A few seconds later, a ragged line of enormous splashes erupted across the channel, each one about ten metres from the next.

'Ah,' continued Thorn. 'That's what I was going to say. I'd pre-range them on the channel and shoot them in salvoes. Getting the range is the most difficult part with those throwing machines. They can swivel them on their bases as you go past, but ranging takes time. So they'll shoot all five at once, and just blanket the channel.'

'There's a gap of ten metres between each one,' Hal pointed out. 'We could slip through that.'

Stig grunted agreement, but Thorn shook his head.

'You might. But that assumes that every shot will fall in exactly the same spot. Depending on the different weights of the rocks they're throwing, the shots could vary by four or five metres either way.'

Hal thought furiously. They were speeding down

to the point where he'd have to turn left into the final channel — which was swept by the catapults. He could see the arms being hauled down again as their crews heaved them back, raising the counterweights that would hurl the rocks at them.

'Gilan, Lydia. Ready to shoot,' he said. 'Stig and Ingvar, get for'ard to the Mangler.'

'What are you planning?' Thorn asked.

Hal glanced quickly at him. 'We're going to make the gap wider,' he said.

Mahmel stood by the trebuchet in the centre of the line of siege weapons. He was screaming orders at the crew, striking out with the flat of his scimitar at those he thought weren't obeying quickly enough.

In his rage and haste, he sometimes allowed the edge to strike a glancing blow at the soldiers labouring at the windlasses that loaded the massive machines. Several of them had blood running freely down their arms. All of them looked darkly at him, hating him for his arrogance and cruelty.

'Sink that ship!' he raged. 'Then get boats ready to drag her crew and passengers ashore. I'm going to roast those cursed escaped slaves in a fire — I'll start with their feet, and then feed them slowly into the flames until they're burned to a crisp!'

One of the soldiers, heaving on the winch that drew up the counterweight for a catapult, scowled at the green-turbaned figure.

'Yes, you son of a pig,' he muttered to himself. 'I'll bet you will.'

Mahmel strode over to the battery commander. He was crouched over a sighting device that let him measure the ship's speed, and the angle at which he would have to fire the five throwers to have the best chance of hitting her. Mahmel flailed at him with his sword.

'What are you waiting for?' he screamed. 'They're escaping! Sink them! Sink them, curse you!'

The commander looked up from his sights, angered by the distraction, and Mahmel's stupidity.

'Lord, the projectiles are in flight for twelve to fifteen seconds. I have to estimate where the ship will be in that time when I shoot.'

'Don't argue with me!' Mahmel's voice cracked in fury. He pointed his scimitar at the ship as she turned left into the final channel. 'There's your target! Sink her now!'

'But —'

Mahmel's voice went into an even higher pitch. 'Do as I order!'

The battery commander hesitated, then turned to his waiting crews.

'Release!' he shouted, and the crews pulled on the trigger levers.

On board *Heron*, Hal swung the bow into the second half of the channel. The wind was now over their starboard quarter, coming from astern. Automatically, Ulf and Wulf began to haul in on the sheets, but he called to stop them.

'That's enough!' he said. 'Ease them a little.'

As the twins obeyed, *Heron*'s speed slackened perceptibly. Hal waited, watching the shore and the line of war machines. Then he heard that rolling, rending crack once more as they all released at once.

'Now! Sheet home!' he yelled and *Heron* surged forward as the sail came hard onto the wind. They all heard the rush of jagged boulders in the air as they passed over the ship to erupt in ragged explosions of white water once more. But the volley fell behind them, the aim thrown off by *Heron*'s sudden change of speed.

'Nice move,' Thorn said. 'But it won't work twice.'

'It won't have to,' Hal replied. 'They've got time for one more volley. Let's make a hole we can slip through.' He studied the massive weapons. Four of them were simple catapults, consisting of a long beam with a counterweight at one end and a bucket at the other to hold the projectile. The other was a trebuchet: a similar design, but with the addition of a rope sling at the end of the throwing arm that would whip over the top like a flail, adding impetus, power and range to the shot. Raising his voice, he called to Lydia and Gilan. 'Concentrate your shots on the trebuchet in the centre of the line,' he said. 'Cut down her crew before they can reload.'

The two were standing amidships, on the port side, weapons ready. They both nodded in unison, then, with breathtaking speed, Gilan loosed five arrows at the trebuchet crew. Lydia wasn't far behind him, with three darts hissing away from her atlatl.

Around the trebuchet, men began to fall. The hail of arrows and darts struck home, seemingly out of nowhere. Four men went down before anyone was aware of what was happening. The others turned and ran, crouching to hide from the deadly storm of missiles arcing down among them. The other machines were ready to shoot but the trebuchet remained uncocked, with its counterweight only halfway through its vertical rise.

'Release!' the commander shouted. But there was no one to trip the trigger lever on the machine in the centre of the line. And when other soldiers tried to get close, the hail of arrows and darts recommenced and drove them back.

The rolling crash rang out once more as the other four machines hurled their rocks high into the night sky. But Hal had steered *Heron* for the gap in the line of missiles — a twenty-metre gap now that the centre trebuchet hadn't released. *Heron* slid smoothly through the disturbed water, although the inner catapult, throwing a lighter rock than before, came perilously close, hurling up a fountain of spray barely three metres from the ship.

He glanced at Thorn, his heart in his mouth at the near miss. 'I see what you mean,' he said.

At the half-cocked trebuchet, Mahmel was screaming insults and orders, driving men back to their posts, ordering them to recommence winding the massive windlass that would raise the counterweight.

On board *Heron* as she slipped past, Stig saw the green-turbaned figure, barely fifty metres away, and recognised him.

'Ingvar! Load one of those scatter bolts!' he called. The Mangler was already cocked and Ingvar dropped one of the pottery-headed bolts into the loading slot. Then as Stig began to walk the massive crossbow around so that it was trained out to port, Ingvar seized the training lever and helped him.

'Left. Left. Left . . . steady there!' Stig called. He was winding the elevation wheel as he spoke, centering the sights on the green-cloaked, green-turbaned figure of the slave master.

SLAM!

The Mangler bucked wildly against its leather restraints as he pulled the trigger lanyard, and the bolt swooped away towards the shore.

Stig's aim was slightly off. The bolt hissed past Mahmel, staggering him as he felt the wind of its passage, and smashed against the wooden frame of the trebuchet. The pottery head shattered, releasing a storm of whirling shards that flew wildly among the crew.

One of them took a jagged, five-centimetre piece in the forehead. It tore a huge flap of skin from his head. Blood gushed out, blinding him, and he threw both hands to his face in pain. He staggered and reached out blindly for something to support him. His hand closed on the trigger lever and he released the half-cocked trebuchet.

But the massive weapon, with its counterweight only half raised, didn't have the force to hurl the sling up and over. It was propelled upwards for a few metres, then, defeated by gravity, it dropped back. The jagged boulder that had been loaded into it lurched a few metres into the air, then fell free. It struck the frame of the trebuchet a glancing blow as it came down and was deflected to one side.

Mahmel never saw it coming. He was still hurling curses at the little ship as it slid past, barely fifty metres away, heading for the open sea, when the huge, crushing weight landed on him.

He screamed once, then he was silent.

One of the trebuchet crew, nursing an arrow wound in his left arm, curled his lip in disdain at the slave master. Mahmel was lying on his back, pinned beneath the heavy boulder. His eyes were wide open, but they saw nothing. An ominous dark stain was spreading across the flagstones beneath him.

'Good riddance,' the soldier said softly. Then he looked up at the slim little ship as she left the channel and slipped into the open sea. The first large roller slid under her keel. She rose to it gracefully, dipped her bow, then slid down the far side, gathering speed as she headed north.

Across the water, the Socorran heard the faint sound of cheering as she moved away.

CHAPTER FIFTY-SIX

It was late in the afternoon when *Heron* slipped quietly into the little bay by the village of Deaton's Mill.

Hal had decided to bypass Cresthaven. The twelve rescued slaves were eager to get home and let their families know they were safe and he was happy to accommodate them. As he headed the ship towards the beach, he sniffed the air. The smell of burnt wood was still evident.

A few villagers were on the beach as *Heron* slid her sharp prow into the sand and rode up a few metres onto dry land. Stefan, as ever, was ready with the beach anchor. He dropped over the bulwark at the bow, ran inland and drove the blades of the anchor firmly into the sand.

The half dozen villagers reacted with alarm at the sight of the ship. She was smaller than a wolfship, but she was built on similar lines. And when Stefan slipped ashore, his clothing marked him as a Skandian.

And Deaton's Mill had all too recently had trouble with Skandians and wolfships.

The bystanders began to run up the beach towards the village. Gilan moved quickly to the bow and leapt up onto the bulwark, his green and grey mottled cloak identifying him as a Ranger.

'King's Ranger!' he shouted. 'You're safe! No need for alarm!'

Two of the villagers kept running, shouting to warn the rest of the village. But the others stopped where they were, looking curiously at the sight of the Ranger perched on the bow of this strange ship.

Then Walton moved into the bow and joined Gilan, although he was nowhere near as sure of his footing as the Ranger. He recognised one of the men on the beach, who was hesitating, still poised to run if necessary.

'Ben Tonkin!' Walton shouted. 'What's up with you? Can't you see we're back?'

The man hesitated, then raised his hands to shade his eyes as he peered at the figure in the bow of the beached ship.

'Walton?' he said uncertainly. 'Is that you, boy?'

'Aye, it's me all right,' Walton shouted. 'And the others who were taken. We're back safe and sound!'

Several of the other former slaves had joined Walton in the bow, waving and shouting to those further up the beach. Tonkin took a few paces closer to the ship, then, ascertaining that it was, in fact, Walton, and that the others around him were all from the village as well, he turned and shouted the good news back to the village.

A small trickle of villagers, warned by the initial cries of those who had fled at the sight of *Heron*, were making their way out of the village and towards the beach, armed with makeshift weapons — axes, hoes and even the occasional spear. They may not have fought before, but they'd spent three weeks repairing the damage Tursgud's men had done, rebuilding the burnt barns, re-thatching the houses where the roofs had been set alight by the raiders. They weren't about to see their hard work go up in smoke once more.

But now as the word spread that the prisoners had returned, they threw the weapons aside and ran to the beach. The trickle became a flood until virtually the entire village were gathered on the beach, laughing and cheering as their twelve friends came ashore, mobbing round them, congratulating them. More than one mother wept openly at the sight of her son or daughter returned to her.

Ophelia was the last to leave the ship. On the voyage home, Edvin had tended to her night and day, using salves and poultices and herbal remedies that he had learned about from the healers in Skandia. The results were remarkable. The girl was able to walk unaided now, and although she winced from time to time if she moved incautiously, she was a far cry from the injured, hesitant girl who had come aboard in Socorro.

'You did a great job,' Hal told Edvin quietly as they watched willing hands lift the girl gently down to the beach. Edvin shrugged diffidently. Then a smile broke out on his face. He knew he wasn't the best warrior on board the ship. But he had taken on the role of healer with determination and enthusiasm. He studied the old scrolls on healing and he assisted the apothecaries and surgeons in Hallasholm whenever he had the time. The reward came when he saw a result like this.

'Yes,' he agreed cheerfully. 'I didn't do too badly at all, did I?'

Of course, there was a celebration feast that night to mark the homecoming of the lost twelve, as they were called. And of course, the crew of the *Heron* were guests of honour.

Several lambs were grilled over a fire pit, and a massive goose was roasted. In addition, there were green vegetables, floury soft potatoes cooked in the coals of the fire pit and fresh fruit from the village's orchards to finish. The Herons were offered all the ale they could drink, but Hal refused politely on their behalf, opting for coffee instead.

During the meal, which was held in the open in the village square, the Herons were treated to a steady procession of mothers, fathers, aunts, uncles, sweethearts, sisters and brothers belonging to the slaves they had rescued, all taking their hands, thanking them and hugging them warmly.

At one stage, a pretty young girl nervously approached the table of honour where the crew were seated, and sought out Hal.

She was wearing a soft woollen dress of pale blue and her dark, shining hair was plaited and coiled on top of her head. With a slight sense of shock, he realised it was Ophelia. Now that she wasn't dressed in filthy rags, and with the drawn lines of pain and fear gone from her face, she was barely recognisable as the miserable creature they had carried out of the slave market and through the back alleys of Socorro.

Hal smiled warmly at her as she stood beside his chair.

'Why, Ophelia,' he said, 'you look beautiful.'

Lydia, a few seats away, curled her lip scornfully.

'Hal, I want to thank you for saving us. For bringing us home. Thank you so much.'

Hal made a self-deprecating gesture, indicating the other members of his crew. 'It wasn't just me. The whole crew helped.'

'Maybe so. But I think you're wonderful,' she said. And leaning in, she kissed him on the cheek. Then, embarrassed at her forwardness, she turned and ran. The crew all cheered and laughed as Hal flushed with embarrassment.

'I think you're wonderful too, Hal!' Stefan said, in a workmanlike approximation of Ophelia's breathless, admiring tones. The crew laughed even harder.

Lydia snorted through her nose.

Thorn turned to study her scowling features.

'What's got your undies in a twist, princess?' he asked, grinning.

She glared at him. 'One day, old man, you'll say one word too many.'

Several hours later, the cook fires were dying down and the villagers were heading for their beds. Celebration or not, there were crops to tend, wheat to grind into flour and animals to be milked, fed and watered first thing in the morning. Gilan found himself sitting with Hal and Thorn as the party wound down.

'We've got an early start in the morning too,' he said.

Hal looked at him, curious. 'What for?'

'The King, remember?' Gilan told him. 'We were summoned to see him some weeks ago. I'm sure he'll understand that bringing the slaves home took precedence over his summons. But now they're safe, it might be wise if we complied with his request.'

'Request?' Hal said, grinning.

Gilan smiled in return. 'Command is possibly more accurate,' he admitted. 'He might get a little testy if we waste any more time. Kings tend to do that.'

'Why do you think he wants to see us?' Hal asked.

Gilan began to shrug, but Thorn interrupted. 'Maybe he wants to knight me,' he said. 'I fancy being Sir Thorn.'

'I doubt that,' Hal said, smiling.

But Thorn shook his head ponderously. 'It's a good chance. Look at it this way.' He held out his left hand. 'On the one hand, he wants to knight me. On the other hand . . .'

He held out the polished wood hook that had taken the place of his right hand and looked at it, feigning surprise.

'Well, what do you know? There is no other hand. So I guess it's a knighting for me.' He smiled at them, pleased with his little performance. They all ignored him. Such a dreadful joke deserved to be ignored.

'What do we call him?' Hal asked Gilan. 'I've never met a king.'

Gilan considered the question for a few seconds. 'Well, you can address him the way we do. We call him your majesty, or my lord. Either of those will do.'

'No,' said Thorn flatly, and they both looked at him in surprise.

'No?' Gilan asked. He sensed he knew what was coming. Skandians were a notoriously independent people, with decidedly egalitarian views. They elected their leader and they didn't believe in the birthright of kings or queens.

'Your king is the equivalent of our Oberjarl,' Thorn said. He looked at Hal. 'And how do we address the Oberjarl?'

Hal shrugged. 'If it's an official occasion, we call him "Oberjarl".'

'Exactly. So we don't show this King any more respect than our own leader. Or any less. We'll call him "King". *Hullo, King,* we'll say. *Delighted to meet you. How are things, King?*' He glared a challenge at Gilan, who held up his hands in a peacemaking gesture.

'I'm sure that'll do just fine,' he said, remembering an earlier occasion when King Duncan had encountered Skandian protocol. 'He'll be used to that. After all, he met your Oberjarl some years ago.'

'Then he'll be ready for me,' Thorn stated.

But now Gilan shook his head and his smile widened.

'Oh, I doubt that, Thorn. I seriously doubt that.'

ABOUT THE AUTHOR

John Flanagan's Ranger's Apprentice and Brotherband adventure series have sold more than eight million copies worldwide. His books are available in more than one hundred countries, are regularly on the *New York Times* bestseller list, and have had multiple award shortlistings and wins in Australia and overseas. John, a former television and advertising writer, lives with his wife in a Sydney beachside suburb.